MOBIUS

VINCENT VALE

MOBIUS is a work of fiction. All names, characters, places and events are divined from the author's imagination or are being used fictitiously.

SOULESTIAL

~PRESS~

Cover Art by Adam Burn

Other works by Vincent Vale:

THE VESTIGIAL MAN

Website: www.vincentvale.com

Email: vincentvale@vincentvale.com

Goodreads: www.goodreads.com/VincentVale

Twitter: @VincentValeNews

REVIEWS ON AMAZON AND GOODREADS ARE GREATLY APPRECIATED

To Sharon and John, my loving parents. Karen, my sister, who was first to read it. And David, whose editorial skills and friendship were lifesavers.

Quantum Threshold

—— 2969 ——

I wasn't alone—I heard a beating heart behind me. Not the soothing sound of mother's blood, but a deep and ominous thudding. *Doom-damn... Doom-damn...* It continued with the cadence of hellish clockwork. *Doom-damn... Doom-damn...* My skin crawled, my stomach clenched.

What was behind me? A man? A monster? I didn't dare open my eyes, didn't dare look back. It couldn't be human. No man's chest could contain such a heart. It grew louder and louder, becoming thunder in my head.

Doom-damn! Doom-damn!

My breathing quickened, forcing me to suck in more of the foul air around me.

What's that stench? I wondered.

I at last opened my eyes—slowly, fearfully. Holo-monitors illuminated the room, displaying ever-changing graphs and numerical data. It meant nothing to me. I looked down and found myself naked, floating in an anti-gravity field above a metal slab.

Where the fuck am I? I thought. *Why am I naked?*

The beating heart continued. *Doom-damn! Doom-damn!*

"Stop! Please stop!" I screamed.

It felt like my skull was cracking. What was behind me? I had to see. The truth would release me.

I tilted my head back. Disbelief! Horror! My small hairs rose. It was a complex beast—half machine, half monster. A great blob of bio-mechanical flesh. Metallic nano-fibers interlaced the pale skin, causing electrostatic discharges that buzzed and sparked.

The beast loomed above me, the height of the ceiling, like a giant animal—but not an animal, an abomination of flesh. It had no appendages and no head, only a great, moist sphincter that puckered mere inches from where I lay.

"Holy shit! Holy shit! Holy shit!"

Escape! Fight! Run! I wanted to do all these things, but my body proved too heavy, too weak. My perceptions distorted. Was the beast growing larger or was I becoming smaller? My stomach heaved and my head spun. My thoughts clouded over and my brief journey into the conscious world ended.

I again awoke, my head pierced by pain, my vision a jumble of blurred shapes and drab colors. My eyes focused. A face. A hideous face hovered above me. Two bulging eyes, stained the color of piss, inspected me.

Who is this ugly fuck? I wondered.

I felt the urge to fight. I lashed out, but the man pinned me down with surprising strength. I thrashed, kicked, screamed.

"Let go of me, you bastard!"

The man held my neck with one hand and produced a hypo-injector with the other. "This will calm you."

I felt the sting of the injection. My face went numb and my anxiety soothed. I looked around and discovered I was in a different place, no longer near that enormous beast. I was lying on a small cot. It felt soft and clumpy beneath me.

I sat up on elbows. "Where am I?"

"You're in the sanitarium, where you belong," replied the painfully close man.

What's he talking about? I thought. *What sanitarium? Why do I belong here?*

From what I could see, I was in a room no more than two lengths of my body from wall to wall. It was lit by a dim node overhead. A single door with a magnetic lock gave passage to the room. It hung open. I heard the whisper of distant voices.

I grabbed the man above me. "Who am I?"

"You're Theron Mobius."

"Theron Mobius?" The name was unfamiliar. "Who are you?"

"I'm an orderly, here to take care of you. I attend to your hygiene, nutrition, and overall comfort."

"You're an ugly fucker," I said.

"That's not very nice, but I know you're confused. Now, let me look you over."

The orderly began poking and pulling at me. I tried to fight him off.

With two greasy fingers, the orderly spread my eyelids apart and peered inward. "Some people think the eyes are the path to the soul, and they're mistaken, for it's the brain itself that gives way to that mysterious entity lurking within each of us."

He spoke a command word and a glowing orb floating near his shoulder descended just above my forehead. It started scanning me with beams of energy. I could feel a searing heat on my face and then in my head as if it was melting my brain. I tried to bat it away, but my arms became heavy as the orb increased the gravity around my body. I felt like I weighed a thousand pounds.

The orb spoke in a female voice, "There are no deviations across the quantum threshold. Atomic neural stability is holding. The fusion is optimal. The specimen is unique."

A wave of energy shot through my body. I flailed my arms and kicked my legs with an unnatural strength that defied the increased gravity. A lucky swing sent the orb crashing into the wall. It flashed and fizzled as it hit the ground and rolled under my cot. I kicked the orderly, sending him through the room's doorway and onto his ass.

"Something's in my head!" I cried. "It claws at my skull! It wants out! It's too great! My head's too small!"

The orderly stood up and signaled down the hall. He was soon joined by a man whose face was a gnarled mask of large features and pale, splotchy skin. He wore a fine black suit, perfectly tailored for his body.

"Doctor," said the orderly, "it appears Theron's undergoing a more difficult acclimation than the others."

Something about the doctor caused a terrifying sensation within me. I didn't know what it was, but I felt it in my stomach, my brain, and my heart. It was unbearable. I gazed into his eyes. They glowed with an unnatural green color as they looked down the length of a long bulbous-tipped nose.

"My brain," I whimpered. "Does it spill from my head?"

The doctor worked my head between his palms. "This is fantastic. He's more affected by the treatment than the others."

"He is," agreed the orderly.

"Take Theron back to the rehabilitation vesicle," said the doctor. "He shows promise deserving of another treatment. I'll be there momentarily."

"Release me!" I cried. "Please!"

"You're in need of another treatment," replied the orderly. He clamped a silver ring around my chest and I floated up, limp and weightless.

I was helpless as the orderly pushed me down a hallway of many doors. At that moment, my mind filled with strange words. I was compelled to speak them aloud, over and over: "A thread of thought, I forge in flesh, I cast it out into the light and await its return to cure the blight..."

The orderly didn't respond to my utterance and soon brought me to the end of the hallway where stood a large metal door protected by a force field. He performed an odd hand motion, causing the force field to dissipate and the door to open.

We entered the chamber of the bio-mechanical creature I had previously encountered. The orderly placed me back in the anti-gravity field above the metal slab, near the beast's great sphincter.

Robotic insects crawled on the creature's terrible flesh, repairing damaged nano-fibers and cauterizing open sores.

"Lie still until the doctor arrives."

I could only repeat those words that filled my head: "A thread of thought, I forge in flesh, I cast it out into the light and await its return to cure the blight..."

When the doctor finally entered the room, my mental fit subsided. "Who are you? What are you doing to me? Why are you torturing me?"

The doctor placed his hand on my chest, at my heart. "We're going to help you rise from the depths of insanity, Theron. You must trust us."

"I'm scared."

"You shouldn't be," replied the doctor.

"What is that thing?" I tilted my head back and recoiled from the sphincter trembling behind me. "Take me away from this abomination! Please!"

"I cannot, my son." The doctor turned to the orderly. "Hold him in place for insertion."

"Insertion?" My jaw dropped. "What do you mean 'insertion'?"

The doctor closed his eyes and remained still as a tendril of glowing nano-fibers emerged from just above the sphincter of the bizarre creature. It stretched out toward the doctor's forehead, where it broke the flesh and pushed inward, joining the doctor to the creature.

"What the fuck!" I screamed.

The great sphincter above me puckered and swelled. Ten of the robotic insects gathered at the perimeter of the sphincter and deployed tiny tractor beams on my body, pulling me in.

"Stop! Please, stop! Fucking hell! No!"

My resistance was useless. My entire body was ingested by the beast.

An unlikely calmness ran through me.

My God, where am I?

Instead of finding myself in the vile innards of the creature, I found myself floating in an expanse of pure light. The bio-mechanical skin of the creature encased another realm. The light surrounding me rippled and stirred in such a way that it seemed alive, or at the very least was something more than just light.

I was mesmerized as a sparkling silver-white wisp caressed my cheek. It was soon joined by another, and then another, until a multitude of glowing wisps constricted down upon me. I felt the wisps of light penetrating my body, creeping into the core of my being.

I opened my eyes. I was slumped in a comfortable chair in a large room. A dozen unkempt and sickly-looking people sat around me. They wore identical green outfits. I suspected they too were patients of the sanitarium. Some sat unconscious, while others spoke in low, weary voices.

Four white orbs hovered at the ceiling. I watched as one descended upon a male patient and scanned him against his will. He tried to resist, but another descended and placed him in a gravity restraint.

This place is a nightmare, I thought.

Then I saw her. She was beautiful. She returned my gaze, smiled, and then approached. She had blonde hair, a spare frame, and large blue eyes. I didn't know what to say.

"Hi... I mean... hello."

"I'm glad you're awake, Theron." Her voice was soft and soothing.

I paused awkwardly. "Who are you?"

"I'm Mage. I kept you company while you slept and stimulated your mind with conversation, though it was I who did all the talking."

"Thank you," I said. "Are you an orderly?"

She laughed. "I'm like you, Theron."

"You're a patient?" I said in surprise.

"I am."

"You're too pretty to be—" I winced.

"To be what? Crazy?" Mage smiled, and then touched my face in a caring gesture. "Are you feeling better?"

Her touch comforted me. "I am now. How long have I been asleep?"

"Many days."

Before I could ask more questions, a young man with darting eyes and a thin face approached. "She's been fawning over your catatonic body the entire time."

"Ridiculous, Sensimion," said Mage. "I merely kept Theron comfortable since the orderlies neglected him. They're only concerned with changing his soiled clothes and forcing food down his throat with a tube."

Sensimion pointed to other individuals slumped around the room. "There are many needy invalids in this shit-hole. Why was Theron the only one deserving of your special treatment?"

Mage raised her nose. "Enough of your jealousy, Sensimion."

I grabbed Mage's hand in an attempt to capture her full attention. I looked around the room neurotically. "I've been molested in horrible ways!"

Sensimion laughed. "He's talking about the sphincter beast."

"Must you call it that? It's such a disgusting name."

"A disgusting name for a disgusting beast," replied Sensimion.

Mage brushed my hair from my forehead. "Theron, don't worry about the rehabilitation vesicle. It's merely a device to help us become well."

Sensimion leaned forward secretively. "This is what the doctor and orderlies tell us, but I believe its true purpose to be something much more malevolent."

Mage shook her head. "Don't listen to Sensimion. He's a paranoid mess."

"I don't understand," I said. "Why can't I remember my life before this place?"

"It's the nature of the process," said Mage. "We're all here to be treated for mental illness, and by erasing our memories when we arrive, we start fresh. There are no past experiences left to corrupt our sanity. The rehabilitation vesicle is then used to reshape our minds, removing any predisposition for deviant thought. After a treatment, the mind is overwhelmed and the patient goes into a catatonic state."

"Am I now cured?" I asked. "Will I be allowed to leave soon?"

"Not a chance," said Sensimion. "Like all of us, you'll continue your treatments in the sphincter beast, unless you can find a way past the main portal of this madhouse and escape." Sensimion indicated a large archway at the other side of the room. "As you can see, the archway generates a force field. It can discriminate the DNA of a person and allow only authorized people to pass through."

"And what lies beyond the threshold of the archway?"

"The doctor has told us the sanitarium's hidden within the vacant sublevels of a MegaCity, away from any people who may find such a facility compromising to their communities."

I felt a chill when Sensimion mentioned the doctor. "There's something unnatural about the doctor. I don't know what it is, but an unsettling aura surrounds him. His presence is oppressive on the mind. Do you sense this also?"

Sensimion tapped at his temple. "He's an overbearing man forcing his strange medicine on us. As far as sensing some kind of oppressive aura from his person, I don't. Nonetheless, your conviction seems genuine. I'll pay more attention the next time he carries his ugly fucking head into my presence."

"I've had no such feelings," said Mage. "It's probably just your weakened mind playing tricks on you, Theron."

"Maybe," I said. I heard a loud computer tone. "What's that?"

"That's the signal for us to return to our sleeping quarters," said Sensimion.

Mage kissed me on the cheek. "I'll see you tomorrow. Sleep well."

I'll never sleep well in this place, I thought.

Weeks passed. I became sluggish from a routine of eating and sleeping. My only pleasure came from conversations with Sensimion and Mage in the congregation room. At night, I pushed my thoughts inward, desperately searching for any surviving memories of my life before the sanitarium. It's a scary thing not knowing who you are, or where you're from. What did I do to belong here? Was I a criminal? A lunatic? Who was Theron Mobius?

One late night in bed, I felt a neuron ignite and a memory was found.

I was awake all night, overwhelmed by the memories that began crowding my mind. I sat on the floor, huddled in a corner, facing the wall. Slowly, I rocked, back and forth while repeating, "One atop another, they pile upon each other..." I laughed hysterically as my mind spun and my senses flared. The void was filling. I felt elation from the genesis unfolding in my mind.

I heard Mage's voice: "What's the matter, Theron? I heard you screaming."

"Ha! You're mistaken. I was laughing."

"At what? Why do you sit in the corner? What are you looking at?"

"The lies and the lives... and the lives and the lies."

"What lies?"

"The lives! I cradle them all. Some are big and some are small. Do you wish to see them?"

"Yes," said Mage. "Show me what you have."

"I have them all—one, two, three, four... six... twelve... twenty-four."

"You're scaring me, Theron. Turn around. What are you cradling?"

"The blood of them all." I turned, allowing Mage to see the truth that I held. My left forearm was covered in a layer of blood.

"What have you done, Theron?"

"Forgive me, it's not the blood. It's what lies beneath." With my right hand, I rubbed away as much blood as possible, revealing a series of symbols I had gouged into my arm with a shard of the broken orb. "Don't you see? It all makes sense now."

"Let me help you, Theron." Mage tore off a piece of her shirt and knelt beside me, trying to tend to the series of bleeding symbols.

"No!" I cried. I began pointing from one symbol to the next, explaining each in turn. "This one's the horrors of war, and this one's the gift of life. Here love was found... and there it was lost. In this one... beautiful faces... but here death erases. I'm a healer in this one... but a monster in that one. So many experiences, so many places. I'm every man, from every land."

Stuttering sounds heaved up from my stomach. I no longer knew if I was laughing or crying. A brightness filled my vision and I frantically looked to Mage, trying to hang on to her image.

I woke up on my cot. Mage was gone. She had wrapped my arm in a strip of her shirt. I turned an ear to the door. Silence. Stillness.

It must be night, I thought. *The door's closed. The light's low. Sleep. Go back to sleep before the memories return.*

I closed my eyes and lay in the dark. Instead of finding sleep, I found that oppressive sensation I'd felt before. When I opened my eyes, I saw the doctor standing above me with a perverse grin on his face.

"How did you get in here!" I cried. "I didn't hear the magnetic lock release or the door open. What do you want?"

"I want to make sure you're feeling well," replied the doctor. "You're a special patient, Theron, and I'm confident you'll soon be cured."

"Actually—" I held my tongue. It would've been a mistake to tell him about the memories. If I concerned the doctor, I might extend my stay in the sanitarium forever, enduring the inner mysteries of the sphincter beast over and over again. "Actually... I feel fine. Now, I'd like to go to sleep."

I rolled on my side and stared at the wall, hoping for the doctor to leave. When there was no indication of his departure, I prepared to voice my anger for the interruption to my sleep, but when I turned, the doctor was gone.

The following day, I was eager to tell Mage of my strange visit in the middle of the night. I went to her quarters and then to the congregation room, but she was nowhere to be found.

I confronted Sensimion. "Where's Mage?"

"During the night, I heard her being taken to the sphincter beast for treatment. They're usually finished by morning, but it seems they're taking longer than usual."

Half the day had passed when Mage was finally brought to the congregation room by an orderly. He dropped her body into a chair and then left the room.

I held her hand. "Mage? Are you all right? Can you hear me?"

She was unresponsive, staring blankly through half-mast eyelids.

I gasped in horror. One of the sphincter beast's robotic insects clung to the side of her head. I tried to pull it off, but its barbed metal legs were embedded under her skin. It buzzed and clicked while moving in an up and down motion.

"What the fuck is it doing to you! I'm here, my friend. Wake up." I continued trying to wake her, but her conscious mind was beyond my reach.

Sensimion approached. "Like Mage told you, this catatonic state is a normal reaction to the treatment. Don't worry about her."

"Don't worry? What about this robotic bug?"

"It's a therapeutic process to help heal her mind. She'll snap out of it soon enough."

I was no less concerned for her. I adjusted her body so she sat with a more dignified posture. I fixed her hair, brushing it back with a gentle hand.

"What are you doing?" asked Sensimion.

"I'm doing what she did for me when I was in this condition."

"Do as you like," huffed Sensimion. "However, when it's I who sit in a helpless stupor, with twisted limbs and tangled hair, I'd prefer not to be stroked and squeezed like a sick puppy."

"I'll try to keep my hands off you, Sensimion."

"As you should!" Sensimion walked to the main portal, where he tampered with the archway by jamming a fork into a seam of its frame.

I continued sitting with Mage, until I decided she wasn't comfortable. I gently lifted her from the chair and carried her back to her sleeping quarters. I carefully placed her on the cot. She truly was beautiful.

"I'll keep you company, Mage. I'll keep you safe."

I placed my face next to her lips and felt her warm breath on my cheek. I rested my head on her chest and listened to her heartbeat. I sat patiently with her, and eventually I slipped into deep thought, staring forth, as if entranced.

Hours later, Sensimion entered Mage's quarters and jolted me. "What's wrong with you, Theron?"

I gazed intensely at him. "Memories have been surfacing in my mind over the past few weeks. But they're unfamiliar, as though I'm remembering the memories of other men."

Sensimion's eyes widened. "What happens in these memories?"

"So many things. They're not memories of my life before this place. Of this I'm certain. It's as though I have the memories of many different lives tangled in my head. The people and scenery of each set of memories are so distinctly different from the next, it's like each set of memories takes place in a different age of history." I shook my head in confusion. "Could I be remembering past lives I've lived? Impossible! Ridiculous!"

"Reincarnation?" Sensimion swung a paranoid look to the door. "Don't let the orderlies hear about this. We must keep this to ourselves. These memories may be a clue as to what's really going on in this place. We must investigate further."

"How?" I asked. "I can't make sense of any of these memories. I know nothing about history or the world beyond the walls of this sanitarium."

"We do have resources, Theron. Follow me." Sensimion led me out of Mage's quarters and back to the congregation room, where he pointed to a table with an inlaid view-panel. "We're allowed access to the library. It contains everything about the world above. Use it to make sense of the memories. Try to identify any names or places you can recall."

"This seems impossible. If they *are* memories of past lives, it could take a lifetime to sort through the details of history."

"Then I suggest you start immediately, Theron."

I touched the empty seat beside me. "Not until Mage is better."

Once Mage woke up, I began my investigation. I spent the better part of the next month studying human history.

I discovered many correlations between my strange memories and the reality of the past.

I informed Sensimion and Mage. "It's like there's a seepage of the past welling up in my mind. I possess the memories of many people, spanning back to the beginning of recorded history, and possibly further. I'm uncertain how these memories can be."

Maybe I am insane, I thought.

Sensimion's mouth hung open. "Whose memories are they? What are the connections between these people, if any? Could it be reincarnation, as you suggested earlier?"

"It's not reincarnation, since some of the people lived at the same time. There is, however, a similarity shared by many of the people. Most were a part of some significant turning point in human history." I brought up the image of a man on the view-panel. "Seven hundred years ago, this man perfected the process of cold fusion. It's odd, for I can recall the moments leading to his breakthrough and the days following. But that's all. I know nothing else of this man, his thoughts, or the life he led."

I displayed another portrait. "This man, in the mid-twentieth century, helped develop the integrated circuit, which gave rise to the computer age." Another portrait was displayed. "And this man, who lived during the twelfth and thirteenth centuries, was a great leader who founded the Mongol Empire. My memories of his life are much more extensive." And another. "This man was a religious icon whose teachings were the inspiration for a religion called Christianity. I have the memories of the last few years of his life."

"Who else?" asked Sensimion eagerly.

"I've made a list of names on this scrap of paper."

"Be careful!" Sensimion snatched away the paper and tucked it into his pocket. "We can't let the doctor know about this. There's something unethical going on in this place, and we're swimming through the thick of it."

"I think you're right, Sensimion." I surveyed the patients in the congregation room. "Why doesn't anyone get visitors? Someone must have loved ones worried about them."

Mage, who had been listening on in silence, spoke up. "The two of you are feeding on each other's delusions. Please, Theron, stop talking about these strange memories."

"I can't ignore what's inside me."

"You must, or the doctor will never release you. If we get well soon, we can be together on the outside."

"We will be," I said. "I promise you, Mage."

She placed her hand on my chest. "Then stop this, Theron."

I displayed another image on the view-panel. "Just look at the things I'm remembering. How is it possible?"

"It's not possible." Tears filled her eyes.

"I'm sorry, Mage. Please, don't cry." I watched sadly as she departed. I wished she believed me, for I felt a strong bond with her. I wanted to share everything with her.

Don't you know how much I care for you?

"She'll get over it," said Sensimion. "Now, what are we going to do?"

I sighed. "The answers are with the doctor. We need to see what happens in the chamber of the sphincter beast while someone's undergoing treatment."

"I agree," said Sensimion, "but it won't be easy. The security door is state of the art. And even if we could bypass it, the doctor and orderlies spend nearly all their time in that room, making it impossible to enter undetected. And don't forget we're locked in our sleeping quarters at night, when patients are treated."

"Don't worry, Sensimion. I have a plan. It doesn't require us to breach the door or enter the room. Remember, we only need to see inside." I didn't elaborate further, since two orderlies entered the congregation room to deliver lunch.

An orderly served me a plate of the usual synthetic slop. I spoke to him like a madman. "Orderly! My sleeping quarters are unfit! The shit and piss of a thousand men have been deposited within. I fear that this human excrement might rise from the cracks in the floor and envelop me." I banged my face on the table, causing my eyes to tear and my nose to bleed. "I haven't slept in days. How can I get well without sleep? I demand a room with more comfort and less stench!"

The orderly grunted in annoyance. "You can relocate to the sleeping quarters next to your current quarters. They're empty."

"Unacceptable!" I exclaimed. "That one's filthy, too. The only clean quarters are at the end of the hall, next to the chamber of the rehabilitation vesicle."

The orderly slid a feeding tube down the throat of a catatonic patient sitting near me. "Fine. I'll unlock it after lunch. Now, eat your meal."

Satisfied, I ate my shitty meal with a smile.

When the orderlies finally left the congregation room, I informed Sensimion. "My plan is unfolding perfectly. When I'm relocated to the sleeping quarters next to the chamber of the sphincter beast, I'll begin drilling a small peephole through the common wall." I nodded my head with delight. "It couldn't be simpler."

"Where will you find a drill?"

"The walls of this place are crumbling. I won't need a powerful tool. The broken medical orb left beneath my cot contains a micro scalpel. I can modify it into a pulse drill. It'll probably take a long time with such a weak tool, but time is what we have in this prison."

"How do you know about such technology?"

"I know things now. The memories have given me experiences and knowledge of many things. I'm more than I was before."

That night, I smuggled the medical orb into my new sleeping quarters and began. I pried open a side panel of the orb and revealed its complicated inner workings. They were so familiar. I looked to the memories that crowded my mind and found the memories of a woman. She was an engineer who designed such robots. I recognized one of six power-nodes and removed it carefully, insulating my fingers with some fabric from my shirt. I located the micro scalpel and followed the circuitry to its control chip. This was all I needed. I disconnected the scalpel and control chip and left the rest behind.

How can I know these things? I wondered, somewhat afraid of myself.

I coupled the power-node to the micro scalpel and began strategically shorting circuitry pathways. When finished, I held my breath for a moment and then used a piece of metal to temporarily bridge two circuits. The micro scalpel shot forth a pulsing beam that made me smile. For some reason, it was the happiest I'd been in the sanitarium.

The next night, I worked out the proper angle and engaged the tiny pulse drill. Despite a slow progress, it functioned perfectly. Worried about an orderly entering my quarters, I positioned my cot against the wall so I could work lying down, with the drill concealed under my blanket.

Every night the peephole got deeper. Occasionally, when the pulse drill's intensity weakened, I'd replace the power-node. On the tenth night, I halted my work when I heard the door opening. I dropped the drill under my cot and pulled my cover over my head.

"Theron?" came a soft voice. "Are you awake?"

"Mage?" I sat up. "How did you get out of your quarters?"

"I tampered with my door's magnetic lock before bedtime. I wanted to see you."

"You're amazing," I said, hugging her close. "But you could get in trouble for such defiance."

"I'm worried about you, Theron." She took my hand and ran a finger over a row of energy burns. "What are you doing in here? You seem exhausted during the day."

I looked in her round blue eyes. *I can't upset her. She doesn't need to know.*

"I know you're up to something." She brushed her hand against my blanket. "What's this dust?"

I can't lie to her.

I moved the blanket away from the wall. "I've been drilling a peephole, so I can see inside the chamber of the rehabilitation vesicle. So I can see the truth."

"This idea of conspiracy is consuming you, Theron."

My head sagged. "If there's no conspiracy and the memories aren't real, then I am insane." I placed a finger to the peephole. "This gives me hope."

She shook her head. "What of me? What of us? With friendship, hope is forged. I can be your sanity. Together, we can live a normal life, despite a few crazy, stupid memories."

I looked at her fondly. *She's the only person in the world who cares about me.*

"You're right," I said. "I've been a fool. I risk our future together. I'll stop. I'll stop for you... for us."

She pulled me down on the cot and I felt her warm body against mine. I was soothed by the rise and fall of her chest as she breathed.

This is right. This is the answer to my madness—the closeness, the companionship, the shared moments, the love.

I sat up. "You must go back to your quarters and fix the magnetic lock."

"Just a few more minutes."

I kissed her with passion and then pushed her to the door. "Go."

She looked back at me. "Is this what love feels like, Theron?"

"I think so." I felt a strange excitement—the chance for a future, for something more, for happiness. I thought of our possible life together, somewhere else, somewhere far from the sanitarium.

After two hours, I heard the sound of activity from the hallway—the scuttle of feet, the squeak of a door, the command of an orderly, and finally the reply of Mage's fragile voice.

"No," I whispered. "She doesn't deserve this, not now."

I struggled with my thoughts. *I must be good. She wanted me to stop.*

I grabbed the pulse drill from under the bed. I had to know.

I need more power.

I took the remaining three power-nodes and coupled them together. I risked an overload that could've blown off my head. I didn't give a shit. I turned it on and it pulsed with triple intensity. An hour had passed when the pulse beam broke through the other side of the wall. I frantically shut it off, fearing the beam had shot through the other side and caught the attention of the doctor and orderlies.

After ten minutes, when neither orderly nor doctor burst through my door, I was confident I had gone undetected. I put the pulse drill down and eagerly gazed into the peephole.

I saw the doctor standing beside the sphincter beast, its nano-fiber tendril extending into the doctor's forehead. Mage was apparently still within the confines of the bio-mechanical creature. I wondered what was truly happening before my eyes. I wondered about my memories of the past.

How can they be? Are they divined from the sphincter beast, the doctor, or insanity?

For hours the doctor was linked to the so-called "rehabilitation vesicle" until he shook with something like annoyance.

"The fusion isn't stable!" he said to the orderly beside him. "The quantum threshold collapsed! She's no longer a possible subject."

I'd heard those words before, when the orb scanned me after my own treatment.

What's a quantum threshold? I wondered. *What's he trying to fuse with us? This isn't about our mental health. This is something bigger.*

A moment later, Mage's limp body spilled from the sphincter beast in an incontinent birthing. I looked on in horror as the orderly approached her, bent downward, and spun her head. A gruesome crunch nearly caused me to vomit. I trembled.

Motherfuckers! Why? She didn't deserve this. I'll kill them. All of them.

"Throw the body into the incinerator," said the doctor. He gestured to the wall behind the sphincter beast and it rose up, revealing a secret chamber.

Within was something so grotesque that I couldn't process what I saw. Many female figures hung from the ceiling connected by a network of transparent tubes attached to their mouths and genitals—some kind of pink nutrient broth flowed through them. Their bellies were swollen. Were they pregnant? Was it some kind of awful experiment? Where were the babies being birthed from these poor, tortured women?

I watched as the orderly carried Mage's body to the center of the secret room and cast her into a dark hole. I heard an intense electric surge and Mage was gone.

My view drifted to the doctor, who swung a look of awareness to the peephole. I shrank back in panic. I quickly hid myself under my blanket and faked sleep for an unbearable period.

I heard the click of my door's magnetic lock and feared I'd been discovered. When no one entered, I realized it was merely morning.

I sat at the library view-panel. My plans had changed. I was getting the fuck out as soon as possible. It didn't matter what was going on. It only mattered that I wanted to live.

Sensimion approached. "Have you had more memories materialize?"

"No," I said.

"Well then, what has your attention so focused?" Sensimion poked his head in front of the view-panel. "Human anatomy? Why do you wish to learn such boring things?"

"Leave me alone."

"What's wrong with you, Theron? You've learned something, haven't you? Did you finish drilling the peephole? What did you see?"

I've seen the work of pure evil, I thought.

"Well?" said Sensimion.

"I haven't broken through," I lied. "You'll know when I do."

At that moment, the doctor entered the congregation room, wearing a white suit with a decorative stitching of interlaced circles and helixes.

"What's going on?" whispered Sensimion. "The doctor rarely gives us the privilege to look at his hideous bulk, unless we're being treated."

"I bring words of encouragement to all," said the doctor with a disturbing satisfaction.

I'll kill you. I'll kill you. I'll kill you, echoed my thoughts.

The doctor continued, "After many invigorating treatments in the rehabilitation vesicle, our friend Mage has at last achieved a new and healthy mental stasis. Last night, I released her to the world. She now flies free like a regal bird toward a promising future."

Sensimion scowled. "You've sent her away without letting us say goodbye?"

"The mental strain of sad goodbyes wouldn't have been good for her. Once one is cured, they must be completely separated from this place so a sense of rebirth can be attained. Remember, Sensimion, if you're confident of yourself and of your treatment, you too shall reach this final goal."

My insides boiled. *Liar! Murderer! Monster!*

The doctor glanced at me for an instant, and I thought to see the corners of his mouth turn up, ever so slightly.

Before I exploded, the doctor briskly left the congregation room. Many of the patients showed signs of enthusiasm for the doctor's brief dialogue.

"Are our suspicions wrong?" asked Sensimion. "Are we paranoid? Your mysterious memories are proof. Aren't they?"

I chewed my lower lip, restraining my anger for Mage's murder. "Don't let the color of the doctor's words paint over the truth."

"Aha!" said Sensimion. "I knew you were acting strange. What aren't you telling me, Theron?"

"I'll tell you everything tomorrow morning." I looked at the force field of the sanitarium's main portal. "Listen carefully, Sensimion. In the morning, make sure you're awake and dressed an hour before your sleeping quarters are usually unlocked. Don't sleep late. Time is of the essence."

"Why?"

"Please, just do it."

"Your mood is troubling, Theron. Why won't you tell me? What do you know? What are you planning?"

"You'll understand in the morning. Right now, I have something important to do."

I left the congregation room and returned to my sleeping quarters. I began my modifications to the pulse drill. I no longer needed it to pulse. I needed a steady, concentrated beam that would kill and cut. After a few modifications, I returned the micro scalpel back to its original function. I tested it on a piece of synthetic meat I had brought back from dinner. It sliced it in half with ease.

"They've driven me to this course of action. They're liars and murderers. My actions will be justified. Afterwards, I'll carry on without remorse." I held my breath for a moment, and then spoke with ultimate conviction: "I'm not insane."

I silently waited in my quarters until I heard the computer tone indicating bedtime. I listened carefully as all the patients were escorted to their sleeping quarters by a single orderly, who then locked the doors, one by one.

I heard the heavy steps of the orderly approaching my door—the last door to be locked—and pushed the door outward with all the weight of my body behind it. The door smashed into the orderly, knocking him out.

I nervously peered down the length of the hallway— no one saw. I took hold of the orderly by the armpits and dragged him into my quarters.

With the micro scalpel in hand, I stood over the orderly.

Am I really going to do this? I thought. *Will I be as bad as them?*

Despite my hate for the doctor and the orderlies, I still dreaded the hideous act I was about to commit. I examined the orderly's face and felt a disturbing comfort.

"It was you... your hands... your action." I smiled. "I do this for Mage."

I tucked my blanket in the crack at the base of the door.

Hopefully, this'll be sufficient. Soon there'll be much blood.

I couldn't believe what I'd done. Despite guilt and disgust, I wore it. Humid and hot, it stuck to my skin. It was heavier than I'd thought it would be and confined me terribly. I could barely breathe within it. I walked down the hall with a labored gait and finally came to Sensimion's quarters. I released the magnetic lock and swung the door open. Sensimion sat up in his bed, his expression that of absolute terror.

I stepped within.

Sensimion drew back. "Who are you? Is this a dream?"

I pulled it away from my face, revealing myself.

"What have you done, Theron?"

"I've flayed, and now wear, the skin of an orderly."

"You've gone crazy."

"No, I haven't," I said defensively. "They didn't let Mage go free. She didn't get well like the doctor said. They broke her neck and threw her into the incinerator like garbage."

"And wearing their skin like a wild-eyed lunatic is your revenge?"

"No. I wear the skin of an orderly so I can pass through the main portal of the sanitarium. It was *you* who told *me* that the force field of the portal can discriminate the DNA of anyone trying to pass through." I peeked into the hallway. "We must escape now, unless you want to join Mage in the incinerator."

Sensimion agreed, and we snuck to the main portal. The doctor and orderlies were nowhere in sight.

I whispered, "I'll pass through first, remove the skin-suit, and throw it back through the portal. When you put it on, be sure to secure these straps to close the openings at the arms, legs, and back. This will ensure your own skin won't be detected by the portal."

Sensimion shuddered.

"Do you understand?" I said.

"Yes."

I tested the orderly's flesh, moving my hand toward the portal's barrier. It passed through freely. Without further delay, I stepped to the other side. I quickly removed the skin-suit and threw it back through the portal to Sensimion.

I stood nervously. *What's taking him so long?*

Finally, Sensimion appeared. He pulled off the skin-suit with panic and revolt. "What now?"

"Let's first get clear of this place," I said, looking down the dim corridor in which we now stood.

We ran for hours through a maze of empty corridors, until at last we arrived at the MegaCity's breathtaking under-workings. I tried to gain my bearings. In preparation for the escape, I had accessed the library view-panel and found pictures and schematics of the MegaCity's structure. In front of us towered monolithic pillars that served to uplift the city's diamond-fiber superstructure to its fantastic height. Between the pillars sat great machines, whirring enthusiastically, keeping the city alive.

I turned to Sensimion. "We should part paths here, and find separate ways to the surface."

"I'd rather not be left alone," said Sensimion. "Why can't we go together?"

"They'll be looking for *two* of us. Also, we should never speak of these events again." I frowned. "I've done terrible things. I've killed and mutilated a man. You're no less guilty, as you've benefited from this sick deed." My lips curled in revolt. "I'll never forget the disgusting confinement of wearing another man's skin. It'll haunt me forever."

Sensimion cocked his head, as if to listen to the MegaCity above. "What do you think's out there?"

"Something better than the sanitarium." I hugged Sensimion. "I'll miss you, brother."

"I'm sorry about Mage, Theron."

"So am I. Goodbye, Sensimion."

DIMENSIONAL
CHAOS

I looked out the window of my apartment on the Brahman Station and admired the magnificence of Jupiter, around which the space station orbited. I looked back to the old framed picture of my wife, Cassandra. It was her birthday today. "I'll see you soon, my love."

I returned the framed picture to the dining table. I touched the window and a control screen popped up.

"How may I help you Mr. Mobius?" came the computer's female voice.

"Upload the program 'Mobius One' to my neural interface."

"I cannot, Mr. Mobius. That program contains illegal SLIP coding that can be both addictive and degenerative to your neural pathways."

I held my hand to the window. "Override safety protocols."

"Verifying credentials…" The computer scanned my identity chip and biometrics. "Level ten authorization accepted. Uploading program now."

I could feel the program stimulating the desired neural clusters. Bright flashes blinded me as the neural activity traveled to my visual cortex. I fell back into my anti-gravity chair and blacked out.

When I came to, Cassandra was standing above me. Her caring blue eyes connected with mine. I felt whole again.

She smiled. "What are you doing my silly, wonderful man?"

"I've been waiting for you, my love. Happy Birthday. Where have you been?"

"You know my birthday falls on the annual genetic medicine conference."

"Of course I know. I'm glad you're back."

She fell into the anti-gravity chair with me, and we comforted each other in a weightless embrace. I sighed in relief as I held her tight. I never wanted to let go. I wanted to feel her heart, her breath, and her warmth forever.

"You smell like honeysuckle."

"Do you like it? It's new."

"It's perfect."

She whispered, "We're perfect."

"I caressed her face with a gentle hand. "I love you so much."

"I know you do."

She pushed me out of the anti-gravity chair and her face turned serious. "That's why you have to let me go. You have to move on."

31

"Why are you saying this?"

"You have to let me go. You have to move on."

"Stop it. You're scaring me. What's going on?"

"Someone murdered me. That's what's going on."

"What do you mean, Cassandra? You're taking this joke too far."

"Don't you remember, Theron? I'm dead." She repeated those words, louder and louder, until she was yelling. "Don't you remember, Theron! I'm dead! I'm dead! I'm dead!"

The window suddenly cracked, Jupiter's image became distorted. I looked back and Cassandra was gone. Fear and emptiness filled me. I cried out for her. Sadness quickly became anger, and I screamed. The window shattered outward and I was sucked into space. I fell into Jupiter, its gravity pulling me faster and faster. At last, I realized the truth. I was in SLIP mode. I was hallucinating.

I bounded out of the anti-gravity chair. "Who the fuck!"

I went to the control screen at the window and accessed the SLIP program. I looked over the coding and realized it had been altered. "Computer, who modified this program last?"

"You did, Mr. Mobius."

I grit my teeth. "What terminal was it accessed from?"

"Terminal 32 in the upper control room."

"Bring up the nearest surveillance recording for that terminal at the time the program was modified."

Another screen popped up on the window and I saw the back of someone's head. Someone's head I knew well. Atticus turned around and waved to the camera, knowing I'd be looking at the recording.

I closed the control screen. "That old bird's going to drive me crazy."

I didn't hold it against him. He just wanted me to move on—to find happiness again. The truth was, it *would've* been Cassandra's birthday today. She died a long time ago. I missed her so much. She was the second woman I'd loved in my life. Mage being the first. Then again, Mage may have never been real. The events in the sanitarium ninety years ago may have only been a dream, or at least I wished they were.

"Computer, display all pictures from album four."

Every smart surface in the apartment displayed Cassandra's image. I picked up the old picture frame from the dining table. It was the best picture I had of her. We just finished rehabbing an old house. She loved getting her hands dirty and didn't think the AI-droids should have all the fun. Our life was just beginning. We were truly happy at that moment, and would be for another ten years, until her murder.

I placed an adoring finger on the picture, touching her blonde hair. I remembered how soft it was and how good it smelled. *Oh, to smell that sweet, honeysuckle scent again.*

"Happy Birthday, darling. They say eighty's the new forty." I laughed. "As long as you can afford the genetic rejuvenation treatments you helped develop."

She was a beautiful genius—her work still renowned. I wondered what she'd look like now, middle-aged like myself.

"You've missed so much in the last thirty-five years. I finished the dimensional gateway. I wish you were here. I wish you could be proud of me."

A computer tone indicated someone was at the door. I returned the picture to its usual spot at the center of the dining table.

"Come in," I called.

Atticus shuffled into the apartment. He was an older man, with silky white hair and a wrinkled complexion untouched by rejuvenation treatments.

I gave him a stern look. "You could've given me a cerebral aneurysm."

"My code was flawless." He looked at my pants. "Hmm… maybe not flawless."

"What do you mean?"

"You were supposed to piss yourself."

"You sick bastard."

I started laughing and he joined me.

"Let me make it up to you, Theron." He held up a small glass vial filled with an amber liquid. "I finished synthesizing your medicine."

I took hold of it eagerly. I needed it bad. "Did you increase the concentration, my friend?"

"I did, and it concerns me, since a tenth of this concentration would be lethal to a normal man. This is the second time in the last month you've asked me to increase the concentration. What's going on?"

I felt embarrassed. "The memories are returning. The insanity, after so many years in remission, is again clouding my mind." I uncapped the vial and let a drop fall into my eye. "For some reason those memories… those non-realities… have been resurfacing over the last month, unhindered by the medicine. A few days ago, I found myself in the bathroom on my knees, reciting some ancient German speech. Unfortunately, I thought the toilet was my microphone. I'm afraid I may again lose myself to the madness."

Atticus showed caring eyes. "For whatever reason these memories have returned, we'll suppress them just as we did so long ago."

34

"I hope you're right, Atticus. I still have many things to do in this life. I don't want to be wandering the streets again, ranting the rant of a madman."

"That was a long time ago." Atticus put a reassuring arm around me. "And even if you do go crazy, I'll still be here for you."

I smiled. He truly was the best of friends. Ever since Cassandra died, Atticus had been the glue that kept me together. Without him, I would've fallen to pieces long ago.

"Don't get emotional on me now, kid. Will you be ready for the maiden voyage through the dimensional gateway? It's only three days away."

"I've sacrificed too many decades of my life for the Brahman Station. I won't let a few bouts of madness interfere with the final realization of our work." I rolled the vial between my fingers. "Hopefully, this new concentration will maintain my sanity."

"Remember that the inauguration party will be held the day before. You'll be expected to say a few inspiring words, as there will be diplomats from Earth, Mars, and Mercury, representing their generous contributions to the dimensional gateway program."

"Don't worry, Atticus." I took a deep breath. "The new concentration's working. Even now, I feel like a new man. I must get some rest. I'll see you tomorrow."

Atticus departed and I went straight to bed. Before I could fall asleep, my communication node chimed, signaling an incoming call. I pulled myself out of bed and trudged across the room. The display screen identified the caller as "Simon Mobius, brother of Theron Mobius."

A prank?

I didn't have any relatives, except for Atticus, who I considered my surrogate family.

Curious, I decided to open communication. I walked to a round cistern recessed in the floor and filled with a liquid matter. I picked up a control sphere and dropped it in. The nano-intelligent matter, by guidance of the control sphere, rose up and took the shape of a human figure. Its form became defined and colors bled through the substance until the figure resembled an almost perfect simulacrum of a man. It had gray eyes, blond hair, and wore a long blue coat.

"Who are you?" I asked. "I have no brothers."

The simulacrum stepped out of the cistern and, moving with all the independence of a real person, shrugged its shoulders. "I had to speak with you, Theron, and I knew such a mysterious communication couldn't go unanswered. Also, I wish to gain your permission to board the Brahman Station using this alias."

"Absurd! Who are you, and what do you want from me?"

"Both these questions must remain unanswered until we can meet in person. This mode of communication can't be trusted. The hyper-signal is poorly encrypted. All I can say is that it's very important."

"What'll you have me do? Invite a stranger aboard a secure space station that's about to launch humankind into the next era of space travel." I waved my hand in disregard. "One who puts blind trust in a stranger is either a fool or has nothing to lose. I assure you, I'm neither."

"That's why I'm going to wait a single day for your decision to grant me permission to board."

"And what in that single day is going to convince me?"

"Do you have a stylus?"

Although puzzled by the request, I guided him to the nearest smart surface. The simulacrum seized the stylus and began sketching something onto my work table. It sketched so quickly that its artificial hand was a blur. When finished, he presented me with a complex schematic.

Intrigued, I shifted the image to my halo-display and it was rendered in three dimensions. I examined it with interest. "My initial instincts tell me it's a lens of some sort."

"You have a quick mind, Theron. You're right. You should have few problems assembling it, since its technology shares a similar physics with your work on the dimensional gateway. In fact, your work was the inspiration for this device." The simulacrum gazed out the apartment window to Jupiter. "When it's assembled, observe the worlds that surround you."

"What exactly will I be looking for?"

"When you see it, you'll know." The simulacrum stepped back into the cistern. The nano-intelligent matter deconstructed itself back to its viscous pre-form, terminating communication.

The next day, motivated by profound curiosity, I attacked the project with determination. In my private workroom, I assembled the lens. It proved to be a complex task, since I had to custom-craft most of the parts. The lens itself was merely an add-on to the station's existing telescope array. As far as I could determine, its function was to modify the array's ability to analyze the eighteen dimensions of the universe.

After an entire day of work, I completed the lens and fully integrated it into the station's telescope array. I directed the newly modified array toward Jupiter and analyzed the data. It showed nothing out of the ordinary. Frustrated by the lack of results, I reluctantly directed the array toward Mars, and again discovered nothing extraordinary.

I became aggravated. My time was being wasted. I repeated the stranger's directions: "Observe the worlds that surround you!" I lifted a fist in anger. "What do you want me to see, goddamnit?"

I finally brought Earth into the eye of the array. There, I discovered something not just extraordinary, but impossible.

"My God, what am I witness to?"

The Earth, by all current indications, was shrouded with a dimension not native to the natural universe. The array displayed the invisible dimension by casting a symbolic sapphire-blue haze around the Earth. All the known laws of dimensional physics dictated this nineteenth dimension couldn't exist.

"Computer, extract all data from the station's main system and upload it to my neural implant."

No one can know of this.

My mind worked long into the night as I tried to understand this mystery. To my dismay, I merely found myself making weak theories on the origin of this impossible and frightening dimension shrouding Earth.

At last, I was tired. I realized I was drowning in an ignorance not to be overcome in a single night. Before going to bed, I sent a message to the security division of the space station, informing them of my guest's anticipated arrival.

The next morning, over two hundred guests from the three planetary nations in the solar system arrived at the Brahman Space Station. They joined the live-in staff of three hundred scientists for the dimensional gateway's inauguration party. It was a grand undertaking held under the stars in the translucent dome of the space station's arboretum, where, amongst its small forest of trees and vegetation, the guests mingled, feasted, and danced. Radiant globes floated among the trees, painting a romantic atmosphere of light and shadow within the arboretum. Ten musicians performed on a stage for the growing crowd. Four dozen dining tables, arranged around a dance floor, were set with the finest silk cloth, silver utensils, and crystal tableware.

By late afternoon, the arboretum echoed with conversation and laughter. I made my entrance, and the crowd greeted me with thunderous applause. It felt good. I had worked hard for this. I found my way to the stage and began.

"To make the dimensional gateway a reality, it's taken nearly fifty years of effort, the resources of three planetary nations, and the most dedicated and brilliant scientists and engineers alive. The success of this endeavor is evidence of humankind's greatness, for soon we'll have all the stars of the universe resting at our fingertips. We'll no longer be bound by the sluggish pace of light-speed travel."

I gazed up through the transparent dome of the arboretum, outstretched my arm, and pointed to a single star. "I foresee a future in which anyone can pick a star in the heavens, and lay claim to it and its planets. Each of us, if we so desire, will have the freedom to establish our own civilization somewhere out there, anywhere, even in another galaxy at the other end of the universe.

"Tomorrow, we'll activate the dimensional gateway, and through it we'll send the first manned pod-ship, which I'll be piloting. The journey, to be only a single light-hour distant, won't be a far journey, but it'll be an instantaneous one. The dimensional gateway does, in fact, have the ability to send the pod-ship clear across the universe. However, the trip would be one-way. Keep in mind that the dimensional gateway housed on the Brahman Space Station is only a prototype. Once we're confident it can consistently create a stable dimensional fissure, we'll be ready to build ships capable of creating their own dimensional fissures, allowing them to travel independently across the universe."

I paused thoughtfully. "Before the celebration continues, I want to thank the generous supporters who provided the resources for this project—notably, the Mars Elitists, the Mercury Miners, and the many officials of Earth." I bowed my head graciously. "Enjoy the evening. I look forward to speaking with all of you."

As I received a final round of applause, I searched through the faces in the crowd, hoping to recognize the mysterious man who had contacted me two days earlier. When I couldn't find him, I set out into the crowd to mingle.

Atticus approached me. "As a matter of etiquette, you should first visit with the heads of the three solar nations."

I looked through the crowd. "I'm not good with faces, Atticus."

Atticus arched his brow. "Theron, I fear you've been cooped up in this space station too long."

I laughed with embarrassment. "So it may be, my friend."

Atticus tilted his head, directing my view. "That extravagantly dressed man is Morion Morpheme, Prime Elitist of Mars. Like most of the Mars Elitists, he looks down on all who are not of his class. He's egocentric, condescending, and, as you'll soon discover, intolerable." Atticus directed my attention to another man. "And over there, standing more than a foot taller than all who surround him, is Orsteen Hunn of the Mercury Miners. Don't let his rugged features and grim expression fool you—his true nature is that of good spirit and kindness." Atticus spun slowly on his heels, so to face the opposite direction. "Standing beside that weeping willow tree and surrounded by her security team is Allienora Chang, Prime Minister of Earth."

I saw her and was speechless.

"I thought you might react in such a way," said Atticus.

"She looks like Cassandra."

"Indeed."

I admired her for a long moment, relishing the similarities she shared with my dead wife—blue piercing eyes, full, sensual lips, and an air of confidence. She wore a vibrant aquamarine gown of ultra-fine fabric. Her golden hair was upswept in a spectacular fashion, as to make it appear like a great cresting wave.

I felt a warmth in my chest that I hadn't felt for decades. "I thought Darius Chang still held the position of Prime Minister of Earth."

"You've got to get your head out of your work," said Atticus. "Prime Minister Darius Chang has retired. She's his daughter and successor. She's been prime minister for over two years."

I moved in her direction, but found her surrounded by many preening gentlemen, strutting about with outthrust chests, all competing for her attention. I decided to hold off on introductions.

I saw that Morion Morpheme, Prime Elitist of Mars, had already engaged Orsteen Hunn of the Mercury Miners in conversation. I approached them and exchanged greetings.

Morion Morpheme smiled at me with child-like enthusiasm. "Mr. Mobius, I'm inspired by your vision of laying claim to a planet in the heavens. Such a whimsical possibility compels me to envision my retirement in a different light. I'll search the cosmos for the perfect planet. On the shores of an alien ocean, I'll build a majestic castle and staff it with butlers, chefs, and concubines." Morion took a profound breath. "I'll live like a king atop my planet, in a style of arcane magnificence."

Even though I'd just said the same thing in my speech—minus the concubines—it sounded insane coming from Morion.

"It sounds like paradise." I turned to Orsteen Hunn. "And what of you, Orsteen? How will your future endeavors be shaped with the entire universe at our disposal?"

"I certainly seek nothing so luxurious, like Morion. I am, however, comforted to know that my people will never be hungry for work. The Mercury Miners will now be able to spread out to new worlds, procuring the unlimited natural resources of the universe."

I saw Allienora Chang approach. She walked with such measured elegance that she seemed to float in our direction.

Be a gentleman. Be interesting. Be calm.

I smiled as she joined us.

"I hope I'm not intruding."

"Not at all, Prime Minister Chang," I said.

"Please, call me Allienora."

"As you like, Allienora." I stood there in an awkward silence.

What the hell's wrong with me? I thought. *I'm a grown man.*

I snapped out of it. "We were just sharing our visions of the future. Orsteen Hunn was remarking on the unlimited resources the universe will soon offer us, and Morion Morpheme was dreaming about a peaceful retirement on a planet he alone would rule."

Allienora looked to the stars. "I don't wish to depress you, but I fear that, with this new freedom, humankind will have the potential to plunge into chaos, unless we can find a way to police these new worlds you envision, Theron. If we allow anyone the freedom to strike their flag into the soil of a distant world, isolated from lawful civilization, then we could soon be faced with a universe full of little dictators and world-mongers." Allienora directed her words to Orsteen Hunn of the Mercury Miners. "Will anyone be allowed to harvest a world of its resources? Who will ensure the preservation of those worlds with unique life?"

"I assure you, Prime Minister Chang," responded Orsteen, "the Mercury Miners are not thoughtless plunderers. We respect the tree that bears the fruit."

"I apologize," said Allienora. "I meant no disrespect. I'm only concerned about the future."

She's right, I thought. *She's as intelligent as she is beautiful. A forward thinker like her father.*

"Let's put business aside." I signaled for drinks and a tray floated in our direction. "Grab a fresh drink and let's dance. This is a celebration, after all."

Allienora smiled. "An excellent idea, Theron."

The party went into full swing, but I found it difficult to immerse myself in the moment. Again and again, my thoughts turned to Earth and the unnatural dimension that shrouded it. I looked repeatedly for the stranger who had contacted me—but, by the end of the night, he had yet to show himself. I was left to retire to my apartment in disappointment.

In the early morning, the computer indicated that someone was at my door. On my doorstep, I discovered a man with the most amazing eyes I'd ever seen. They were brilliant hyper-blue spheres that shimmering and glowed. I leaned in close, transfixed on them. With a close enough view, I could perceive their level of complexity. Small pinpoints of light traveled along pathways throughout the nano-architecture. I could only glimpse the surface of their depth. Their sophistication was breathtaking. The integration of such synthetic eyes into a human body was no small feat. The real question was: What the fuck did they do?

The man, despite his surreal synthetic eyes was sickly-looking. His pale skin accentuated the two eyes and the energetic luster that poured from them.

"May I help you?" I said, still preoccupied with his eyes.

"I'm the one who contacted you two days ago."

I paused, focusing on his facial features. "You don't look like him."

"I prefer not to display my true face when using simulacra."

"Come in," I said, strangely excited. "We have a lot to talk about. I can't begin—"

The stranger held up his hand. He removed a small device from his pocket, placed it on a nearby table, and activated it. "We're now free to talk without worry for eavesdroppers."

"Who are you?" I asked.

"Don't you recognize your dear friend? It's me, Sensimion. Surely you remember the sanitarium."

My thoughts raced. *The sanitarium. The doctor. The sphincter beast. Mage. He lies.*

I turned away. "Often, my mind betrays me with many unreal memories. I've tried my hardest to forget the sanitarium. I'm not even sure it was real."

"If it wasn't real, then neither am I."

"I remember doing horrible things in that place." I turned back to face Sensimion with an insane look. "Did I really kill and skin that orderly?"

"I have proof, Theron." From his pocket, Sensimion removed a laminated scrap of paper. He handed it to me.

My mouth drooped open. It was a list of names I'd written down many years ago. "Where did you get this?"

"I think you know, Theron. I took it from you in the sanitarium." Sensimion paused. "Believe it. All of it was real."

"What happened to us there? Were we really imprisoned for insanity, or was there something more going on, as we suspected?"

"I too questioned my sanity after we escaped. I began doubting our conspiracy theories and wondered if our escape was harmful to our mental health. Even though I didn't feel insane, I knew the truly insane are unaware of their diseased minds. Some years passed and I sought out the credentials of the sanitarium. Since I knew it by no other name, and I knew neither the doctor's nor the orderlies' names, public records were useless.

"I did, however, remember the sanitarium's location. When I returned to that place in the far depths of that MegaCity, I found nothing. Even the walls had been torn down, leaving me to question, like you, the reality of the sanitarium and my experiences within it." Sensimion pulled the list of names from my hand. "If not for this scrap of paper, which I kept in my pocket at all times, I probably would've truly gone crazy." Sensimion gazed into the distance. "I submersed myself in the lives of these people, studying their significance in history. But the names revealed nothing. I was no closer to solving the mystery of the sanitarium and the torture we endured there. I lingered for thirty years, depressed, until I saw you giving a presentation on your theories of dimensional physics. At that moment, my heart was filled with purpose. I realized your life held the answers I sought, since it was from your memories that this list of names was compiled."

"Why didn't you contact me sooner?" I asked.

"I wanted to observe you, study you. Whatever was done to us in the sanitarium, it affected you more than I."

"So I had a few odd memories. What of it? I don't understand where you're going with all this, Sensimion."

"I believe I've discovered the significance of this list of names."

I looked fearfully at the scrap of paper in Sensimion's hand.

"Are you all right, Theron?"

"Yes." I breathed deeply, trying to avoid a panic attack. "Continue."

"In order to explain the significance of the people you listed, Theron, I must return to that point of my life when I thought *you* were the key to the answers I sought, some fifty years ago. At first, I merely hung in the shadows of your life, spying on you. It was when I paralleled your work in dimensional physics that the mystery deepened a thousand fold, for that's when I discovered Earth was surrounded in a dimension not natural to the universe. To ensure the discovery wasn't a miscalculation, I invited other minds to help me understand what I'd found. Soon, I formed a purposeful and secret society."

"Are you saying that my memories from these historical figures are somehow related to this unnatural dimension surrounding Earth?"

"Please, bear with me," said Sensimion.

I nodded.

"We worked for years, trying to further understand the dimension around Earth. At last, we achieved a breakthrough. We developed a lens of even greater sensitivity. It allowed us to detect not only the unnatural dimension around Earth, but also the presence of an indefinable and exotic energy that occupies the dimension. Only then did we discover that there are human imposters walking among us. We observed the cloud of exotic energy producing human forms. These manifestations mimic human beings perfectly."

"Imposters? Manifestations? You're fucking joking, right?"

"Not at all." Sensimion pointed to one of his hyper-blue eyes. "These synthetic eyes allow me to see the exotic energy forming these human imposters."

"Let me get this straight," I said. "These human imposters are literally formed from this exotic energy?"

"Exactly. We're calling this cloud of exotic energy and the unnatural dimension suffocating Earth 'the Fume.'"

"Quite ominous," I said. "Why are these manifestations of the Fume among us?"

"That's the question. We believe they're taking human form so they can manipulate humankind."

I realized my connection to this revelation. "And you believe the people from my memories were all manifestations, as you call them?"

"I do."

I felt ill, as if my stomach were in my throat. "Why would I have their memories? Surely you can see with your synthetic eyes I'm not one of these manifestations of the Fume."

"Whatever was done to us in the sanitarium was the work of the Fume's manifestations, and your memories are a result of them altering your mind."

I went to my nutrition unit and had it dispense two ounces of Red Ethanol. Despite the audible warning for moderation, I chugged it down. "What else do you know of them?"

"From what we've observed, they can't pass beyond the boundaries of the unnatural dimension they've created around Earth. It seems they're connected to it in some way."

"Have you attempted to contact any of the Fume's manifestations?"

Sensimion was silent for a moment, as if struck by a devastating memory. "When we first discovered them, my closest associate and friend made a terrible mistake. He believed if we confronted them with our knowledge of their existence, they might reveal something of their purpose and plot. I was against such a bold tactic, but I couldn't persuade him otherwise. I watched on with a surveillance drone in Earth's orbit as he confronted one of the Fume's manifestations. My friend spoke right to the point: 'I know you're not of this world. I demand to know why you sneak among men and manipulate humankind.' The manifestation responded with a calm gaze, and my friend soon after burned to ash."

"Then they are powerful beings," I said.

"Powerful enough to turn a man to ash in the blink of an eye." Sensimion shook his head sadly. "I blame myself for the tragedy. I shouldn't have allowed the interaction to occur, since my experience in the sanitarium was a clear indication of the manifestations' threatening nature. Ever since this powerful display, my people haven't set foot within the dimension around Earth. We've hidden ourselves in a remote location of the solar system."

Is this truly Sensimion? I thought. *Can these revelations be real?*

"I can sense your doubt, Theron. You must believe me."

How could I? I looked out the window to Jupiter. "I stand here on the highland of my life. To finish the dimensional gateway, I've worked with all my soul. Why do you come to me, now, with these world-shattering revelations?"

"I'm not here by coincidence or bad timing. I've come here to help preserve this project you hold so close to your heart."

"How?"

"Exactly one week ago, my people detected a trace of the Fume's exotic energy on the Brahman Station."

"I thought you said these manifestations can't pass beyond the boundaries of the unnatural dimension around Earth?"

"We don't know how yet, but the exotic energy we detected only lasted a few minutes and then vanished. If it were a manifestation of the Fume, there would still be traces of the exotic energy—which there isn't."

"What does it mean?"

"We don't know," said Sensimion. "Nevertheless, we believe the Brahman Station may be in some kind of danger. And that, old friend, is the reason I'm here."

"Certainly you don't expect me to abandon the maiden voyage? People will think I'm crazy if I tell them what you've told me."

"I wish only to be given access to the Brahman Station during the maiden voyage. I'll be able to detect the presence of any exotic energy with my synthetic eyes."

"Giving you such access would raise suspicion among my colleagues."

"Don't worry. I'll be able to look over the entire station from these quarters." Sensimion removed a large ocular device from a pouch. "This spatial rendering sensor can see through walls. If I detect something sinister transpiring, only then will I move through the station. I would, however, like a tour of the station and proper introductions to any important people."

"With those eyes?"

"These are amazing times, my friend. Everything is new. If they ask, tell them they're experimental. Tell them I was blind."

I groaned. "How shall I introduce you?"

"As your brother, Simon Mobius."

"I've known the people on this station a long time. They know I don't have any family. It'll be much simpler if I introduce you as a friend from my youth, who's like a brother." I checked the time. "The day has begun. Once I'm ready, I'll take you out into the station, where you'll stay close by my side. Understood?"

Sensimion nodded.

"Are you all right, Sensimion?" There was definitely something wrong with him. "You look sick."

"A side effect of these synthetic eyes. They require a lot of energy, which is drawn biochemically from my body. They're a tolerable burden, given the reward of seeing the unnatural dimension and exotic energy of the Fume."

I made my way to the main control room of the dimensional gateway with Sensimion. I was scheduled to meet with some of the more important guests, and give them a private tour of the dimensional gateway.

"Good morning," I said, greeting about twenty guests, which included the Prime Minister of Earth, Allienora Chang; Orsteen Hunn of the Mercury Miners; and Morion Morpheme, Prime Elitist of Mars.

All in the room looked with seeming fascination at Sensimion.

A stocky man with slicked back hair approached me. "I'm the Defense Minister of Earth, Renworth Vole. I wish to congratulate you on your achievement, Mr. Mobius." He held out his hand.

I shook it and was surprised to feel nano-intelligent matter. He was a simulacrum. "It's unfortunate you couldn't be here in person."

"Seeing the event via simulacrum will have to suffice. I have many important things to do here on Earth." Renworth Vole stared into Sensimion's eyes. "And who's this?"

"This is Simon," I said, simply.

"It's a pleasure to meet you, Simon," said Renworth Vole.

Sensimion squinted. "Have we met before?"

"I don't think so," replied Renworth. "I would remember a man with such exquisite eyes."

"Where's Atticus!" I shouted nervously. I glanced around the room, and then beckoned a nearby technician. "He was supposed to be here ten minutes ago."

The technician responded, "He's making a last minute round of the gateway."

"Then I'll have to begin the tour without him."

I led the guests to a great oval window in the upper control room. It overlooked a massive chamber, constituting half the volume of the Brahman Station.

"Below us is the dimensional gateway engine. As you can see, there are eighteen enormous dimensional augmenters arranged in a circle, twenty meters in diameter. When they're activated, they'll generate the dimensional fissure, which will span the twenty-meter circle. If you look overhead, you'll see the pod-ship I'll be piloting. Once the dimensional gateway is open, I'll fly the pod-ship down into the dimensional fissure, and be instantaneously transported to the designated coordinates, one light-hour away. And this, as simple as it sounds, will be the entire event you'll be witnessing today."

"Are you certain your trip through the dimensional gateway won't be dangerous?" asked Allienora Chang, stepping close to me. "The human body is a sensitive thing."

She smells fantastic, I thought, detecting the scent of vanilla.

"We've already sent an assortment of primitive life forms through the gateway, and have yet to see any complications. If there were a possibility of harm, I wouldn't be so eager to be the first man to journey through it."

A woman in a white business suit stepped boldly in front of Allienora. "The public has questions, Mr. Mobius."

I noticed the small media orb floating just above her shoulder.

Great, I thought. *Here comes the accusations.*

The media just wanted scandal and reaction shots. If they couldn't find real scandal they did their best to create it. I hated these media skaggs. I wished I could shoot her out an open hatch into space. That's where they all belonged.

"I'm here to answer all your questions, Ms...." I looked to her I.D. badge. "Ms. Pendike."

"As you know, Mr. Mobius, your biography was just released in the *Neofrontier Chronicle*."

"Actually..." I interrupted, knowing it would piss her off. "I didn't know. I'll be sure to upload a copy."

"Anyway," she continued. "Your relationship with Atticus Roth is detailed greatly. He rescued you from the streets, mentored you both morally and academically, and eventually became your colleague in your pursuit to build this dimensional gateway."

"This is true. He has made me the man I am. I trust him implicitly. He's a friend and a father. He's the biggest influence in my life."

"What isn't documented in your biography..." She took a deep breath to accentuate that something important was about to spill from her over-plumped, genetically engineered lips. "Is that Atticus Roth manipulated and deceived you."

Chatter filled the control room.

Allienora stepped forward and held up her hand in a call for silence. "What are you talking about, Ms. Pendike?"

"Sixty years ago, Atticus Roth stole a prototype neural accelerator chip from the Tetrion Corporation. This is months before Theron received his first neural interface—when they were just hitting the market at the turn of the millennium. I believe Atticus secretly integrated this stolen tech into Theron's implant. I believe Atticus made Theron the man he is, so he could reach the fame and fortune he has now attained. Theron's breakthroughs in dimensional physics were only achieved after he was implanted with the hyper accelerated neural interface."

Holy shit, I thought. *How did she find out?*

She was pretty close to the truth. She got two things wrong. I was willingly implanted with the device and I even helped Atticus steal it. It wasn't about the money, though. It was about so much more.

Allienora moved closer to Ms. Pendike, who took an uneasy step backwards. It was exhilarating to witness the power Allienora held over people that stood in her presence. I found myself even more attracted to her.

"You still haven't provided us proof, Ms. Pendike."

Ms. Pendike held up a data node. "Here's my proof."

Allienora took it from her. Before she could uplink with it, her personal guard stopped her.

"Prime Minister. That is an untested data node. There could be malicious coding on it."

"I'll be fine," she said, touching the node to the back of her neck to trigger the uplink. Her eyes fluttered as her neural implant took in the data and transferred it to her conscious mind. "This is hardly proof that Atticus was involved. All you have here are leaked documents from the Tetrion Corporation, confirming the theft of the prototype neural accelerator chip and its schematics. Nothing in them implicates Atticus."

I felt relieved until Ms. Pendike revealed a neural analyzer.

A smug look distorted her over-altered features. "Then Theron won't mind if I test his neural implant."

Allienora grabbed it from her hands. "I'll test Theron."

What do I do? My heart raced. *This could ruin everything.*

Allienora separated the two halves of the analyzer. She placed one on the back of her neck and one on the back of mine. I didn't resist. I just tried to play it cool. Though, I probably should've said something.

Allienora activated the analyzer and her eyes again fluttered as she took in the data. It was the longest ten seconds of my life. Her eyes finally stopped fluttering and she looked at me intensely. She must have seen the data imprint from the chip.

What is she going to do?

She smiled ever so slightly. "There's nothing there. No trace of the neural accelerator chip."

"Impossible!" shouted Ms. Pendike. "Let me look!"

"I'm the Prime Minister of Earth, Ms. Pendike. Are you questioning my ability to use a simple neural analyzer? There's nothing there." Allienora signaled her personal guard. "Get her off the station."

What just happened? How did she not see it?

"The theatrics are over," announced Allienora. "Theron, please continue."

"Very well," I said, breathing easier. I looked through the faces. "Before I take you down for a closer look at the dimensional gateway, I must know who among you would like the privilege to be aboard the rendezvous ship, which will be present at the pod-ship's emergence point? You must decide now, since it'll take the rendezvous ship an hour to get there at light-speed. Otherwise, you may remain here to see my departure with the rest of the guests."

"Definitely I," said Morion Morpheme, with an oddly impatient enthusiasm.

Allienora stepped forward. "If only a limited few will be present at the emergence point, then I too would like to be on hand to witness the spectacle." She turned to Orsteen Hunn of the Mercury Miners. "Will you accompany me, Orsteen?"

"It would be my honor."

"Very well," I said. "Once your tour's completed, you'll be taken to the rendezvous ship."

I finished with the leaders of the three solar nations and saw to their departure aboard the rendezvous ship.

Allienora was last to board.

She signaled her personal guard to board ahead of her. "I want a private moment with Mr. Mobius."

I grew nervous as we stood there alone at the docking gate. Her large blue eyes examined me—as if she were measuring the depths of my being. It became clear what she was thinking.

She knows.

My head sagged in guilt. "Why didn't you tell them?"

"Because it doesn't matter. I don't care how you did it, Theron. You're about to change everything. Humankind will never be the same. This is the beginning of something great, and we have you to thank for it."

"What about Ms. Pendike? She won't give up."

"I'll take care of her. I'll make her understand. I have ways of dealing with her kind."

"I'm sorry, Allienora. I hope I didn't disappoint you."

"People have done worse things to achieve their goals. You didn't hurt anyone, Theron."

"I hope I'll see you after the maiden voyage."

"You can count on it."

She gave me an unexpected kiss on the cheek.

I smiled. "Safe travels."

"You too. Good luck."

I returned to my apartment, where Sensimion was setting up various monitoring equipment for his lookout during the maiden voyage.

I went to a console. "These are the access codes to the entire station. You may upload them to your neural implant."

While Sensimion interlinked with the console, I administered a drop of amber narcotic into my eye. It was early for another dose, but I had to make sure the memories wouldn't return during the maiden voyage.

"What's that, Theron?" asked Sensimion.

I relaxed as the liquid permeated the membrane of my eye. I then tucked the vial back into my pocket. "With this drug, I've found relief from those haunting memories, which were an unbearable undertow of pain."

"Astonishing," said Sensimion. "I hope when your maiden voyage is complete, you'll consider cleansing yourself of this drug, so we can analyze the full scope of these memories. They could be our best means to discovering the motives of the Fume's manifestations."

"I suppose, if it would help. But it would have to be for a short period, since I'd begin to lose the clarity of my own true memories, which define me."

"I understand," said Sensimion. "Now, if you don't mind, I must begin my surveillance of the station."

"As you wish. I must see to a few things before I journey through the gateway."

In truth, I had very little to do. My only obligation was in two hours' time, when I'd sit in the small pod-ship, direct its nose toward the dimensional gateway, and plunge. In the meantime, I set out to find Atticus, who I hadn't seen all morning.

Strangely, I couldn't find him.

I ate a light lunch in the dining hall and then dressed myself in a flight suit. Just as I was about to make my way to the pod-ship, I paused. "What the fuck are you thinking, you fool?"

I quickly returned to my apartment.

"What's the matter?" asked Sensimion.

"Nothing," I replied, moving straight to the dining table.

I retrieved the picture of my dead wife and took it into the bathroom, away from Sensimion. I breathed a sigh of relief as I relished her image.

"I almost forgot, my dear Cassandra."

I removed the back of the picture frame and retrieved the thin silver necklace hidden within. I held it up and admired its delicate pendant—a fine, filigreed, cobalt-blue metal in the shape of an infinity spiral. I had given it to her instead of an engagement ring. After accepting my marriage proposal, she wore the infinity spiral over her heart, never removing it—until death.

"If anything happens..." I placed the necklace around my neck. "...we'll be together soon."

I tucked the pendant under my flight suit and left my apartment.

I went to the docking platform of the pod-ship, where I at last found Atticus on-hand to see me off.

"We've worked hard for this day, Atticus."

"Nothing will be the same after you pass through the dimensional gateway."

"Allienora and I were just talking about that." I looked down on the ring of eighteen dimensional augmenters. "Humankind will see great change."

"You have no idea, Theron," uttered Atticus.

I found Atticus' response a bit perplexing. I placed my hand on his shoulder. "You seem tense, my friend. When I return, we'll calm your nerves with toasts of champagne."

Atticus' stomach growled. He clutched his abdomen with both hands, as if to contain any further volatility. "Excuse me."

"Don't be nervous. I'll see you soon, Atticus." I waved farewell to the hundreds of spectators sitting within the many observation rooms surrounding the chamber of the dimensional gateway. I heard their muted cheers from behind the glass windows. I boarded the pod-ship, and sat comfortably in the control chair. Looking through a porthole, I discovered Atticus had departed the docking platform.

Over my communication node came the voice of a technician: "We'll be activating the dimensional gateway in exactly thirty minutes, Mr. Mobius."

"Very well," I replied. "My neural implant is interlinked with the pod-ship. I wait for your signal to descend into the dimensional gateway."

With only thirty minutes until the dimensional gateway's activation, Sensimion continued to search for anything out of the ordinary. His ocular device allowed him to see through walls and spy into every corner of the station. He saw Theron in the pod-ship, the many spectators sitting on the edges of their seats, and the engineers, scientists, and technicians carrying on with their duties. Nowhere did Sensimion detect, with his synthetic eyes, the sapphire-blue glow of the Fume's manifestations, or any other exotic energy or unnatural dimension.

All seemed fine, until Sensimion scanned the personal apartments of the live-in staff. There, he saw something in the hollow space of a wall—the inactive figure of a man slumped into an awkward pile. Due to the angle of the man's position, Sensimion couldn't see his face.

Sensimion grabbed a plasma gun and headed to the apartment. He bypassed the lock on the front door with the access codes Theron had given him. Within, he noticed a wall panel slightly askew. He pulled it open and found the inactive man. Beside him sat a bizarre organic mass that Sensimion couldn't classify. It was shaped like a giant egg. Its outer husk had the texture of charred flesh. A fracture ran up its length, allowing Sensimion a view of its insides. The husk was hollow, almost as if something had been hatched from within. Sensimion turned his attention to the incapacitated man. He was still alive.

Sensimion pulled him from the wall and laid him on his back. He recognized the man as Theron's friend and colleague, Atticus. There was a metal device lodged in his nostrils. Sensimion delicately extracted it and Atticus showed signs of wakefulness. Sensimion helped the process along with stern words: "Open your eyes! Do you hear me, old man? Wake up!"

Atticus made inarticulate sounds until, at last, he spoke. "What's that awful smell?"

"Never mind your smell," said Sensimion. "Why have I found you unconscious in a wall?"

Atticus sat up from the floor. "I was at my desk, reviewing dimensional vector calculations for the maiden voyage, when I heard a thumping coming from inside the wall. When I removed the wall panel, I found myself face to face... with myself. A doppelgänger, if you will. I stood there in shock, until my double knocked me out." Atticus stood up. "What day is it?"

"It's the day of the maiden voyage," said Sensimion.

"I've lost almost an entire day!"

"If that's true, then this doppelgänger, as you call him, has been impersonating you all day." Sensimion suddenly remembered that fifteen minutes ago he had spotted Atticus. He now realized it was his doppelgänger. He had been making adjustments to one of the dimensional augmenters. "The station's in danger! Atticus, get to the control room and tell them to abort the maiden voyage. They must not activate the dimensional gateway. I'll find your doppelgänger and stop him."

Sensimion moved through the Brahman Station with speed. When he reached the expansive chamber of the dimensional gateway, he moved with a more deliberate gait, so not to startle the doppelgänger into desperate action.

He located Atticus' doppelgänger and stood out of sight, trying to gain a general understanding of his meddling.

The doppelgänger stood at an open panel of one of the dimensional augmenters, giving him access to its inner workings. Sensimion watched on in secret as the doppelgänger performed a strange act—he placed his hands on his belly and began kneading the meat of it, as if adjusting its contents to his better comfort. He continued to work his belly thoughtfully, and then released a disgusting progression of belches that evolved into gagging. Immediately, something of substance began rising from the bowels of the doppelgänger. A significant bulge could be seen at his throat as the object traveled upward, until finally it came to rest in his mouth.

A rich yellow light spilled from the doppelgänger's mouth as a glowing orb breached his lips. He snatched it from his mouth with a three-fingered grip and held it on fingertips, admiring its swirling, plasma-like nature.

Sensimion sensed it was a thing of force and leveled his weapon. "Move and you die!"

The doppelgänger turned. An evil expression spread across his face.

"Who are you?" asked Sensimion. "You're not one of the Fume's manifestations. You don't emit the signature exotic energy."

"When you speak of 'the Fume,' I assume you're referring to my master."

"And you're his minion?"

"I'm his loyal servant, yes."

"Why does your master wish to destroy the dimensional gateway?"

The doppelgänger chuckled, as if the question were humorous. "I doubt I can answer this question to your fullest satisfaction. You see, when my master created me, he gave me only the necessary thoughts and emotions required for my mission."

"It seems you've failed him, since I've stopped your sabotage."

"You're late with your heroics. This is the last orb I must deposit within the eighteen dimensional augmenters."

"Remain still," commanded Sensimion, anticipating the doppelgänger's desire to lunge toward the dimensional augmenter. In the short while the doppelgänger had been holding up the radiant orb, Sensimion had gained a small understanding of its power, for it exuded such acrid force that it caused bloody lesions to tear across the skin of the doppelgänger's face and arms as it shined forth so brilliantly. "You don't look well."

"Since you force me to stand here, I must endure the effect of being so close to the orb."

"Yet it's been in your stomach for at least an entire day."

"My master specifically designed my stomach to contain the powerful energy of the orbs."

"You reveal too much!" said Sensimion triumphantly. "Now, swallow the orb! Unless you wish me to thrust it down your throat with the full extent of my arm."

"My life has been short, but one of purpose," proclaimed the doppelgänger. And as the doppelgänger's mouth gaped wide in a toothy grin, he launched the orb with the flick of two fingers into the open hatch of the dimensional augmenter.

The doppelgänger's sudden movement caused Sensimion to discharge his weapon, sending a plasma molecule toward the doppelgänger's head, where it impacted in an explosion of face, brain, and skull. Atticus' doppelgänger fell dead.

I waited patiently in the pod-ship, unaware of what was transpiring below me. I heard Atticus' cries over the control room intercom: "Abort! Abort the maiden voyage! There's a saboteur aboard the station! His disguise is amazing—he looks exactly like me! I don't know how or why, but he has tampered with the dimensional gateway!"

"The station is safe," said a technician. "We haven't activated the dimensional gateway."

I felt a chill up my spine. Sensimion's concerns for the station's safety were right. I spoke to Atticus over the intercom: "Where's the saboteur now?"

"I'm uncertain," replied Atticus. "Only ten minutes ago, a stranger with pale features and mesmerizing blue synthetic eyes rescued me from inside a wall, where I've been unconscious for almost an entire day, drugged by my doppelgänger. Even now, my savior's trying to catch the saboteur."

Just as Atticus began to elaborate on his encounter with his doppelgänger, the dimensional gateway came alive.

I heard Atticus yelling at a technician: "Are you deaf? Why have you activated the gateway?"

"I haven't," pleaded the technician. "It activated on its own."

I looked down on the ring of dimensional augmenters and saw the formation of the dimensional fissure. Dancing facets of rich magenta and brilliant white light emanated from the center of the gateway, until a blinding light exploded outward, and then receded. The dimensional fissure, although now imperceptible, was fully formed.

I heard Atticus' panicked voice: "This data is impossible. The dimensional augmenters are over-distorting the tertiary dimensions. Dimensional symmetry is chaotic.

"Shut it down!" I called, horror-struck as the dimensional augmenters made a hideous sound, like the sustained cry of a dying animal.

"I can't," replied Atticus.

I moved close to the communication node to ensure Atticus would hear me. "Shunt the power of the fusion reactors away from the dimensional augmenters."

"I've already tried," he replied. "Wait, I did it!"

But Atticus' howl of success was premature, as one of the fusion reactors ruptured. A plume of superheated plasma curled up toward the pod-ship. It impacted with terrible force, disabling the gravity drive and causing an internal explosion, which sent a hail of molten shrapnel into my left arm.

"Fucking hell!" I screamed, as my arm burned.

The pod-ship was still attached to the docking platform by a single clamp—it dangled without power. The gravity wake of the dimensional fissure pulled the pod-ship downward. The docking clamp tore free and my pod-ship entered the dimensional fissure.

GODS
AND
MONSTERS

I woke up, barely able to see. My vision was distorted. It felt like I was in bed. It was dark. I tried to clear my eyes but couldn't. My right arm was a stump. It flailed back and forth.

"My arm! Where's my arm?" Doubt and despair overwhelmed me. "Where am I!" I screamed. "Of course I know my name! I'm Cheung Po Tsai, son of a fisherman, captain of this vessel."

No one responded.

I jumped from bed and crashed to the floor—my legs collapsed from my own weight. "What is this place? Where's my crew?"

I stood frozen in a confused moment. Strange lights surrounded me. At last, I recognized the glow of computer consoles and medical equipment. What the hell was I thinking? I wasn't a captain, or the son of a fisherman. I remembered now—the pod-ship, the explosion, the pain of molten shrapnel.

I lifted myself up and sat at the edge of the bed. *What's wrong with me? I'm broken, fractured, flawed. Help me, God. Help me, anyone.*

I repeated a mantra that helped me through such bouts: "I am Theron Mobius. I am myself. My mind is my center..."

I need my narcotic.

I pushed the memories of the pirate captain from my mind and cleared my eyes with my existing arm. I was in a hospital room. Nearby, a glass incubation cylinder contained a half-grown replacement arm. I continued to search the dim room for my amber narcotic. Someone was sitting at a table.

"You there!" I called. "Why do you sit in the dark? Where are my clothes, my personal effects?"

After no response, I called for the lights and discovered it was a computer-guided simulacrum, working on the construction of a rehabilitation mesh for my soon-to-be arm.

I found my vial of amber narcotic among the shredded remains of my flight suit. I fumbled impatiently to open it—my current one-armed condition made it hard. I administered a generous dose and my mind soon became clear.

Eager to learn the state of the Brahman Station, I made for the door, but found it locked from the outside. After pounding on it to no avail, I paced the room in frustration.

At last, the door unlocked and Allienora Chang entered. I was glad to see her.

"Why was I locked in this room? What happened to the Brahman Station?"

Allienora paused in a strange way. "There are many questions to be answered, Mr. Mobius."

"How do you mean? What happened? I can't remember anything after the explosion crippled my pod-ship."

"After the explosion, your pod-ship successfully passed through the dimensional fissure and arrived at its chosen emergence point."

"We did it! This is fantastic."

"For you, yes. Unfortunately, the Brahman Station was soon after pulled into Jupiter's atmosphere."

"What are you saying?"

Allienora stood silent for a moment. "The Brahman Station was destroyed."

I fell back on the hospital bed. "Survivors?"

"Only you and those aboard the rendezvous ship, which included me, Orsteen Hunn of the Mercury Miners, Morion Morpheme of the Mars Elitists, and a few others of your staff."

With trembling fingers, I cradled the infinity spiral pendant that hung from my neck.

Now I've lost Atticus as well.

Allienora went to a view-panel and brought up four side-by-side video images. "This is the scene of the station after you passed through the dimensional fissure."

I watched the four recordings of the Brahman Station as chaos ensued. People screamed, alarms buzzed, and the dimensional gateway made a deep, gut-wrenching noise as it headed for meltdown. Computers spoke calm warnings of imminent doom, while the crew darted about, making every last effort to silence the storm. I could barely watch as my life's work crumbled before my very eyes.

I watched an external video of the station taken from a nearby ship.

Allienora explained, "The dimensional fissure created an unanticipated gravity wake."

The Brahman Station was pulled closer and closer to Jupiter. In a hopeless tug-of-war, the station's gravity drive screamed as it tried to counteract the gravity between Jupiter and the dimensional fissure. The Brahman Station moved with increasing velocity toward Jupiter and I heard Atticus on the recording send out a signal to abandon ship. Such an alert, however, came too late, and the station vanished into the brown and beige turbulence of Jupiter's upper atmosphere.

The recordings ended and I stood silent. I lost everything—my life's work, my friends and co-workers, and Atticus, the closest person to a father I'd ever known.

What is this cruel force working against me? I could only painfully wonder.

Allienora seemed unusually cold. "Once your arm has been replaced, you'll be brought before a panel of officials for an inquiry."

"I don't understand. Are you suggesting I'm somehow responsible for this?"

"Due to a case of blood poisoning from the shrapnel lodged in your now-amputated arm, you've been unconscious for a week. During this time, we've discovered that just before the sabotage, you invited a man named Sensimion aboard the Brahman Station and gave him the access codes to the entire facility. This man was the reported leader of a rogue group that has assassinated various members of Earth's government."

"Jesus Christ! Why would I help sabotage my life's work? You're wrong about Sensimion and his motives aboard the station."

Allienora held up her hand. "Save your defense for the inquiry. Until then, you'll remain in this room."

I couldn't believe what she was implying. "And where the fuck is this room, Madam Prime Minister?"

"We're in a secret undersea military base just beyond the flooded ruins of Old New York City, off the coast of North America." Allienora signaled to one of her personal guards, who had been watching on from just outside the doorway. "Get this man some clothes. We can't have him in his underwear during the inquiry."

After a week of being held like a prisoner, my replacement arm finally reached full maturity. After the surgery, I lay on my hospital bed, still drunk from the anesthesia. The simulacrum began fitting a rehabilitation mesh onto my new arm.

"Must you do this now?" I slurred.

It didn't respond and continued its task while reciting instructions for the rehabilitation mesh. Midway through its instruction, the simulacrum became oddly still. Its eyes, which were filled with the murk of a thoughtless drone, became clear.

It looked at me with new spirit and spoke: "Theron Mobius, my time is brief, so listen carefully. As we speak, a fleet of one hundred and twelve Obelisks head for Earth."

"Who are you?" I sat up on elbows. "What do you mean Obelisks?"

"They may be ships, they may be weapons, they may be something else. We're uncertain. However, we believe the Fume controls them. It's essential you get to these coordinates within four days." The simulacrum repeated a set of numbers two times. "If you don't, you'll be damned with the rest of the Earth's population to an unknown and possibly unfavorable fate."

"I don't know who you are, but I'm a prisoner in this place. I'm not going anywhere. They think I'm responsible for the destruction of the Brahman Station."

"My leader, Sensimion, knew otherwise, as do I. Go to the underwater launching bay of this base. It should become active when they learn of the inbound Obelisks. One more thing..." The simulacrum reached under the hospital bed and revealed a hidden hypo-injector. It then grabbed me by the neck and injected me with its full dose.

"Motherfucker!" I screamed. "What the hell was that?"

"Trust no one save your eyes."

Before I could further question the simulacrum about the glowing silver content of the hypo-injector, it stepped into its holding cistern. The nano-intelligent matter of the simulacrum deconstructed itself into its viscous pre-form.

I rested for another three days in the hospital room. Instead of finding revitalization, I grew ill. My arms were weak and heavy, my face was pale and ghostly, and my brain ached with the sensation of a hundred piercing needles.

What the hell was in that hypo-injector?

Despite my worsening condition, two guards escorted me to a room attended by twelve officials. All exuded a self-righteous air, suggesting they were diplomats and military personnel. They sat in a row at one side of a large smart table, across from a single lonely chair to which I was directed.

Of the twelve faces before me, I could only identify two—Allienora Chang and Defense Minister Renworth

Vole, the gentleman I had met through simulacrum on the Brahman Station, only hours before its sabotage.

I took my seat and experienced an irksome sensation. It wasn't related to the illness induced by the injection from Sensimion's colleague, but rather it was a sensation somehow dreadfully familiar. I couldn't remember when I had felt it before. It warped my mind in a terrifying way. The sensation flowed through me, and twisted in my stomach like a coiling serpent.

Before I could put my finger on the familiar sensation, Allienora began the inquiry. "We gather on this day to address your involvement, Theron Mobius, in the sabotage of the Brahman Station."

I pounded my fist on the table. "Goddamn you all! I've lost everything from this tragedy. Why do you wish to further plunge me into this quagmire of misery? I've done nothing wrong!"

"Don't jump to conclusions, Mr. Mobius," said Defense Minister Renworth Vole. "We're not here to incriminate you for the events on the Brahman Station. We don't believe you were directly responsible. Yet, we do believe you were deceived by this fellow, Sensimion, so he could gain access to the Brahman Station. From the recordings we have of the events, we're certain Sensimion was behind the sabotage."

"I'm confused," I said. "If you have recordings of the events on the station, then you have the recording of Atticus crying out just before my pod-ship was damaged."

"What are you referring to, Mr. Mobius?" asked one of Renworth Vole's advisers.

"Just before the dimensional gateway was activated, Atticus spoke about his doppelgänger. There was someone aboard the station impersonating him. Atticus also indicated that Sensimion was trying to stop the saboteur."

"There are no such recordings," said Allienora. "You were badly injured, Theron. Could these events be a hallucination?"

"No! These events happened before I was hurt."

Renworth Vole drummed large fingers on the table. "Maybe Atticus was also a part of this conspiracy."

"A possibility we should look into," said Renworth Vole's advisor.

I stood tall out of my chair. "How dare you implicate Atticus! He was a good man! He was my friend! My family!"

"Calm yourself," said Renworth Vole. "Tell us how Sensimion coaxed you into giving him access to the Brahman Station."

I'll tell them everything. I'll clear Atticus' name. I'll tell them of the unnatural dimension shrouding Earth and the manifestations of the Fume that manipulate humankind.

But, as my lips formed words, I hesitated. I remembered the oppressive sensation that afflicted me minutes ago. The only other time I had felt such visceral dread had been in the presence of that bastard doctor from the sanitarium. And if I took all Sensimion's theories for fact, then the doctor from the sanitarium was a manifestation of the Fume—and, by some mysterious ability, I was able to sense the presence of these manifestations. If this was indeed the case, then I sensed another manifestation at this very moment sitting across the table from me.

One of these twelve officials is a monster. A monster I will kill! Kill! Kill!

I froze in anger. The true saboteur of the Brahman Station—and demolisher of my life—sat with confidence

73

before me. I now knew why there were no recordings of Atticus' outcries before the sabotage. The manifestations of the Fume were attempting to blame Sensimion.

"Are you all right, Theron?" asked Allienora. "It's not a difficult question."

"But it is, Prime Minister Chang—" Before I could continue, I fell back into my chair. "I apologize. Many emotions clutter my mind. Where's the bathroom?"

Allienora stood up and held out her hand. "I'll show you."

I took her hand. Her skin was soft. As I stood up, I again smelled vanilla. She walked me down the hallway, but suddenly stopped.

"I want to set the record straight," she said.

"About what?"

"This." She pointed back to the room of officials. "I'm not in charge of this."

"In charge of laying blame?"

"Little do you know, Theron. I've been your biggest supporter. I've followed your work more closely than you can imagine. I know everything about you and your project."

"Then why don't you help me?"

She bit her lip, as if frustrated with me. "Let me tell you something you don't know. When I came into office, nearly all the nations' leaders wanted to halt the funding for your project. I had to pull a lot of favors to keep the money flowing. You may think I'm just a pretty face, but I do command power."

"If you're behind me, then why don't you tell those fuckers they're wrong?"

"This is just formality. I'll look at all the evidence and make the final judgment." She leaned close to me and whispered, "Don't worry. I still have faith in you, Theron."

Something happened when I felt her breath on my ear. I don't know what, but something changed inside me. Or did she just remind me too much of my dead wife? I didn't know.

"Are you all right?" she said.

My knees suddenly buckled and I caught myself against the wall. Something was wrong with me. My headache had become unbearable. "Where's the bathroom?"

"Down the hall and two doors to the left."

I walked unsteadily to the bathroom and locked the door behind me. I stood in front of the sink and splashed cold water on my face. I saw my reflection in the mirror and became terrified by a strange development— hemorrhaging capillaries radiated throughout the whites of my eyes, forming two bloody web-works. My eyeballs felt as though they were ready to burst from my skull.

I sat slumped on the floor and rubbed my palms into my eye sockets, attempting to massage away the pain. Ten, maybe twenty, maybe thirty minutes passed. Time moved slowly. I at last snapped out of it when someone knocked at the door.

"I'll be right out!" I called, lifting myself to my feet. I made one last glance to the mirror and found myself confronted by a familiar phantom. I now shared a similar appearance with that of the late Sensimion—my eyes were synthetic hyper-blue spheres. They glowed with brilliant blue and white light. I rather liked my new look—half man, half machine. I may have felt like shit, but I looked like some kind of superhero, eyes glowing with power.

The injection administered by Sensimion's colleague gave me the synthetic eyes that would allow me to see the manifestations of the Fume lurking in my presence. And although this would surely prove to be a useful ability, it also created a dilemma of immediate gravity.

If I go back before the inquiry with the synthetic eyes of Sensimion, I'll be condemned as a traitor and imprisoned. The Fume's manifestation's plan to accuse Sensimion will be achieved. I must act now.

I had to follow the instructions of Sensimion's colleague. There was only a day remaining to reach the Earth coordinates given to me.

I cracked open the bathroom door and discovered a single guard attending me. I left the door open, hunched over the sink, and called out in pain.

The guard entered the bathroom. "What's wrong with you?"

"Look at my arm!" I cried.

The guard looked down and my fist came up with full force, hitting his forehead. He fell unconscious to the floor and I took off his clothes.

In my new military outfit, I moved as casually as possible down the corridor, in the opposite direction of the group of officials. My only hope for escape hinged on Sensimion's colleague's prediction that the underwater launching bay of the base would be opened, so to allow me passage up through the waters of the Atlantic Ocean. As I searched for the launching bay, I hung a tired expression on my face, exposing only a thin line of my electric hyper-blue eyes. It proved a successful tactic as my eyes went unnoticed by two people passing by.

I took a wrong turn into a storeroom. It contained an assortment of forgotten oddities and artifacts I would've expected to discover in a secret military base—prototype weapons, AI-droids, and various other secret technologies. To my astonishment, I came upon a row of cryo-cylinders, packed and plugged with people being stored like fine wines. From what I could tell, it was a repository of people thought to have historical importance—past prime ministers, scientists, scholars, musicians, and writers. If not for the placards naming them, they would've been impossible to recognize through the cloudy cryo-gel preserving them.

Before moving onward, I grabbed a plasma gun, a string of marble-sized explosives, and an anti-gravity belt that I secured tightly around my waist.

I must be prepared for anything.

I finally found the launching bay's large security door. I interlinked with a control panel and, surprisingly, found the door to be unlocked. It opened to a chamber of profound dimension. Hundreds of anti-relativity warships hovered above, near the twenty-story high ceiling. They resembled a school of hibernating fish lingering in cold waters. Below them sat assorted equipment, computers, and machinery. A giant deuterium isolator piped down the ocean waters and separated deuterium to fuel the ships. AI-droids monitored the equipment and serviced the warships. At first glance, I didn't see any people. Only when I looked to a far wall did I realize I wasn't alone.

The horror, I thought. *I've seen it before.*

Across the wall hung hundreds of people. A network of transparent tubes connected them all together. The tubes were fused to their mouths and genitals, feeding them a pink nutrient broth and carrying away waste matter. Mechanical insects patrolled their flesh, cutting away necrotic tissue and sealing open sores. I could see fiber-optics coming from the backs of their necks, possibly indicating that their neural interfaces were hardwired to a computer mainframe.

Defense Minister Renworth Vole's voice came from behind me: "Your absence from the inquiry had us worried. I see now you're just lost, Theron."

I turned. With my new eyes, I saw Renworth Vole glowing with the sapphire-blue haze indicative of one of the Fume's manifestations. I stumbled a few steps backward, regained my balance, and then put on my most fearless face.

"I'm not surprised you're the Fume's manifestation. That's why you had to witness the maiden voyage via simulacrum. Being one of the Fume's manifestations, you're confined within the unnatural dimension around Earth, and couldn't travel in person to the Brahman Station."

He ignored my statement. "You look dreadful, Theron. Are you sick?"

"I've never been better. With these eyes I can see what you truly are. I can see the exotic energy that forms you." I gestured to the people hanging gruesomely on the wall. "I also recognize the handiwork of one of the Fume's manifestations. I've seen such cruelty before by one of your kind."

"I admit it—human manipulation is my obsession. However, these individuals are much different from the individuals you saw in the sanitarium. These men are remote pilots for these anti-relativity warships. The individuals in the sanitarium were something altogether different."

"Sensimion was right! There *was* one of your kind—a manifestation of the Fume—running the sanitarium."

"I deplore this nickname you've given me. It hurts my feelings. Nevertheless, I must correct your perception of me. There's only *one* of my kind, and he is I. I'm every manifestation. I *am* the exotic energy you detect with your eyes. I am the Fume, as you call me. And as you guessed, I too was the doctor in the sanitarium."

"What do you want from us? Why are you here?"

"You're given to a second misconception. You're assuming I'm alien to this world, and your people. You, Theron, should know better than anyone that I've been among you since the beginning. Don't you have some of my older memories? Don't you experience them like they were your own?" The Fume paused, as if pleasured by my discomfort. "Yes, Theron, they are real memories—not madness, not fantasy. You've seen what my eyes have seen."

"Why have you shown me these things! Why do these memories haunt me?"

"There's some of me in you."

What does he mean? He wishes to confuse me. Manipulate me.

"What's your purpose on Earth?" I asked. "What do you want?"

The Fume paused thoughtfully. "There's greatness in the minds of men. I'm here to promote it."

I waited for further explanation, but none followed. "I won't be satisfied with your cryptic shit."

I peered into the Fume's eyes. They swirled and eddied like chasms into hell. An awful emotion slithered through my guts and I became paralyzed. I felt as if an arc of electricity connected us. The memories of all the Fume's past manifestations spilled back into my mind. One in particular rose to the top. I experienced it in perfect clarity as it unfolded in my mind.

"What is this hallucination?" I said. "Where am I? The past? I'm in the Victorian house that Cassandra and I built. But something's wrong. I'm not me! These aren't my clothes. These aren't my hands. I can smell apple pie in the air. Cassandra loved to cook apple pie. I'm sneaking through the hallway toward the kitchen. I turn the corner and see Cassandra. Her back's turned. Her hair's a mess. I see the clock. It's noon and she's still wearing pajamas. Wait! What am I doing? I creep up behind her. I grab her by the neck. I strangle her. Why do I strangle my dear Cassandra? Stop this! Please! Damn you! Stop!"

In my mind, Cassandra went limp and her neck slid from my grip. In my hands remained her engagement necklace. The infinity spiral. The symbol of our love. It was the last time she'd ever wear it. From the murderous hands, it dropped to the floor like something worthless.

The memory ended and I puked on the launching bay floor. I glared at the Fume, my fists clenched, my lips trembled. "They said it was a drifter, but it was you. You killed my wife all those years ago, you bastard! Now you torture me with this memory. It's as if I killed her myself. I felt your hands clutching her delicate neck." I swallowed back a second urge to puke. "You fucking monster! She was pregnant!"

"Children are a distraction." The Fume smiled deviously. "I'm surprised you've gleaned this memory. I didn't think you'd be able to see things that have occurred during your lifetime."

As I stood there trembling, a commotion erupted from the remote pilots. They twisted and swayed as they became strangely excited. The warships hovering above whirred with power as their fusion reactors cycled up.

A circular segment of the launching bay's ceiling slid open, revealing the aqua-green waters of the Atlantic Ocean. A force field was now all that kept the entire weight of the ocean from plunging into the launching bay. A giant force field emitter, near the opening, propelled a powerful beam up into the ocean waters. It expanded, thus parting the seas and creating a massive tubular column, through which a movement of air could be felt as the pressure of the cavern equalized with the upper atmosphere. The tubular force field remained steady and the anti-relativity warships began their ascent through the sluice gate.

Just as I prepared to trigger my anti-gravity belt and flee through the sluice gate, Allienora entered the launching bay with two of the Fume's human minions following behind her.

She'll see my eyes, I worried, turning away as she approached.

"Sir Vole, what's going on?" asked Allienora.

"I was giving Mr. Mobius a tour," replied the Fume.

"There's no time for tours," said Allienora. "A hundred and twelve vessels of extraordinary size are headed for Earth. They overtake Saturn as we speak. At current velocities, they'll arrive here within twelve hours. Your guidance as defense minister is required."

"I'll be there momentarily, Prime Minister."

I turned to the Fume. "Defense Minister Vole, you don't seem concerned about this threat. Could it be you knew of this visit?"

Allienora gasped. "What is this, Theron? Your eyes are the same as the traitor Sensimion."

"It's not what you think, Allienora."

"I believed in you, but I was wrong." She pointed upward. "Are you also in league with these vessels headed for Earth?"

"You should ask Renworth Vole," I said. "He's the one responsible for this mysterious fleet."

The Fume snapped his fingers at his minions. "Take Mr. Mobius to my special workshop."

"I don't think so!" I cautiously stepped backward as the minions came toward me. I could sense they were a dangerous sort, filled with a volatile combination of small thoughts and big egos. I realized I'd be no match for them and grabbed the string of explosive marbles concealed in my pocket. In one fluid movement, I scattered the marbles on the ground, interlinked with my anti-gravity belt, and sent myself flying toward Allienora. I snatched her up and we flew in the direction of the sluice gate.

Seconds passed and the concussion of explosive marbles jarred my senses. Allienora thrashed and kicked in my arms.

"Stop moving!" I cried. "Do you wish to fall to your death? Look downward. We're a hundred feet up, and fly higher!"

"Help me!" she yelled.

"I'll save you, Cassandra. Just be still and I'll take you away from here."

"Who's Cassandra?" screamed Allienora.

I didn't know what I was thinking. She looked so much like Cassandra.

"He's not human," I said. "Look back and see the monster, Renworth Vole. No human could've survived that explosion."

The two minions were disfigured, toppled into grotesque mounds—all blood and gore. Between them stood Renworth Vole, unhurt by the explosion. He held his hands over the remains of his human minions, as if praying for them.

I turned my attention to the sluice gate, while Allienora continued to look back.

"They're alive!" she yelled. "By some impossible reflux of life, the defense minister's men live. Did you see?"

"No," I said, concentrating on our escape. "The warships have departed the launching bay! The sluice gate is closing! Hold on!"

I implemented the full thrust of my anti-gravity belt and we rocketed up through the ocean depths. Just as we rose above the water's surface, the sluice gate released its tubular force field from the ocean waters, sending a tremendous gust of wind upward as the ocean collapsed in on the remaining void.

I idled my anti-gravity belt, and we floated on a breeze in midair. We overlooked a turbulent ocean in all directions. I looked up and became enchanted by the sapphire-blue light spilling across the sky from horizon to horizon. I marveled at this sentient entity that shrouded Earth.

"Has it truly existed with humankind for so long, undiscovered?"

"Release me, you lunatic," screamed Allienora. "What are you looking at? Why do you stare at the sky like a madman? Do you hear me? Release me!"

"If I release you now, you'll drown. A storm brews in the east and will be here soon. We must fly."

Allienora glanced eastward and roared angrily.

"Such spirit, Prime Minister." I smiled. "I like it."

"Why are you doing this?"

"You have to trust me."

"Impossible!"

"Only an hour ago, you said you had faith in me."

"Things change. You're fucking crazy!"

"You're too beautiful for such language, Allienora."

I was about to move in the direction of the coordinates given to me by Sensimion's colleague when a small transport ship caught my eye. It descended in a freefall, like a fishing lure dropped from the heavens. In an instant, it came to rest exactly beside us. A window opened and a haggard head appeared. The pilot's lustrous hyper-blue eyes instantly identified him.

"Open the door," I called.

The pilot didn't comply. He lingered in silence and inspected Allienora, who hung tightly around me.

"Drop the woman in the ocean and I'll open the door."

"Are you totally heartless? She's an innocent bystander. Let us in, goddamnit!"

The pilot grunted and then opened the door. We entered the small transport and fell onto a plush velvet bench.

"They'll be here soon," said the pilot. "We must move fast, so our destination isn't revealed." He engaged the transport ship toward North America.

Allienora pulled wind-tangled ringlets of golden hair from her face. "You maniacs won't get far. You realize I'm the Prime Minister of Earth? An army will be here in moments."

The pilot lifted his hand in a careless manner. "I'm a clever man, Prime Minister. I've planned for the worst."

I felt hardly reassured. "Exactly what are these Obelisks, where are we headed, and what's the plan?"

84

"Save your questions until we're off this planet. We're still uncertain as to the scope of the Fume's powers and perceptions."

"Are you aware the Fume is a single entity, which controls every manifestation?"

"We are," said the pilot. "When the Brahman Station was being sabotaged, we were monitoring the interaction between Sensimion and one of the Fume's human minions, who implied this fact when he called the Fume his 'master.'"

"You're both crazy," said Allienora. "You're talking nonsense."

"Listen carefully," I explained. "There's a powerful presence on Earth. It has secretly existed with humankind for millennia. It commands powers beyond mere mortals, including omnipresence, possible mind control, the ability to turn a man to ash with a gesture—and, as you've witnessed, it's immune to the effects of explosives. It manipulates humankind as if it were a machine to be tweaked and adjusted. To what end? We don't know. But it's possible the Obelisks are a move toward the Fume's final plan."

Allienora held up a flat palm. "Gods and monsters? You're insane."

The transport ship traversed the American continent and headed out into the Pacific Ocean on a course for Asia.

"We have company," announced the pilot.

I peered through a porthole and discovered a ship flying alongside us.

"They've come for me," said Allienora triumphantly. "You'd be smart to surrender." She tapped the smart-glass of the porthole, magnifying the nearby ship. "It's impossible! I thought I was confused!"

"What?" I asked.

Allienora displayed less hostility. "After you gruesomely murdered the defense minister's men, I thought I saw them stand up from death, as if resurrected." She gestured through the porthole. "I thought I was hallucinating, but it must have been real. One of the minions sits, quite healthy, within that ship."

I spotted another ship barreling down from the sky. "It looks like his buddy's joining him."

"Hold on!" said the pilot, taking evasive maneuvers. "It's hopeless. Their ships are faster. It's time for a more extreme plan."

"Well," I said. "What's your plan?"

"There are anti-gravity belts and personal cloaks at your feet."

"You want us to abandon ship?" I said. "These cloaking devices are just visual camouflage. They'll find us immediately."

"They won't think we've left the ship—we'll leave bodies behind."

"What do you mean?" I asked.

"There's a compartment under your seat."

Allienora and I stood up and lifted the cushion. Surprisingly, we found two men inside. At first glance, they appeared dead, until I noticed the slight rise and fall of their chests.

I inspected the faces of the two sleeping men. "You've indeed prepared for the worst by cloning the two of us."

Allienora's eyes flared at the pilot. "How can you expect me to trust you when you perpetrate such crimes? Cloning is a capital offence."

The pilot waved a hand in disregard. "Truly, this is no time to nitpick, Prime Minister. Or have you yet to realize our lives hang from a thread."

"Your plan's flawed," I said. "There are only two clones."

"You should have dropped Allienora into the ocean."

Allienora leaned forward. "You're not going to leave me behind, are you?"

"It's the obvious choice," said the pilot. "Besides, don't you wish to be free from us?"

Allienora shook her head wildly. "I don't know! I don't understand what's going on!"

The pilot sighed. "You and Theron will go. I'll deal with the Fume's human minions. They won't think to differentiate the life signs within this ship. Now, get ready to fly. The coast of China isn't far off."

While Allienora and I prepared our cloaks and anti-gravity belts, the pilot pushed the small transport ship to its limits in an effort to reach landmass.

"You must go now," said the pilot. "More ships approach. Stand behind the bench above the emergency-hatch and prepare to eject."

I grabbed Allienora's hand and activated our cloaks. "We must fly together so our cloaking fields are merged. I don't want to lose you in the unforgiving lands of China."

The pilot glanced back to me and Allienora. "Do you remember the exact coordinates, Theron?"

"I do. What will we find there?"

The pilot didn't answer. He looked to the sky with his glowing synthetic eyes wide. "Despite all its ominous overtones, the dimension and exotic energy filling the sky is quite beautiful. Isn't it?" With that said, he triggered the emergency hatch, sending us into freefall.

I activated our anti-gravity belts and we floated just off the coast of China. We watched from a distance as four ships surrounded the small transport. Moments later, the transport ignited into a fireball, apparently caused by an internal explosion.

"My God!" screamed Allienora.

I held her tightly. "The pilot knew they'd eventually force the vessel down and discover our absence. This act of sacrifice will allow us enough time to escape."

"Why is your life more important than his, Theron?"

I looked with conviction in the direction of our destination. "Hopefully such a question will be answered at our final destination within the Khingan MegaCity."

OUT OF PHASE

We flew for hours into the northeastern regions of China. Allienora had passed out from exhaustion. I held her in my arms. Her head rested on my shoulder. It was comforting. I hadn't felt such real intimacy in years. My addiction to SLIP code had turned me into something sad. Finding intimacy in hyper-realistic fantasies just wasn't like the real thing.

We are all just halves, until we become whole. I stole a kiss from her sleeping lips. *I want to live again.*

She woke up after a while. Her lips trembled. She might have been in shock.

"Are you all right?" I asked.

Her large eyes glistened. "I don't understand what's going on, Theron."

"You must trust me, Allienora. We must move forward. The Obelisks are coming."

"What are they?"

"I don't know."

"What of the defense minister's men?" she asked.

"They haven't discovered us yet." I scanned the hilly landscape. "Perhaps the pilot's daring plan was successful."

"Successful, though costly," she replied. "How much farther?"

"I don't know, but the day's ending." I looked at the sun sitting on the Khingan Mountain range.

Allienora cringed. "What's that smell?"

We became drenched in a putrid gas cloud. Below, we discovered the source of the sickening stench. The land below was split open, revealing a ten-kilometer chasm into the heart of an ancient dumpsite, exposing the decaying remnants of five hundred years of human waste. I pointed out giant robotic machines. They worked to process the toxic garbage. I flew us higher to avoid the smell.

The sun set and the barren lands below were painted in gray tones. Halfway through the night, as the crest of the mountainous horizon rolled toward us, a magnificent light pierced the dark landscape. The Khingan MegaCity had revealed itself.

In the dawn's light, we marveled at the MegaCity. It had an air of power over the surrounding mountains, like a bejeweled king among peasants. The MegaCity's diamond-fiber superstructure was the foundation for an ever-growing and changing habitat for the two hundred million inhabitants.

I considered the size and complexity of the MegaCity as we neared its perimeter. I halted our flight in midair.

"Why have we stopped?" asked Allienora.

"I need to access my neural implant to find the coordinates in the MegaCity." I closed my eyes and gazed inward. My neural implant showed me the best route to our destination.

Allienora started shaking me. "Look, Theron! Something's happening. Thousands of ships are leaving the MegaCity."

I focused on the outside world and, looking slack-jawed to the sky, found the cause of the mass departure. "The Obelisks have arrived!"

Before us, one of the one hundred and twelve Obelisks descended into the atmosphere. It was the width of the MegaCity and four times the height.

"It's enormous," uttered Allienora.

"Have I gone crazy, or does it lack substance?"

The Obelisk itself seemed a thing of illusion. It was translucent like a phantom, causing me to question whether it was real.

"It's as if it's out of phase with reality," said Allienora. "I can see right through it."

"We should find safety within the MegaCity." I interlinked with my anti-gravity belt and we continued towards the MegaCity at best speed.

I guided us into the lower regions of the MegaCity, hoping to buffer us from the Obelisk's descent. We became lost in a labyrinth of old construction long since forsaken and left for the poor and homeless.

I landed us on a wide street lined with buildings in various stages of disrepair. Above and beyond, the newer and more magnificent architecture of the MegaCity could be seen. It was a beautiful creation, a larger-than-life artwork composed of the soft sheen of metal and the cool glow of electric light.

"Our view of the Obelisk is blocked," said Allienora.

"Don't disengage your cloak," I instructed. "This is a dangerous place and chaos is upon us."

Preparing for the Obelisk's impact, we remained in the open, hoping to be safe from falling debris. When many minutes passed and neither winds nor quakes brought us to our knees, I decided we must continue. I again interlinked with my neural implant.

"We must be quick," I said. "Our destination is much higher, at the peak of the MegaCity."

"Watch out!" screamed Allienora.

Before we could again make flight, a transport sphere struck us from behind. We crashed to the ground—our arms and legs wrenched by the force. Our cloaks disengaged from the impact, revealing our limp bodies.

The transport sphere stopped and someone got out.

I couldn't move. I looked to Allienora and discovered the driver of the vehicle on her. He was an ugly little fuck, with drooping jowls and pale pink skin. His arms were lined with synergistic implants. She'd be no match for his enhanced strength. I tried to get up, but couldn't. I watched as the man ran his finger along Allienora's neck.

"My caress pleases you, doesn't it?"

Allienora squirmed beneath him. "Get your hands off me, you pig!"

The man pulled himself even closer, presenting her with two beady eyes and a perverted smile. "I thought I might have a taste."

Allienora continued to struggle for freedom. The man dragged his tongue, like a wet slug, across the base of her neck. "Mm... vanilla," he lusted.

Allienora kicked him in the balls.

Instead of pain, he showed satisfaction. "Mm... again you please me. You're like an angel of ecstasy. You're what I dream of when I sleep, and when I pleasure myself."

"Get off her!" I screamed, forcing myself to stand. I moved to intervene, but Allienora's molester jammed a prod-like device against my arm, injecting something beneath my skin. I became paralyzed. He did the same to Allienora. I couldn't move, but I was wide awake.

Neeble, as he introduced himself, inspected us. "My brother will reward me for capturing such fine specimens. Especially ones with so many precious technologies—anti-gravity belts, cloaking devices, and a plasma gun."

Neeble came face to face with me. His breath smelled like meat and shit. "Pretty eyes. Too bad they be stuck in that hideous head. My brother might help you remove that hideous head, then you just be pretty eyes."

I watched as he retrieved two long silver fibers from his vehicle and tied them to our waists like leashes. "The impact of my transport sphere must've damaged your anti-gravity belts. Don't worry, my brother teaches me about such devices. He's a wise man. His head is overstuffed with many brains." He tinkered with our anti-gravity belts for a moment. "You see, I already fixed them."

Allienora and I floated upward. We hung at the ends of the silver fibers like two queer balloons. Neeble left his vehicle behind and pulled us by hand down the street.

Neeble took us through dark alleys, condemned buildings, and at last we arrived in the basement of a huge spiral tower. There, Neeble loaded us into a hidden anti-gravity lift, which catapulted us into the upper regions of the MegaCity.

The lift door opened and I saw a warehouse of old junk—neural interfaces, a wall of half-assembled AI-droids, stasis chambers, medical paraphernalia, synergistic implants, and illegal genetic alterers.

"Brother!" called Neeble. "I bring choice specimens from the lower slums!" After no response, Neeble pulled us through the warehouse and into a large workroom, where a man, in front of a panoramic window, was talking excitedly to himself.

I understood the man's excitement, when I saw the wondrous and surreal view. The window looked out beyond the MegaCity, upon the looming Obelisk that had landed only miles away. Its translucence was just as we had observed during its descent. The morning sun, although blocked by the Obelisk, could still be seen as a great, distorted entity through the strange substance. It acted like a prism, filtering the sun's light into a spectrum of rich colors.

Neeble's brother examined the Obelisk with a large ocular headset.

"Did you witness its majestic descent, Neeble? With such disturbing silence, it floated down to Earth, like a feather falling in still air." His headset extended two bulbous lenses forward. "It is. But it is not. It can be seen. But it cannot be touched. Even now, a flock of oblivious birds flies through the Obelisk as if it presented all the risk of a cloud in the sky."

Neeble's brother danced about on two thin legs. "Neeble, aren't you stunned by this amazing event, or are you an oblivious bird?"

"I didn't notice," said Neeble. "I was catching these fine specimens from the lower slums. Our paths, quite literally, collided."

"You've done well, Neeble. Set them on the examination tables."

Neeble guided us to two metal tables. He cradled Allienora like an infant as he laid her down, disengaged her anti-gravity belt, and then extracted the electrode inducing her paralysis. "It's all right my angel. I'll take care of you. Yes, my gentle caress is for you, my love."

"Quit fucking around, Neeble!" commanded his brother.

Neeble crashed my floating body to the other metal table like a sack of rocks, and then removed my paralysis electrode.

"Done, brother! They're secure." Neeble gave Allienora a longing glance and moved to his brother's side.

I wriggled my fingers and toes, trying to regain motor function. I prepared myself.

Strike hard. Strike fast. One... two... three.

I tried to leap to my feet, but was bound to the table by a gravity restraint.

I grunted angrily. "Why have you brought us here!"

"First, let me introduce myself," said Neeble's brother. "I'm Vega, a scientist and scholar. I'm a man propelled through life by great aspirations. You've been brought here to be the subjects of experiments that'll change the very nature of human existence. You see, I'm on a quest to attain superiority of mind and body, and, ultimately, immortality of person. To achieve this goal, I utilize many promising technologies in both genetics and the use of AI-droids as sustained vessels for the mind."

"You can't be serious," I said.

"Don't worry—when I've achieved immortality, your deaths will be meaningful."

I fought against the gravity restraint. "That's a hackneyed manifesto, fitting for inner-city garbage like you. Do you think you're an innovator of such ideas? Much more brilliant minds have tried and failed. Additionally, your shitty lab is sub-standard for such science."

"'Innovation in the face of adversity' is my motto," said Vega. "I'll take humans to a new level of perfection."

"More! More! More!" screamed Allienora unexpectedly. "Why must we keep wanting more? The stars! Immortality! How far must we go to find happiness? The void cannot be filled if nothing fits!"

Allienora's statement struck a chord in me. Even in this moment of peril, I couldn't help but wonder about her. It was a strange declaration coming from her.

What void is she talking about?

"Calm yourselves," said Vega. "I must confirm you're both healthy before I can put the automated surgeon to work." He indicated a complex yet barbaric mechanism hanging from the ceiling. Its robotic metal arms were equipped with an assortment of surgical tools stained with dried blood.

"Let's have a look at these synthetic eyes of yours." Vega, still wearing his ocular headset, replaced the eyepiece with a different one, and then peered into my eyes. "What's this? These aren't mere ocular implants, but rather some sort of advanced bio-machinery—organic lenses, molecular circuitry, and..." Vega adjusted his eyepiece. "...it appears they obtain power by drawing chemical energy from your body. I suspect this is the reason for your pale complexion. What's the function of these amazing eyes? What do you see with them?"

"Your ugly face," I said.

Vega looked up euphorically. "On this, I'm overwhelmed by wonders. This technology will definitely advance my work by quantum leaps." Vega's enthusiasm faded. "Who are you people? You're not the usual bottom feeders that Neeble catches from the lower slums."

"We're merely travelers," I said. "We lost our way in the chaos of the descending Obelisk."

"No! There's more to the two of you." Vega cradled Allienora's chin in his hand, turning her head from side to side, inspecting her. "It can't be you. It's impossible. Yet, here you are, Prime Minister Allienora Chang, before my very eyes."

Vega gestured to a giant view-panel that simultaneously displayed twenty news broadcasts, all covering the one hundred and twelve Obelisks that had descended across the globe. "It's only logical you're responsible for this amazing occurrence. This is surely the Earth government working some master plan on its helpless sheep. You've already herded us into these claustrophobic MegaCities as if to quarantine a plague. What's next for the underlings of Earth?" Vega smacked Allienora in the face. "Tell me! What's this monstrosity outside my window?"

"Why would I tell you anything?" she said. "You're nothing but a kidnapper, a murderer, and a lunatic."

Vega moved toward me with a sinister grin. "If you don't tell me, Prime Minister, I'll have to use tactics of persuasion. Does this man mean anything to you?" He touched a control panel on the side of the metal table, causing me to be sucked down harder. The increase in gravity began crushing my body.

I won't let this worm see weakness in me.

"Have you ever seen a person's lungs implode under extreme gravity?" said Vega. "It's very gruesome. The best part isn't the chest caving in, it's the beautifully terrible expression on the victim's face as they try to draw an impossible breath."

"Please!" cried Allienora. "We know nothing of the Obelisks."

"Ridiculous! Do you think I'm stupid?" Vega increased my gravity restraint.

I flexed every muscle in my body, struggling for each breath.

"From the depths of my heart," said Allienora, "I swear it's the truth. Please, don't harm him."

"Then why were you roaming the lower slums?"

"We were forced to abandon our transport ship, and sought refuge from the Obelisk. Please, stop this! You should release us now, before the rescue team locates us and discovers your illegal acts. You'd be crazy to think no one's looking for the Prime Minister of Earth."

Vega reduced the intensity of my gravity restraint and began pacing back and forth.

I took a deep breath and then carefully inspected the room. *What can I do? How can I stop this? Think, damn it. Think.* Nothing obvious came to light—until I noticed my vial of amber narcotic, which showed as a bulge in my pocket. I wondered if Vega was so completely delusional that he'd believe anything to attain his dream of immortality.

I set a plan into motion by defying the gravity restraint; my heavy hand moved with obvious intent to hide the telltale bulge of the vial.

Vega noticed my stray hand and jumped to my side. "What have we here! Do you think you can hide something from *me*, Vega the Great?" Vega plunged a long-fingered hand into my pocket and revealed the vial. "What's this liquid?"

"Nothing," I said.

"You can't fool me!" cried Vega. "I'll find out its purpose, one way or another. I'll implement the basest of tortures. I'll flush your intestines with flesh-eating nanites. I'll make you scream!"

I sighed heavily. "You're right. I can't fool you, Vega. It's ironic that the formula we're transporting should fall into *your* hands, an innovator of longevity."

Vega raised an eyebrow of suspicion. "Moments ago, you called me a hack and a lunatic."

"Hollow words," I said. "We feared the threat of your great intellect on our mission and the formula. You're known throughout many circles of scientists and scholars, and are considered a formidable competitor in the race for longevity."

"Well... I... I didn't realize my work had leaked out to such elite scientific circles. What's this formula in my possession?"

"My colleagues and I call it the 'Elixir of Life.'"

Vega's eyes opened wide. "Intriguing."

"One drop into your eye will grant you eternal life. However, beware—eternal life can be an arduous existence. I advise profound contemplation."

"I'm not a coward. I can handle anything set before me." Vega opened the dropper and peered at the amber fluid with greedy eyes. "Just one drop, you say?"

"Just one," I cautioned.

It was a wicked measure, but I saw no other way. I had been taking the narcotic for close to eighty years, during which time I slowly increased the concentration. Its potency would kill Vega instantly.

Vega slowly moved the dropper to his eye. Before a drop was released, and Vega's own self-infliction of death carried out, the window providing the view of the Obelisk melted away like wax, and with the in-rushing wind came the Fume's two minions, propelled by anti-gravity belts. They wore black-scaled battle garb and carried plasma guns at the ready.

Neeble, who had been hovering over Allienora, scurried to a dark corner of the workroom.

"What's this!" screamed Vega. "Why do you come into my home and threaten me with weapons? What's your business with me?"

"Our business lies on your tables, you fuck," said one of the minions. "Do you know who you're holding prisoner?"

"They're not my prisoners. They're my guests. This is Allienora Chang and her escort, or someone of that sort."

"You're half right," said the other minion. "Look closely and you'll recognize the great scientist Theron Mobius. He and the prime minister are traitors. We're here to detain them."

Vega focused on me. "My God, you *are* Theron Mobius. I didn't recognize you with your bio-electric eyes." Vega turned to the minions. "Theron Mobius, a traitor? Lies!"

"They're responsible for the destruction of the Brahman Station."

"We're innocent," I said to Vega. "They only want the Elixir of Life."

The minions seemed confused by my statement. One declared, "Your cries of innocence are useless, Mr. Mobius! You're coming with us."

I looked desperately to Vega.

Vega resealed the vial of amber narcotic and guarded it with two hands. "Jabberwocky!" he yelled, causing force fields to fall from the ceiling like curtains of energy. The minions were trapped in a grid of cells. "As you can see, I'm in charge now. Don't fire your weapons. The resonances of these force fields cause a nasty ricochet." Vega glared at the two minions demonically, teeth grinding, nostrils flaring. "Your intrusion into my home was a mistake. I'll deal with you two momentarily."

Vega, able to pass freely through the force fields, moved to my side. "Forgive my conduct, Mr. Mobius. Your work, despite its recent setback, has taught me that anything can be achieved if a man puts his heart into it. Your life has inspired me to continue my work despite all obstacles. If I had recognized you, I wouldn't have acted with such disrespect. I'm at your service, my friend." He disengaged the gravity restraint, releasing me from my invisible bonds.

I was stunned by Vega's change of heart, but quickly utilized it. "You're forgiven, Vega. I can't hold a grudge against such a dedicated innovator, so much like myself."

Vega stuttered from excitement. "I too have always thought we were alike, cut from the same cloth and all."

"I must be honest with you, Vega," I said.

"How so?"

"Had I known earlier of our impending friendship, I would've never misled you to believe that the Elixir of Life was complete. The formula, as it is, has many dangerous side effects. I can't allow my new friend to be put in danger. I promise to send you the formula once it's safe."

"You're as kind a gentleman as I had imagined," said Vega. "Do you need me to do anything for you?"

"Take care of these animals who have desecrated your home. Also, may I have back the defective Elixir of Life?"

"As you wish, Theron Mobius." Vega hesitantly returned the vial to me. "You and Allienora Chang are now free to move through the force fields."

"The Master will find you, Mr. Mobius," said a minion. "You're no match for the Master."

"Is this the same master who sent you two idiots to retrieve me?" I turned away from the minions and attended Allienora, helping her from the table.

Allienora looked around. "You've done the impossible, Theron."

"It was pure luck."

She smiled at me.

She thinks differently of me now, I thought. *If only we weren't in this mess.*

I took her hand. "Let's get out of here."

While I retrieved our anti-gravity belts and plasma gun, Vega dealt with the Fume's minions. "Neeble, engage the automated surgeon."

"As you say, Brother."

"We're going to have fun with these two fellows." Vega turned to me with a look of genuine madness. "We've been having great success with the brain's sustained consciousness in a state... devoid of body."

Was I really going to let him torture these men? I looked to the minions, paused, and then to Vega. "Good luck."

I took Allienora's hand and we soared through the window, into the MegaCity, toward our destination.

Our destination was at the opposite end of the MegaCity. We flew fast and watched as the people below were given to madness. Fires emanated from many windows of the high-rises and looting could be seen on the promenades of multi-leveled habitats. Murder, rape, and violence raged across the MegaCity.

"It's sad," I said. "When death descends upon us, and terror, like an incurable disease, rules the actions of men, only then can we truly see the ugly potential of the human condition."

Allienora shook her head in similar dismay. "I wonder if humankind will ever be better."

"Who knows?"

We at last reached the coordinates, arriving at the peak of a great tower. We set down on a narrow ledge. Our foothold would have proven unsteady if not for our anti-gravity belts, which provided stability against the heavy winds.

"There's nothing here," said Allienora. "Did they tell you what we're looking for, Theron?"

"They told me nothing," I said, admiring Allienora. It looked like she was having fun. And why wouldn't she be? She probably had never known such adventure, then again, neither had I. I smiled and then walked along the perimeter of the conical spire, which tapered up to a pin-head.

"Are you sure these are the coordinates?" she asked.

"Yes. Latitude, longitude, and altitude are precisely as I was told."

"Here!" she called. "There's a recess leading inside." She stepped into the opening, but was stopped by an invisible barrier. "There's a force field blocking the passage."

I moved toward it, and, amazingly, my synthetic eyes operated as a key and granted us entrance. Within was an empty chamber. Its walls tapered upward with the contours of the spire.

"Goddamnit! We missed it."

"Missed what?" asked Allienora.

"I don't know." I turned in a circle. "The pilot died for nothing."

I walked to the center of the empty chamber and nearly broke my neck as I tripped over thin air. Allienora rushed to me, and also tumbled to the ground.

I searched for the cause of our clumsiness, and soon discovered an object uncloaking. It was a sleek black transport ship less than four meters in length and two meters wide. The top slid open to reveal its inner compartment. Its lining was molded to fit two bodies side by side.

"No way!" Allienora shook her head. "I'm not crawling into this oversized coffin."

I ran my hand across the surface of its exterior. "Holy shit! I've never seen such a small anti-relativity drive. Someone crammed a lot of tech into this tiny ship. We've come this far, Allienora. Why end our journey now? Unless you want to stay with the Obelisks and await their surprise."

"You're right, Theron." Allienora's eyes grew large. "We'll see it to the end. Everything has changed. Alien objects out of phase with reality have fallen from the sky—the world is under attack. I shouldn't be excited, but I am." She jumped into the small ship like a kid on a carnival ride. "Are you coming?"

I smiled and quickly joined her. We proceeded to lie down, side by side, in the small vessel. Its lining expanded around us, securing us in place. The top slid closed, trapping us within. A node of light at our feet provided illumination.

I turned to Allienora. "I'm sorry I brought you into all this, but I couldn't leave you with the defense minister."

"I don't blame you, Theron. You were thinking the best for me when I thought the worst of you. Besides, I'm having fun now."

Who is this girl before me? I thought. She had suddenly become more interesting, even fascinating. I reflected over the past day. *I won't soon forget her soft body wrapped around mine, floating over the world, as if in a dream.*

We looked at each other for a suspended moment. The dangers we had experienced together created an intimacy. I touched her cheek, and then moved to kiss her. But, before our lips touched, the inner compartment of the vessel began filling with a viscous fluid. Our moment was lost.

Allienora pounded on the lid of the craft. "What's happening?"

"The craft is filling with cryo-gel and we're being placed into stasis. If you relax, the process should be painless."

"Where are they taking us?"

"I don't know," I said, "but I'll see you there."

Two mechanical claws came down from the lid of the vessel and gripped our necks like shackles. Needles and probes pierced our veins, arteries, and nerves. I felt a deathly calm as I went into stasis.

THE FRACTAL
SKYLARK

I felt a rush of energy—my state of living death lifted. I convulsed and coughed up a throat-full of cryo-gel. My lungs burned as I breathed in fresh air.

My first thought came quickly: *Where's Allienora?*

The ship's lid was open and she was no longer beside me. I sat up from the cryo-gel and strained to see my surroundings. At last, I saw her. She was revived, sitting on the floor with arms hugging legs. She was like a beautiful bird pulled from an oil slick. Her hair was a slimy mess and her clothes hung heavy with the muck.

A large man lifted me out of the vessel and set me next to her.

"Who are you?" I asked in a raspy voice.

"Orsteen Hunn of the Mercury Miners. We met on the Brahman Station."

"I remember." I swabbed away a glob of cryo-gel from behind my neck. "Where are we?"

"You're in the docking bay of my private estate atop the great Scarp of Mercury. It's nearly morning." Orsteen gestured through a window. It overlooked the gray-cratered landscape of Mercury, which enjoyed a gentle illumination from a predawn light. The thin atmosphere revealed the landscape in perfect clarity. Its desolate and still-virgin terrain reminded me of the moon before man populated it.

Allienora raised her head, muttered, and then fell back into a daze.

"You'll be all right, Allienora." I rubbed her back. "It's just post-stasis sickness."

Orsteen stuck a medical sensor on my forehead. "You look of death, Theron. You're so pale and your eyes..." Orsteen hesitated. "Where did you get those eyes? What do they do?"

"I've been getting that question a lot." I didn't know why we were on Mercury. I wasn't about to tell him everything I knew. "We all have our enhancements."

I gestured to Orsteen's arms and legs. The Mercury Miners' bodies were laden with synergistic implants. Strength and endurance were essential to survival on Mercury. At least two hundred years ago. Now, they were probably just a cultural norm.

"Well, whatever their function, they're sucking the life out of you." He pulled the sensor off my forehead. "You'll live for now, though. Relax while I revive the others."

"Others?" I asked.

Orsteen attended the first of two similar stasis vessels. He opened a control panel and minutes later the lid slid open to reveal a man. Orsteen tried to remove him but couldn't. The half-conscious man stubbornly gripped a large diamond-fiber case lying beside him. In one great heave, Orsteen lifted the man and case out of the vessel and onto the floor. The man pulled the bulky case closer to his body as if to protect it from theft.

From the second vessel, Orsteen removed a man I recognized. It was Morion Morpheme of the Mars Elitists. He too had come alone and was traveling with a case, although one of even greater size. Orsteen grunted as he lifted the large case from the vessel.

I rose unsteadily to my feet. "Why are we all here, Orsteen?"

Before Orsteen could answer, Morion spoke frantically: "This slime! It's suffocating! It's vile! Get it off me!"

"I apologize," said Orsteen. He walked past Morion and lifted Allienora off the floor. "I shouldn't allow Allienora's beauty to be soiled another minute."

Orsteen took us into the living quarters of his estate. Nano-intelligent matter rose up from holding cisterns and formed four female-gendered simulacra. They took us to a decadent washroom of sonic showers and dermal regenerative baths. It was an unexpected treat after all the recent stress we'd endured. As the simulacra applied nourishing oils to our skins, I couldn't help but look at Allienora's nude figure. Her skin had a soft sheen like silk. My heart beat faster as I looked from her breasts to her abdomen to her shapely hips and down her perfect legs. I looked up and found her blue eyes peering back at me.

I turned away. *How long did she see me spying?*

I looked back and found her smiling. She looked down at my own nude body, and then shrugged her shoulders in a joking way.

I smiled back at her. We hadn't known each other long, but I felt a strange comfort around her.

Once dressed, Orsteen led us to a living room. The walls displayed a hyper-real tropical setting. It was as if the room was in the middle of a beach, with waves crashing on one side and palm trees swaying in the wind on the other. We sat in fluffy chairs around a holo-projector.

A simulacrum that looked like a native islander, presented Orsteen with a levitating tray of five glasses and a bottle of clear liquid. Orsteen poured the bottle and handed out the glasses.

"This should prove an effective stimulant," said Orsteen. "Drink up."

I inhaled the beverage without concern for flavor. "Why have we been brought to Mercury?"

Orsteen activated the holo-projector. It showed a recording of the Obelisks landing on Earth. "As you all should know, the solar system has been visited by a fleet of mysterious Obelisks. They currently sit inactive on Earth. Before they landed, the Earth government sent out their warships to intercept the Obelisks. Unable to communicate with them, the warships implemented all their great weaponry to destroy them. However, the attack was unsuccessful. The Obelisks appear to be untouchable by physical force. Shortly after the Obelisks landed on Earth, I received a secret communication from a group calling themselves the 'Scions of Sensimion.' They told me they had a plan to eliminate the threat of the Obelisks, and that I should wait for your arrival."

Morion Morpheme stood from his chair in objection. "The Scions of Sensimion?" He turned to me and pointed to my eyes. "Is this the same Sensimion that Theron Mobius helped sabotage the Brahman Station?

It's this league of underhanded men responsible for the Obelisks. They're assassins and anarchists."

"Ridiculous!" I replied. "You think Sensimion's colleagues are behind the invasion of Obelisks? First, the Obelisks appear to be out of phase with normal dimensions, a scientific feat unexplored by humankind. Second, the amount of resources needed for such constructions would be extraordinary. Do you believe that any human association could build such a fleet without the notice of the rest of the solar system?"

Orsteen nodded in agreement. "The Mercury Miners would be the first to notice, since it would take all the precious elements of Mercury to construct such a fleet. It would seem logical that the Obelisks aren't born of our solar system."

Morion didn't reply and sat back down.

I briefly admired Allienora, who tugged awkwardly at the over-large clothes she'd been given. I then focused on the stranger sitting next to her. He had thin features, a sliver of a nose, and sharply angled eyes.

"I'm curious as to everyone's purpose," I said. "I'm acquainted with everyone except you, sir. You've been sitting quietly, assessing the situation with paranoid eyes. Who are you and what's in your diamond-fiber case?"

"I'm Thirm Bastile. I know nothing of the Obelisks, or the Scions of Sensimion. I'm not here to save the world or fight off villains. I'm merely an arms dealer from the Lunar Colonies, here to deliver my merchandise to an anonymous buyer." He indicated his case with a delicate touch. "Now, which one of you is to take delivery of this case—and, more importantly, pay me my one billion notes?"

"One billion notes!" said Morion. "We'll need to know what we're purchasing, first."

Thirm Bastile looked cautiously to everyone. "If I'm betrayed, there'll be consequences."

"Get on with it!" said Morion.

"Within this case is a Level-4 Quantum Bomb."

Orsteen scooted away from the case. "Possession of such a device is highly criminal."

"I'm an honorable man," said Thirm Bastile. "The criminal isn't the arms dealer who delivers the weapon, the criminal is he who'd dare use the weapon. In all my life, I've killed no one. What you do with this device when my bounty is paid is between you and your god."

I pointed to the hologram between us. "Even with such a destructive weapon, there'd be no effect on the Obelisks. Not to mention, we'd need one for each Obelisk." I looked to Morion. "Why are you here? I saw you also brought a case."

Morion lifted his head to a proud angle. "I wouldn't have come if they had identified themselves as the Scions of Sensimion. However, like with Thirm Bastile, they chose to remain anonymous. They said that I, Morion Morpheme, Prime Elitist of Mars, was invited to be a part of a secret mission that would save humankind from the Obelisks. This was an irresistible proposal, since I've always craved a life of heroics." Morion stared dreamily into space. "Once I've walked the path of a hero, I'll bask in the glory of my deeds and live forever in legend. Even in death, I'll be remembered."

"Putting your dream of glory aside, what's in the case?" I asked.

"They wanted me to bring one of my people's failed endeavors—an artificial black hole generator. It's a fairly worthless device. Why anyone would find it useful to create a micro black hole for less than a millisecond is beyond me."

"Impossible," I uttered.

Allienora touched my hand. "What is it, Theron?"

"Before the dimensional gateway was a glimmer in my mind, I conceived a doomsday weapon." I gestured to Morion. "You see, Morion's device warps space much like a black hole. Yet, it's not a true black hole and doesn't have the same destructive properties. However, I theorized if you directed an explosion of enough energy into this quasi-black hole, it could gain enough gravitational force to draw in an entire planet. Since the mass of a single planet couldn't sustain the black hole, it would quickly collapse into normal space and spit out the remaining worldly pulp."

"I'm confused," said Orsteen. "Even if such a weapon could be assembled, it wouldn't be the logical weapon. It would destroy Obelisks, Earth, and all."

"You're right," I said. "It doesn't make sense."

Morion refilled his glass. "Thirm Bastile and I are here for obvious reasons. What's your part in all this, Theron? Moreover, what could the Prime Minister of Earth possibly contribute to this situation?"

"Your tone's insulting, Morion." Allienora stepped in front of him, grabbed his drink, and chugged it down. "Theron and I know the true mastermind behind both the Obelisks and the sabotage of the Brahman Station."

"This is significant information," said Morion, frowning at his empty glass. "Who's responsible?"

Allienora turned to me. "Tell them, Theron."

I told them of the Fume and his exotic energy within the unnatural dimension around Earth. I told them of the manifestations posing as human beings to manipulate the human race. I felt, however, that it was in my best interest not to tell them of my long association with the Fume, beginning in the sanitarium of my youth. As well, I wasn't going to tell them about the Fume's memories that cursed me.

When I had finished, the group looked at me with disbelief.

Orsteen was first to respond. "If there is some otherworldly entity on Earth, driving humankind's evolution to an unknown end, why now has it chosen to bring down its final plan? If that's what the Obelisks indicate."

"I believe the Fume's been forced to act since Sensimion discovered his presence and developed the means..." Here I indicated my synthetic hyper-blue eyes. "...to see his various manifestations."

"I want nothing to do with these disturbing events," said Thirm Bastile gruffly. "Give me my one billion notes and I'll be headed to a location of far-off safety."

Orsteen topped off Thirm's glass. "I apologize for your inconvenience, Thirm, but you must collect your money from the Scions of Sensimion, since your deal is with them."

"Where are they?"

"We're meeting them in the underground city of Ironwrought." Orsteen pointed to a three-handed clock. "We better leave now, since the sun sits just below the horizon. When daylight comes, we must be gone from the surface—temperatures will become smoldering."

I looked out a window at the light on the horizon. Mercury was slow on its axis. Nighttime remained for eighty-eight Earth days, the same length as daytime. During this long day, the Miners take refuge in the underground cities, where they mine precious ores.

Thirm Bastile grumbled, as if to stress his inconvenience.

"I don't have your money, Thirm," said Orsteen. It's only a short journey to Ironwrought—there you'll find your riches."

The group boarded a small craft that, despite Orsteen's great wealth, was dented and old.

Morion touched a finger to an unsettling crack in one of the windows. "Don't you own a less dangerous craft?"

"Don't worry," replied Orsteen. "She's an ugly can, but flies true in all directions."

We disembarked and flew along the great Scarp of Mercury, which meandered into the distance for over a hundred kilometers. Embedded in the steep face of the Scarp were many homes, perched high like the nests of cliff-dwelling birds. At the moment, a great migration was occurring—Mercurials abandoned their homes as the season of night came to an end. At the upper plateau of the Scarp sat foundries, acclimation centers, and a spaceport that sent the minerals off-world. Empty air scows embarked for the underground mines, where they'd become full with the precious ores of Mercury.

My attention focused upward. My heart raced as I saw shimmering lights coming from the sky.

"My synthetic eyes are detecting something!"

"Don't worry, Theron. It's not the Fume. It's an aurora effect. We've been working on a large project here on Mercury. We've been trying to generate a magnetic field strong enough to counter the radiation of the solar winds. We've so far created a twenty-kilometer dome—a mini magnetosphere. The power required is enormous."

"I had no idea you were working on such a bold endeavor. How strong is the field?"

"About fifty percent of Earth's."

"How are you powering it?"

Orsteen made a long pause. "We all have our secrets, Mr. Mobius."

Orsteen took the craft down to the base of the Scarp and flew toward a huge hole. Above it sat an enormous sign of twisted metal displaying the name "Ironwrought." We entered the hole with speed, plunging downward into the depths of Mercury. After a ten-kilometer descent through darkness, we came to a series of force fields. Orsteen explained how they acted as atmospheric containment gates.

Once through, our craft entered an expansive cavern. It was unbelievably large and was illuminated by the ambient glow of the city Ironwrought—a place reminiscent of an earlier time in Earth's history. The city's cobblestone streets separated intimate city blocks occupied by modest stone structures, all artfully built. Homes, taverns, bistros, and storefronts each presented their own unique character and sophistication.

Orsteen pointed to the perimeter of the city. "We're in Ironwrought's main cavern. From here, tunnels radiate outward, leading to smaller communities and mining complexes."

An anti-gravity field about twenty meters thick lined the domed wall of the cavern. Hundreds of drones hovered on guard, removing fallen rocks and boulders that collected in the anti-gravity field.

Orsteen landed the craft on one of the city streets near the edge of the cavern, and we got out. The air was cool and carried a rich mineral smell that seemed almost therapeutic. I took a few deep breaths and looked to Allienora. She was grunting in annoyance as she pulled up her sagging pants. At last, she ripped off the base of her shirt and tied it around her pants like a belt.

Thirm Bastile continued to carry his diamond-fiber case in a paranoid manner. He looked suspiciously at passing Miners on the street. "Why do they stare at me?"

"They probably find you interesting," said Orsteen. "We don't see many foreigners in our cities." Orsteen removed Morion's black hole generator from the craft and attached an anti-gravity node to it. He pushed it through the air to Morion. "I leave you in charge of your case."

Morion reluctantly accepted it.

"What's that?" I asked, pointing down the street, where marched a parade of giant, monster-like puppets. Long poles, driven by Miners, animated the creatures with thrashing limbs and gnashing jaws.

"They represent demons and long-toothed monsters fabled to dwell in Mercury's depths," explained Orsteen. "The Daylight Festival will continue for the next few Earth days. It would be smart to stay by my side. Drunken Miners are quick to brawl."

"How can they celebrate in the streets when we're faced with invasion?" asked Allienora. "Aren't they concerned about the safety of humankind and the threat of the Obelisks?"

"It's by my instruction that they carry on with their normal routines. But don't underestimate Mercury's preparedness—on a moment's notice, we'll be ready for anything. If the Obelisks spill forth hordes of alien conquerors, have no doubts, the Mercury Miners will be there to smash heads with the best of them."

Allienora didn't seem convinced, until Orsteen removed a small holo-projector. "Mercury is more ready than you know, Prime Minister."

He displayed a holo-image of a thousand ships of unfamiliar design.

"We have an armada of anti-relativity warships waiting to be launched from a nearby military base." Orsteen looked thoughtfully through the streets. "These are just citizens. Unfortunately, I can tell the Obelisks weigh heavy on their minds, as the festivities appear unusually lame."

Orsteen led us through the streets, which presented six hundred years of Mercurial culture. We passed stone effigies to old leaders and small monuments made of twisted metal paying homage to some past achievement. The physiology of the people also told of their history. Their considerable stature and rugged features alluded to the harsh beginnings on Mercury, when only the strongest could tolerate a Miner's life.

We at last approached the outer envelope of the city. I marveled at the cavern's towering rock dome. A beautiful collage of figures was carved into its surface. The stone portraits stared with proud expressions toward the great city of Ironwrought.

Orsteen held a respectful hand to his heart. "It's tradition that when a Miner dies, they're immortalized in stone, so to become a part of Mercury. It's believed their eternal vigilance protects the city from cave-in."

"Quite romantic," said Allienora.

I noticed children among the portraits. "So many young."

Orsteen shook his head. "There were sad times in the beginning."

"Unfortunate," I said. "But there are always risks when conquering new frontiers."

Thirm groaned impatiently. "Where are you taking us, Orsteen?"

Orsteen indicated the mouth of a small tunnel in the rock wall ahead. "It's not far."

We entered a tunnel filled with an intoxicating odor of sweet organic matter. Our way was lit by small but brilliant light sources scattered about the tunnel walls.

"What are these lights that guide our way?" asked Morion. "They're like gems filled with internal fire."

"Their beauty is beyond words," said Allienora.

"They're bioluminescent slugs," said Orsteen. "They live in these tunnels, surviving on the chemosynthetic moss that grows beneath their feet."

I was a bit mystified when a tiny robotic spider approached one of the slugs and scanned it. It then gently picked the slug up and carried it away.

We continued deeper into the surreal environment of slug and moss. Orsteen navigated us through tunnels that split again and again into smaller and smaller passageways. At last, our tunnel ended at a round metal door on enormous hinges. Above it, a holo-sign advertised "The Scented Slug."

Orsteen swung the door open, and we entered a tavern full of loud-mouthed and beer guzzling Miners.

Orsteen sang in a deep baritone, "The mighty men of Mercury, we toil our hands and our fingers bleed. The sun's harsh glow takes us below, but our retreat is no defeat. We drink! We eat! We never sleep!"

The crowd pounded their mugs and shouted warm greetings: "Lord Orsteen Hunn has arrived! How about a round for the house, Master Orsteen? Who are these *smallies* you bring for our amusement?"

Orsteen hushed the crowd. "Today you're graced by the presence of four brave souls. They're on a mission against the Obelisks. Please, treat them with respect." He smiled broadly. "Now, carry on with passion—our lives shouldn't be wasted in dull moments!"

The crowd again became excited, guzzling their drinks in a collective toast.

Allienora moved close to Orsteen. "Do you think it's wise to announce our intentions? The Scions of Sensimion have gone to great lengths to keep our presence on your world a secret."

"Our presence won't be known," said Orsteen. "I've disabled the city's telecommunication nodes. We're completely isolated from the rest of the solar system."

"I shouldn't have questioned you," said Allienora.

"You think of the welfare of the group. A worthy cause for second-guessing."

We sat at a large, round table, where an AI-droid took our orders. It returned with five heavy mugs brimming with amber ale and a platter of small, gooey balls. All in the group, except Orsteen, sat like miniatures at the huge table. I noticed a single bioluminescent slug roaming the table's surface. Its pulsing glow reminded me of the exotic energy that exuded from Defense Minister Renworth Vole.

A man approached the table. He was the smallest Miner I'd seen.

"Master Orsteen!" he said in a high-pitched voice that suited his small size. "You bring me new customers from the reaches of the solar system. My establishment will no doubt become legendary throughout all the worlds of men."

Orsteen wrapped a friendly arm around the man. "Everyone, this is the owner of The Scented Slug, Glum.

His family has been tossing drinks here for over four hundred Mercurial days. He's a good friend, despite his tendency to dabble in questionable endeavors." He looked to Glum nostalgically. "If I recall the last incident correctly, you were in trouble for selling cheap swill obtained from a criminal from Blackrot City. The beverage wasn't just disgusting, it also caused an epidemic of crawling hives."

"In all fairness," said Glum, "I wasn't aware of the swindler's reputation. Not to mention, I sampled the shipment myself and was immune to the illness." Everyone glanced at their drinks and Glum continued. "Don't worry, I've learned my lesson, and now only serve the choicest of swill." He let out a cackling laugh that pierced everyone's ears.

Orsteen's face became serious. "My friends and I are here to meet a group called the Scions of Sensimion." Orsteen gestured to me. "Have you seen anyone with such brilliant blue eyes in your establishment?"

"No," said Glum, looking at me curiously. "Such eyes would've caught my attention. However, let me ask the AI-droids. They notice many more things than I. While I'm at it, I'll fetch you our premium ale."

Glum returned with five fresh mugs and five empty bowls too small for serving food. "This is twenty-day-old Grobblemoss ale. Drink lightly or your heads will swim. And here are some smoking bowls in case you decide to indulge in the slug."

I pushed the bowl away. "Have your AI-droids seen anyone suspicious, Glum?"

"Only a group of Far Reach Miners. They were spotted an hour ago. If their appearance is relevant, you must decide. Excuse me. I must return to my other guests. Profit awaits." Glum bowed his head and departed the group.

Morion stuffed his mouth with a gooey purple appetizer. "Who are these Far Reach Miners, Orsteen? Could they be our contact?"

"Unlikely," responded Orsteen. "They're a community of Miners that rarely come into the public eye. They're a strange bunch. Their words are few and their expressions are vacant. It's thought inbreeding is the cause of their strangeness. I don't think they're involved with the Scions of Sensimion." Orsteen pushed the platter of appetizers closer to Morion. "It's good to see you're enjoying our cuisine."

Morion held up one of the purple balls and inspected it. "I tend to consider myself a bit of a gastronome and have never tasted such a flavor. What are these delicious tidbits?"

"Coagulated cave creature blood mixed with spices. They're exquisite in taste but lack nutrition."

"Er... interesting." Morion promptly signaled the AI-droid for more ale.

Allienora took a sip from her mug. "How much longer must we be strung along by these Scions of Sensimion? Can we truly place the fate of the Earth in their hands?"

Morion licked his lips clean. "From what Theron has told us of the Fume's supernatural powers, it would seem the Scions of Sensimion are overconfident. Do they think we can retaliate against such a powerful entity?"

"And what do we really know about the Scions of Sensimion?" said Orsteen. "It's remarkable we were all so easily persuaded here."

"Doubt will get us nowhere," I said. "In grim times, it's better to entertain any small promise of hope than to give in to hopelessness. We all live our lives to endure the unrelenting gnaw of death. It'll swallow us whole one day. Until that day, I'll fight for my place in this universe."

"Theron's right!" said Thirm, slamming his mug down on the case holding the Level-4 Quantum Bomb and causing everyone's eyes to widen. "We must think positive. The Scions of Sensimion have thus far acted with admirable foresight."

Orsteen leaned toward me. "Let's get to the meat of the matter, Theron. Tell us about your interactions with Defense Minister Renworth Vole—or the Fume, as you call him? Are you sure he didn't indicate his motives?"

"Again, I can only tell you that the Fume has been manipulating humankind for thousands of years, preparing us for something." I paused, wondering if I should continue. "This may sound dramatic, but when I was standing near his unnatural aura, it felt like my mind was being twisted to his will—or *its* will." I shuddered. "He's pure fucking evil."

Everyone stared at me.

"I'm not delusional!" I said.

"These are stressful times," said Orsteen.

I should tell them how the Fume murdered my wife and unborn child. This will convince them. I took a chug of ale. *No! They can't know I share his memories.*

Allienora placed a comforting hand on my shoulder. "I was standing with you, next to the defense minister, and didn't sense such evil. Nevertheless, there's something about that interaction that's been nagging me. With the Fume's ability to either kill or resurrect a man with a gesture, how did we escape?"

"I've also wondered that. Why allow us to escape? What purpose could we possibly serve?"

My thoughts lapsed back to the sanitarium. Then, too, I had escaped the Fume. Was my path into the world just another of the Fume's manipulations?

Over more drinks, we started guessing the Fume's motives. We touched on all the scenarios of alien encounters imagined by cheap fiction and daydreamers—from the gathering of resources, to the encroachment into a habitable world, to the enslavement of mankind, and even to the revolting possibility of humans as food.

Gradually, our moods lightened from the ale and the conversation shifted to less consequential matters. While Allienora argued with Thirm Bastile about his illegal arms business, I listened to Morion's thoughts on the perfect woman.

Morion spoke with spirit: "I need a woman with ample breasts, a face of innocence, and an ass of inviting dimension."

"These are fleeting qualities," said Orsteen. "With time, the breasts sag, the face becomes haggard, and the ass become flat. I seek a woman of intellectual character, one who will challenge my own intellect and bring a spring to my step."

Morion indicated a female Miner, who flaunted her goods around the tavern, moving from Miner to Miner, speaking sexual innuendos. "I believe I've found a woman whose fleeting qualities could satisfy my desires."

Orsteen threw down some Mercurial bits in front of Morion. "Such women can be had for the right price, my friend. This tavern serves more than food and drink. But if you're shy about the real thing, Glum deals some quality SLIP code."

"The real thing will do," said Morion with scheming eyes. He collected Orsteen's money, rose from the table, and swaggered with obvious intent toward the woman.

I watched as Morion whispered in her ear. Her eyes lit up and she quickly escorted Morion from the tavern's main room.

With Morion gone, the rest in the company continued in leisurely conversation. I removed myself from the discussion and sat in silence. The extravagant functions of my synthetic eyes had drained my energy.

I gazed into my half-empty mug. *This ale is strong. I'm drunk.*

I observed my surroundings with a twisted perspective and noticed the bioluminescent slug still wandering the table. It had accomplished nothing since our arrival. If it was on a quest for food, Morion had beaten it to the blood balls. If it was in search of a mate, there was none in the area to romance with its luminous display. Despite all its beauty, it had two sad eyes resting on long, slender stalks. It seemed to stare at me, as if to say, *The whole weight of the universe bears down on my dorsal.*

I thought, *We're one and the same, my friend, two beings drowning in the mysteries of life.*

As I pondered the slug's significance in the universe with respect to my own, Orsteen snatched it up with two fat fingers and threw it into the small bowl before him. The bottom of the bowl vaporized the slug into a puff of thick smoke. In one deep inhalation, Orsteen sucked in the totality of the slug's existence. As I mourned its departure from the universe, I realized the slug's pungent, sweet smell explained the tavern's name.

An hour later, Morion returned to the table with a limp. "I think I've been abused... dominated."

Orsteen laughed. "It's a risk you must take with the females of Mercury. Especially when they're bigger than you."

While the company talked of Mercurial customs, my attention drifted to Allienora. *My God, she's beautiful.* I covertly fawned over her, admiring her subtle mannerisms that made her even more attractive—the curl of her lip when she smiled, the inflection of her voice when she spoke with passion, and the innocent expression she made when embarrassed.

Allienora noticed my gaze and returned a demure side-glance. I immediately looked away, but a moment later I was again drawn in by her allure.

Once again, Allienora noticed my stealing looks. "Have I sprouted another head?"

"Do you feel it, Allienora?" I asked.

"What?"

"This," I said, pointing back and forth from me to her. She smiled. "Is this our first date, Theron?"

"Maybe our second. Our first was at Vega's, being tortured."

"You're right," she said. "And afterward we slept together... in a box of cryo-gel."

I smiled and took her hand. "I've been under a lot of stress, lately. But, through it all, I find myself thinking of you, even when you're an arm's length away." My head whirled and my legs went numb. I felt like a youth again. I peered into her blue eyes. "I really like you, Allienora. I haven't felt like this in a long time."

Allienora leaned close to me and whispered, "I feel it too, Theron, but I'm afraid you're drunk."

"Possibly. However, these feelings are real. I had them before we started drinking. I hope I'm not making an ass of myself."

Our date ended when the tavern door swung open, revealing a Miner with an unshapely head and strange facial features. Most in the tavern made expressions as though the Miner weren't welcome. A few cautious patrons covered their mugs, as if to guard from any diseased particles that might shed from the ugly Miner.

"Observe," said Orsteen. "An example of the Far Reach Miners I described earlier. Notice how his face remains in a single static expression."

"He's coming this way," I said in surprise.

The Far Reach Miner stood at our table and took interest in the cases brought by Thirm Bastile and Morion Morpheme. "Are these the devices requested?"

"They are," said Thirm. "I demand to be paid. I'm done with your secretive games."

"You'll get paid when the device is authenticated," said the Miner calmly. "All of you must come with me."

Thirm threw up his hands and rose from the table.

I signaled everyone to remain seated. "You don't resemble a Scion of Sensimion."

"You must trust me, I'm a Scion of Sensimion, pledged to fight against the Fume. Other than this, I can't prove my identity. Although, Theron, you can see I don't exude the glow of the Fume."

"This means little, since the Fume can't go beyond the confines of the dimension shrouding Earth. For all we know, you're one of his human minions."

Allienora introduced herself to the Miner. "I'm the Prime Minister of Earth, Allienora Chang. Before I was Prime Minister, I worked for a special intelligence unit that was tracking the Scions of Sensimion."

"Really?" I interrupted. Allienora continued to surprise me.

"I didn't just become Prime Minister because of my father, Theron. I worked my way up. I had to prove myself."

The Far Reach Miner held up his hand. "I'm aware of the position you held, Prime Minister. You even helped capture some of our people. They were executed for treason because of you."

"At the time, we thought the Scions of Sensimion were anarchists. They killed various members of government and industry."

"Those were the Fume's human minions," replied the Far Reach Miner.

"Now we know," said Allienora. "If you *are* a Scion of Sensimion, you should know details of the attacks."

"Give me your best shot."

"On July 9, 3054 the Scions of Sensimion planted a Tetrion explosive under Senator Robert Clay's transport. My division captured your man and destroyed the bomb on site."

"I remember the event vividly," said the Far Reach Miner. "It was a Sunday."

"I was there that day," said Allienora. "I saw the device before it was destroyed. One detail never made it into the report."

"I'm waiting."

"What color was the bomb's reaction chamber?"

"Is that it?" said the Miner. "The chamber was an old micro-fusion core. It was yellow."

Allienora looked to me and nodded. "He's right."

"Of course, I'm right. I made the bomb."

I put my hand on Morion's case. "We know you're putting together a very powerful weapon. And before we give you the means to build such a weapon, we must understand how you intend to use it against the Fume and the Obelisks. Orsteen pointed out earlier that such a weapon would destroy Obelisks, Earth, and all."

The Miner inspected the tavern's patrons. "Forcing me to reveal our plan in public would be careless."

"Easily solved," said Orsteen, rising from the table. He led the company to a back storage room. "You may now speak without worry of enemy ears."

Apparently satisfied, the Scion of Sensimion reached into his bag and produced a small disc. He held it on his palm and it cast a hologram of the solar system into the upper air of the storage room. He moved a searching finger through the planets. "Mercury, Venus, Earth, Mars, the outer planets, and here, beyond Pluto, lurks the source of the Obelisks."

It was a breathtaking spherical construct.

Morion stood directly below it. "It looks like some kind of alien craft."

"It's an interstellar vessel, as big as Mercury," replied the Scion of Sensimion.

Hovering on one side of the vessel was an orb of blue energy a quarter of the sphere's diameter. I didn't know what it was but it was something powerful—a technology thousands of years ahead of us. Its surface pulsed, swirled and shifted. It was like a condensed ball of pure energy, somehow contained and harnessed by the giant vessel. "What's that?"

"We think it's a dimensional gateway engine. A lot like yours, Theron. But powerful enough to create a dimensional fissure that could accommodate the planet-sized vessel."

"It's beautiful," I uttered.

"And the Obelisks came from this planet-sized vessel?" said Allienora.

"Indeed," replied the Scion of Sensimion. "And this is what we want to destroy with the weapon."

Orsteen pointed to Thirm Bastile's case. "Even with such a powerful weapon, how can you be certain it'll be destroyed?"

"Unlike the Obelisks, it's not out of phase." The Scion of Sensimion adjusted the hologram, enlarging the vessel and revealing the details of its beautifully constructed surface. "Also, we've detected openings that'll allow us passage within, where we hope to deposit the weapon to ensure maximum damage."

I shrugged. "Even if you destroy this vessel, how do you know its destruction will affect the Fume's plans?"

The Scion of Sensimion turned off the hologram. "I guarantee nothing. If you insist on questioning our counterattack, do so on the way to my ship. We must move forward."

Orsteen settled our bill with Glum and we departed The Scented Slug. We followed the Scion of Sensimion through caverns and tunnels, and eventually boarded a small conveyance that flew us through deep tunnels to the far reaches of Ironwrought.

We arrived in a secluded community of metal habitation modules. The townspeople went about their daily lives with a strange calmness. I noticed a pair of Miners in the process of assembling a new module. They worked together in an unnatural silence; neither seemed to acknowledge the other's presence. Yet they worked with a steady precision. Nearby, in the street, a group of children played a game of gravityball with obvious disinterest. Something was definitely wrong with these people.

We followed the Scion of Sensimion to a habitation module built into one of the cavern walls. We ascended the front porch, where sat an elderly Miner. He greeted us without concern as we walked past him and entered the module.

We approached the rear of the module and came to a dining room, where sat a family of four Miners eating dinner. The man of the house—a humungous Miner—rose to his feet and angrily protested the intrusion.

"Our apologies," said Orsteen, who then addressed the Scion of Sensimion who'd led us within. "Why do we disturb these people?"

"Don't worry over this man's feelings," said the Scion of Sensimion. "He's programmed to carry on with such a performance."

"What do you mean?" asked Allienora.

"None of these people are real. They're simulacra."

Morion approached the massive Miner and, out of nowhere, grabbed his nose.

"He's telling the truth," said Morion. "His nose is the texture of nano-intelligent matter."

Orsteen stiffened. "Are you saying this community of Far Reach Miners is fake?"

"It's been the perfect camouflage for our secret outpost. Now, follow me." The Scion of Sensimion walked to a wall of shelves holding ornate dishes, crystal goblets, and an assortment of curios. Without hesitation, he walked, unhindered, through the mass of the shelves and disappeared.

The rest of the group followed him through and arrived in a secret cavern. At the center sat a stunning spaceship plated in radiant scales. About its perimeter were people with pale faces, thin limbs, and hyper-blue synthetic eyes.

Orsteen pointed a scolding finger at the Scion of Sensimion. "This is illegal use of Mercurial territory. Unlicensed excavation of underground territories is a very dangerous and careless crime."

"Justifying this outpost would take too long. I can only offer my apology." The Scion of Sensimion stepped into a simulacrum holding cistern.

"You too are a simulacrum?" I asked.

"Not altogether." His face and body began to lose color and cohesion as an outer layer of nano-intelligent matter melted away, revealing a frail female figure within. She removed a mask that allowed her to breathe, speak, and see, and exposed the synthetic blue eyes and pale features of a Scion of Sensimion.

Morion licked his lips. "Such an ugly disguise for such a strangely beautiful woman."

"My name's Rozlyn," she said, ignoring Morion's creepy comment. "Since Sensimion's death on the Brahman Station, I've been in charge of the efforts against the Fume."

I took a step toward the ship. "Will this ship avoid detection when we near the alien vessel?"

"This is the *Fractal Skylark*. It's equipped with an advanced cloaking technology we've been developing for the past decade."

"How is it," asked Allienora, "that your little group has achieved so many technological advancements? Surely such pursuits aren't cheap."

"Everything we've accomplished can be credited to Sensimion. He was brilliant. If you posed him a problem, he could summon a solution by desire alone. In addition to being the source of our intellectual inspirations, Sensimion also financially supplemented our efforts against the Fume. I'll let you in on a secret. Before

Sensimion discovered the Fume, he developed the biotechnology of neural implants, which all of us use for an easier life. Still, to this day, the proceeds from this achievement are the source of our financial independence."

One of Rozlyn's colleagues approached the group. "Are these the devices to complete the weapon?"

"They are," said Rozlyn. "Take them aboard the ship, verify their quality, and then couple them to the auxiliary unit."

Thirm Bastile held his diamond-fiber case tightly. "What of my payment?"

"Don't worry," said Rozlyn. "My colleague will bring your money when the device is verified."

Thirm breathed deeply and finally released his case. "Very well."

Orsteen scowled as he scrutinized the secret base. "What else goes on in this place besides the construction of awful weapons?"

"I'll show you. Follow me." Rozlyn gave us a tour of the secret outpost. It was bigger than I initially thought. She led us into another cavern full of people sitting in front of view-panels. "This is the heart of our intelligence, where we monitor the Fume's eighty-six manifestations presently on Earth."

"How do you obtain such thorough surveillance?" asked Allienora.

"We've hidden numerous telescopes around the solar system, all with sights on Earth. Additionally, we've infiltrated nearly every computer system on Earth, giving us eyes and ears into any location with some level of technology."

I approached one of the monitoring stations. An attendant studied the image of a man engulfed in the sapphire-blue aura that betrayed his human disguise. The attendant logged the Fume's every word and action.

My stomach twisted. *The Fume. My torturer. My nemesis. I need my drug.*

"What of the Fume's human minions?" asked Allienora. "Do you track their movements as well?"

"We do," said Rozlyn. "However, they prove more elusive, since, unlike the Fume, they're able to travel beyond the dimension around Earth. If we can't track them by passive means, we send out field agents."

"What of the nature of these minions?" asked Morion. "Are they human?"

"Honestly, we don't know," said Rozlyn. "Yet, we do know the most essential aspect of their nature—they bleed and die like men."

I studied the Fume's many manifestations, whom I knew from experience didn't die like men. Some, as expected, were prominent figures in government and industry, while others were insignificant people commanding little influence on the world.

"What have you learned about the Fume's manipulations?" I asked. "Are there any indications of his motive or design, Rozlyn?"

"A difficult thing to figure out, given our brief surveillance. Compared to the grand scope of the Fume's time on Earth, we've seen only a fraction of his manipulations. Nevertheless, over the last three decades, we've seen strange behaviors from the Fume. Nearly all his recent manipulations have promoted the success of the dimensional gateway. This has been confusing, since, after all his efforts, he sabotaged the gateway. Such counterproductive behavior boggles the mind. What did the Fume accomplish? Who knows?" Rozlyn looked to me with something like optimism. "Many of us here have been waiting for you to join us, Theron. Sensimion always felt that your memories burdened upon you in the sanitarium were the key to further understanding the Fume's greater scheme. However, Sensimion was hesitant to interfere with your work on the dimensional gateway, since the Fume seemed so intent on its completion. Before asking you to join us, he wanted to see why the dimensional gateway was so important to the Fume. When we detected that brief burst of exotic energy on the Brahman Station, Sensimion was eager to contact you and gain access to the station, so to more closely observe what was happening."

"What's this about a sanitarium?" asked Allienora.

"Nothing," I said nervously. I pulled Rozlyn away from the group and spoke to her privately. "Don't talk about my past in the sanitarium. I don't want them to know of my close association with the Fume."

"As you wish, but that list of names Sensimion obsessed over was an amazing assortment of historical figures. If they are indeed memories of the Fume's past manifestations—"

"They *are* his memories," I said. "I verified this much on my last encounter with him on Earth."

"Astonishing!" said Rozlyn. "You must tell us about every last memory. Better, we can connect you to a neural interface, which Sensimion developed. We'll suck every one of those memories from your head."

There was a sudden commotion among the attendants monitoring the Fume's manifestations.

"What's going on?" asked Rozlyn.

A man at the nearest station worked deft fingers on a control pad. "We've lost all surveillance feeds. Notice how all the images are frozen in a single frame."

"It's impossible," said Rozlyn. "All the telescopes send out independent signals. How could they have failed at the same time?"

An older gentleman, overseeing the stations, approached Rozlyn. "Everything's functioning properly. These images are accurate and to the moment."

"Then why aren't we seeing the surveillance?"

"We are."

"I don't understand," said Rozlyn.

"Observe." The older gentleman went to one of the surveillance stations and, manipulating the telescope's view, zoomed out so the entire Earth was displayed. "Notice the satellites orbiting the Earth. They move smoothly, in a steady, unhindered fashion." He then zoomed in on a MegaCity of Earth and panned through the streets. We saw inhabitants of the city standing still, as if they had turned to stone. "This may sound impossible, but it appears the Obelisks have placed Earth in a field of temporal stasis."

Everyone gazed in amazement at the view-panels.

"Temporal stasis," repeated Rozlyn in surprise. "The Fume's plans are advancing ahead of our counter-efforts. If you'll excuse me, I must see to preparations."

"What about my one billion notes?" asked Thirm Bastile.

"Here they are now," said Rozlyn.

An individual approached, handed Thirm Bastile a bag, and then addressed Rozlyn. "The devices will conform perfectly to our needs. We'll complete the weapon's assembly on the way to the target."

"I must leave now," said Rozlyn. "You've all acted selflessly for the welfare of humankind. Theron, I hope you'll remain here and tell us about your memories."

"I haven't come this far to rehash some bad memories. I'm boarding that ship with you. I want to see with my own eyes the destruction of the planet-sized vessel and the unraveling of the Fume's plans."

"I agree with Theron," said Morion. "I too wish to immerse myself in these grand adventures."

Orsteen and Allienora acted no less enthusiastic and demanded to be a part of the mission. Thirm, however, stood calmly, with the comfort of one billion notes cradled in his arms.

"And you, Thirm Bastile?" asked Rozlyn. "Do you wish to be part of this? Your knowledge of weapons could be useful."

"I'm not one to interfere in the affairs of my clients, who usually consider me all grit and greed." Thirm took a long breath. "Yet, I'm intrigued by what you might find in the alien vessel. Perhaps changes in my rules are in order. Count me in."

"Very well," said Rozlyn. "Everything we'll need is aboard the ship."

Rozlyn called for the immediate departure of the *Fractal Skylark*, sending a rush of people in all directions.

Before we boarded the ship, I stopped Rozlyn. "How do you plan to leave the depths of Mercury? This ship's too large to navigate through the tunnels that led us to this secret outpost."

"Darkness can be deceptive." Rozlyn pointed above the ship to the darkness clouding the upper parts of the cavern. Guide lights suddenly ignited, illuminating the mouth of an upward tunnel that appeared to lead to the surface of Mercury.

Orsteen shook his head in disbelief. "We'll have much to discuss when we return."

INSIDE
THE
SPHERE

The *Fractal Skylark* embarked on its journey to the edge of the solar system, where the alien vessel drifted. We hit light-speed in no time—Mercury vanished and the sun faded behind us.

The ship's accommodations were sparse—most of the interior was allotted for the construction of the black hole weapon. Its construction went smoothly and was expected to be completed within the eight-hour trip to the alien vessel.

We spent most of our time talking in a small galley. I sat at a table, swallowing back the urge to vomit. I felt worse than ever. My eyes were like molten balls in their sockets.

I'm coming undone, I thought. *I need relief.*

I glanced to Allienora, who was talking with Rozlyn. Just looking at her made me feel better. Since we escaped from Vega's, she hadn't been the same person. She was more carefree, more spontaneous. Tasting death will change anyone. I continued to watch her.

"What are your goals for the mission, Rozlyn?" asked Allienora.

"Obviously the destruction of the alien vessel," replied Rozlyn, as she dispensed a beverage from the nutrition unit. "However, before this is accomplished, we'd like to explore its interior. If the destruction of the alien vessel doesn't stop the threat of the Obelisks, our future efforts will only benefit from additional intelligence."

"What do you think we'll find inside?" asked Orsteen.

"Your guess is as good as mine," said Rozlyn. "Once within, we're prepared for anything. The *Fractal Skylark* is full of weapons and survival equipment. If we can't navigate the ship through the inner realm, we'll travel by foot and anti-gravity belt."

I was about to ask a question, but paused—my eyes became unfocused. A chill scuttled up my spine and my head fell to the table. After a moment of pain, I lifted my head with great effort.

Allienora attended me. "Theron, what's wrong?"

"Possibly death," I uttered.

"This is the worst I've seen you," said Allienora. "Your face is so pale."

"It's a terrible task to carry these eyes," said Rozlyn. "Don't worry, there's a treatment to restore your health. Follow me to the medical bay."

Allienora helped me along and we followed Rozlyn through the ship's narrow corridors and into a small nook, where a hospital bed extended from the wall. I crawled onto it and Rozlyn prepared a syringe. Allienora ran her fingers gently through my hair, comforting me.

"What are you giving him?" asked Allienora.

"I'm giving him a dose of sympathetic nanites. They enhance the body's metabolic rate. This will allow him to tolerate the eyes."

Rozlyn inserted the needle tip directly into my right eye. I didn't feel it enter, but watched as Allienora cringed. She squeezed my hand—her pain was apparently greater than mine.

Once the treatment was complete, I slept.

A couple hours later, I woke up. My physical condition had improved, but I was again haunted by the Fume's memories. They grew in my thoughts like a virus. The memory of my wife's murder was the clearest and most toxic. I tried to suppress it. I tried to forget.

I am Theron Mobius... I am myself... My mind is my center...

It was useless. I took out my vial of amber narcotic. As I administered a drop into my eye, the medical bay door opened.

Allienora stood there with a questioning look. "More nanites for your eyes, Theron?"

I gazed to the floor, embarrassed by my addiction. "No. This is for my sanity." I tucked the vial into my pocket. "I have problems, Allienora. I think I need help."

Allienora's soft hands touched my face. She tilted my head up and I looked into her blue eyes.

"It'll be all right, Theron. Why are you so sad? I want to know everything about you. Even the secrets you hide."

"You might not like what you hear."

"I won't judge you."

I wanted her to like me as much as I liked her, but I feared what she'd think if I told her my secrets.

She held her hand to my cheek. "You can trust me."

I smiled. She deserved to know who I really was. "I'll start at the beginning."

I told her the story of the sanitarium, the doctor, and the treatments in the sphincter beast. I told her of the aftermath of unreal memories and my loss of sanity.

When I finished, Allienora seemed confused. "Why would the Fume want you to know of his past manipulations?"

"I also wondered this—ever since I found out they were the Fume's memories and not madness."

"And your drug erases these memories?"

"Well enough," I said. "Without the amber narcotic, my mind would become muddled with them."

Allienora crawled into bed with me.

I wrapped my arms around her. "I feel like I've known you forever."

"That's an old one," she said, smiling wide.

"The classics are always the best. Did it work?"

"Maybe. But what do you really know about me?"

"I've been doing research." I tapped at the back of my head, at my neural implant. "I've been up-linking to the library every chance I get."

"Textbook reading, huh? The socialite. The scholar. The humanitarian. The prime minister's daughter turned into her father. Everyone knows that stuff about me."

"I read your books."

"My social and political theory won't tell you much."

"I read *all* your books."

"Really?" She paused.

"Even the one you didn't write."

"I don't know what you mean." She smiled. "The one I didn't write?"

"The one written by Olive Forlorn."

"How did you find out about that?"

"It was something you said when Vega held us captive. 'The void cannot be filled if nothing fits.'"

"Of course, the last line of the book." Allienora's eyes grew large with an endearing sadness. "What does it tell you about me, Theron?"

"It tells me everything. You long for something different, something more. But you don't know what it is. Every time you find something comfortable, something good, you begin to crave for something better—if such a thing even exists. You're trying to fill that *void*, but nothing fits."

Allienora wept softly. "It doesn't make sense. I've had everything in this life. Why do I feel this way?"

"We're a lot alike, Allienora."

"Do you know what it is, Theron? What I'm searching for?"

"I only know we're all searching for it." I put a hand on her cheek. "Maybe we can find it together."

She smiled. "I'd like that."

I held her tight. *This is becoming more? She cares for me. Maybe I'm not alone anymore.*

I felt at peace and soon fell asleep.

A knock at the medical bay door startled me awake. My arms were empty of Allienora's slight figure. It saddened me. I wanted to hold her forever. She had apparently left while I slept. Another knock brought me to my feet. I opened the door and found Rozlyn.

"We're nearing the alien vessel," she said. "You should eat before we try to enter."

"I am kind of hungry."

I went to the galley and sat beside Allienora. "You were gone when I woke up."

She smiled. "I enjoyed our talk."

"So did I."

"Are you feeling better?"

"Yes. I feel... lighter—now that there aren't any secrets."

Rozlyn approached and handed me a small, unidentifiable loaf. "Despite its blandness, it's highly nutritious."

"Mm... delicious," I mumbled during my first bite. It tasted like shit.

Morion was the only person in the company not eating scantily. Despite his expression of utter revolt, he ate like a pig. "It's a mistake to dine on such flavorless food before a dangerous mission. What if it's our last meal? One shouldn't depart for the afterlife with a stomach full of sludge."

"Enough!" said Orsteen. "Do you want to curse us?"

"I agree with Morion," said Thirm Bastile. "A more adequate meal should've been considered."

The group began talking about the perfect final meal.

I looked to Allienora and we exchanged secret glances. *What is she doing to me? Can I truly feel such feelings again?*

I suddenly became aware of the infinity spiral pressing against my chest. In a moment of confusion, I withdrew my gaze from Allienora and continued eating.

One of Rozlyn's colleagues entered the galley. "The weapon's assembly is complete."

I choked down my last bland bite. "Are you confident it works?"

"I am," said Rozlyn's colleague. "Yet it wouldn't hurt to say a prayer to your gods."

"Then there's no reason to delay," said Rozlyn. "Follow me to the control cabin."

Rozlyn escorted us to the forward cabin of the ship, where she discharged the current pilot from a control chair and took his place. On a massive view-panel, we saw the alien vessel. The image of the planet-sized vessel was crystal clear. The surface was constructed like a complex machine of black and gray composite. Great conduits of light ran along the surface of the sphere, possibly the method for channeling power. But it was the orb of blue energy, a quarter of the alien vessel's diameter, that truly took our breaths away. It was like a glowing moon of energy hovering just above the surface of the planet-sized vessel. Rozyln had theorized it to be a massive dimensional gateway engine like the Brahman Station's.

"What kind of readings are you getting from the smaller orb?" I took a step closer to Rozlyn. "At this distance you should be able to determine if it's a dimensional gateway engine."

"Give me a minute," said Rozlyn, interlinking with the ship's sensor matrix. The view-panel indicated the ship's sensors were analyzing the orb of blue energy. The structures of subatomic particles popped-up on the screen until at least a hundred were displayed. "Subatomic particle decay indicates the presence of a negative Higgs field. Dimensional symmetry is distorted."

I couldn't help but smile. "That's one big, fucking beautiful dimensional gateway engine."

"Beautiful but terrifying," said Allienora.

My smile subsided. "These aliens are giants compared to us."

"I don't think we should go inside," said Thirm. "Couldn't we detonate the weapon at the surface? This would be less dangerous."

"It must be detonated inside," said Rozlyn. "We only have one chance with the weapon."

"Where do you plan to enter?" asked Orsteen.

Rozlyn zoomed-in on the alien vessel. "There are thirteen openings on the visible side. There's little difference between each. I'll choose randomly."

The opening was no more than a pore on the face of the gargantuan craft. All in the group were silent as the *Fractal Skylark* entered the planet-sized vessel's gravity field and neared the opening. At last we entered, but were soon confronted by a barrier. It was the color of quicksilver and undulated in a gentle, fluidic fashion.

"What is it?" asked Orsteen.

"Whatever it is, it blocks our way," I said. "Rozlyn, what does the sensor data show? Is there a way around it?"

My question went unanswered. Rozlyn was in a catatonic state, her eyes wide in an empty gaze.

"What's wrong with her?" asked Morion.

I tried to grab her, but my arm recoiled from the bite of electricity. "She's guarded by a force field."

Allienora stared at the view-panel. "She's not slowing our course. We're going to hit the barrier."

"She's being influence by them!" shouted Thirm.

"I'll stop her." Orsteen flexed his muscles in anticipation of the electrical shock. His fists hit the force field and he crashed backward. "That bit the bone! I hope my sympathetic implants aren't shorted."

Allienora helped him up. "If you remove her now, we'll all die. Do you know how to fly this ship?"

"You're right," responded Orsteen. "I wasn't thinking."

"We're out of time, in any case," I said. "Hold on!"

Surprisingly, the *Fractal Skylark* didn't crash into the quicksilver barrier with the force we were predicting. Rather, it sank into the fluid-like mass, moving through its depths with a sluggish speed.

Everyone relaxed when Rozlyn became responsive. "Everything's fine. We're safe."

"Why didn't you respond?" I asked. "And why were you shielded?"

"My mind was busy in calculation. The shield's a safety precaution while I'm in such a state. Without it, a saboteur could've slaughtered me."

"Your actions were reckless," I said. "The next time you plan to put us in danger, I think we should talk about it first."

"While I was interlinked with the sensor matrix, I realized the barrier wasn't dangerous. It appears to be a containment gate." Rozlyn paused. "But if you insist, we'll put our next course of action to a vote."

I looked to the view-panel just as the *Fractal Skylark* emerged from the quicksilver barrier and saw inside. "My God, it's beautiful."

We were confronted by an unlikely inner landscape. A lush alien forest splayed out before us. Enormous plumes of pink, feathery umbrellas, reached high into the air, creating an amazing canopy. Below it, a spongy forest floor was overgrown with spiraling fronds and red prickly bushes. Green vines with amber pods grew unbridled, choking a variety of other strange plant life. Scattered among the wild vegetation were large pillars of technology. Rozlyn scanned the structures and the view-panel showed them to be gravity generators.

Above it all hovered great spheres of artificial light, like a series of miniature suns. They floated in an ominous ashen haze which veiled whatever loomed beyond.

Orsteen moved close to the view-panel. "Are we in a basin, or something of this nature? In the distance, the forest rises up into the mist above."

Rozlyn reviewed the sensor data. "We're in some kind of tubular forest channel, nearly fifty kilometers in diameter. The gravity contours with the inner walls, so all surfaces are flat ground."

Morion's eyes widened. "I didn't think it would be so splendid. Maybe we shouldn't destroy this amazing habitat."

I held up my fist. "Don't forget Earth."

"I'm landing the ship," said Rozlyn. "We should do an initial survey before we proceed."

Rozlyn submerged the ship under the forest canopy and landed.

"Is the atmosphere breathable?" asked Allienora.

"It is, but we should remain cautious and use breathers while remaining cloaked. We don't want to be detected." Rozlyn sat up from the control chair. "Come. Let's suit up."

I put on an environmental suit, which was also a cloak. "This looks like an amazing piece of technology, Rozlyn. Nothing like the old kind."

"The cloak will also negate the sound of your voice. You'll need this communicator." Rozlyn jammed something in my ear and then addressed Thirm. "You'll be in charge of transporting the weapon."

Thirm's face puckered as though he smelled something bad. "I'm not a mule."

"This isn't the time to question," replied Rozlyn. "The weapon's been equipped with an anti-gravity lift for easy movement and a cloak for concealment."

"Fine," said Thirm.

With the black hole weapon, packs of provisions, plasma guns, and anti-gravity belts, the company of six departed the *Fractal Skylark*. We walked out into an atmosphere full of murk and shadows. The occasional shaft of light filtered down through the forest canopy.

"Unsettling," said Allienora, grabbing my hand.

"Agreed." I momentarily removed my breather and sampled the air. I smelled many rich and complex odors from the surrounding forest life.

"Activate your cloaks," said Rozlyn.

I did so and immediately felt a dry static on my face. "I don't think they're working. You all look like gray shadows."

"They have interactive fields," said Rozlyn, "allowing you to see your fellow travelers."

Allienora hadn't activated her cloak. "They're working fine. I can't see any of you, though I can hear the crunching of forest detritus below your footsteps."

I found a sensor device in my pack and pointed it upward. "Beyond the mist, the forest splits into two great channels. As far as these readings show, one channel moves toward the center of the alien vessel, while the other heads somewhere along its outer fringe."

"Let's get a closer look at this gravity generator," said Allienora.

I could see her perfect figure, like a gray silhouette, moving toward it. The rest of us followed her.

The gravity generator was twenty meters high. As we approached, it again became clear that we were out of our element. The surface of the structure seemed to contain a tremendous level of complexity, as if every square centimeter held a microcosm of technology. I scanned the surface and was blown away.

"The micro-structure of the material is like a living organism. Arteries run throughout the material transporting a super-dense plasma filled with an array of base elements. The elements are being used as building blocks. I can detect the atomic reorganization of the elements on the surface of the structure."

"How are the elements being reorganized?" asked Allienora.

"By a force that can't be detected by this scan pad." I looked upward. "This gravity generator is literally being grown. The nano-intelegent matter of our Similacra is nothing compared to this. These aliens can grow a complex and functional machine without lifting a finger."

"This is priceless technology," said Morion, removing a scan pad from his pack. "It's possible this entire planet-sized vessel was grown with this technology."

Rozlyn commanded silence with a hiss. "There's movement in the distance. Be still."

Three figures like tailless monkeys bounded through the forest toward us.

At first, I thought they were foraging wildlife, but as they came closer, I noticed they were covered in protective armor, obviously forged by unnatural means.

"Fascinating," whispered Rozlyn. "Although strangely proportioned, they have two arms, two legs, and a head. Quite similar to us."

The large bulge that Rozlyn called a head was also covered with armor. We had no way of knowing what was inside. In the center of the so-called head was a single golden crystal, inlaid into the armor. It stared forth like a fiery eye.

Morion made a small laugh. "Our solar system has been invaded by a race of Cyclops monkeys."

"Shall I give them a stomp?" grumbled Orsteen. "They'll squish below my boots."

"We'd be revealed," I said. "It's too soon to risk the mission. Stay still."

One of the aliens perched itself on a branch and swept its golden eye across the forest landscape. The other two stood nearby, also giving attention to their surroundings. Far-off squawks and howls of unseen beasts heightened the situation. I was getting anxious and began to sweat. My hands thoughtlessly reached for my plasma gun. If the aliens came closer, they'd stumble upon the cloaked ship, which would stop them dead in their tracks.

With my plasma gun in hand, I nervously waited for the aliens' next move.

During the stillness, brown and jade centipede creatures stirred from the underbrush. With long, grasping mouthparts they munched on fallen fruits and forest debris. A specimen the size of a human arm approached my cloaked leg. With two rows of sticky feet, it climbed upward.

I suppressed the urge to kick it away, for fear the creature would cause a commotion as it tumbled on the ground. The aliens continued inspecting their surroundings. I wondered if they had noticed the centipede's disappearance as it crawled up the length of my leg and into my cloaking field.

The giant centipede became still, clinging to the length of my leg with its mouthparts at my hip. Just when I thought it couldn't get worse, the centipede began chewing on my environmental suit.

Holy shit!

The centipede spit bile on me. The acidic fluid dissolved one of my pockets and worked its way through my suit. The control node for my cloak was only inches from where the centipede feasted. I prepared to strike it with the butt of my plasma gun—but, before I could act, the centipede fell from my leg and out of the cloaking field. It twisted and writhed, causing a commotion that captured the attention of the three aliens.

The alien on the branch jumped toward me and landed on the centipede. It was only a meter away. I squeezed the grip of my plasma gun. The alien snapped up the centipede with an armored hand and inspected it with its golden eye. In an instant, the armor surrounding the alien's head shifted into an unseen dimension, revealing its weird alien face. It inspected the centipede with two bulging, emerald eyes, below which dangled a tan snout. Like a tiny elephant trunk, it extended outward, probing and smelling the centipede.

I breathed faster. It still hadn't seen me. I held up my plasma gun, ready to fire. Everyone else aimed at the other two, which remained nearly ten meters away.

"Don't fire," whispered Rozlyn. "We're not in danger yet. Our cloaks also mask our smell. Their long snouts shouldn't detect us."

With its two armored hands, the alien cracked open the centipede, exposing its frothy innards. It continued its examination and then immersed its hand into one of the gory ends, pulling from it my vial of amber narcotic. My heart raced. The centipede had eaten it along with the fabric of my pocket. It was now empty—the lid had apparently dissolved from the centipede's corrosive bile.

As the alien held up the empty vial, I grew angry. I needed my drug and this alien made me lose it. It would pay. I was ready to gouge out its bulging, emerald eyes and tear its slippery snout from its head.

"I'm going to kill it," I growled. "It found my vial. Take aim at the other two monkeys."

"Control yourself, Theron!" cried Allienora. "It's obvious their armor will protect them. You may be able to kill yours with a shot to the head, but the other two may be impervious to our plasma guns."

"They're aware of us," I said, studying the alien's reaction to the vial. "They have evidence."

The alien smelled the vial and then extended its snout toward the forest. It was apparently searching for a similar scent. At one point, I swore its bulging, emerald eyes met my own.

I couldn't stop thinking about my amber narcotic. *Without it, he'll torment me. Without it, he'll twist me to his will. Without it, the Fume will take my sanity.*

The alien suddenly stopped its search, relaxed its long snout, and shifted its head armor back from an unseen dimension. Its fiery, crystal eye again gazed forth. Without further investigation of the vial's origin, all three aliens vanished into a puff of blue light, which I suspected only Rozlyn and I could see with our synthetic eyes. They seemed to command an advanced form of dimensional travel.

I trembled with rage, fear, and madness. "I can't believe they didn't find us. We might not be so lucky next time. Let's deliver the weapon as quick as possible."

"They must have detected the *Fractal Skylark*," said Rozlyn. "We better travel by anti-gravity belts from here on out."

"We'll be more productive if we divide into two groups," I said. "The forest splits into two channels. One group can move to the center of this inner-world with the black hole weapon, while the other group takes the channel along the outer fringe to perform reconnaissance."

"Sounds good," said Rozlyn, inspecting everyone. "Since I'm the only one familiar with the black hole weapon, I'll take it to the center. Thirm Bastile can help me."

"Very well," I said. "Our paths split here. Assuming it's a straight course to the center of the alien vessel, twenty-four hours should be sufficient to rendezvous back at this point. Set the black hole weapon to detonate with enough time to allow our escape. Good luck. The future of humankind rests in your hands."

With the black hole weapon in their possession and their anti-gravity belts engaged, Rozlyn and Thirm took flight through the feathery canopy and into the mist above.

I looked to Allienora, Orsteen, and Morion. "Shall we be off as well?"

"Wait!" called Orsteen. "I'll stay here and protect the ship. The three aliens may return for a second look."

"The crew of the *Fractal Skylark* can handle such a task," I said. "Don't you want to discover the mysteries before us?"

"I can't fly," admitted Orsteen. "I'm a Mercury Miner. We don't have a propensity for such flight. Would you put wings on a rhinoceros?"

Morion laughed. "You know your limits, Mr. Hunn. However, don't worry. It's not that hard. When you become airborne, don't struggle. Let your legs go limp and have faith in the anti-gravity belt around your waist."

Orsteen interlinked with his anti-gravity belt and rose from the ground. His immediate response to flight was the opposite of Morion's instructions—his legs struggled to find solid ground, causing his body to waver to and fro like a buoy tossed amidst ocean swells.

"I'm going to overturn!" yelled Orsteen. "Miners are top-heavy!"

I joined the others in laughter, momentarily forgetting about my drug. *A small amount of humor might get us through this.*

Allienora flew in Orsteen's direction and took his hand. She pulled him along slowly and he stabilized. "You're safe, Orsteen. Let's fly together."

Orsteen soon became confident of his new wings and allowed Allienora to leave him unattended.

At great speed, we began our journey through the forest channel. I couldn't help but appreciate the beauty around us, even though it was the enemy's ship. I thought about the aliens we just saw. "What's the connection between the armored aliens and the Fume?"

"I don't know." Allienora flew next to me. "And do they have the same powers as the Fume? Can they kill with a thought or resurrect a dead man? Do they command omnipresence like the Fume?"

"If these aliens are like the Fume, then I'm confused." I reflected a moment. "My eyes detected the three armored aliens' use of an advanced form of dimensional travel. Yet, they didn't exude the exotic energy which identifies the Fume. Additionally, why is the Fume bound to the strange dimension around Earth, while the aliens aboard this craft are apparently free to roam the universe? My only proof may be the twinge in my gut, but it seems like we're dealing with two totally different animals."

Orsteen smiled proudly as he flew between me and Allienora with amazing precision. "Perhaps the Fume's in control of these aliens, like he is with his human minions on Earth."

"Maybe," I said.

"Or..." said Allienora, "the Fume isn't in charge. As far as we know, the three armored aliens are in control of the Fume."

"Whatever the case," said Morion, "we've gained no answers within this alien vessel. We've traveled for over five hundred kilometers and haven't found anything but vegetation and primitive wildlife. Where are the conquering armies, the great machines that will rape the Earth of its resources, or the storage containers that will preserve the human race for later consumption?"

"There's still time for answers," I said. "Let's continue."

Six hours passed and we still hadn't found anything. Maybe there was nothing to find.

"We'll have to turn back in less than four hours," I said. "Or there won't be enough time to return to the *Fractal Skylark* before the weapon's detonated."

"Not yet!" shouted Morion, flying ahead of everyone. "There's a clearing in the forest canopy. There's something ahead—something large."

I squinted curiously in the direction indicated. The canopy receded, giving way to a barren terrain. Within it, I saw a white structure.

We nervously flew onward. As we neared, I experienced a sense of recognition for the structure. *Why is it so familiar?*

When we finally got close enough to distinguish details, I was confronted by an improbability I couldn't have anticipated—there was never hope, there was never a prospect. But there it was—a ghost that made my heart race. I could only pray it was real.

"Allienora, do you see it?" I said with eyes wide.

"I do," said Allienora. "It's the Brahman Station."

We carried on toward the ghost of the Brahman Station.

"Could it truly have been saved?" A hopeful realization came to my mind. "They could still be alive."

"If they are, then we have a problem," said Morion.

I glared in his direction. "What do you mean?"

"Have you forgotten our mission? If your friends and colleagues are here, alive and well, how do we rescue them before the black hole weapon's detonated? The *Fractal Skylark* won't carry a tenth of the passengers that were aboard the Brahman Station."

"Then we must stop Rozlyn and Thirm from detonating the weapon." I frantically attempted communication with them.

"They're out of range," said Allienora. "There's too much interference in this maze of forest channels."

"Then we must turn back." I halted in midair, ready to reverse course. "I can't suffer the death of my friends for a second time."

"Your emotions are clouding your judgment," said Orsteen. "If we don't destroy this alien vessel, we risk the future of Earth. Are saving the lives of five hundred people worth the sacrifice of an entire world?"

"Nothing's certain!" I shouted. "We don't even know if destroying this alien vessel will stop the Obelisks, or the Fume. Hell, for all we know, the Obelisks have already destroyed Earth, or they're culling our resources, or placing the population into slavery. I won't sacrifice the Brahman crew for uncertainties."

Allienora flew close to me and put a hand on my shoulder. "Before we decide, let's look at what's left of the Brahman Station. We're only a short distance from learning the fate of your friends."

Allienora's voice calmed me.

"All right," I said, "but let's move. Our time's running out."

The forest canopy receded, and we flew above a terrain absent of vegetation. The structure of the great vessel was exposed—the same amazing composite that made up the gravity generators. We quickly realized something was being grown from the ground up.

"It almost looks like the foundation of a city," said Morion. "Imagine this technology on Mars. The Elitists could build a glorious empire—cities built overnight."

I kept my eye on the Brahman Station, which sat at the center of the growing structure. But as we neared, my optimism faded. The scene ahead grew more and more remarkable. The station, being removed from the weightless environment of outer space, had been propped up by pillars of the self-constructing composite, preventing it from rolling over.

Around the station was a massive gathering. As far as I could estimate, there were at least ten thousand figures moving about. Some of the figures traveled up alien-grown escalators attached to the station's docking bays, making for easy access into the station.

"I doubt those are the passengers of the Brahman Station," said Orsteen. "There are too many."

"So it seems," I said, disheartened.

We landed not far from the masses around the Brahman Station. I could now distinguish the figures ahead. They weren't human. "These aliens are different from the ones we encountered earlier. There must be a hundred different species before us."

"I may be wrong," said Allienora with a roving eye, "but this gathering of aliens has the feel of some weird festival."

"Indeed," said Orsteen.

I thought back on my days as a student. I always found evolutionary biology remarkable, and often daydreamed of what life would be like on alien worlds. The crowd before us showed a wide range of physiological diversity. Regardless, I felt less than interested by their odd forms, since their presence was part of an invasion.

I focused on the Brahman Station. "Let's move closer."

Still cloaked, we snuck through the crowd, passing various booths offering goods and services of one sort or another.

One booth in particular was extremely crowded. Behind the counter stood an alien with a head divided into two lobes, each equipped with a compound eye like a small pile of diamonds. Its mouth puckered as it whistled a complex melody—it seemed to speak in musical notes. With gangly arms, the alien reached over the booth's counter and accepted multi-colored beads from the crowd and dispersed vouchers in return.

Behind the cloven-headed attendant were ten horizontal tubes tinted different colors. They spanned the length of the entire booth. Attached to the end of each tube was a chamber containing a melon-green insect that fluttered about in defiance of its confines. When the attendant collected a sufficient number of beads from the crowd, he quickly pulled down a lever that simultaneously opened each of the insect chambers, allowing the insects to race down their tubes. The first insect to reach the end of its tube was apparently declared the champion, and the attendant paid winning vouchers, while losing vouchers were flung to the ground.

"Unbelievable!" I said. "They play carnival games while Earth's attacked."

"We play a similar game on Mars," said Morion. "However, our champions are small rodents, rather than insects."

"Let's continue toward the Brahman Station," I said angrily.

We continued on and soon found ourselves captivated by a group of tall, lanky aliens. They walked with a strange gait—their legs bent at an angle opposite the human form, giving their stride the appearance of a persistent forward kicking. We moved toward them for a better look. They didn't seem real. Their skin had the gloss of something artificial, and as we got closer, I saw the pattern of circuitry. As if the lines of organic and mechanical were blurred.

"An alien like a machine... and a ship like an organism." I looked to Allienora. "We have found the future."

Morion grabbed Orsteen's arm. "You're synergistic implants are archaic by comparison."

"That would be too far," said Orsteen, touching one of his synergistic implants. "At what point does one question his humanity?"

I stopped in front of a series of archways, each five meters tall and half as wide. "These archways seem to be the method of transportation used by the aliens."

At random moments, groups of aliens appeared below the archways and moved into the crowd. A parallel row of archways functioned as departure points, whisking away those who stepped within.

Allienora strayed toward a booth offering alien goods. Orsteen, Morion and I continued inspecting the archways with fascination.

My synthetic eyes became active. "Every time a traveler comes through an archway, my eyes detect a flash of blue light, indicating a dimensional disturbance. Their use of dimensional travel appears to be as ordinary as using a doorway."

"I've found something!" said Allienora over our communicators. "Come quick!"

She was standing in front of a small booth. Within hung an array of masks—not unlike ones worn to a masquerade or mystical ceremony.

"Why did you call out, Allienora?"

She pointed to an arrangement of four masks. The first looked like my friend Atticus, the next like Sensimion, and another like Renworth Vole. The final mask looked exactly like me.

"What's their purpose?" asked Orsteen. "What do your faces matter to them?"

"Could they be souvenirs of Earth's conquest?" suggested Allienora.

Not far from the booth, a small alien with the features of a fat child wore the mask that portrayed Atticus. It capered about on two stumpy legs, flaunting its newly acquired mask to all who passed by. Two frog eyes peeked over the mask—the alien's facial structure prevented it from looking through the human eyeholes.

"That little frog-faced fuck," I said, repulsed by the spectacle. If my longtime friend Atticus was indeed dead—a sad thought becoming ever more likely—then to wear such a mask and dance around was a mocking of his life.

I restrained myself from striking the little creature. "We waste time among this freak show. It's time to learn the fate of my friends."

I took the lead towards the Brahman Station.

We mounted an alien escalator and were brought to a docking bay, where we entered the station. Within, we found aliens wandering around, as if the station was an exhibit.

We walked through the halls of the living quarters.

"I spent many years in this station," I said. "Something's not right."

"How do you mean?" asked Allienora. "Everything looks the same to me."

I pulled at my chin. "I can't figure it out, but there's something off-balance."

The others acted indifferent to the surroundings, apparently unable to detect the strange air I described.

"It feels like I'm in a dream," I said. "The walls seem to loom at a height larger than life. The doorways, panels, floor tiles, and windows seem more detailed and fancy."

Morion impatiently gestured to the surrounding aliens. "It appears the crew and guests aren't here. We should return to the *Fractal Skylark*."

"Not yet!" I blurted. "We just got here. Let's explore the dimensional gateway chamber and then the main control room on the upper level."

"Very well," said Allienora. "Let's hurry."

We came to a lift. I touched the control panel and nothing happened. It was broken. We continued down the hallway and then stopped short. There was a line of aliens waiting to board what appeared to be a floating cart similar to an amusement ride. Its destination was a makeshift hole in the wall.

"Things grow more bizarre by the moment," commented Orsteen.

We moved closer to inspect. A group of aliens loaded into the cart, which then flew into the hole.

Morion peered curiously within. "It goes to the upper levels of the station."

I stepped closer. "Since the lift's broken, this appears to be our ride up. Orsteen and I will explore the upper levels. Allienora and Morion, the two of you should continue searching down here."

An empty cart emerged from the hole, and a waiting group of aliens boarded it.

"Take hold of the back," I said to Orsteen.

A groove on the back of the cart allowed us to get a foothold. Due to his size, Orsteen struggled to stay on. The cart took us on a route that transected the station through walls and floors, until finally we arrived in the dimensional gateway chamber.

We had found the crew! Or so it seemed for an instant. "This is unbelievable, Orsteen."

I almost started laughing. Playing out before us was a theatrical re-creation of that day I held so painfully at the tip of my mind. The performers were human-like, but not at all human. They wore white uniforms, much like the ones that had been worn by the crew. They played the roles of technicians, preparing the station for the maiden voyage. They acted like mimes, moving with large gestures and exaggerated expressions.

To complement the theatrics, three aliens, removed from the performance, played music on elaborate instruments—a spiraled horn sounding from six outputs; a box of deep, thudding percussion; a device so complicated it could only be described by the high-pitched plucks, coos, and whines that filled the parts of harmony and rhythm.

Prompted by the music, a character jumped out from behind one of the eighteen dimensional augmenters. He moved with an enlarged, sneaking stride, which instantly translated his sinister motive to the audience. His stained face was a parody of Atticus. If this was an accurate re-creation of the events on that day, then this was Atticus' doppelgänger.

A replica of a replica, I thought.

The saboteur snuck past technicians and continued on his way to another dimensional augmenter. There, he proceeded to remove a small, yellow orb from his mouth. Suddenly, another character appeared. He played the part of Sensimion. His eyes were two brilliant blue spheres, and his face was stained to a haggardly effect. He approached the saboteur in a single bound, raised his hand in disapproval, and then mouthed something inaudible. The rendition was apparently a silent one. The saboteur spun around and hurled the glowing yellow orb into the dimensional augmenter.

Sensimion's character discharged a plasma gun that shot confetti rather than plasma molecules. The saboteur promptly threw himself to the ground, where he underwent an exaggerated and comical death.

"This is all so confusing," said Orsteen. "Why put on such a production?"

"For demented amusement," I suggested.

The cart flew toward the main control room.

Orsteen shook his head. "We better leave now or we won't make it back in time to escape."

"All for the better, Orsteen. I've seen enough. Follow me."

I jumped from the back of the cart and led Orsteen to an emergency passage, which took us down to the lower levels.

We quickly found Allienora and Morion.

Morion held up a hand in excitement. "We've discovered something!"

My heart beat faster. "What?"

"After the two of you left, Allienora and I continued our search. We decided to interlink with a data orb, so we could learn what happened to the station after it fell into Jupiter's atmosphere. We found one and attempted to interlink with it, but it was nonfunctional like the lift. We then decided to extract a data-storage unit and take it with us, in hopes of later deciphering what happened.

"When we pulled back the panel below the data orb, it was empty—there was no data-storage unit, or, for that matter, any internal components. And it wasn't as if they'd been removed, but as if those components had never been installed." Morion held his breath, looking with anticipation to me and Orsteen.

I was in no mood for further drama. "Get to the point!"

"Don't you see?" said Morion. "The station's fake. Your initial impression of the station was accurate, Theron. This place is a flawed replica, with missing parts and inaccurate dimensions. Since this isn't actually the

Brahman Station, we can be certain the crew and passengers aren't here."

I took a moment to inspect the station more closely. "Why?"

"This is a question we can contemplate later," said Orsteen. "The black hole weapon will be detonated soon, and we have a long journey back to the *Fractal Skylark*. Let's go."

I gave a final sad inspection of the station's interior. "I find this whole situation beyond my comprehension. We're birds trying to understand the ocean's depths."

We left the station and made our way through the crowd.

I looked around. "Let's not fly until we reach the edge of the alien crowd."

Allienora shook her head. "Our quest has only raised more questions. It's unfortunate we didn't discover the motive of these aliens and the Fume."

"Unless," said Morion, "their motive is the relief of mere boredom."

"At least we've learned of our enemy's nature," said Orsteen.

"Nature?" Morion raised an inquisitive eyebrow. "What's your impression of these aliens' nature, Mr. Orsteen?"

Orsteen briefly thought over the question. "Well, for the most part, I don't believe they're all that different from us. They appear to find excitement in gambling. And as Theron and I saw, they enjoy music and theatrics—humor, drama, pathos, and all." Orsteen pointed to a booth serving food, where an individual with an oversized head ate an oddly-colored meat. "They obviously indulge in their sense of taste, relishing food's flavor."

Morion held up a questioning finger. "How can you be sure that alien's enjoying its food, and not merely satisfying its hunger?"

"Do you see the unused napkin in its left claw?" said Orsteen.

"Yes."

"He decidedly licks his claw clean rather than use the napkin. He wishes to relish every last taste." Orsteen lifted a hand high. "Apparently, the pursuit of pleasure is a constant throughout the universe."

Morion slapped Orsteen on the back. "You're more perceptive than I had previously thought, Mr. Orsteen. Maybe even the flair of a Mars Elitist."

"I'm not stupid," said Orsteen, raising his brow in an uncharacteristically arrogant manner. "I studied twenty Mercurial days with Master Fjiorn of the Prime Caverns. He's Mercury's greatest philosopher, scientist, sociologist, and ontologist."

Morion gave Orsteen a respectful nod, and then asked my opinion.

"I agree with Orsteen to some extent," I said. "They seem much like us. The fact that such fundamental traits as desire, greed, and gluttony can be seen between species of separate origins means a great deal in the scheme of convergent evolution, both mental and physical. It was possible we could've encountered beings so different in cognitive function that they could've been much like a colony of bees with no purpose but honey and stings." I shook my head sadly. "We could've learned a great deal from these aliens. It's tragic we've discovered them under such hostile circumstances."

"Hold that thought," said Allienora. "The three armored aliens are back."

I saw them standing in the distance. "I doubt they're here for the festivities."

"We must fly!" declared Morion.

"No!" I exclaimed. "They may be detecting the use of our technology. I have an idea."

I led everyone back toward Brahman's duplicate and returned to the booth selling exotic masks. While the attendant stood oblivious, I stole four masks. I handed them out. "Put these on. When I signal, we'll disengage our cloaks and walk away in plain sight. Carry yourselves with a swagger, like you own the place."

I thought it only fitting that I wore the mask of myself, while I gave Allienora the mask of Sensimion. When choosing for Morion, I couldn't help myself, and I selected a mask with three goggling eyes that surrounded a long phallic nose hanging limp to the chin.

"My mask is one of buffoonery," complained Morion, slipping it on with hesitation. "Orsteen's would be more to my tastes."

Orsteen stepped back, defending the rights to a regal, black-beaked mask.

I smiled under my mask. "I thought, with your extravagant Martian tastes, you'd savor something between humor and grotesquery."

Morion grunted.

I surveyed the aliens around us, trying to judge the right moment to disengage our cloaks.

"Now," I signaled.

We disengaged our cloaks and remained still, fearing the three armored aliens might see us. Fortunately, we were undetected and we began walking to the ends of the crowd, where we would re-cloak and take to flight.

While moving with a confident gait, I looked casually through the crowd for the pursuing aliens. I had lost sight of them, hopefully for good.

We continued for a brief while, but once again the aliens materialized. They were closer than ever, standing next to a row of dimensional archways. Their crystal eyes stared forth, following our movement. It felt as though their golden eyes were capable of examining my very substance.

In tandem, and with no cue but a possible psychic moment, we all drew our plasma guns. Our hands shook as we fired a stream of plasma molecules at the aliens. To our dismay, they stood unmoved as their armor absorbed every molecule, leaving them unhurt.

We ceased fire and stood motionless, surrounded by hundreds of aliens who stared at our four masked faces. Reactions from the alien crowd were unreadable, but their silence was clear.

To the side of the armored aliens, I noticed one of the dimensional archways had been hit by a stray plasma molecule and now lay in ruin.

"I have an idea," I said urgently. "Follow me into an archway!"

I ran forward at best speed, with the rest of the group following behind me. I jumped head-first into an archway and disappeared.

NEURO-RAPTURE

I found myself in some kind of intermediary dimension—a transcending place of pure thought, devoid of body. I saw a panorama of the universe. Elliptical galaxies, spiral galaxies, and barred-spiral galaxies encircled me like radiant chandeliers. Then, I heard it, a whisper coming from the center of my consciousness: *My thread of thought I forged in flesh, you journey far into the light. I await your return to cure my blight.*

Before I could put further thought to the oddly familiar whisper, all but one of the galaxies shrank back into the depths. My consciousness raced toward the remaining galaxy. A jarring convergence of body and mind made me whole again and I belly-flopped on the surface of an alien planet.

I lifted my face from a maroon-brown soil and then picked myself off the ground. I watched as the others spilled from the archway, one by one.

Before the armored aliens followed, I fired at the archway until it was a pile of broken parts. I hoped this would slow them.

We removed our masks and brushed ourselves clean. Morion looked disdainfully at his phallic-nosed mask and then threw it on top the pile of broken archway.

We were on a new world. It was night and we stood atop a sea cliff. It overlooked a calm ocean illuminated by two swollen moons, each hanging low on the water. Against the two brilliant, meteor-scarred faces, wisps of clouds lay silhouetted, moving gently across the sky as if traveling the serene ocean waters for mere pleasure. It was an intoxicating scene that bested the most fantastic of dreams. A cool, salty breeze blew in from the ocean and greeted us.

We turned away from the ocean and found a primitive town sprawled out behind us. Simple wooden houses with circular windows, square doors, and red-shingled roofs lined a central plaza. At its center, a bonfire blazed, casting dancing light on the houses.

"It's a bit primitive for aliens with dimensional travel," I said.

Allienora gazed up to the stars. "I wonder where we are, and how far we've come."

I gestured to the ruined archway. "From the amazing journey we experienced through the archway, it seems we traveled to a different galaxy. It truly was an exhilarating ride."

"What do you mean?" asked Allienora. "I experienced nothing when I passed through the archway."

"What about you, Orsteen?" I asked. "Didn't you find your thoughts traveling through space?"

Orsteen shook his head in bewilderment. "My journey was instantaneous."

"There's no time to talk!" said Morion. "Aliens are coming. They must have heard Theron destroying the archway."

The aliens were tall and thin and moved with an urgent gait. With the light of the bonfire at their backs, they looked like shadows racing closer.

"Quickly," I said. "Take cover!"

We rushed to the nearby tree line and hid behind some bushes, where we spied on the six aliens. I recognized their backward bending knees and the gloss of their bio-mechanical skin and the circuitry-like pattern embedded in it. We had encountered similar aliens in the crowd around the Brahman Station's double.

The aliens inspected the ruined archway. One of them outstretched an arm like a tendril and grabbed Morion's phallic-nosed mask from the remnants. He shared his out-of-place finding with his companions.

The aliens discovered our trail of footprints. They turned threatening glances to the forest, but didn't seem to know our precise location. They kicked their way to the tree line, while emitting a high-pitched noise from two rows of polyps along their cheekbones.

"Let's get out of here," I said. "There may be more on their way."

We pressed into the dark woods, where the sound of chattering insects surrounded us. I pushed through branches and bushes. I heard the scuffling of nocturnal wildlife and feared we might stumble into the waiting jaws of something large and hungry.

After a long distance, far from the alien colony, I stopped the group near a hole in the ground. "My scan pad indicates an underground network of caves extending as far as the sea cliffs, to our right."

Allienora surveyed the hole. "You think we'll find safety in the ground? We have no idea what's down there—hibernating beasts, venomous serpents."

"Better to be met by a sleeping beast below than a stalking beast above."

A distant rustling of leaves caused Allienora to jerk her head toward the dark foliage. "Good point." She removed a small electric lantern from her pack and then took the lead into the opening.

Morion, obviously exhausted from our flight, gasped for air. "I'm not as easily convinced this is the best plan. Crawling into a dark hole like a petrified mouse is no solution. More importantly, I'm vastly claustrophobic."

I pushed him toward the hole. "We'll only stay below until daylight comes."

I waited for Orsteen to enter and then took up the rear. At first, the tunnel was narrow, but it soon gave way to a wide cavern. The sound of dripping water echoed from all directions. We weaved around stalagmites and stalactites, delving deeper into the cavern. At last, we found a suitable area to settle down, devoid of puddles and wetness.

Orsteen nodded his head in approval. "Theron, you've found us a cozy spot. I feel like I'm back in the belly of Mercury. How about something to eat?"

"Good idea, Orsteen." Allienora removed a set of rations from her pack and handed them out. I waved away her offer, but she insisted. "You haven't eaten in over twelve hours."

"I feel sick. These eyes are again taking a toll on my health. I need another injection." I removed the syringe and vial from my pack and administered the prescribed dosage of nanites, which, though helpful, wasn't the medicine I truly craved.

Damn that wretched centipede creature. Damn myself. I'll be strong. I'll fight the memories.

I scrutinized the vial of nanites. There might have been a hundred doses in it. After that, and without proper care, I'd have one of two choices—die from the degeneration of my health, or remove the eyes from their sockets.

Allienora again put food in front of me. "Please, eat."

She truly cares for me, I thought, allowing myself to smile. "As you wish."

We sat in a bubble of dim light produced by our lantern and ate our flavorless food. Morion devoured his share in a few thoughtless mouthfuls, and then proceeded to grope at the cave floor, frequently turning his head to the unseen ends of the dark surroundings.

"You seem anxious, Morion," I said.

"I told you I was claustrophobic."

"Why do you grope at the cave floor?"

Morion scoffed. "To ensure I'm not being overtaken by anything that crawls or slithers. Those puddles are infested with small gelatinous-filled-sacks-with-legs. They hop from puddle to puddle, spreading their stench."

Orsteen turned in the direction indicated. "Such things may have the potential to be eaten... or smoked, if we're lucky. Let me know if your groping turns out to be fruitful."

I moved the lantern closer to Morion. "I believe you're safe from such creatures, Morion."

"I'll be the judge of that!" said Morion, eyes shifting back and forth. "Do you think I can't manage my own safety? And, just so you know, I believe the walls have decided to cave in on us. See there!" Morion stabbed a finger toward the cave's ceiling. "That stalactite—it attempts to wobble free, so to impale me."

"Merely a play of light and shadow," I said.

Morion started to come to his feet, as if preparing to escape back to the surface.

I pulled him back down. "You're having a panic attack. Be calm. We must remain here."

"Here!" barked Morion. "Here, where you've condemned us. Your madcap getaway has stranded us. What now? Do we wander the forests and caves of this alien world forever?"

"You should be thanking me rather than blaming me. We needed to escape the alien vessel before the black hole weapon was detonated. Coming here saved us."

"Silence!" said Allienora. "Such bickering is pointless. We must learn to adapt, so we can survive. Forget the comforts of your past lives and anticipate hardship. Let's just hope this new life wasn't delivered in vain. We must pray the alien vessel will be destroyed. Now, as to your claustrophobia, Morion, I noticed some tranquilizers in my pack."

"I have something better," said Orsteen. "It'll instantly cure your claustrophobia, Morion." Orsteen revealed a metal flask. "I never go anywhere without my reserves. It's a comforting concoction that I sip before bedtime. Ingest only a small quantity. It slides down the pipes like a knot of thorns."

Morion grabbed the flask and took a big drink. His face puckered, and he was overcome by a strenuous cough that raised arteries in his neck and forehead. Morion extended the flask to me. I gracefully accepted it and drank with similar intensity.

"A powerful drink, Orsteen," I said through clenched teeth. I passed it to Allienora, who handled it with more charisma.

Before Orsteen took a drink, he raised the flask high. "To Thirm Bastile and Rozlyn. May they deliver destruction to the alien vessel and escape unharmed."

I nodded in approval and received the flask for another drink.

After a few more rounds of the flask, my body numbed and the cave floor softened. We rested on our backs with sprawled arms and legs, enjoying the effects of Orsteen's drink.

My lips and face tingled. "There's no coming down from this alcohol, Orsteen."

"Like a bird floating on air," said Morion, no longer showing concern for the looming stalactites and scurrying cave creatures.

"It's not alcohol," said Orsteen. "It's a hallucinogen."

"What!" said Allienora with concern. "It's not addictive, is it?"

"Absolutely not. What's more, you'll have no hangover in the morning."

"What's in it?" I asked.

"I'm not sure," said Orsteen. "It's used by our young when performing their rites into adulthood. As leader of Mercury, I'm allowed special access to it. It's called Neuro-Rapture, said to elevate the mind from youthful ignorance to mature wisdom."

"Then there's indeed hope for Morion," said Allienora jokingly.

"Unfortunately not," said Orsteen. "The mind must still be youthful. It's far too late for Morion to undergo the transition."

We were silent for a while, each of us enjoying our altered states. I found my mind going to strange places— both fantasy and nightmare. But I quickly focused on reality when Allienora inched her way toward me. I accepted her in my arms with pleasure.

Morion raised his head from the cave floor. "I couldn't help but notice the intimacy the two of you share, and something unsettling occurred to me. If we're going to be stranded here for the rest of our lives, then we have a problem."

"Which is?" I asked.

"The composition of male to female is askew. Two of us gentleman will be living a very lonely existence."

"You're right," I said, now pulling Allienora's warm body closer.

"I propose," said Morion with a grand tenor, "for the health of our little tribe, that Allienora relocate her feminine comforts every other night between the three of us, so we may all share in her fruits. Additionally, she won't play favorites and will remain vigilant to the schedule of rotation—this, in effect, will avoid any jealousy among the three of us men."

"You've lost your mind," said Allienora. "I won't be passed around like a whore. You can find comfort from that stalagmite at your feet. Fondle it to your heart's content."

Morion smiled crookedly. "My proposal wouldn't be unreasonable to a woman of Mars."

"This isn't Mars. Your perverse ways are irrelevant." Allienora smartly turned her gaze from Morion.

Morion stroked his hair in contemplation. "Then, I immediately declare this planet in the name of Mars. Thus the rituals and social customs of Mars immediately apply."

I raised my hand in objection. "I was first to arrive through the archway, and it's this essential detail that gives *me* ultimate authority. Thus, I declare Allienora will act as she pleases and pursue any affairs she wants."

"If this is how it must be, then I warn you, Mr. Mobius, I plan to charm her with all my secret ways."

"As you like, Morion, but remember—impossible pursuits require impossible efforts." I exaggerated my tender embrace with Allienora, so to let Morion know who held the upper hand.

Allienora pulled away from me. "Neither of you will enjoy my company. It seems Orsteen is the only gentleman among you." She proceeded to lie next to Orsteen, who was sound asleep and snoring.

I saw a gelatinous-filled-sack-with-legs hopping near me and smiled deviously. I snatched it up, took aim, and launched the slimy creature into the air. It landed with a splatter on Morion's face, who screamed in revolt.

I laughed to myself and found Allienora shaking her head in disapproval. She, too, then laughed.

The night passed.

I awoke to a shaft of morning light that slipped into the cave and warmed my face. I stood up and inspected a previously unnoticed opening, which overlooked the ocean. The cave we inhabited was within the face of the sea cliff, close to the surf. I watched the alien sun rise at the ocean's edge, spilling an apricot light across the gentle fluxing waters. Winged creatures, like bald ferrets, flew above the water. One by one, they crashed down to catch small bundles of gray tentacles from just below the surface.

"It's beautiful," said Orsteen, approaching from behind me.

"Indeed."

"It means much to you. Doesn't it?"

"What do you mean?" I replied.

"The necklace," said Orsteen. He indicated the cobalt-blue infinity spiral that I caressed thoughtlessly. "I can tell it's important to you. You've been checking its safety more often than the narcotic in your pocket."

"My drug is gone," I said tensely.

"And the necklace? What's its significance?"

"It was my wife's."

"Of course," said Orsteen. "I read your biography in the *Neofrontier Chronicle*. I've also lost a wife."

"I'm sorry, Orsteen. How did it happen?"

"She was supervising a mining excavation when a subterranean tremor caused a cave-in."

I looked thoughtfully to Orsteen. "I think I understand you now."

Orsteen tilted his head inquisitively. "How so?"

"We're all stricken with tragedy in this life. This is part of what defines us as mortal beings. It's how we choose to have those experiences shape our lives. After the tragedy of your wife's death, you chose to become a leader, someone who protects those in need of protecting. From her death came something positive... *someone* positive. You're a good leader, Orsteen."

Orsteen placed a hand on my shoulder. "You've given me a different perspective, my friend. Thank you."

I looked out to the ocean.

What of my own choices? I wondered. *Orsteen made good with his tragedy. What did I make with mine? I closed my heart to love. Lost myself in my work.*

"Are you all right, Theron?"

"This life can be cruel and beautiful at the same time. Who knows if it means anything at all?"

For a while we stood in silence, admiring the view.

I thought about Allienora. "We should wake the others."

We found a bunch of the gelatinous-filled-sacks-with-legs hopping carelessly on Morion's sleeping form. Orsteen and I laughed. Apparently, during the night, the creatures had made a nest of silver webbing on Morion's chest. Thus, the day began with Morion in a rage, slaughtering the cave creatures. He crushed them against the cave walls, and those that dared to hop at his feet were instantly stomped. The rest of the creatures fled to the opening illuminating the cave. They toppled over the edge of the cliff and into the surf below.

Morion trembled. "Didn't I tell you these disgusting hobgoblins were out to get me? They've soiled my clothes. I now reek of their foul secretions."

Once Morion calmed down, we journeyed out into the alien morning, keeping a lookout for our armored pursuers.

While Morion and Orsteen looked for food, Allienora and I ventured to the far perimeters of our surroundings to assess the risk of further alien encounters. We realized we were on a small peninsula of tropical forest. Sea cliffs, like castle walls, formed the outer edge of the peninsula and protected against the ocean tides.

When we arrived at the tip of the peninsula, we discovered, to our breathtaking surprise, a floating city in the shape of an enormous teardrop. It hovered above the water, a few kilometers off shore. We could see a glowing, crimson beam of energy being shot from the base of the teardrop city and into the water's depths.

"What's it doing?" asked Allienora.

I found an ocular headset in my pack. Looking through it, I saw aliens traveling on walkways that wound up and around the great structure. The floating city was at least a thousand meters tall and shimmered with a golden luster.

"I don't know what the beam of energy is, but you should see the opulence of the architecture. The finely crafted railings lining the walkways, the robust columns supporting the various levels, even the enormous windows seem to reflect the light with an abnormally enchanting flare."

Allienora took a turn with the headset. "Quite picturesque. What one might expect from the Romans of old, had they ascended to an age of technology."

"Picturesque indeed." I took the ocular headset from Allienora and pointed it toward her.

"What are you doing?" she asked.

"Taking a picture. If we ever return home, I'll need a memento."

"I've never looked worse."

"You've never looked better. You're an adventurer now. The first woman to stand on an alien world."

"I like the sound of that."

I waved her back a step. "Quit fidgeting and smile for me."

The sun had risen to its zenith and now began its leisurely descent.

Allienora and I returned to the cave and found Morion alone, sitting next to a small fire. He held a sharpened stick, on which were impaled a number of gelatinous-filled-sacks-with-legs. He hummed a tune as he cooked them delicately over a small flame. He turned to us with wild eyes and grinned.

"You're just in time for the feast. I've taken my ultimate vengeance upon these hobgoblins. I believe if you eat them, you'll absorb their powers!"

"What are you talking about?"

Allienora picked Orsteen's flask off the ground. "He drank all the Neuro-Rature."

I shook my head at the idiot in front of me. "What if you eat me, Morion? Will you absorb my powers?"

Morion's eye widened. "Your statement has blown my mind." He looked at the skewer in his hand. "I'll need a bigger stick."

"You're insane, Morion. Snap out of it!"

He raised up the skewer of gelatinous-filled-sacks-with-legs. "Power or no power, they've turned out to be quite tasty. Their gelatinous centers cook nicely into a white meaty texture. Sit. There's plenty for all."

"Where's Orsteen?" I asked. "Didn't you return together?"

"Orsteen's the insane one, not me. He decided to spy on the community of aliens we encountered near the archway. I told him such boldness could get us captured and we parted paths."

"How long ago was this?" asked Allienora.

Morion tested the firmness of the gelatinous-filled-sacks-with-legs and then spoke through a crazy smile: "Roughly five rounds of my little hobgoblin friends."

I gave him a fierce look.

Morion cleared his throat and straightened his posture. "At least two, maybe three hours ago."

I attempted to contact Orsteen over the communicators, but he didn't respond.

"Do you think he's lost?" asked Allienora.

"I don't know," I said, "but he'll have to find his way back alone. Morion's right. We can't risk being captured."

"Sit and eat," said Morion, handing us each a skewer of cave creatures and some small green fruits. "The scanner in my pack showed these fruits to be edible— however, my initial trials found them to be the cause of uncontrollable flatulence. Eat at your own risk."

I ate scantily and told Morion the great teardrop city, which floated over the ocean.

Finally, after hours of waiting for Orsteen to return, we gave up and slept.

In the middle of the night, Orsteen charged into the cavern, his expression that of a lunatic. "They've arrived! All three of the armored aliens! I was at the edge of the alien community, observing customs and routines to get better acquainted with our new neighbors. Without warning, the armored aliens arrived in the center of town, as if still in hot pursuit. They immediately sought counsel with the native aliens. At that point, I raced back here."

Orsteen caught his breath and then snatched up one of the green fruits Morion had harvested. I grabbed desperately for it, but Orsteen devoured the fruit in a single gulp.

"We're doomed," uttered Morion, lying on the floor like a corpse. "Inform the aliens of my surrender."

Morion seemed unable to filter his thoughts. I had the urge to throw him into the sea, but decided against such an indulgence. "Must you be so negative, Morion?"

Orsteen puffed out his chest. "It's time to fight."

"Agreed," I said. "But how? Our plasma guns are useless against them."

"I don't know," replied Orsteen.

What could we do? Our resources were limited. I became distracted when Morion started talking to himself. The effect of the Neuro-Rapture had apparently diminished, and Morion again cast paranoid looks to the looming stalactites.

"Your claustrophobia has inspired me, Morion!" I collected everyone's anti-gravity belts and carried them to the corridor giving entrance to the cavern. I took apart three of the belts and removed their anti-gravity nodes, which I then placed around the walls of the corridor. I adjusted their emitters so they projected their anti-gravitons to the ceiling, causing the upper region of the corridor to be void of gravity.

I located ten of the biggest stalagmites. One by one, I attached the remaining anti-gravity belt and uprooted them from the cave floor with a blast from my plasma gun. I carefully positioned the stalagmites within the weightless upper region of the corridor. I then interlinked with the anti-gravity nodes and manipulated their sensors.

"At the first sign of the aliens, the anti-gravity nodes will disengage, sending the crushing weight of ten stalagmites down on them."

"Very creative, Theron," said Allienora.

With the plan in effect, we huddled in a dark corner, waiting like skittish chickens. With each drip of water, we flinched. With each scurrying hobgoblin, we reeled. The two moons at the ocean's edge poured a rich light through the opening, into the cavern, and down the corridor. Our one chance for survival was held in the weight of a hulking mass of mineral deposit. Despite the uselessness of our plasma guns, we held them at the ready.

I glanced sidelong to Allienora. Her face glowed in the moonlight. I noticed her hands trembling and attempted to steady them with my own. She smiled timidly and then looked back toward the corridor.

A concussion jarred my senses. In a daze, I realized the trap had been tripped. The impact shook the cave with such intensity that a mass of rock collapsed in upon the opening, leaving us in total darkness. I turned on our electric lantern.

"Did we get them?" asked Morion. He held his plasma gun close to his body, turning frantically this way and that way. "Do you see them? I see none. Did we get them? Did they get past?"

I crept up to the pile of toppled stalagmites. "At least one hasn't escaped." An armored leg splayed out from the pile. I poked at it with the barrel of my plasma gun and it remained still. "I'm not sure about the other two."

From the shadows, one of the aliens jumped toward me. With tremendous strength, Orsteen struck it, sending it flying. Before hitting the cave wall, it vanished into a blue light that only I could see.

"Thank you, Orsteen." I rushed to the blocked opening that had overlooked the ocean. "Quickly, let's clear this rubble so we can escape."

"I'll hold off the aliens," said Orsteen, as another sprang from a dark hole. He successfully wrestled it away and it retreated back to the shadows.

As Allienora and I worked to gain access to the outside, Morion came forward with plasma gun in hand. "Stand clear! I'll blast it open."

Allienora pushed down his weapon. "Are you crazy? You'll cause an avalanche that'll sweep us all into the ocean with a hundred tons of rock."

Morion grunted. He tucked his plasma gun into his belt, and continued to clear away rocks, piece by piece.

Orsteen stood in a defensive crouch, arms held at guard. He cursed the two remaining aliens as they hurled themselves forth from the shadows. He moved fast and caught them by their heads with his massive hands. He lifted them high into the air, roared angrily, and then cast them to the ground as though to drive them to the very depths of Hell.

The two aliens merely bounced on the ground and rolled back into darkness. An instant later, one of them reappeared and performed an unexpected dance. As Orsteen watched in disbelief, the other alien came out of hiding and jumped on his back. In an instant, both Orsteen and the alien disappeared.

I launched a boulder toward the remaining alien. It dodged it effortlessly.

While Allienora and Morion continued clearing the opening, I grabbed a splinter of stalactite from the pile of rubble and poked and prodded at the alien, trying to keep it at bay. The other alien reappeared from wherever it had taken Orsteen.

"Allienora! Morion!" I screamed. "Behind you!"

Allienora smashed a rock over its head. Morion, in a panic, fired his plasma gun, only to miss the alien. The plasma molecule shot to the ceiling, where it broke free a slender stalactite. It fell like a spear down on Allienora, goring her through the abdomen. Her face froze in absolute horror. She grabbed the stony sliver extending from her belly, exhaled a profound breath, and fell to the floor.

Before Morion could fire another shot, the alien jumped onto him and they crashed down on Allienora's body. A second later, the three disappeared.

My emotions swelled. *Kill them! Murder them!*

Allienora's deathly expression fueled my rage. I lashed out at the remaining alien with all my substance, smashing rock and fist upon the little creature. Despite all the strength and speed I summoned, I couldn't harm it. I punched it away, but a moment later it returned with twice the effort. It leaped and plunged at me, snatching and grabbing with armored hands, trying to take hold of me.

Defeating the alien no longer seemed possible. I pulled out my plasma gun. "Fuck you, you little troll!"

I sent a stream of plasma molecules to the ceiling. Rock and stalactites rained down, and the cave began collapsing in on itself.

I waited for the end.

The alien darted around, trying to avoid the falling rock. It could've easily escaped with the use of its transporter, but, for some reason, it chose to risk life and limb to capture me.

By some divine favor, the pile of rubble blocking the cave's opening gave way, and moonlight spilled through. I rushed through the opening, and threw myself over the cliff's edge into air. A ten-meter drop took me to the cold waters below. I hit the water with a jolting whack. I struggled to stay afloat—I was tangled in a mesh of alien seaweed.

I flailed at the water's surface, trying to grab a nonexistent edge of land. Beginning to sink, I realized something had my foot and was pulling me down. It crawled up my legs. I felt what I knew to be two armored hands. The alien had followed me down. I kicked to no avail. Before I became fully submerged, I took a deep breath.

MOBIUS

I continued trying to break free, until the reflex to breathe overpowered me. In a violent contraction, cold water overwhelmed my lungs. My head filled with a burning pressure and my consciousness failed.

BIOLINGUISTIC
LOBE

I woke up to a dream, to a nightmare, to an afterlife—I wasn't sure. I hung in an upright position. A cold metal restraint pressed against my naked chest. I felt like a deflated balloon—weak and flimsy.

I saw a figure, like a shadow, passing in front of me. It came closer. It was one of the lank aliens with backward-bending knees. A closer look revealed its sophisticated skin. The surface was glossy and nearly transparent. Embedded within the skin were fiber-optic-like filaments, causing the skin to glow ever so slightly.

It must be a machine, I thought.

It turned its tall, narrow head in my direction, as though it heard me thinking. Two oversized eyes looked at me intensely—they seemed almost human. Polyps around its small mouth quivered with a high-pitch trilling sound and I heard a whisper, "I am alive. I am sentient."

I couldn't respond.

It suddenly revealed a vicious-looking mechanism ending in two metal talons. I shuddered as the talons veered toward my eyes with a slow, deliberate motion. They spread open like those of an eagle before snatching prey. I tried to close my eyes, but they refused. I tried to beg the alien for mercy, but my mouth failed me.

The two talons grasped the tender orbs of my eyeballs. Pain! Horror! My mind screamed. I heard a bloodcurdling crunch and pop before again losing consciousness.

I stirred after what seemed an eternity of slumber. Still half-asleep, I had the wishful thought that the past few weeks were just a fading dream. Sadly, everything flooded back and I remembered what happened to Allienora.

I've lost you already, my dear. Everyone dies in my path.

I was still in an upright position, bound and paralyzed. I inspected my prison. The walls glowed with an electric-yellow light. Below me sat a large basin of fluid, in which floated unusual masses of tissue. Their gray, glistening substance resembled brain matter. I tried not to think of their purpose or origin.

Upon a small table sat an assortment of strange surgical tools, including the two-talon mechanism I had believed to be a figment of a passing dream.

What have they done to me? Why can I still see?

I realized the ill-effect of my synthetic eyes was gone, leaving me to wonder if the aliens had replaced them with new ones.

There was something behind me. I felt strange emanations. It was like I was secured to some kind of machine. Something penetrated my skull, possibly linking me to that machine.

I hung there for a while, staring at the air in front of me. All I could think about was Allienora and the short time we had spent together.

My sweet Allienora, I thought. *You deserved longer. Ever since we met, I felt something I hadn't felt in a long time. Life is so much better when you have someone to share it with. We could've been happy together. I'm sorry, my dear.*

Allienora's soft voice filled my head: *Such passionate words. If we're being honest, I think you may be a little too old for me. But as they say, love has no boundaries, right?*

Allienora? You're not dead?

I don't think so. Unless in the afterlife you're paralyzed, and forced to stare for eternity at a wall of blinding yellow light. Allienora's words became intense: *Is that you, Theron? I thought I was hallucinating.*

How is it we're communicating? I thought. *My mouth doesn't move, yet you hear me.*

I don't know, came Allienora. *However, my thoughts are what you perceive as well. Are you also hanging from some great machine?*

Yes. We must be close, since the walls are the same glowing yellow you described. I suddenly felt tears in my eyes. *I'm glad you're alive.*

So am I.

Hold on, I interrupted. From the electric-yellow wall, a previously undetectable crack expanded into an oval doorway. From it, one of our captors appeared. *One of the aliens enters.*

"Excellent, you're awake," said the alien in a perfect English dialect. "I was beginning to fear you had brain damage from the operation."

As it spoke, I noticed its mouth didn't move. However, the polyps surrounding its mouth trilled in sync with every word I heard.

It continued, "It was possible you weren't going to wake up."

Unable to move or speak aloud, I stared at the alien.

"Forgive me," said the alien. It approached a control podium and tapped on it, triggering my release.

I felt a network of fibers retract from the back of my head—it was a weird sensation. The metal restraint at my chest released, and I fell to the ground in a mound of bent joints and loose muscles. I picked myself up and stood proudly, unashamed by my nakedness.

"What have you done to us, you evil fucks?"

The alien's expression shifted. "I admit that my skills with such procedures are that of a novice, but 'evil' is a harsh term to use considering I've saved your lives. I was the only person on this planet with the skill to help you. I only did as the two Oryxes instructed."

"And how is it you speak my language so fluently?"

"I don't," said the alien. "Besides repairing your mortal injuries, I was also asked to implant a biolinguistic lobe within your brain. This will allow you to communicate with any other species with such a lobe. It works by a sort of psychic transmission. In short time, you'll master its use, so not to mingle your thoughts with your intended communication." The alien gestured to a tangle of metal on the table. "Unfortunately, I couldn't implant the biolinguistic lobe without removing your primitive neural implant. This setback may have been the reason you were comatose for so long."

"Comatose?" I said.

"You've been unconscious for two hundred days."

"Impossible."

"Don't worry," continued the alien. "If you had any appointments to keep, you won't miss them. This room is contained within a temporal bubble, which dilates time. For every day that passes within, only a minute passes outside."

"Remarkable," I said. "And where is outside?"

"We're in the floating city of Azimoir, not far from where the Oryxes found you."

"What of my companions? Where are they?"

The alien again tapped at the control podium. The machine from which I had hung was in the shape of a large cube. It revolved, revealing the naked figures of Allienora, Morion, and Orsteen.

"They're all alive," said the alien. "The female is healed, and everyone's biolinguistic lobe is functioning properly." The alien pointed to me. "You were the most troublesome of my patients. I had to remove your artificial eyes. They sucked the life right out of you. Though I must say, they were a lovely albeit imperfect design." The alien ran a hand along his arm, showcasing his glowing skin. "Your people may someday achieve total systematic integration."

"So you're not a machine?"

"Organic or mechanical, we're all machines. But to answer your question, my people are mostly organic."

"What else did you do to me?"

"Your tissues were saturated with poison. I tried to flush it from your system, but your brain is dependent on it. Thus, I grafted a gland to your pancreas to supplement your system."

With new eyes and the amber narcotic in my blood, I now knew why my mind was so clear.

"What's next for us? Why have we been taken captive?" I realized there was a much greater issue. "Why have you invaded Earth?"

"I know nothing about this place you call 'Earth,' or the invasion you describe. Yet, the name is somehow familiar." The alien rubbed one of its quivering polyps with a long finger. "I consider myself a well-traveled man, acquainted with many civilizations, and, still, I've never seen beings quite like you. Moreover, I've never heard of a species not born with biolinguistic lobes." The alien extended his long finger upward. "I must reference the compendium." He stood at the control podium, and after a few minutes formed an expression like shock. "The Oryxes didn't tell me who you were. You'll have to talk to them. I'll let them know you're awake."

The alien manipulated the control podium and Allienora, Morion, and Orsteen all fell from their bondage. The alien walked briskly toward the electric-yellow wall. It generated an opening that immediately sealed shut once he passed through.

We stretched our weary limbs and rolled our heads, attempting to regain our flexibility. In all, the machine that had sustained us during our sleep prevented any serious atrophy.

I found everyone's clothes on a nearby table.

Allienora stood in a timid pose, shielding her nakedness to the best of her ability. She looked at me and smiled. "It's good to see the color of your real eyes, Theron. Hazel always suited you."

"It's good to see you with them."

From behind her, Morion ogled her pleasing form. *The things I'd do to you. The positions I'd have you in.*

Allienora glared at Morion in revolt. "Your thoughts are easily heard with our new biolinguistic lobes. I assume this is the case for all weak-minded souls."

"So, our thoughts have become one." Morion smiled wide. "What a turn of events. In light of our new psychic connection, I'll explore your thoughts and discover your true feelings for me. They're likely pent deep within you, my lovely Allienora." Morion modeled his nude figure, arms akimbo, chest heaving, belly drawn in, and face twisted in a perverted grin. "Look at me! And reveal your emotions!"

I laughed at Morion's absurd pose and his look of stupid concentration as he tried to read Allienora's mind. "I think you're going crazy, Morion."

"I'm a dreamer, Mr. Mobius!"

"Whatever you are, it's good to know you're capable of bringing humor to any situation. Every company of travelers should have a clown on hand. It's good for the spirit."

Morion released his breath and let his stomach fall forward. He grabbed his clothes from me, and then turned away with slumped shoulders.

The armored aliens—or Oryxes, as we now knew them—would arrive shortly. I put on my clothes and went to the table of surgical tools. I selected some kind of scalpel. When I pushed a button on it, the blade glowed red as if the molecules became energized.

"This should do the trick," I said, sliding the tool under the tight fabric of my sleeve. "They better keep their snouts away from me."

I grabbed at my heart as I felt a strange emptiness. I realized my wife's necklace was missing. Thankfully, I found it among the surgical tools. I held it tightly in my hand, hesitating to put it on. I looked to Allienora who currently argued with Morion.

My feelings for her are growing, I thought. *Am I being unfaithful to Cassandra?*

Orsteen apparently noticed my preoccupation. "You must move on with your life, Theron. Would Cassandra want you to mourn forever?" Orsteen tilted his head toward Allienora. "Be happy in the moment. There's enough room in your heart."

I admired her for a moment and then tucked the necklace into my pocket.

As Orsteen nodded in approval, the walls of the room drained of their electric-yellow light, quivered momentarily, and then vanished. We now stood in a large room, surrounded by many thick marble columns that seemed more decorative than functional.

I walked out on an attached balcony, which afforded a panoramic view of the ocean. In the distance, I saw the cliffs of the peninsula we had stayed on two hundred days ago. I corrected my perceptions.

It was only yesterday.

From an arched doorway came the two Oryxes. Instead of their armor, they wore smocks of a delicate white cloth. At first, I thought they were in a calm mood, with snouts long and relaxed. But as they neared, something in their round emerald eyes conveyed intense emotion.

"You've been quite frustrating," said one of the Oryxes. "The proverbial bug in our bed!"

"The same could be said of you," I replied.

I contemplated the moment. *They stand without their armor. I'll move fast. Pull the surgical tool from my sleeve and get my revenge for the Brahman Station.*

"Your trap in the cave was wickedly ingenious," continued the Oryx. "Poor Bergus never saw those stalagmites coming." He let out a sad snort, like a sob. "Before we entered, I advised him to engage his head armor, but Bergus was a stubborn fellow."

The other Oryx gave his snout a passionate tug. "Our friend wasn't deserving of such a meaningless end! Your ignorance killed him!"

I threw up a hand in protest. "You accuse us of ignorance! Who are you to judge? Your attack on Earth is why we're here. We merely tried to stop you."

"Your efforts were too ambitious. Your companions didn't succeed at destroying our vessel with their weapon. We were able to contain the spatial disturbance when it was detonated. Your friends, unfortunately, didn't survive, and like poor Bergus, they too died a needless death. You must now understand that we're not the hostile force you believe us to be. We're not planning to harm you or anyone on Earth."

"Ha!" I scoffed. "Over five hundred crew members and guests aboard the Brahman Station died from your act of sabotage! You may inform their families of your pacifism!"

The two Oryxes began snorting and grunting in an awkward laugh. "You're mistaken. Your friends weren't killed when the Brahman Station fell into Jupiter. And, the Brahman Station wasn't destroyed."

Is it true? I thought. *Are they still alive?*

I grit my teeth. "We saw your replica of the Brahman Station. You can't fool us twice."

"You're right, it *was* a replica. The real Brahman Station and its passengers are... somewhere else, safe. This, I promise you." The two Oryxes engaged their armor, which appeared from nowhere. They held out their hands. "Come, it's time to show you how the universe has come to be."

I hesitated. "Where do you plan to take us?"

"Back to our vessel near Earth," said the Oryx.

I looked to the others, who appeared no less confused. I then reluctantly accepted the Oryx's hand. The rest of the company gathered around.

Everyone shifted through space.

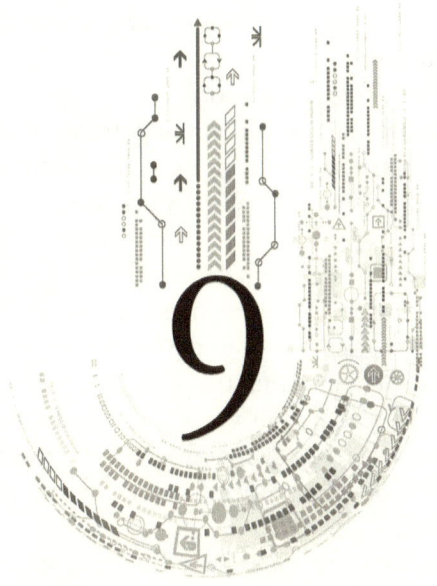

9

DECA-HELIX

I was baffled by our new surroundings. We stood in a comfortable living room no different from one found in a human home. It was furnished with oversized couches, wooden tables, and gaudy lamps that lit the room in a pale light. Paintings of alien landscapes hung from the walls and statues of unusual animals were positioned randomly about.

"This is the alien vessel near Earth?" I asked.

"Yes," responded one of the Oryxes. "This is the sphere ship just outside your solar system. We're in the Impresario's personal residence within Central City."

"Central City?"

"A city at the center of the sphere, where all the forest channels intersect."

"And who's this Impresario?"

"The Impresario is the administrator of this sphere. You'll find your answers with him. If you'd excuse us, we have other things to do." Without pause, the two Oryxes vanished.

While we waited for the Impresario, we snooped around the room. I approached a set of tall shelves crowded with leather-bound books and oddments, noticeably ancient. Among the shelves sat a cage, perhaps for a bird. From it, a faint voice emanated: "Bring an end to my dismal existence. Show me mercy. Smother me in a clenched fist, or cast me into space for the journey into cold eternity."

I approached the cage for a better look and found a pathetic creature, no more than a foot tall. With feeble fingers, it gripped the bars of its cage, pushing and pulling its body back and forth, struggling with its confines. It gazed up with weary eyes. "You! Large fellow! I beg you—bring me relief."

"Are you held against your will?" I asked. "I'd be glad to free you from this cage."

It heaved a profound sigh. "This measly, wretched, constricted, corporeal state is my cage. This body is my burden. My mind desires freedom. It seeks a higher plane."

Perplexed by the miniature character, I could only stare in curiosity as it opened the door of its cage and hopped to a nearby shelf, where it sat on edge, with elbows on knees and head slumped into palms.

As we marveled at the sad creature, we noticed an intense light spilling from around a corner. We turned the corner and found a giant archway that led to a brightly lit room. A group of aliens sat at a table—all unique in physiology. They were obviously in conversation, but we couldn't hear them talking. One of the aliens with a fantastic horse-head looked at us for a moment and then returned to the conversation. I suddenly became disoriented as I looked out the large window of the other room. I saw a beautiful city of glass buildings. Alien air-cars flew by. In the distance, a bloated orange sun sat on a horizon. The archway must have been a dimensional gateway, but one that allowed you to see the other side. Just a step away was an alien planet. I grabbed a book from a nearby shelf and tossed it through the gateway. It landed on the other side and the entire table of aliens looked at me with something like annoyance. They went back to talking and I started to step across the threshold of the archway.

"Stop! I wouldn't do that!"

I turned and found the little creature from the cage.

"You don't have any shielding and you're a double-helix species. You'd require a lot of genetic repair if you step through that gateway. Only deca-helix species with self-repairing genetic strands can tolerate the amount of radiation on that planet."

"Why can't we hear them?" asked Allienora.

The little creature looked at Alleinora as if she were joking. "Sound can't travel across a dimensional threshold."

"How far away is that planet?" I asked.

"Please no more questions," said the little creature. "I don't have time to babysit the four of you. I was just about to kill myself, and need to get back to it."

A moment later, the alien with the fantastic horse-head walked through the dimensional archway. He spoke in a deep voice. "Greetings, travelers! Sorry to make you wait, but I had an important meeting with some other Impresarios. Big events are upon us."

We stood there in awe of him. He had an exquisitely shaped skull, two great hollows for cheeks, and a large jutting jaw. Blue velvet garments draped from his body. His lofty stature and upturned chin gave him a regal appearance.

"I see you've met Stimple. I hope he didn't bring you down. He's been a bit sad lately. Once every thousand years, he suffers a fit of depression. It'll pass in a year, maybe two."

"You're the Impresario?" I inquired, staring in wonder at the alien's fantastic horse-head.

"I am. You may call me Fandoral." Fandoral inspected each in the company, rubbing his massive chin.

His gaze was oddly joyful. I wondered if there were cages somewhere for us. Was Fandoral planning to add us to his collection of curiosities and miniature men?

"It's a favor of fortune that the four of you have arrived here, and now." Fandoral applied his attention first to Orsteen. "Ah... Orsteen Hunn of the Mercury Miners—unrefined, hard-working, and loyal." He stepped to Allienora, examining her soft features. "Allienora Chang, Prime Minister of Earth and the last of royalty— elegant, beautiful, and mysterious. Morion Morpheme, Prime Elitist of Mars—a connoisseur of fine living, verging into gluttony, vainglory, and excess. And, finally, Theron Mobius—"

"Enough!" I protested. "What's this all about? What do you want from Earth?"

"This will take some time. Come, have a seat." Fandoral gestured to a low table surrounded by couches of a heavy, green fabric. We sat in awkward silence.

Fandoral remained standing. He cleared his throat and adjusted his blue velvet garments. "The things you've seen in the Guardian Sphere are not what you think. My people, this place, and the Obelisks we've sent to Earth, are not related to the Fume and his presence around Earth."

"Bullshit," I said.

"It's true," replied Fandoral.

"What of the sabotage of the Brahman Station?"

"Also the Fume. It was his human minion who planted the devices on the Brahman Station, not us."

"The Oryxes assured me the crew and passengers of the Brahman Station are unharmed. Does this mean you saved them from the Fume's sabotage?"

Fandoral smiled. "No. In a sense... they weren't saved."

"Then what happened to them!" I yelled. "You and the Oryxes speak in circles!"

Despite my outburst, Fandoral's smirk remained. He raised and whirled a thick-jointed finger, and a node rose out of the table in front of us. It projected a holographic image of perfect clarity.

I jumped to my feet when I saw Atticus. He was alive. His face was drawn and withered, but he was alive.

The hologram became animated and Atticus spoke: "It's been hard times, to say the least, since the sabotage of the Brahman Station two years ago."

I looked to Allienora and the others, confused by the stated interval of time.

The image of Atticus continued: "I've decided to create this log to document our experiences. Hopefully, it'll someday be found and our times here won't be forgotten. When we first arrived here through the dimensional fissure, the Brahman Station was greatly damaged. We had suffered over a hundred casualties. Currently, we're adrift, a thousand light years beyond the rim of a galaxy on the other end of the universe. Earth is so far away. The crew has become restless. I don't know if we'll survive this. People are losing their minds.

"Sensimion and I have come to believe that the devices planted by the Fume's human minion were intended to destroy the Brahman Station. But, by some miracle, we were instead sent through an unstable dimensional fissure, and our lives were spared.

"We spent months analyzing galactic orientations, attempting to figure out our new location in the universe. We soon realized that the Doppler shifts of the galaxies were off. At last, it became obvious why we were having trouble deciphering our location. We had traveled back in time at least twenty-one million years and the galaxies here have yet to orient themselves as we know them." Atticus looked up in reflection. "If my boy, Theron, were here, I know he'd be excited by the discovery of time travel. I wish he were here. He'd probably have some brilliant idea to get us home." Atticus began to cry and the image dispersed.

"Holy Shit!" I said, realizing what I just heard. "Time travel?"

I stared inward, trying to hypothesize the mechanism, the equation, or the force that would make such a fanciful notion possible. "And your people found the Brahman Station, twenty-one million years adrift?"

"No. The Brahman Station's crew and passengers didn't die on the cold edges of some distant galaxy." Fandoral pointed a large finger upward. "They rose up from hardship and saved themselves, ever since thriving. *We* are the descendents of the Brahman crew and passengers."

"Everyone?" I said in astonishment. "The Oryxes, the bio-mechanical beings with backward-bending knees, the many aliens gathered around the replica of the Brahman Station?"

"Yes, all of them," said Fandoral. "We're the product of twenty-one million years of human evolution, beginning from the four hundred and one survivors of the Brahman Station. To relieve your earlier confusion, the replica of the Brahman Station was a commemoration of our beginnings. There are now over a million worlds throughout the universe inhabited by the descendents of the Brahman Station's survivors."

"And why only *now* have you returned?" asked Allienora.

"When you tamper with the universe, as time travel does, she becomes a volatile thing. You see, the totality of my existence and the existence of the rest of the people descended from the Brahman Station's survivors has been teetering for twenty-one million years on the edge of oblivion. Our fate has rested on the unaltered reoccurrence of a single event caused, unknowingly, by the Fume. Simply put, if we had interfered with the sabotage of the Brahman Station, we would've ceased to exist."

"This is all too unbelievable," I said.

"Unbelievable, but true," said Fandoral. "It was your companion Sensimion that laid the foundation for preventing paradox. His foresight and ingenuity has kept us all safe. I'll allow his words to convince you further." Fandoral again whirled his thick-jointed finger, activating another hologram.

An image of an old man appeared. His gray beard was so dense that it seemed capable of smothering his every breath.

"My name is Sensimion," he said with surprising energy. His eyes were no longer hyper-blue synthetic spheres—they were now forest-green and real. "One thousand-nine hundred and twenty years have passed since the Brahman Station was sent back in time twenty-one million years. I've lived so very long. All the original survivors of the Brahman Station are long since dead. I don't know why I've lived so long. I sometimes wonder if my treatments in the sanitarium caused this unnatural longevity." He paused, looking out a window. "After the Brahman Station was sent back in time, we spent years repairing the dimensional gateway. We were eventually able to travel to a planet we named Brahman. At first, the atmosphere proved mildly noxious, but the second generation—those born on Brahman—were genetically engineered to tolerate the atmosphere. Since then, our civilization, a population of now thirty million, has ascended to a technological era comparable to where Earth was." Sensimion laughed. "Or will be.

"The present is a peaceful time, but it's the future I fear. Our population grows restless, longing to explore the universe by means of the dimensional gateway technology, which has lain dormant, since the construction of a new society has taken precedence. This inherent need for man to explore and spread to new frontiers has motivated me to create an army of protectors—guardians who will protect the Brahman descendents against obliteration. For if during the next twenty-one million years, there's contact with primal Earth or the Fume, we may hypothetically cause a paradox. The repercussions of such an event can hardly be fathomed, for the science of time travel is still a mystery.

"We've discovered that the Fume isn't unique to Earth. We've developed long-range dimensional telescopes to detect the Fume, and have thus far identified his telltale dimension and exotic energy around a thousand alien worlds. Fortunately, the Fume seems confined to a small corner of the universe—a conglomerate of seven galaxies. Avoiding this area of the universe must become dogma.

"If we're capable of abiding by these laws for the next twenty-one million years, we may avoid paradox. But who can tell what such a vast quantity of time may bring?

"As the dimensional gateway technology is used to search for new worlds, it'll be the duty of the Guardians to police its use. In addition to preventing paradox, the Guardian Army will be in charge of monitoring the Fume using unobtrusive methods. We must learn of this entity, and understand its function in the universe and its threat to humankind."

Sensimion approached a workbench, where laid a sophisticated device shaped like a giant turtle's shell. He placed his hand fondly upon it. "This miniaturized dimensional transporter will give the Guardians free range to roam the universe. Once it's attached to an individual's back and interlinked with the brain, it can be shifted into an alternate dimension, thus leaving it invisible and weightless. Without the constraint or conspicuousness of a ship, the Guardians may travel across the universe and arrive at any location in complete secrecy."

The distant voice of a young girl interrupted Sensimion's report: "Father, I'm finished with my listening exercises. I can't take it anymore. The volunteers were thinking awful things about me. They think I'm ugly."

From behind Sensimion a girl approached. Her appearance couldn't be regarded as mere ugliness. Rather, she suffered some kind of hyper-cephalic condition, in which her head had grown uninhibited into a gnarled and unshapely mass, no less than twice the size of a normal human head. Sensimion wrapped an endearing arm around her.

"Say hello to the people of the future. They wish to meet you. People of the future... this is Nara-Narayana."

The girl pushed close to the recording sensor, and presented a great pink eye that, from the influence of her overgrown skull, bulged wildly from its socket. "I hope you've become better people in the future, with proper and healthy thoughts." She paused thoughtfully. "I'll be watching you." She proceeded to laugh with girlish glee.

"That's enough, Nara. You must get back to your listening exercises. The volunteers have sacrificed a great deal to help you reach your potential."

"Their thoughts are unmanageable," said Nara. "Strange and horrible things rise into their minds. It curdles my blood."

"You must learn to tolerate all manner of thought, good or bad. Evil thoughts will always plague the minds of men and women, no matter how pure the soul. Judge a person by their actions, not thoughts. Now, run along. We'll study more about moral psychology after you finish your listening exercises."

She went on her way and Sensimion continued his report. "Nara-Narayana is something special. She'll someday lead the Guardians. She'll live a life of near immortality, in a hidden realm, where she'll look over the Brahman descendants. And, if all goes according to plan, she'll protect them for the next twenty-one million years until the threat of paradox has passed. The complexity of her mind and genome is beyond that of any human. When I conceived of her, it was a moment of divine inspiration, nothing less.

"But enough about Nara; I cannot divulge the details of her abilities, or where she'll reside for the next twenty-one million years. This knowledge must remain secret, so to protect her from outside influences that may someday wish to corrupt her. I'll provide future updates when necessary. Goodbye."

The hologram ended, evaporating into air.

"And as the story goes," said Fandoral passionately, "twenty-one million years passed—without paradox, but not without difficulty. And, at last, the Brahman Station's descendents have returned home."

"Amazing," said Allienora. "And now that you've returned? What next?"

Fandoral breathed deeply. "We're going to stop the Fume's manipulation of humankind."

"Tell us about the Fume," I said. "What is it? Where is it from?"

"We exist in a multiverse," said Fandoral, holding up a hand, as if gesturing to the heavens. "There are countless universes unseen and unaffected by each other. Long ago, the Fume arrived from another universe. His consciousness spread around Earth, and he began changing and shaping the Earth as he saw fit. With time and the seemingly infinite patience of the Fume, humankind evolved. But man's biological evolution wasn't the only thing influenced by the Fume, for he also began manipulating man's social evolution."

"Hold on!" said Allienora. "Are you saying the Fume is the creator of humankind? A god of sorts?"

Fandoral smiled widely. "The Fume is indeed the creator of humankind—however, he's not a god. The Fume doesn't stand the test of any orthodox definition of a god. His powers are quasi-omnipotent. His manipulations, while they've generally advanced the human condition, have also caused many terrible repercussions."

"And what of these manipulations?" I asked.

"As I said, the Fume began manipulating humankind's social evolution. To do this, he took on human form, producing some of the most influential characters in human history. Through these various manifestations, he inspired wars, religions, prejudice, human arrogance, and so on and so forth, complicating the world in an effort to control humankind's progression into the future."

I knew these historical icons well. They haunted my memories. *How did these memories become rooted in my mind? Do I possess some supernatural clairvoyance? Am I somehow in tune with the Fume? What was done to me in the sanitarium?*

Fandoral halted. "Theron, you seem more disturbed by these revelations than your companions. Are you all right?"

"It's nothing," I said. "What does the Fume want from us?"

"Even after twenty-one million years, his final goal is still a mystery. Earth hasn't been his only focus—there have been over a thousand planets in the seven galaxies that he has manipulated. We've witnessed the rise and fall of many non-human species, which he has created and controlled. He'll take them to great heights, both technologically and socially, and then, in more cases than not, he'll eradicate them, as if they had failed some standard he was trying to achieve." Fandoral smashed a fist into palm. "The simple fact is that humankind and other civilizations under the Fume's control are ultimately deprived of their autonomy, with no freedom to grow and evolve naturally. In the end, all seem to face extinction by a disgruntled maker. This won't be the fate of Earth!"

Orsteen chewed on his tongue. "The significance of this is almost too great to swallow."

"If he even speaks the truth," said Morion.

"I've given you the facts," said Fandoral. "It's an extraordinary occasion to learn of your divine maker, only to look up and find your limbs are attached to strings, wielded by that maker, who's just a puppet master jerking and pulling with a malevolent grin. But, do not fear. We've come to drive the Fume out of our universe. All who suffer under his control will be freed, and their autonomy regained."

I sat forward. "And you have the means to accomplish this?"

"Why do you think we sent the Obelisks to Earth? We haven't endured twenty-one million years to bring Earth a collection of monuments. And, like Earth, we've also brought Obelisks to each of the one thousand and twenty non-human planets shrouded in the Fume's outpocketings. Currently, the Obelisks hold Earth in temporal stasis until all the Obelisks, throughout the seven galaxies of the Fume, are in equilibrium. Once this occurs, the Obelisks will create a dimensional barrier between our universe and the Fume's."

Fandoral extracted a metal bottle from a decrepit case on the table. He pressed a button on the bottle and the top opened, releasing a hiss of pressure. He poured its black, ethereal contents into six bulbs. "This is a monumental time—when you, the ancestor, and I, the descendent, stand side by side." Fandoral distributed the bulbs to each in the group.

Stimple, who had mounted the tabletop by means of a small ladder, claimed a tiny remaining bulb.

Fandoral swirled the contents of his bulb under his nose. "I rescued this bottle from the ruins of a planet whose inhabitants—descendents of yours and some distant cousins of mine—were a hundred millennia extinct. I now propose a toast." Fandoral raised his bulb high. "To the expulsion of the Fume from our universe. His meddling has gone on too long—"

Before the toast was completed, Morion took a premature drink from his bulb. Unable to cope with the volatile liquid, he convulsed, sending the contents of his mouth across the table and onto the little creature, Stimple, who looked down sadly at his wet clothes.

"The drink is detestable!" proclaimed Morion, lips puckering.

I stopped the bulb short at my lips. "Or our sense of taste has yet to evolve to appreciate the drink's complexity."

Fandoral grumbled in amusement. "Be bold, Theron Mobius, and have a drink."

I took a small drink from the bulb. Like Morion, I found it disgusting. Regardless, I forced the thin liquid down my throat with a resisting gulp. "It's very sour. Maybe it's gone bad."

Fandoral laughed. "It hasn't gone bad. This is a unique drink. Its subtleties can only be enjoyed after suffering the first repulsive gulp, in that it changes your tongue in preparation for the next." Fandoral took a second drink from his bulb, and then licked his lips clean.

I took another taste, and was surprised by the spectrum of flavors that coated my tongue. "Interesting, Fandoral. Once the tongue becomes altered, the drink takes on a whole new personality. You're then able to taste flavors previously undetectable—almond, persimmon, and essence of ocean."

"I'm glad you like it, Mr. Mobius." Fandoral replenished the contents of Stimple's tiny bulb.

Everyone finished their drinks and Fandoral rose to his feet. "Come, there's time before the Obelisks are aligned. I'll entertain you with a fine meal of our local cuisine."

"Splendid," I said. "I still have many questions."

"Very good, Mr. Mobius. This way. It's only a brisk walk down the Corridor of Guardians." Fandoral lifted Stimple onto his shoulder and proceeded through the doorway.

We followed Fandoral down a corridor of tall glass walls, behind which were entombed armored figures standing at attention. There were thousands, arranged into rows stacked upon rows. On their backs hung the bulky transporter carapaces usually concealed in an unseen dimension.

"What is this place?" I asked.

"This," said Fandoral, "is a repository of Guardians. They stand dormant in temporal stasis until their services are required. As you learned from Sensimion, the Guardian Army has been the key to preventing paradox for the last twenty-one million years. They've been recruited over the eons from numerous worlds in the Brahman Sprawl. They've given up their lives and pledged themselves to preventing paradox."

"Are so many needed?" asked Orsteen.

"What you see here is only a fraction of a fraction." Fandoral nodded gravely. "You'd be surprised at how many have plotted to destroy our existence, attempting to make contact with the Fume or visit Earth—maniacs, iconoclasts, anarchists, religious zealots on a quest to find their creator. Every sort throughout the ages has attempted. All that's needed is an unauthorized dimensional gateway and a celestial map leading to the seven galaxies of the Fume."

"It's an awesome achievement," I said, "that with all the worlds that have sprouted from the Brahman Station's survivors, none have become known to the Fume."

"Indeed," said Fandoral proudly. "And now that paradox is no longer a concern, these fine protectors will be allowed to retire."

We left the Corridor of Guardians and came to a balcony that overlooked Central City. It was like no city I'd ever seen. Enormous spherical structures floated in fixed positions—apparently the buildings of the city. Some were clumped together and connected by great walkways. Dimensional archways were prevalent on nearly every balcony of every floating structure, allowing anyone to be transported to their desired destination. I looked to the far surroundings of the floating cityscape and saw, in all directions, the mouths of the various forest channels. At the center of each opening was a glowing sphere like an artificial sun. The Oryx had said earlier that Central City was at the center of the Guardian Sphere, where all the forest channels intersected. It was a beautiful feat of engineering. It was the future of humankind. A testament to our greatness.

I thought Fandoral was guiding us to a dimensional archway, but he took us to a small air-car.

"There's no dimensional archway where we're headed," said Fandoral.

The air-car took us away from Central City, into the mouth of one of the forest channels. We flew over the pink plumed canopy until we saw the most fanciful restaurant. It was no more than a giant platform hovering in air. People sat at tables on its large, round surface, eating and drinking in a merry fashion.

Fandoral rubbed his hands together in anticipation. "This is one of the finer establishments in the area. I urge you to sample their steamed snout beetles stuffed with sweet jelly."

We docked the air-car at the side of the restaurant and got out. After seating ourselves, a fat fellow, with magenta-toned skin and bulging eyes, attended our needs. "The drink of the hour is Gray Nectar Liqueur. May I bring you a pitcher?"

Fandoral nodded eagerly. "Additionally, bring three platters of your finest local delicacies."

"With pleasure." The waiter moved swiftly considering his plumpness, and promptly returned with both drinks and platters.

All in the company proceeded to eat and drink with enthusiasm.

My gaze wandered through the crowd, finally fixing upon a group of girls on a nearby dance floor. They moved in an intricate dance of high kicks and handclapping. "It's amazing these are human descendents. Though they look different, they carry themselves like any other human of Earth."

Morion made a perverted grin. "And their exotic forms aren't at all unappealing. I believe I'm developing a fondness for our newfound descendents. Tell me, Fandoral, would it be inappropriate to mingle with these other races in a less than innocent fashion?"

"By all means, mingle to your heart's content. There are many races here from throughout the Brahman Sprawl celebrating this great time. But, be careful what you say. A few misplaced words may arouse insult—or more severely, may bind you to some verbal contract in which you may find yourself married."

"I'll heed your advice." Morion rose from the table and looked down at his clothes. "This environmental suit is unfit for the celebration. I'm embarrassed to be mingling in such rags. Mr. Orsteen, I require your presence on the dance floor. Your great stature may take notice away from my dreadful outfit."

"If you insist," replied Orsteen. "Let me first refill my mug." Orsteen signaled the waiter, who rushed a fresh pitcher of Gray Nectar Liqueur to the table. Orsteen grabbed the entire pitcher and followed Morion to the dance floor.

The rest of us continued to eat and drink. I munched on a biscuit slathered in a rich pâté of meat, or insect, or possibly some kind of fleshy vegetable. I was uncertain. I laughed as I watched Stimple walk across the table and refill his tiny mug by dipping it into my larger mug.

I proceeded to drink heavily, attempting to calm the commotion of so many revelations occupying my head—time travel, multiple universes, and alien creators.

I finally felt more relaxed. "Fandoral, you said the Obelisks will be aligned soon?"

"Correct," replied Fandoral, popping a steamed snout beetle in his mouth. "I'd approximate within the hour."

"Then this is the climax of twenty-one million years of preparation. I'm impressed, even worried, at how calm you are. Are you so confident in your plans? Additionally, aren't you concerned the Fume will retaliate?"

Fandoral wiped his large mouth. "I'm calm for two reasons. First, the Obelisks have been effective at keeping the Fume trapped in temporal stasis. Second, he has no way to retaliate, since he cannot manifest himself beyond Earth. His powers in our universe are limited only to the planets where he's formed an outpocketing of his consciousness. At this distance, we're beyond his reach. As well, every planet shrouded in the Fume's outpocketings—that's over a thousand in the seven galaxies—is being held in temporal stasis. Once the Obelisks are aligned, the dimensional barrier between our two universes will be created, and our lives will proceed without the Fume."

I couldn't help but think Fandoral was overconfident. I took a drink, and suddenly heard the sound of water trickling nearby. I looked down and found Stimple pissing off the side of the table, whistling a happy tune and swaying uncontrollably from side to side.

Fandoral apologized for Stimple's behavior and then reached across the table and poked him. "It's good to see your spirits higher, my little companion. However, there are bathrooms by the kitchen for you to relieve yourself." Fandoral helped the tiny drunkard to the floor and nudged him on his way.

I returned to our conversation. "You described the Fume's presence around Earth as an outpocketing of his consciousness. This confuses me, Fandoral. What kind of entity are we dealing with?"

"Indeed," said Allienora. "I'm also curious."

"Forgive me," said Fandoral. "I've neglected to explain the fundamental nature of the Fume. Firstly, the universe that the Fume's native to is nothing like ours. It's a universe filled entirely with the Fume's consciousness—a single conscious universe. If you visited it, it would be like traveling through the neural pathways of a brain, the structure of which is a complex web of exotic energy that extends to infinity. Even the dimensional symmetry of the universe is different. The fabric of his universe has twenty-seven dimensions, not eighteen—and they are weaved in a pattern nothing like ours. We couldn't even occupy the space of his universe, our matter would be unstable, it would dissociate at a quantum level. Only the exotic energy of his consciousness can exist."

"There are no stars or galaxies?" asked Allienora. "No matter of any kind within his universe?"

"Precisely so," said Fandoral. "There's only his matrix of consciousness."

I took a large gulp of Gray Nectar Liqueur. "So, the exotic energy that occupies the unnatural dimension around Earth is only a fraction of the Fume's being?"

"Exactly," said Fandoral. "His consciousness is as vast as his universe."

"Remarkable," I uttered. "Then the Fume truly is a being of great power."

Allienora shook her head. "Earlier, Fandoral, you said he wasn't a god. Yet a being that encompasses an entire universe seems godly to me."

"Not at all," said Fandoral. "He may be all-powerful in his universe, but he's the god of no one. There are no mortal beings under his command. No one worships him. There's nothing but himself."

Allienora took a contemplative sip of her beverage. "It would seem a deprived and lonely existence, having only yourself in an entire universe. Sad, wouldn't you say?"

"Possibly," responded Fandoral, "but we shouldn't be concerned with the Fume's introverted existence. Besides, he's kept himself entertained by playing god in our universe."

I reflected on my memories of the Fume's past manifestations. "As far as the Fume's social manipulations on Earth, do you have any detailed records of his actions?"

"With our advanced methods, we were able to maintain a complete record of humankind's history, including the Fume's manifestations."

"I'd be eager to have a look at these records," I said, "so to better understand the Fume's motives."

Fandoral laughed so hard he coughed. "You, Mr. Mobius, wouldn't be the first man to give his attention to this subject. There have been more theories than stars in the sky. But..." Fandoral gave a noncommittal shrug. "...I see no harm in letting you look. I'll send you the surveillance archives when you've settled into quarters."

I nodded graciously and emptied my mug at a gulp. I sat at ease, absorbing the colorful landscape that spread beneath and around the floating restaurant. In the distance, I could see the floating structures of Central City. In that moment I felt privileged.

What wonders I've seen in this life. I looked away from Central City and then to Allienora. *Some wonders more beautiful than others.*

A loud electronic voice echoed from all directions. I couldn't understand the alien language.

"It's time," said Fandoral. His eyes glowed.

I leaned close to him and noticed a film over his eyes, apparently displaying a large amount of numerical data to him.

"The Obelisks are aligned?" I asked.

"They are. Everything looks good."

Above the restaurant, a large hologram of Earth appeared. Its atmosphere was unmoving as it remained in temporal stasis. The image revealed the presence of the Fume's outpocketing with the standard sapphire-blue aura.

The crowd of the restaurant roared enthusiastically. I felt more nervous than excited as the Obelisks initialized, energizing the atmosphere with a growing white light. The luminous spectacle continued for just a minute and then faded. The sapphire-blue aura of the Fume's outpocketing was now absent. Again the crowd roared. Success was apparent.

I admired the image of Earth. It spun on its axis and glowed with its normal blue-green pallor. For a moment I felt strange, almost cathartic, as though an imponderable burden had been purged from my mind. I was free. I looked to Allienora and smiled.

Suddenly, a collective gasp could be heard across the restaurant. The Fume's outpocketing returned with a growing intensity that startled everyone.

"This doesn't look good," I said.

"To say the least," replied Allienora.

I found Fandoral shaking his head and mumbling in disbelief. His eyes were great white spheres, glowing bright as data passed quickly along the ocular film.

Allienora pointed across the restaurant to the dance floor. "There! Something's appearing."

An unidentifiable mass materialized. Its substance twisted and swirled in a strange evolution to find solidity.

"It's the Fume!" I said. "He attempts to manifest himself beyond the limits of Earth."

From a pocket of his blue velvet garment, Fandoral retrieved a small eyepiece that glowed red around the edges. He placed it over his eye. "You're right. I'm detecting his exotic energy. Wait... it's gone."

What remained was a large black cinder of flesh. A hot, rancid steam emanated from its charred surface.

Fandoral lowered his eyepiece. "You were correct, Mr. Mobius. But the Fume's attempt has obviously failed. I'm not detecting his exotic energy anymore."

I approached the smoldering mound of flesh. Its odor was extremely pungent. I avoided breathing through my nose. Allienora joined me to examine the fleshy bulk.

"It's horrendous," said Allienora, turning away in revolt. She peered from the edge of the floating restaurant to the forest below. "There's another one down there! Do you see it, Theron?"

"And more!" I pointed throughout the forest.

Fandoral and the waiter who'd been serving us approached the charred cinder of flesh.

"What is it?" asked Fandoral.

"I don't know, but it might still be alive," I said, observing subtle pulsations at its surface. I retrieved the surgical tool still concealed under my sleeve. The blade became energized and I stabbed the burnt flesh. It reacted, contorting away from my assault. "Whatever it is, we should destroy it. Do you have a weapon, Fandoral?"

"No, but I'll call a Guardian for assistance." Fandoral fled the scene.

The waiter stood close to the pulsating mass of flesh, prodding it with a long finger.

"I wouldn't stand so closely," I said.

The fat waiter ignored my advice and continued to poke at the horrible thing. "The surface here rises like an enormous blister. I think something's moving inside."

As the waiter moved closer to inspect, the swollen membrane ruptured, discharging a cloudy fluid. From within, a great set of jaws sprang forth, tearing the head of the waiter clean off his neck. Immediately the jaws retracted, disappearing into the mass of charred flesh, along with the waiter's head.

I grabbed Allienora and pulled her away from the creature.

From the depths of the forest channel echoed a frightening roar, unlike any of the native wildlife. I looked up in terror as a wave of large winged beasts, like black reptiles, swooped down on the restaurant, snatching up people and devouring them in midair.

Panic overtook the restaurant. Everyone rushed for their air-cars to escape.

"Watch for flying beasts, Allienora. I'll keep an eye on the charred mass."

Suddenly, its outer casing split open to reveal the powerful winged creature within. It uncurled from a fetal position. Thick mucus dripped from it. It spread its fleshy wings to full extension—their span was impressive and threatening. I noticed a large bulge residing at the neck of the beast, evidently the waiter's head embarking on its journey to digestion. When I saw the things black skin, I knew it was the Fume's creation. A network of silver nano-fibers were embedded in the surface of its skin— the pattern and color was just like the sphincter beast from the sanitarium. It was a terrible reminder of the past.

The beast cawed and lunged at me, snapping its jaws. With the surgical tool in hand, I spun around the beast, fell to a knee, and stabbed at the base of its sinewy back. The beast reacted angrily and turned to me with a toothy snarl. As its jaws bore down on me, an explosion of flesh left the head of the beast a gruesome wad. It instantly fell dead.

"Holy shit!" I screamed.

I looked up and found Allienora with some kind of energy gun in her hands.

"A woman's job is never done." She winked and then helped me up.

"Thanks," I said, trembling from my near death experience. "Where did you get that?"

"A new friend," she said, waving to an alien behind the bar. He looked like a gorilla without hair.

I didn't want to say it out loud, but she was damn sexy with that gun in her hands. "Prime Minister, adventurer, and monster killer. Are we having fun yet?"

"I've never felt so alive, Theron." She grabbed me unexpectedly and kissed me.

Her lips were soft. I hadn't tasted a woman in a long time. It took my breath away.

She pulled away from me. "Sorry, it's probably not the best time."

I was speechless. She started firing at a second wave of winged beasts that descended on the crowd.

Suddenly, a group of Guardians appeared, weapons blazing. They were excellent shots and didn't need our help to hold down the restaurant.

Allienora returned the energy gun to the gorilla-like bartender and we regrouped with Orsteen and Morion. Soon after, Fandoral returned in his air-car.

"Get on!" he called.

Stranded patrons of the restaurant closed in upon the small craft.

"We can hold a few more!" I said.

Fandoral engaged an energy bubble around the craft. "They'll be safe with the Guardians. No need to increase our load."

We sped out into the forest channel, in the opposite direction of Central City. Fandoral flew the air-car close to the top of the pink plumed canopy.

I looked down at the forest. It was infested with black beasts. "We've underestimated the Fume, Fandoral. Instead of manifesting himself within the Guardian Sphere, he sent an army of his own creation to kill us."

"It's definitely a problem," said Fandoral. "There are a lot of them out there."

"At least we know they can be killed," said Allienora.

"The Guardians are highly trained," said Fandoral. "They'll eradicate these monsters in no time."

"What then?" I asked. "How will you proceed against the Fume?"

"I don't know." Fandoral hesitated. "I must consult with Nara-Narayana."

"Nara-Narayana!" I said in surprise. "Are you saying that Nara-Narayana, the child from Sensimion's log, is still alive?"

"Indeed. She's still the leader of the Guardian Army."

Allienora's eyes widened. "The things one could learn from such a person. What wisdom has she gained from twenty-one million years of existence?"

Fandoral steered the air-car into an intersecting forest channel. We came upon a populated area resembling a medium-sized city of Earth. The black beasts could be seen stalking the city streets. The inhabitants were nowhere in sight. They had obviously taken refuge in their homes.

"Where are we headed?" I asked.

"I've arranged for you to stay with a friend. His stronghold will ensure your safety."

"We're not useless," said Orsteen. "We can help in this battle."

"No need to be hasty," said Morion. "The Guardians seem quite capable. I'm delighted Fandoral would go out of his way for our safety."

"I don't question your courage," said Fandoral, "but I'm certain the Guardians will soon have everything under control. There's no need to put the four of you in harm's way."

I gazed down at the passing city, surveying the many sturdy structures, any of which would seem to fit Fandoral's description of a stronghold. Fandoral, however, didn't seem intent on landing the air-car anytime soon. He kept a straight course, flying past the city and into another forest channel. The globes that gave light to the inner world became dim, emulating a soft moonlight. The vegetation and trees were much different from the previous forest channel, as if we'd traversed an ocean and now came to a new continent of wildlife.

Fandoral took the air car down and landed in the densest part of the forest channel. Magnificently-sized trees loomed high on fantastic root structures like stilts, propping the trunks above the land.

"Why have we landed here?" asked Morion nervously. "In the middle of nowhere. Where's the stronghold?"

"You don't see it?" said Fandoral facetiously.

"Of course not," replied Morion. "All I can see are these gangling roots and the gray colors of darkness. Do you insult my perceptions?"

"Your perceptions are accurate, Morion." Fandoral disengaged the energy bubble surrounding us, hopped to the ground, and pointed to the tree with the most impressive root structure. "Your stronghold awaits."

I pushed a strained gaze through the darkness. I saw the faint flicker of light coming from the window of a wooden bungalow erected within the root structure. "And you're confident we'll be safe in this... stronghold? Not far back, I saw a trio of winged beasts. They seemed a stronger breed than the ones we encountered earlier."

Fandoral gestured to the bungalow's front door. "Knock hard. My friend Bardio is deaf in his left ear."

"You plan to leave us on a stranger's doorstep?" said Allienora.

"There's no time for introductions," said Fandoral. "I'll return when the situation's resolved." He leaped back into the air-car, which immediately rose up and away.

THE ONE VOICE

We crept up the stairs of the wooden bungalow. I knocked at the door and waited. From within, I heard footsteps and a progression of mumbles.

A large peephole slid open and a pudgy face was revealed. "If you're selling junk, sell it elsewhere. If you're looking for Bardio, he isn't here. If you're here to rob me, I've got an Intersplit gun pointed at your belly."

"Fandoral brought us here," I replied. "He said Bardio would help us."

"And which of you is Fandoral?"

"None," I answered. "Fandoral left for important matters. Do you know when Bardio will return?"

The man didn't reply. His face remained fixed in the peephole and his eyes started to close as if he were falling asleep.

"Hey!" said Morion, poking the man's fat cheek through the peephole. "Let us in. It's not safe out here."

His eyes opened wide. "You said Fandoral?"

"Yes," I said.

"Well, I *have* been a bit lonely. You can join me for dinner."

A bolt slid free and the door opened, revealing a short man with a potbelly, arms too long, and legs too short. In his hand was a carrot-like vegetable, not an Intersplit gun.

With a hobbling gait, he led us into a rustic living space illuminated by a fire blazing in a stone hearth. A ladder in the center of the room led up into the trunk of the tree, which had been hollowed for a sleeping loft.

"Sorry about my earlier hostility. We don't get many people out in the swamp, and when we do, they always have an agenda. I'm Bardio."

"It's a pleasure to meet you. I'm Theron. This is Allienora, Orsteen, and Morion."

"I hope you like swamp weasel." Bardio tended an animal carcass turning on an electric spit in the hearth. He then looked up to Orsteen. "You're a big one, aren't you? Be a good giant and fetch a cylinder of Aqua Vita from the kitchen. Tonight we'll dine in proper fashion. Luckily, my wife isn't here. She's a bossy hag who'll be out hunting swamp weasels until tomorrow."

I thought about the Fume's beasts and looked out the window. "Are you aware the Obelisks have failed against the Fume? The dimensional barrier wasn't created between the two universes."

"This is bad news," responded Bardio. "My father worked his entire life on the Obelisks, as an engineer.

He's probably very upset. Come, we'll discuss this tragedy over a delicious meal."

Bardio served his golden-brown roast with a side of sautéed roots, a salad of aromatic flowers, and a dessert of sweet dumplings.

We sat at a crowded table and ate sparingly, while filling in the gaps with Bardio's Aqua Vita—it was a refreshing but potent liquor. When the meal was over, Orsteen and Morion retired early to the sleeping loft, leaving Allienora, Bardio, and myself to share conversation over cups of hot tea.

"Have you lived in the Guardian Sphere long?" asked Allienora. "It seems unnatural, living in a place with no sky, shielded from the infinities of the universe."

"I need not look past the boundaries of my bungalow and swamp to find peace. I relish the small things life has to offer. As well, I have my thoughts to keep me occupied. And my wife, despite all her intolerable qualities, provides certain... *services* that keep me in the pink."

I took a contemplative sip of tea. "Such is the way, hopefully sooner than later, I'd like to find the conditions of my life. It would be a peaceful change, living each day with only the necessities."

"Really?" said Allienora. "I'm surprised by your desire to lead such a reclusive and simple life, Theron."

I gazed inward. "Bardio's right, though, isn't he? It *is* the small things. It's about looking across the room and seeing love for the first time. It's about that feeling you get when you help someone in need. It's about finding pride in your children." I paused, thinking about the child I could've had with Cassandra—my unborn child killed by the Fume. I would've been proud of that child. I would've loved it with all my heart.

"What's wrong, Theron?" Allienora held my hand.

"I'm fine."

Bardio uncapped a cylinder of Aqua Vita. "What of you, Allienora? Have you so far lived the life you've always dreamed of?"

"True happiness is hard to find. So far, I've lived the life laid out before me—a life of public servitude, as my father did before me."

"It's never too late for change," said Bardio.

"Change may not be necessary," I said, looking deep into Allienora's blue eyes. "Maybe we just need to be more aware of those small things, those small moments that fill our lives. We need only to recognize them as they happen."

"Moments like this one?" said Allienora.

"Just like this one," I said. "Happiness may be right in front of us."

A loud snoring interrupted our conversation and we laughed. Bardio had passed out with the cylinder of Aqua Vita dangling in his hand.

I grabbed the cylinder and added a splash to our tea. "This small moment isn't over yet, my dear."

In the morning, all in the bungalow woke up to the screams of a stout woman. She stood over our cots aiming a sophisticated weapon. "I should feed you all to the swamp. I don't take lightly to squatters. Before I throw you out on your asses, where's my worthless husband? Have you killed him? Speak fast—my Intersplit gun has a hair-trigger."

I looked around for Bardio. He was nowhere to be found. "Hold on, lady! It's not what you think. We're guests of your husband Bardio, who speaks highly of you."

"You're a liar. If my husband spoke highly of me, it would be him drudging in the swamps to feed his fat belly. It would be me sitting on the porch enjoying the subtleties of life. He cares only about satisfying the hunger of his stomach and loins, both at the cost of my toil."

Morion, apparently faking sleep to avoid the woman, stirred from his silence. "These are hungers a man shouldn't neglect. Otherwise, he may become susceptible to ill health and psychotic episodes."

The stout woman turned to Morion, fixed a hard gaze upon him, and then aimed her Intersplit gun between his eyes.

"Dolia!" exclaimed Bardio, climbing up the ladder of the loft. "What's the meaning of this? Put away your gun. Do you wish to scare our guests?"

Dolia aimed the Intersplit gun at her husband. "Bardio, you're a stupid and gullible man. Who are these trespassers?"

I slowly got out of bed. "We were brought here by Fandoral, who assured us you'd be happy to give us shelter."

"Fandoral, you say?" Dolia's eyes grew large. "This is even more reason to send you packing. It was Fandoral who sent me Bardio. And, after two hundred years, he's yet to retrieve him. I'll be sure to inform him I'm not a sanctuary for every common vagrant."

I put my hand on my heart. "Please, madam. We won't be here long."

Dolia paused, released a sigh, and then lowered her Intersplit gun. "Clearly, I've become soft in my old age. I'll allow you to stay."

"Thank you," I said.

"So... who are you, and why do you seek shelter in my swamp?"

"We're from Earth and her sibling planets," I said. "We seek shelter since the Guardian Sphere is under attack by an army of black-winged beasts controlled by the Fume."

Like Bardio, Dolia seemed indifferent to the revelation. "Well, we mustn't let such things ruin our appetites. It's coming on lunchtime, and I have many swamp weasels eager for a swim in the stew pot."

Days passed, and with no word from Fandoral, we became restless. The black-winged beasts, though unseen, weighed heavy on everyone's mind. Orsteen and I, for the majority of our time, kept a lookout on the porch. We maintained our sanity by talking with Bardio and drinking Aqua Vita at a leisurely pace.

Presently, night fell on the swamp and we ate a dinner of swamp weasel stew. Everyone sat at ease except for me. I felt unsettled and jittery and at last my patience wore thin.

"Why hasn't Fandoral contacted us?" I said. "Who knows what's going on out there? We need to find out. Bardio, how do you communicate with Fandoral?"

"He's easily contacted with this." Bardio revealed a small tile and handed it to me.

I took the device and held it close to my mouth. "Fandoral? Are you there?"

"What are you doing?" said Bardio with a smile.

"Trying to communicate with Fandoral."

"You squeeze it."

I squeezed the tile and the table we were eating at split in half. A translucent orb rose up and floated between us.

A female face appeared in the orb and spoke, "How may I help you?"

"Who are you?" I asked.

"I am the One Voice of this Guardian Sphere. I oversee all its vital core systems. How may I help you, Theron Mobius?"

"You know my name?"

"Of course. I'm a very old consciousness. My data-sphere is vast."

"We need to speak to Fandoral."

"Contact with the Impresario is currently limited to authorized personnel."

Bardio leaned forward. "I, Bardio, wish to speak to him."

"I'm sorry, Bardio. You're not authorized either."

Bardio's face suddenly transformed. He seemed more dignified, more intelligent. "I'm a class one deca-helix architect. I helped build your consciousness. I'm older than you, and your superior."

"You retired a long time ago, Bardio. I apologize for the inconvenience."

Bardio growled. "What's happening on this Guardian Sphere?"

"A state of emergency has been issued. All inhabitants are advised to remain in their homes."

"Show me Central City!" said Bardio.

"Data feeds are limited to authorized personnel," replied the One Voice of the Sphere. "Please remain calm."

Bardio stood in anger, his face blood-red. I looked to Dolia and she seemed impressed, even aroused, by Bardio's passion.

"This only amplifies my fears," I said. "We must leave this place. The time for waiting is over." I pushed my bowl of swamp weasel stew forward and stood with purpose. "Where's your craft?"

"We have no craft," said Bardio.

"How do you acquire supplies, food, clothes, tools?" said Morion.

"As I've said, we live a frugal life. We live off the land, seeking nothing extravagant." Bardio's mood strangely went from anger back to apathy. He returned to eating his swamp-weasel stew. I wondered how old he was and if he suffered from a touch of dementia.

"Then we'll hike through the forest channels to Central City," said Orsteen.

Bardio licked his bowl clean. "Such a journey would be far too difficult and take many weeks."

"And what would you know of this, Bardio!" said Dolia harshly. "The extents of your journeys are not beyond the outhouse. Your laziness is evident to all, as your ass has become flat from sitting." Dolia turned to me. "Despite my husband's uselessness, he's right. The nearest dimensional archway is a hundred kilometers away. You may be able to use our neighbor's craft, but he's a bitter old hermit who'll probably deny your request."

"Then we'll take it by force," replied Orsteen.

"You've already been over-generous, Dolia," I said. "Would it be too much to ask you to guide us there? On the way, we could assist you in hunting swamp weasels."

"It would be refreshing to have a competent man hunting by my side." Dolia squinted at Bardio, who stared back with indifference.

"When do we leave?" asked Allienora.

232

"We'll leave tomorrow." Dolia inspected Allienora from head to toe, apparently taking stock of her slim figure. "Although, it would be wise if Theron and I go alone. The swamp isn't friendly to delicate specimens like you."

"Is that so?"

"You'll only slow us down."

Allienora and Dolia's eyes met in an awkward moment and Allienora finally responded: "If it must be, then I'll wait here with Bardio, who may enlighten me with his fascinating intellect."

Dolia, ruffled by Allienora's subtle remark, wrenched Bardio from his seat and marched him to bed.

I poured a splash of Aqua Vita into Allienora's cup. "Don't let her bother you. I know your capabilities. I've seen you kill monsters before."

Allienora slugged down her drink, smiled at me, and then turned to Orsteen and Morion. "It looks like the three of us will get to sleep in. Grab another cylinder of Aqua Vita from the kitchen."

In the early morning, Dolia outfitted me with a pair of rubber waders that, despite cutting off circulation in my legs, provided a watertight seal and protection from the elements.

Dolia led me out into the cool air and pointed in the direction of the neighbor's bungalow. "It's a half-day's journey in that direction, Theron."

I sprang forward, but was stopped short by Dolia, who veered off the specified path. "We must take the long route, as the weasel swims. Although terrestrial, they spend most of their time in the depths of the swamp, hunting snails."

I suppressed my impatience and trudged close behind Dolia into waist-high water, each footstep a tug-of-war against the suction of swamp muck.

The morning progressed with a rigorous hunt for swamp weasels. Dolia instructed me in the proper technique of flushing out the critters, which simply involved running through the water with high, knee-kicking strides. During my chaotic march, Dolia fired upon the resulting frenzy of swamp weasels.

Once satisfied with our catch, we returned to solid ground, each lugging a full string of swamp weasels over our shoulders. We now took the straight course to the neighbor's home.

Dolia was a quiet woman when not in the presence of her husband. She was a breed of obvious distinction from Bardio, with a thick frame, short arms, and large breasts. Possibly a different species from Bardio altogether.

Dusk approached as we completed the final leg of our journey. Immediately upon our arrival at the neighbor's bungalow, we heard weapon-fire and smelled smoke in the air. We hid behind a bush and assessed the situation.

Dolia readied her Intersplit gun. "Do you see anyone?"

"I can see nothing with so much smoke."

A roar emanated from the fog.

Dolia aimed her gun at the sound. "That wasn't the mating call of the swamp weasel."

We again heard the blast of weapon-fire, and then the grisly wail of a man.

Dolia, taking stock of her surroundings, sampled a nose-full of air. "Prepare yourself, a wind approaches."

And as predicted, a wind blew, taking with it all the smoke surrounding the bungalow. A black-winged beast was revealed, and in its claws hung the limp body of a man.

"Poor Wimser," said Dolia, adjusting her aim. "This beast will pay."

I pushed down her weapon before she could get off a shot. "Revenge won't bring back Wimser. And your attack will only make things worse."

"I'm no bungler when it comes to putting a shot between the eyes of an animal."

"This may be true, but if you look beside the bungalow, you'll discover the reason for my apprehension."

Dolia allowed her eye to wander from her gun's targeting needle, and I pointed to two additional winged beasts inspecting a small air-car.

We returned our attention to the first winged beast, which had yet to release Wimser from its claws. It studied the form of the carcass, pinching its soft tissues with stubby digits.

Dolia hissed with outrage. "He plays with Wimser's remains like a curiosity."

"I fear what comes next."

I cringed in horror as the black beast made a meal of Wimser. It gorged first on his legs, and then on the ample meat of his belly. The beast cast the half-devoured carcass to the ground and began undulating in a wave of violent spasms.

I couldn't help a small smile. "It appears Wimser's getting his revenge, by inflicting a powerful case of indigestion on the beast."

"I don't think it's indigestion," said Dolia.

The beast underwent a disturbing transformation, its bones cracking and re-fusing. Its slumped posture straightened, its clawed digits lengthened into fingers, its long snout flattened, and, finally, its wings petrified, broke free, and fell to the ground like withered leaves.

We watched in wonder as the beast, now more humanoid, approached his companions and let out a belch of apparent communication. The two beasts showed understanding and then inspected their companion's new form. They marched to a pen holding small pig-like animals and gorged themselves. They, too, then underwent similar transformations, becoming more humanoid.

One of the beasts stumbled upon Wimser's Intersplit gun. At first, it handled it with an awkward grip, due either to unfamiliarity with such advanced weaponry or inexperience with its own newly developed fingers. After a brief examination of the weapon, it held it with a normal grip, and then fired it carelessly toward the air-car we had hoped to commandeer. The other two beasts looked at the explosion with something like amusement.

"Damn it!" I said. "The air-car's destroyed. We're not dealing with mere beasts. They have the ability to adapt, change, and think both logically and independently."

Dolia raised her Intersplit gun and displayed a brave expression. "It's time to test my mettle." Without pause, she fired her Intersplit gun so quickly and so adeptly that the three shots were perceived as a single resonating blast. Each energy blast drove home, into the skulls of each of the three beasts. We waited for them to fall. But, as it happened, the beasts went unharmed. Their silver nano-fiber ingrained skin absorbed the blasts.

With the sound of the shots betraying our position, we had no time to run. The beast with the Intersplit gun moved toward us swiftly.

I watched as the beast placed the weapon to Dolia's chest and fired. She stumbled backward, looked down at the wound between her breasts, and then up to the beast, which displayed a frightening grin of sharp teeth.

I caught her from behind and she exhaled her last words: "Theron... tell Bardio a real man would avenge my death."

I set her down and grabbed the Intersplit gun hanging loosely in her hands. I fired a shot at the beast's own gun, which shattered to pieces.

The beast discarded the remains of the weapon and prepared to beat the life from me. Then, stopping short, it made a peculiar expression, as though some forgotten memory had surfaced in its thoughts. It held a long gaze on me. I stood my ground.

I'll move fast if it strikes. I won't cower. I inhaled. *Good god, it fucking stinks.*

Unexpectedly, it turned to its companions and released a roar of communication. On lurching strides, all three beasts disappeared into the depths of the swamp. I stood astonished, pondering the strange turn of events.

What the hell just happened? Why didn't it kill me?

With the bungalow burning and the air-car destroyed, there was nothing for me to salvage. I looked down at Dolia's body, thinking how life could be taken so easily. Despite her rough exterior, Dolia had showed kindness to me and my friends. She took us into her home, fed us, entertained us. I wasn't a religious man, but I said a prayer for her, wishing her well on her journey into the afterlife, wherever it led. Hopefully, it was somewhere better.

I salvaged a panel of the destroyed air-car and used it as a sled to transport Dolia's body. Pulling her behind me, I began my journey back to Allienora and the others.

I arrived at the bungalow, dragging Dolia's body behind me. Bardio stumbled down the stairs of the porch, collapsed at his wife's side, and wept. I knew Bardio's pain, since thirty-five years ago I had found my own wife lying on our kitchen floor, strangled to death.

Such tragedy can eat a man from the inside out.

I had dealt with my own pain by immersing myself in my work on the dimensional gateway. I looked up in realization.

Could this be the reason the Fume murdered Cassandra? The Scions of Sensimion had said the Fume was intent on having the dimensional gateway completed. Could Cassandra's murder have merely been the Fume manipulating me to work harder on the gateway? That bastard killed her to control me!

I looked with angry determination to the others. "We must get out of this swamp."

"I have an idea," said Orsteen. "I've been looking at some of Dolia's hunting maps and I think if we build a small skiff, we can travel down the main body of the swamp, through a tributary, and onward to Central City."

"It's better than doing nothing," I said. "I saw some old wood planks behind the bungalow."

Morion pointed to a shed. "There are tools in there."

Allienora placed a hand on Bardio. "While the three of you are building the skiff, Bardio and I will bury his wife."

After a few days, we finished building the skiff. It was small and slender and would move smoothly through the swamp's placid waters. Its design made for limited space, allowing only Orsteen and I to partake in the journey.

Morion confronted me about his exclusion. "I find it offensive that I get no respect! You give me no consideration for the journey, as though I were some grand coward. I'm a very capable man and if I feel the need to replace either of you on this journey, I'll do so."

"You're acting ridiculous," I said. "There's no conspiracy among us to belittle you or diminish your reputation. If you want to paddle for days on end, with the probability of finding yourself in the grips of a black beast, then I'll be glad to give you my seat."

Morion held up his hand. "You need not go so far. I only sought reassurance of our friendly standing, which you've now given and I accept."

I sighed in annoyance.

Orsteen approached. "If the two of you have mended your relationship, I'm ready to depart. The skiff's loaded with food, clothes, and two of Dolia's Intersplit guns."

"Very well," I said. "I'll be there soon. Let me say goodbye to Allienora."

I went into the bungalow and found Allienora feeding Bardio a bowl of soup. I stood quietly for a moment, admiring the kindness she showed.

"We're leaving," I said.

"Already?" Allienora's face was full of concern.

"Don't worry. We'll be back soon with a more suitable craft."

"You'll be careful, won't you?" She placed a hand on my chest. "I don't want to lose you. We've only just found each other."

I pushed a stray curl of her golden hair behind her ear. "Can I be honest with you?"

"Always."

"When we first met, you reminded me of my dead wife... with all your beauty, elegance, and intelligence. Since then, something has changed inside me. You've cleared the webs from my heart." I looked into her large, gleaming blue eyes with passion. "When I look at you now, I no longer think of her, I think of you—only of you. I wanted you to know that."

"You're honesty means a lot to me, Theron." She looked at her hands—they were dirty from digging Dolia's grave. "Life feels different now. The things that have happened, the adventure we've seen. I've found a different side of me—someone brave, someone happy. You've helped me discover the new me, Theron. Life has been better with you in it."

Allienora moved closer and our lips met. I felt a youthful exhilaration, as though it were my first kiss ever. I held her tight and wished to never let go. I felt safe. I felt right. I felt love.

Orsteen's voice echoed through the bungalow, calling for me. I eased away from Allienora's soft, sensual lips with great hesitation.

"I'll be back soon," I whispered.

She smiled a crooked, wonderful smile. "And I'll be waiting."

Orsteen and I boarded the skiff. It lurched to one side as Orsteen's weight was greater than mine. Once confident of our balance, we rowed the skiff into the swamp. I watched Allienora waving from the shore until a thick fog caused her to vanish. She was gone from my sight.

"You'll see her soon, my friend," said Orsteen.

I smiled, thinking about the kiss we had shared. "I think I love her."

"You *think*?"

"I *know* I love her," I replied.

The skiff glided through the still waters. We rowed at a measured pace, trying not to become tired before the journey was completed. We alternated turns rowing and resting, so our progress continued without stopping.

A day passed, then two, and we had yet to encounter a black beast. On the third day, while Orsteen slept, a rustle of leaves from the above canopy captured my attention. I woke Orsteen.

"Something stirs above. Be on guard."

Orsteen stared upward, weapon ready. "It's Fandoral's craft! He's come to rescue us!"

I rowed the skiff into the open, while Orsteen shouted and waved. The small craft descended until it came to rest beside the skiff, hovering just above the water. Its shield disengaged, allowing us to board. The shield reengaged and I realized we forgot our Instersplit guns.

"Wait! Our weapons."

"You won't need them," replied Fandoral. He looked awful. His blue velvet robe hung tattered and dirty. His hood was drawn and his face hung in a tired mask.

"It's good to see you," I said. "The Fume's black beasts are going to be more challenging than we thought. I encountered three of them in the swamp, feasting on one of the local inhabitants. After eating half the man, the beasts underwent a grotesque transformation, mimicking a more humanoid form."

Fandoral released an unexpected laugh. "Forget your worries. The beasts have been taken care of. We killed them all."

"This is splendid news!" said Orsteen.

I noticed a bloody gash near the edge of Fandoral's face. "You're hurt. It seems they didn't give their lives easily."

"It was a good fight." Fandoral drew his hood tighter around his face, concealing the wound. "But come, these are things I'd rather not discuss. We must return to my residence in Central City."

"Allienora and Morion are still at Bardio's bungalow," I said. "I promised we'd return as soon as we found a craft."

"They'll be safe where they are," said Fandoral, flying the craft in the opposite direction of Allienora and Morion.

Orsteen's face puckered. "What's that smell?"

"I don't smell anything," said Fandoral.

I caught a whiff of the foul stench. "We'll probably need a change of clothes."

Orsteen looked back in the direction of Allienora and Morion. "What's so urgent that we must abandon them in the swamp, Fandoral?"

"We're in the process of implementing the Obelisks in a second attempt against the Fume."

"Really?" I said. "I thought we only had one shot with the Obelisks."

"Not so," replied Fandoral. "Even now we push the Fume out of our universe forever."

Fandoral guided the craft through the forest channel, passing towns and small cities, all of which seemed strangely quiet. At last, we arrived at Central City, where all the forest channels intersected. We made for the largest floating structure, which housed the Hall of Guardians and Fandoral's personal residence. Fandoral landed the craft on a balcony and we continued on foot.

As we walked on, we saw scattered dead everywhere.

"Victory wasn't without cost," I said.

We came across a trail of countless dead Guardians, whose bodies were gruesome tangles of bloody flesh and broken armor. On their backs hung the great carapaces of their dimensional transporters, which apparently shifted out of their concealing dimension upon death.

"I don't see a single black beast lying among these Guardians," said Orsteen. "The casualties don't match up. How is this?"

"We took thorough precautions, burning the remains of the beasts."

I again detected a bad odor. "Tell me, Fandoral, is your little friend Stimple as cheerful as ever?"

"Yes, yes. He's always in high spirits. A commendable fellow."

I stopped at a dead Guardian, who still had an Intersplit gun gripped in his hand. I kneeled at his side.

"Fandoral, this Guardian still lives!" I exclaimed.

Fandoral hunched over the body. And as he began speaking his doubts of such a possibility, I jammed the Intersplit gun into the gaping mouth of Fandoral's great horse-head and blew the brains from his skull.

"What have you done!" shouted Orsteen, taking a step away from me.

I drew back Fandoral's blue velvet robe, exposing the black, nano-fiber ingrained flesh of the Fume's beast. "They seem to carry an unmistakable stench, which I remembered from my earlier encounter." I pulled back the hood, and touched what appeared to be Fandoral's face. "This monster has flayed our friend's face and wears it as his own. A technique I've regretfully seen used before."

"It's an awful disguise." Orsteen's face distorted in disgust. "I feel sick. How do we proceed?"

I surveyed our location. "Considering the beast's desire to lead us to Fandoral's personal residence, perhaps we should continue there."

"Why?" asked Orsteen. "It's probably an ambush."

"We'll gain nothing from lurking in the shadows, slaughtering one beast at a time. Besides, if this beast wanted to kill us, he could've done so at any time. This is more than just leading us into a simple ambush. We now have the advantage of knowing our arrival is expected."

"If you think this is our best course of action, I'll trust you, Theron." Orsteen grabbed an Intersplit gun from another dead Guardian. "But I get the next kill."

I patted Orsteen on the shoulder. "We'll see about that, big guy."

We made our way through the Hall of Guardians, which was now vacant. When we at last approached Fandoral's residence, we heard cries of profound grief. With cautious footsteps, we entered the front door and found the source of the cries. We discovered Fandoral's body on the floor lifeless and mutilated. His face, as we expected, had been flayed, revealing his naked skull. On top of him, Stimple lay sprawled, grasping Fandoral's chest with open arms.

"Come back to me, my friend," cried Stimple. "My sweet companion, come back. Don't leave me. I'll be alone without you."

"I'm sorry, Stimple," said Orsteen.

Before I could give my condolences, a disturbingly familiar voice came from behind us: "You've at last arrived."

I spun around and discovered a hologram above the table in the center of the room. It displayed an unfamiliar face, but I knew the thing well.

I scowled. "So, here we are again, face to face, as it were. Who are you now?"

The Fume bowed. "Judas Kern, overseer of Earth's antiterrorism forces."

"I'm glad you're having fun, you demented fuck."

"I'm having a lot of fun. I'm in charge of exterminating a terrorist group called the Scions of Sensimion. I believe you were helping them." He wagged a finger of disapproval. "Naughty, naughty. I don't like being watched."

"Enough of your games." I approached the image. "I've learned a lot about you."

The Fume made an expression not unlike fondness. "You've come far in your time, my child. You probably have many questions. Don't worry—I have all the answers you require."

"How uncharacteristic of you." I smiled wryly. "I've pondered my entire life the twisted condition of my mind, which has driven me in many directions, both good and bad. I've pondered too long my purpose. Why now would you give me these answers?"

"Must a father give reason for every kind act?"

"You do in fact believe you're some kind of god, the father of all creation. I'm not your child. I'm your enemy."

"Oh... but you *are* my child. I brought you into this universe. I crafted the intricacies of your being. Why do you think you can't remember anything before the sanitarium? You weren't born like others, Theron. You were manufactured like an instrument, which I've consequently utilized to my benefit."

"Why have you done this to me?"

"To help you find your destiny."

"Which is?"

"You must discover this yourself."

I felt my stomach in my throat. "Has every moment, every link in the chain of my life, been forged by you?"

"I set you on your way, and thereafter made minor adjustments. However, all taken with all, I don't control minds. I can only implant ideas."

"From what I understand, you have your hand deep-seated in the puppet's rear. Why do you manipulate these planets and their inhabitants? What's your grand design?"

The Fume seemed to ponder whether to reveal his plans. He took an indulgent look around the room. "Your universe is like a tree preparing to bear fruit. A fruit that's most nourishing to my consciousness. You see..." The Fume paused. "...I'm here to consume the entirety of your universe's energies, making them a part of myself."

I scoffed. "These are grandiose plans."

"Big things cannot fit in small minds. You mortals always have difficulty with the greater things. Do not forget that, in the beginning, your universe was but one singularity of energy."

I walked around the hologram casually. "If you're as powerful as you claim, then shouldn't the snap of your fingers suffice? Feed away! Who's stopping you? Aren't you a god?"

"There are certain steps that must be followed. Your universe is still in a primitive stage. For me to absorb its energies now would be like you trying to gain nourishment from eating rocks and drinking sunlight. In order for it to be digested by my expansive consciousness, it must first be changed. There's more to your universe than just energy and emptiness. There are intangibles that pulse and seethe through the cosmos, connecting all and everything."

"And this change would entail?"

"The evolution of your universe's energies into something like me."

I looked sadly to Fandoral's remains. "Fandoral described your being as an entire universe of consciousness, composed of a complex web of exotic energy extending to infinity."

"He spoke with an elegant tongue. His statement was simplistic but essentially correct. This is the state to which all universes progress." The Fume held up his hands in a profound gesture. "What do you think this is all about? Do you think this universe is just a playground for mortal creatures to play? This universe is the embryo of a god, slowly maturing. And I'm merely accelerating this natural process, which I prefer to call the Apotheosis of the Universe."

"Apotheosis of the Universe?"

"You must look at your universe as a single, evolving entity. When it was first formed, it was but a scattering of primordial energy and elements. It soon began to organize itself, forming galaxies, stars, and then solar systems with planets. And on some of these planets, the next great leap of your universe's evolution occurred— life. The organization of matter that, even in its simplest forms, is millions of times more complex then the raw materials first put forth in the universe's beginnings. Still, life in its primitive forms was just the foundation for something greater, for life soon became aware of itself."

"Consciousness," I said.

"Exactly," said the Fume. "Conscious matter. The organization of the universe weaves tighter and tighter. From energy and elements... to galaxies and solar systems... to planets of wind and water... to life... and then to consciousness. But even consciousness, in the grand picture, is a relatively primitive state." The Fume directed a crooked, holographic finger toward my head. "It's the soul that's the most important and complex step in the universe's evolution, for it's the soul that connects your consciousness to the very fabric of the universe. The soul is a level of organization that goes beyond the tangible. The soul is power. The soul is the divine. The soul is the precursor to godliness."

"And somehow the soul of man will lead to the final evolution of the universe, in which all energies will transform into a single consciousness?" I paused. "The birth of a god?"

The Fume nodded in confirmation. "And when this godly evolution is complete, I'll absorb these divine energies—they will become a part of me."

"If my understanding's correct, there'll be no survivors after this evolution—except you."

"The individuality of each creature in this universe is inconsequential. They are but the cogs of a greater device. If it brings you any comfort, their essences will survive in me."

"Essence and life, although interconnected, seem two very different states."

"Such discriminations are pointless in the grand order."

"You reveal your plans with such arrogance. I can only wonder if you're simply bluffing, trying to distract from the damage caused by the Obelisks and the Guardian Army." I paused. "They won't allow you to succeed."

The Fume tilted his head back and laughed heartily. "I'll admit, they've proven to be a nuisance, for they're a willful evolution. But they're naïve to think they could stop me. And even more naïve to believe I was unaware of their existence."

"You knew of this attack?"

"Don't forget who you're speaking to. Of course I knew."

I shrugged. "Nonetheless, the mere fact that your sabotage of the Brahman Station went wrong is proof that your manipulations aren't perfect."

"Are you sure it went wrong?" The Fume inclined his nose ever so slightly. "*Time* is simply another instrument for me to utilize in my endeavor."

"You're aware of the over one million worlds spread among the thousands of galaxies in the Brahman Sprawl?"

"These worlds and their inhabitants are all a fundamental necessity for the final evolution of the universe. As for the worlds I surround, the worlds the Guardians attempt to free, they don't matter anymore. Their usefulness has passed. It's the descendents of the Brahman Station who I now manipulate."

"If you have everything under control, then why have you sent your army of beasts to kill us?"

"There are reasons for everything I do. Every wave of my hand holds significance."

I could somehow sense something like insecurity from the Fume—a stray twitch of the mouth, an uncontrollable blink of the eye, a spasm of the eyebrows, or possibly an imperceptible quiver in his voice.

"So, how does this proceed?" I asked. "What are the steps to this final evolution?"

"A magician doesn't reveal his secrets to every inquisitive fool. I am, however, disappointed that you haven't realized the plans I've orchestrated. The answers sit at the tip of your mind."

I compressed my lips into a thin line. "Then at least tell me when this Apotheosis of the Universe is going to begin."

The Fume smirked. "Soon enough."

"Why do you dangle your motives before me? What do you want from me?"

"You've already done great things for my cause—however, there's more to be done, and you're just the man for the job."

"Tell me! Now! What do you want?"

"As I said before, I only want you to continue on the path of your destiny. This is all."

"Destiny!" I scoffed. "Whatever you've done to me, whatever you think I'm going to do, you can go fuck yourself. I'd sooner kill myself than let you win."

"I doubt this very much." The Fume reached out to me, as if to touch my cheek with a holographic hand. I stood my ground, but soon found myself lunging backward as I thought the hand had substance.

"Why do you haunt me?" I clutched my head in my hands, thinking back on the torturous memories and the plague of unrest.

If the Brahman Station's temporal displacement was, in fact, premeditated, then was it the Fume's manipulation on my mind that motivated me to build the dimensional gateway? Does he really control me this much? Where does he end... and I begin?

"What have you put inside me? I just want to find peace." I aimed my Intersplit gun to my head. "I'm tired, you know."

"If you believe your death will stop my plans, then carry out your suicide. Though, as a consequence, there'll be no one left to rescue your dear Allienora."

I lowered my Intersplit gun. "What are you talking about?"

"While we've been debating the fate of your universe, I've informed my loyal soldiers—who aren't the brutes you perceive them to be—to capture Allienora Chang. I believe she's become the object of your affection."

"Damn you!" My heart pounded.

"So," said the Fume, "do you kill yourself to possibly save your universe, and condemn your new love to death, or shall you continue on in an attempt to save your universe and allow yourself the chance to rescue her?"

I struggled with the choices the Fume presented, and their equally damning possibilities. "Do you pleasure in my suffering? First you killed Mage, then my wife Cassandra, and now you take Allienora from me. Why!"

"Like you, Theron, she has a special purpose in my plans."

My fists clenched, my heart raced. "I know you killed my wife so I'd work harder on the dimensional gateway. Is it the same with Allienora? Are you trying to manipulate me into doing something? What is it? What do you want me to do?"

"I only want you to follow the path of your destiny."

Without warning, Orsteen smashed his fist into the node that projected the hologram of the Fume's embodiment, ending the transmission.

"What have you done!" I cried.

"You're right," said Orsteen. "He's luring us to go somewhere or do something. His words have the power to persuade. They may even distort our perceptions of reality."

"This is insane, Orsteen!" I felt my eyes bulging from my head. "Why take Allienora from me? What purpose does she serve in his outlandish plot? Hell, what purpose do I hold in his plot? How can he predict what I'm going to do? Am I so much his pawn that he can send me off wildly and still maintain confidence I'll do his bidding and achieve this false destiny, whatever it may be?"

"He admitted two important things," said Orsteen. "First, he doesn't control minds, and second, each of us has a soul. And I believe the soul is what gives us the ability to create our own destinies. He can't anticipate each fickle current of thought flowing through your head."

"You're right, Orsteen. I am Theron Mobius. I am myself. My mind is my center."

"Calm down, Theron. You're head's going to pop if you don't."

"I'm conscious of my thoughts, who I am, and what I'm doing. And I have you, my friend. You'll make sure I don't do anything crazy. You'll make sure I don't betray the human race. If my behavior changes, do whatever it takes to stop me."

"I promise you, Theron. If you turn on us, I won't hesitate."

I knelt beside Fandoral's body, where Stimple still mourned with heavy-heartedness.

Stimple lifted his head from Fandoral's chest. "There are procedures for such emergencies. I tried calling the proper medical authorities, but waited to no end. I tried to contact a Guardian, but no one responded."

I looked to Fandoral's remains. "Nothing could've been done."

"You're wrong! All injuries can be healed, even fresh fatality, so long as the brain is preserved." Stimple shook his head hopelessly. "It's been days, and by now his brain's stricken with decay." Stimple lifted his small hands and shook them angrily. "If I weren't the useless homunculus I am, I could've saved him. Do you see that chamber in the corner of the room? That's Fandoral's stasis chamber. If I were a man of sufficient stature, I could've simply carried him three meters and his life would've been saved."

"If you were of greater stature, you would've been killed, too."

"So it should have been," countered Stimple.

"In life, loved ones can be taken from us wrongfully. I've felt this pain. Luckily, it's in our power to treat ourselves to justice, or, if so desired, revenge. We need your help, Stimple."

Stimple looked to me, inhaled deeply, and regained his composure. "The Fume spoke to you with false confidence. Before Fandoral was killed, he was in communication with the other Guardian Spheres and discovered the Obelisks are fully functional on the other planets, successfully sealing the outpocketings of the Fume. Earth is the only planet where the Fume still has an outpocketing into our universe."

I remembered the girl, Nara-Narayana. "After the failure of the Obelisks on Earth, Fandoral said he was going to consult with Nara-Narayana. We must contact her at once and let her know of the Fume's plans to evolve and then absorb the energies of the universe. She could be our best hope."

"Impossible," said Stimple. "Only Guardians and Impresarios are permitted to communicate with Nara-Narayana."

"You were Fandoral's best friend," I said. "You don't know how he contacted her?"

Stimple shook his head.

"What do you know about her?" asked Orsteen.

"All I know is what I've heard from rumor and fable. As you saw from Sensimion's log, Nara-Narayana is the first and eldest of all the Guardians in the Brahman Sprawl. They say her genome is a hundred times more complex than a deca-helix species. Her creation was the most critical step in preventing paradox, for she can see and hear all that occurs in the Brahman Sprawl."

"How does she monitor the entire Brahman Sprawl?" I asked.

"I don't know. If you believe in children's bedtime stories, then you'd fear her ability to hear every immoral thought that roams in your head. It's said that if she's displeased with your thoughts, she'll stop your heart when you sleep."

"If you can't contact her, then I assume you don't know where she is."

Stimple placed his small hand on Fandoral's chest. "Not even the Impresarios know where she's kept."

"Then we must contact another Impresario to relay this information to Nara-Narayana."

"We'll tell everyone." Stimple gently removed himself from Fandoral's chest, crossed the room, and climbed up the side of a desk with a small ladder. There, he manipulated a control panel, causing an iris to open at the floor. A translucent orb displaying a face rose out of it.

The One Voice of the Guardian Sphere spoke: "How may I help you, Stimple?"

"Open communication with every Guardian Sphere. I wish to send out a general communication to everyone."

"I'm sorry, Stimple, but you no longer have permission to utilize the trans-dimensional Guardian network."

"What do you mean?" replied Stimple.

"All authorizations have been revoked."

"By who?"

"By the new Impresario of this Sphere."

"Who's that?" I asked.

"I believe you were just speaking to him," said the One Voice of the Sphere.

I lifted my Intersplit gun to the orb and fired, shattering it into pieces.

"This is worse than I thought," said Stimple. "The Fume has corrupted the One Voice of the Sphere. You'll have to travel to another Guardian Sphere by means of a transportation archway, and relay your message in person. If you give me a ride on your shoulder, I'll lead you to the Antechamber, where the restricted dimensional archways are secured."

"Sounds like a plan," I said. "But, first, we need to return to Bardio's bungalow and find out about Allienora. Maybe she escaped the Fume's beasts. We also need to check on Morion Morpheme. If he's alive, we can't abandon him, no matter how intolerable he's proven to be."

I flew Fandoral's air-car through the forest channel, trying to evade detection.

"These black beasts are obviously in close communication with the Fume," I said. "We can't be spotted by them."

Orsteen looked down at the passing landscape. "I haven't seen one in a while. It's strange, considering there were thousands roaming the forest channels less than three weeks ago."

We returned to the swamp and I saw the great tree that housed Bardio's bungalow. I flew the craft down. As we descended, I saw a figure ten meters from the bungalow, squatting and hunch-backed, hands groping in the soft mud of the swampland. As the craft neared the ground, I could see it was Morion. He'd yet to notice our descent and jerked a clenched fist from the depths of the swamp mud. With a deranged grin of satisfaction, he examined a plump white grub wriggling in his grip. Without hesitation, he stuffed it in his mouth.

With Stimple on my shoulder, I got out of the craft and approached Morion. Morion turned and presented us with two cow-eyes, continuing to chew slowly.

"Where's Allienora?" I asked, fearing his response.

Morion stopped chewing and blinked. "We depleted our food reserves, and Allienora insisted I was to blame. She said I ate more than I required. She then wanted *me,* Morion Morpheme, to wander into the pale murk of the swamp and hunt swamp weasels. I informed her I wasn't bred to perform such drudgery. I recommended Bardio for the task, but he's as worthless as a pile of entrails. I then recommended that she take on the responsibility. In a brooding silence, she suited up and marched into the swamp. And as you can see, she has yet to return, leaving me no choice but to degrade my dignity and root through the mud for grubs like a mongrel."

I grabbed Morion by the throat, enraged. "You've outdone yourself, Morion Morpheme. You're a thoughtless coward. How could you let Allienora wander off into the swamp, with the sphere overrun by black beasts?"

Morion squeezed rasping words through his constricted airway: "I'm not her keeper, and she's not a child."

I released Morion and he fell into the mud.

"I'm sorry," I said, offering him a hand. "I'm angry, confused. I didn't mean to hurt you."

Morion took my hand and I pulled him up.

Orsteen approached. "Have you spotted any beasts lately, Morion? Or heard any noises from the swamp?"

"No beasts," said Morion, rubbing his neck. "There was a scattering of birds early this morning, but I gave little thought to it. And last night, while I slept, I heard a frightening howl that filled the darkness. It caused me to shrink deep under my covers."

We searched around the bungalow, looking for any traces of struggle. I called desperately into the swamp, but my words fell flat on the dense vegetation.

After a few hours of searching, Orsteen stopped me. "It's no use, Theron. She's gone."

"She's smart. She could've eluded them. Maybe she's hiding." I turned back to the swamp.

"Look at me," said Orsteen. "You must accept this. We must move forward."

"Fucking hell!" I chewed on my tongue nervously. I could feel tears welling in my eyes. "Let's say goodbye to Bardio."

Bardio sat on a bucket next to his wife's grave, sipping from a cylinder of Aqua Vita and mumbling. He didn't seem to notice our approach.

I handed him an Intersplit gun. "Find strength, Bardio. You'll have to eat."

"Why? What's left?"

"Dignity, respect... her memory. Let her live on in you."

Bardio reluctantly grabbed the weapon from my hand. "Find your girl, Theron. Don't ever give up. Happiness is a hard thing to lose."

I nodded and thought, *I've lost it more than once.*

As we left, Morion pulled me aside. "I'm sorry about Allienora. I can be selfish now and again, or most of the time, if not all the time. I realize that a selfish man is a lonely man. If you can forgive me, I'll do my best to change."

"I forgive you, Morion." I looked into the far distance. "Hopefully we can all find change very soon."

Quantum
Control Plexus

"I'll drive," said Stimple, jumping to the front of the air-car. The controls reconfigured around him, accommodating his small size. The energy shield activated around the craft and we sped out into the forest channel.

I looked back to the swamp, desperate to see Allienora hiding among the trees. She was nowhere in sight.

I turned to Stimple. "Where are we headed?"

"To the forbidden realm of the Guardian Army. There we'll find the Antechamber, where the restricted dimensional archways are secured."

To my surprise we returned to Central City. "The realm of the Guardian Army is in Central City?"

"Look closer," said Stimple.

He manipulated the air-car's controls and a filter was applied to the front window. A giant floating structure appeared like a ghostly vision. It was out of phase like the Obelisks that landed on Earth. It was huge—its mass enveloped all of Central City.

"You people do things differently," said Orsteen.

Stimple smiled. "A city beneath a city."

"How do you do it?" I asked.

"It's the same technology developed by Sensimion to conceal the Guardian's dimensional transporters. It's a matter of transforming a few of the lesser eighteen dimensions into clones of the three prime dimensions."

Morion leaned forward. "You can get us inside this hidden realm, little man?"

"I may be as useless as a placenta after birth, but I'm older than most in this Guardian Sphere, and I've acquired several privileges throughout the millennia." Stimple yanked open his shirt, exposing his small chest. A glowing ring was embedded in his skin.

"What's that?" I asked.

"It's the key to the kingdom," said Stimple proudly. "Fandoral entrusted me with it a long time ago."

Stimple ran his finger along the circumference of the glowing ring and something began to materialize in front of the air-car. Before us floated a magnificently crafted portal—a circular dimensional gateway floating in air. At its apex was the body of a majestic bird, its wings drooping down to form the ring of the portal. It gazed forth with frightening intensity. It felt like it was judging me, scrutinizing my worthiness as we prepared to pass into the sanctuary of its sprawled wings.

We flew into the gateway, passing through the wings of the great bird. When we arrived on the other side, the massive floating structure that housed the realm of the Guardian Army was no longer a ghostly vision, it now had substance.

Stimple landed the air-car on a balcony and we proceeded by foot. Stimple rode on my shoulder and guided us into a long corridor lined with towering statues.

Each was a humanoid figure distinctly different in physiology from the next, and all held a radiant globe in the hand of an upraised arm. The globes illuminated the corridor with a ghastly effect, splashing long shadows in every direction.

Morion pointed to the five-meter-tall statues as we passed. "They're breathtaking. Look at the craftsmanship in the faces—chiseled with such detail that you can almost tell what they're thinking."

"These are portrayals of the various races throughout the Brahman Sprawl," said Stimple. "In their hands they hold representations of their home worlds."

The corridor split in the distance.

"Which way?" I asked.

"We must proceed down the left passage," directed Stimple. "It'll lead us to the Antechamber, where we'll gain access to the restricted dimensional archways."

"And the passage to the right?" inquired Orsteen.

"It leads to the training facility of the Guardian Army."

I heard distant footsteps. "Someone approaches from behind us. Take cover."

We concealed ourselves in the shadows and waited as the rhythm of footsteps grew louder. I peeked out with Stimple on my shoulder. We saw a troop of the Fume's beasts passing.

Stimple whispered in my ear. "How did they gain access to this realm? Even though the Fume controls the One Voice, they still shouldn't have been able to gain access. The systems of this realm are independent from the Guardian Sphere."

I watched as the beasts passed by. They had changed considerably since my previous encounter, and were now of two general forms. The first were of great height, comparable to the statues lining the corridor. They had bulging muscles and a thick, calloused skin that was still ingrained with silver nano-fibers. They lumbered onward at an incline, heads thrust forward, to the effect that they seemed perpetually on the verge of tipping to the ground, only to be propped back up at the last moment by each forward footstep.

The second kind was of slimmer form, at half the height of their fellow beasts, yet still taller than Orsteen. They walked with a more controlled and regal stride. Three of them led a group of twenty of the larger beasts. They seemed more intelligent. I guessed they were the leaders of the Fume's onslaught.

The larger beasts carried weapons and equipment— cumbersome energy cannons, communication devices, and power cells. A few at the rear dragged bundles of bodies tied together by ropes. I felt ill as I was reminded of the bundles of swamp weasels I had captured with Bardio's wife. To my horror, I noticed a few of the bodies at the tops of the bundles still squirmed with life.

The beasts moved to a comfortable distance and we relaxed.

"Did you notice the three smaller beasts leading the pack?" said Orsteen. "They wore the armor of the Guardian Army."

"This situation becomes worse by the moment," I said. "They're adapting fast, assimilating the technology of the Guardian Army."

"We must stop them," said Stimple.

"This seems unlikely," I said. "We're no match for such giants."

Stimple pointed in the direction of the beasts. "If they gain access to the gates of the Antechamber, all will be lost. They'll be able to travel to all the Guardian Spheres."

We quickened our pace, following the troop of beasts, occasionally ducking behind a statue to escape notice. We came to the gates of the Antechamber and realized our worst fears. The gates were open.

We hid behind a statue next to the entrance of the Antechamber and were afforded a view of the interior. The Antechamber itself was an enormous cylindrical chamber. Around the perimeter, a six-meter-wide walkway wound around and up, disappearing into a mist thirty stories above. At shortly spaced intervals along the walkway were the dimensional archways, apparently leading to the other Guardian Spheres. There must have been five hundred archways before the walkway vanished into the mist above.

"We're too late," I said.

Within the Antechamber were thousands of black beasts. They walked in a slow procession up the walkway, making their ways through the dimensional archways. Many of the beasts carried Instersplit guns that had been modified for some unknown reason. The whole procession was extremely organized, with the beasts forming into troops of twenty or thirty.

Where the spiral walkway began, a third kind of beast stood at attention, as if on post. It had the typical black, gnarled flesh with ingrained nano-fibers, but was much smaller than the other two types, with a bulbous head and large, glistening eyes. It looked thoughtfully upon a tablet it held, poking it with a long finger. To each troop that passed its post, it would call out a command in a strange language. The troop would then proceed up the spiral walkway and eventually find their way to an archway.

"Allienora!" I called. My heart nearly stopped when I saw her golden hair among the crowd of beasts. "Do you see her? She hangs over the shoulder of a beast, high on the walkway."

I lunged forward, but came to a halt as Orsteen stopped me with a large hand. "Don't be a fool, Theron. You can't rescue her now. You wouldn't make it a single step through this crowd of monsters."

I remembered the psychic moment I had shared with Allienora and now gave all my concentration to send out my thoughts.

I'm here, Allienora. Don't worry. I'll rescue you if it's the last thing I do. Do you hear me? I won't give up.

I waited, but she didn't reply.

"Why doesn't she respond? She's heard my thoughts before." I watched the beast carry her through an archway. "She's gone. What do we do? We have to follow her."

"We'll find her, Theron." Orsteen looked through the gathering of beasts. "We must find another way to a different Guardian Sphere. Stimple, do you have any suggestions?"

"The only other way to a Guardian Sphere is to find a Guardian who still lives."

"Good luck," said Morion. "The only Guardians we've seen are those lying dead in our path."

"That's it!" said Orsteen. "We can use one of the dimensional transporters lying around us. Surely the dead Guardians won't miss them."

Stimple jumped on Orsteen's shoulder. "You can't just strap a dimensional transporter to your back."

"Then where do the Guardians become equipped with such units?" I asked.

"Of course!" said Stimple. "Just down the other corridor, within the training facility of the Guardian

Army." With the backside of his heel, Stimple gave Orsteen a hard kick. "Forward, big fellow!"

Orsteen returned a cold stare.

"Sorry," said Stimple. "When I'm not in the abyss of depression, I'm stimulated to the point of insanity."

Orsteen gave a nod of forgiveness, and then proceeded to follow Stimple's command.

We evaded two more regiments of black beasts and then entered into an open realm that felt like a university campus. We moved down a central boulevard lined with small buildings constructed with an almost gothic architecture. Each building was labeled with a sign engraved with a strange set of symbols.

Stimple pointed down the boulevard. "It's this way to the armory."

Scattered along our path were many half-eaten and decaying Guardian bodies. I felt respect for them.

"It's utterly noble giving oneself to the welfare of humankind." I turned to Stimple. "How did these brave souls become Guardians?"

"With great difficulty," said Stimple. "After an applicant submits their life to the cause of the Guardian Army, they're thoroughly investigated to ensure their motives are honorable. Then, it's said that Nara-Narayana herself approves the applicant's admission. Once admitted, they undergo genetic therapies to alleviate the aging process and to enhance strength, endurance, and mental vigor. They then embark on a painstaking education." Stimple pointed to each of the buildings we passed. "Brahman Anthropology... Transcendental Theosophy... Temporal and Paradoxical Dynamics...

Scientific Verities of the Universe... The Ten Tomes of the Guardian Army... and so on, and so forth. They're also taught in the use of weapons, hand to hand combat, spacecrafts, technological comprehension and improvisation, and the intricacies of military combat and strategy."

"It sounds exhausting," said Morion. "How long does this training take?"

"About two hundred years," said Stimple, now indicating a structure we approached. "This is the armory."

Two magnificent spires stretched upward at either side of the windowless facade.

"The front door's open," I said.

Immediately upon entering the armory, we overheard muted voices coming from a room on the opposite side of the foyer.

"Stay here," I whispered. "I'll check it out."

Stimple hopped on my shoulder. "I'll come with you."

With Stimple on my shoulder, I crept to the entrance of the room and peeked around the doorframe. We discovered a scene of torture and cruelty.

A slender female figure lay naked on a table, strapped in place by her wrists and ankles. She seemed old— withered in the eyes and loose in the skin. Her small, round face was drained of all color, unless such was her natural complexion. On her head, instead of hair, three crests of bone emerged from her skin, and ran from her forehead to the back of her skull. Tears fell from the corners of her eyes. She was in pain. Her skin was covered with sores.

One of the smaller and more intelligent-looking beasts hovered over her. Its large eyes burned with rage.

I listened to a conversation I only half understood. The female, obviously of the Brahman Sprawl and born with a biolinguistic lobe, could be understood perfectly, while the black beast spoke in strange clicks and jibbers— apparently the female's native tongue.

Stimple, fluent in the language, translated the beast's side of the conversation into my ear.

The beast spoke: "I care about nothing except serving my god. I have no compassion for you. If need be, you'll suffer an eternity of my jagged touch. Now! Tell me! What's the pattern of the Obelisks' dimensional frequencies?"

The female bit her lip in pain. "Must I tell you again? The pattern cannot be deciphered by any man, beast, or god."

The beast filled a syringe with a toxic-looking substance that released a yellow vapor on contact with the atmosphere. Every muscle in the woman's body tensed as the beast injected a small bubble of the liquid under the skin of her abdomen.

The beast growled. "I'm both annoyed and impressed by the will you command within that frail form."

The woman opened her eyes fearlessly. "Tell me, you vile creature, how is it your god can penetrate the dimensional barrier on Earth, and nowhere else in the seven galaxies?"

"I'll ask the questions!" roared the beast. "However, as a gesture of good faith, I'll tell you. My god has the ability to focus the totality of his divine energies on a single point in your universe, so to break through the dimensional barrier created by your Obelisks. Consequently, he tires of exerting himself. Now, tell me what I want to know—or else."

"You'll kill me regardless." The woman closed her eyes.

"Don't shut your eyes! I'll cut off your eyelids!" The beast turned away from the woman in a frustrated manner and faced a podium. "This compendium of data tells me everything except the pattern of the Obelisks' dimensional frequencies. It even tells me you're one of the senior designers of the Obelisks, and that you know exactly what I ask. Maybe it'll tell me the most painful way to extract this information from your mind."

While the beast occupied itself with the compendium, I prepared to attack.

My Intersplit gun's useless, I thought. *Its black, gnarled flesh is too thick. Yet this particular breed of beast seems less of a fighter and more of a thinker. Its large bulbous head... is it as soft and supple as it appears?*

I readied my weapon, but quickly froze when I saw something unsettling in the corner of my eye—next to a rack of transportation carapaces, in a dark alcove of the room, stood a shadowed figure as tall as the ceiling. It was one of the goliath beasts. Its eyes pierced through the shadows and seemed to look in every direction at once.

I withdrew from the doorway and Stimple and I regrouped with the others.

"There's a woman," I said softly. "She's being tortured by one of the smaller beasts. I think we could kill it, if not for the goliath beast standing guard in the shadows. We must speak with this woman. She may be our last hope."

"I have a plan," said Orsteen. "The three of you will hide, while I cause a disturbance to lure the goliath beast outside."

"What then?" I asked, doubtful of his plan.

"It'll come to me as I go. Now, hide in that room."

"Wait," said Morion, grabbing Orsteen's arm. He made a strange expression, almost one of real courage. "I'll go. I owe as much."

Orsteen nodded and handed Morion his Intersplit gun. "Be quick on your feet and even quicker with your wits."

"We'll see you soon," I said, strangely proud of him.

The rest of us hid in a nearby room. With the door slightly open, we watched as Morion exited the armory, crossed the boulevard, and took position in front of a domed structure. I saw him standing idly, as if contemplating his next course of action. Morion then aimed his Intersplit gun back across the boulevard, toward the door of the armory, and fired. Hitting his mark, the door flew off its hinges, causing a ruckus that successfully captured the attention of the goliath beast. It bounded to the door of the armory and searched for the source of the disturbance. Morion fired again, hitting the beast in the chest. Unfazed, the beast moved toward Morion. The chase was on.

We quietly returned to the doorway where the thinker beast tortured the woman. It removed a strange metallic bug from a chamber on a workbench.

Stimple again translated the clicks and jibbers of the beast: "This is a synthetic parasite you use to interlink with a patient's biolinguistic lobe. Essentially, it'll open your mind to me. I find myself disappointed at the simplicity and painlessness of the process."

The black beast applied the synthetic parasite to the woman's head. With a barbed tentacle, it began boring into her skull.

I crept up behind the black beast, which seemed fascinated by the work of the parasite. I lifted my Intersplit gun to the back of its head.

"Excuse me," I said calmly.

The beast turned in surprise and I fired. The weapon's discharge passed through the beast's eye-socket and into its large, melon head, making a hot mess of its brain.

Orsteen freed the restrained woman who, in a frenzy, clawed at the parasite clinging to her head.

"You couldn't have come at a better time," she said, knocking the parasite to the floor. "I would've told the beast everything if the parasite entered my brain."

"You're safe now," I said, handing the trembling woman her clothes.

She looked suspiciously at us. "If this is a trick to get the secrets of the Obelisks, I'm on to you."

Stimple climbed on top of a nearby table. "It's not a trick, JarNay."

"Stimple! Who are these people?"

"This is Theron Mobius and his companion, Orsteen Hunn."

"Theron Mobius?" said JarNay in surprise. "How is this possible? How have you been brought here?"

"It's a long story," I said. "Right now, we're trying to get important information to an Impresario."

"What of Fandoral?"

Stimple's eyes drooped. "He's been given to the next plane of existence."

"My sympathies, Stimple." JarNay turned back to me. "As for your need to contact an Impresario, I can't help. The Fume's minions have overtaken most of the vital systems on this Guardian Sphere and have corrupted the One Voice. We can communicate with no one."

"Can you transport us to another Guardian Sphere?" I said.

"I cannot."

"Aren't you a Guardian?" I asked. "Don't you command a transportation carapace?"

"Unfortunately, I only design and outfit them for others."

"Then you can outfit me with one," I said. "We have little time to spare."

"Clearly you're ignorant about such devices. In order to utilize a transportation carapace, one must undergo strict mental training for a hundred years. You see, in order to move from planet to planet and galaxy to galaxy one must think in tandem with a quantum control plexus. Mind and machine must become one. The mind must be altered severely for this to happen. Only then will the universe come into focus." JarNay paused for a moment. "And not to sound insulting, but you're only a double-helix species. You're lacking the neural sophistication required to think in tandem with a quantum control plexus."

I sighed, aggravated by the constant obstacles along our journey. "Can you contact another Guardian on this sphere?"

"Like I said before, communications are down, even within the sphere." JarNay's head dropped. "And, unfortunately, I don't believe any Guardians have survived on this sphere."

I indicated the dead beast. "How is it, JarNay, that the Guardian Army was defeated by the Fume's minions? From what I've seen, their armor makes them nearly invincible, and their ability to transport in an instant makes them impossible to capture."

"At first, the Fume's beasts were easily killed. Then, they began to change, adapting their cellular composition to absorb the energy of our weapons. They are a versatile creation. I was able to examine one earlier in the battle."

JarNay displayed a three dimensional hologram of one of the Fume's beasts. The computer highlighted the silver nano-fibers that ran through the beast like a second nervous system.

"This network of nano-fibers is how the beasts are able to transform. When the beast wishes to change, molecular instructions are sent through the nano-fiber system to every cell in its body. The necessary metabolism for such transformation is powered by radioactive isotopes infused in the DNA of the beast. But this ability to adapt was only part of their victory. Only when they gained access to the compendium and its vast data were we doomed. They were then able to construct weapons capable of disabling the Guardian's armor and pushing their transportation carapaces out of dimensional concealment, thus immobilizing the Guardians."

I fell into a nearby chair and sat thinking. I looked to JarNay stoically. "The people of the Brahman Sprawl have had millions of years to ponder the human condition, to explore the meaning of existence. What do you know of the human soul?"

"The human soul?" JarNay shook her head. "You're free to access the compendium on religion in the Brahman Sprawl. Death is still the bane of human existence. Such beliefs are still prevalent in calming the fear of the unknown."

"No," I said. "I don't seek faith or fairytales. I seek scientific proof of the soul."

"If such an inner force exists, it has yet to be discovered, even after twenty-one million years of human existence. Why do you ask such a thing, especially now?"

"The human soul is the reason the Fume manipulates humankind."

JarNay's eyes lit up. "You've discovered the Fume's motives?"

"We have. And this is the reason we seek an Impresario. We had hoped someone in the Brahman Sprawl could utilize this knowledge."

"Please," said JarNay eagerly. "Tell me what you know."

I stood up and began pacing the room. "First, you must know that the temporal displacement of the Brahman Station and the evolution of humankind in the Brahman Sprawl didn't happen by accident. Everything has unfolded as the Fume planned."

"Why would he want this?"

"The Fume claims that it's the people of the Brahman Sprawl he now manipulates."

"How? To what end?"

"He's planning to use the souls of the Brahman descendents to birth a god, a being of the same exotic energy as himself. It'll be the end of the universe as we know it. All the energy of the universe will be transformed into this god. The Fume will then be able to cannibalize its divine energies."

"I'm speechless," said JarNay. "The truth has surpassed the wildest speculations of the past." Her eyes gleamed with wonder. "What is the soul? How can the souls of all humankind birth a god?"

"I don't know," I said. "But the Fume said some things that resonated deep within me. He said the soul connects the consciousness to the very fabric of the universe. He said the soul is a level of organization that goes beyond the tangible. He said the soul is the precursor to godliness."

JarNay leaped in front of the compendium. "I'm struck by inspiration. It may be possible to modify a transportation carapace to function like an archway, but it'll only allow a single trip."

"How do we choose our destination?" said Orsteen. "With the Fume's beastly minions on their way to the other Guardian Spheres, there's no telling which sphere has an Impresario who still lives."

"Instead of finding an Impresario, you'll find Nara-Narayana herself. This information is far too important for anyone else."

I shook my head with uncertainty. "From what Stimple has told us, Nara-Narayana isn't one to be located—if she exists at all."

"Few people can attest with confidence that Nara-Narayana is indeed a genuine entity. Fortunately, I'm one of the privileged few."

"Then you'll send us directly to her?"

"No, I don't know her location. But I'll send you to the only living Guardian who knows how to find her."

"Very well," I said. "But you must hurry with your modifications. Our companion, Morion Morpheme, has been keeping one of the Fume's goliath beasts occupied. There's no telling how long he'll stay ahead of the game."

JarNay nodded, acknowledging the urgency of the situation. "First, one of you must volunteer to receive the quantum control plexus at the base of your biolinguistic lobe."

I raised a sarcastic eyebrow. "I thought us lowly double-helixes couldn't think in tandem with a quantum control plexus."

"That's why I'm programming it to resonate with the proper coordinates to guide the transportation carapace."

I stepped forward. "You can implant me."

"It may take a few minutes to construct a properly calibrated quantum control plexus," said JarNay. "Orsteen, you should stand guard at the front door, in case the Fume's beast returns."

"Can do," said Orsteen, who left the room with Stimple on his shoulder.

As JarNay worked at a console, inputting the specifications of her design, I laid stomach-down on the table, preparing myself for the procedure.

"It's ready," said JarNay, removing a red glowing node from a chamber. She then retrieved a sliver of metal from the counter. "Using this probe I'll insert the quantum control plexus through the back of your skull. During the process, I recommend you calm your body and mind." JarNay put on an ocular device. "It'll take a moment to analyze the pathways of your brain and biolinguistic lobe to determine the exact placement of the quantum control plexus."

JarNay applied an anesthetic and began. I felt a large pressure in my head as JarNay pushed the probe into my brain.

"It's done," said JarNay. "The quantum control plexus will automatically establish the proper neural linkages. I must now tend to the modifications of the transportation carapace."

"Are you coming with us?" I asked.

"It'll be best if I remain here, since there's no one of authority left on this sphere."

"Then you should tell me about our destination."

"The world's called Fallgate," said JarNay, continuing to work on the transportation carapace. "It's in the Crux Galaxy and sits among a cluster of backwater worlds spaced many light years apart. Due to the moral decay of this region, as well as the general acceptance of a lawless society, there are no dimensional archways by mandate of the Guardian Army. However, these planets do command the use of spaceships, thus there's trade done between them. Since each of these worlds has maintained their own unique physiology, you won't be met as oddities regarding your appearance.

"Once you arrive, you must seek out a Guardian named Fanbert Manderwall. He's worked many years as an observer on this planet, and maintains residence in the port city Neubius. Though he won't look it, he's very old. Such a post is considered his retirement, for there was little chance that anyone in this technologically primitive region would ever gain the means to contact Earth or the Fume. Not to mention the fact that these planets have long since forgotten the truth of the Fume and the temporal displacement of the Brahman Station. In all likelihood, they've evolved their own fictitious account of their origins. Keep this in mind when you're locating Fanbert and come into contact with the local inhabitants."

"And when we find this Fanbert Manderwall, what do we tell him?"

"Speak my name, and tell him you seek the forgotten world where the Prophets sleep. Inform him their waking is overdue."

"These Prophets can lead us to Nara-Narayana?"

"Indeed. They're the only beings in the Brahman Sprawl who know her location." JarNay put the final touches on the transportation carapace. "My modifications are complete, but I must warn you, you may find yourself in the cold darkness of space. These modifications are the best I could do in such little time."

"I understand," I said. "Your best is good enough for me."

JarNay touched the transportation carapace. "You and your company need only to gather around the unit and trigger this switch. Now, let me confirm that the quantum control plexus successfully melded with your brain." She again put on her ocular device, which made a fuss of noise. "Strange."

"What is it?" I asked.

"Your brain... it's being pervaded by filaments of energy. From what my oculars can perceive, the filaments are lengthening at a rate of one one-hundredth of a millimeter an hour. They've just recently found their way to your new biolinguistic lobe." JarNay went to the compendium. "It's impossible!"

"Tell me what you've discovered!" I demanded. "Why are you looking at me like that?"

JarNay's slight figure became rigid. Her findings, whatever their significance, seemed to have dissolved any trust I had thus far gained from her. She was on the verge of calling for help.

I sprang to my feet and seized her by the arms. "What frightens you?"

"You're seeded with the Fume's exotic energy. And this I can't explain, since the Fume cannot manifest himself beyond the realm of his outpocketings in our universe. It would be no different if I cut out a piece of my brain, cast it into the ocean, and expected it to return with the secrets of the deep. A mind, no matter its nature, must remain whole in order to function properly."

"I promise you, I'm not the Fume. I'm Theron Mobius."

"Promises are uttered by desperate men and liars."

I remembered when I asked the Fume why I was burdened with his memories. The Fume had replied: 'There's some of me in you.' He was speaking quite literally. The memories were now explained. I felt a great anxiety.

The Fume's inside me. Like a disease, I'm infected. I repeated my mantra in silence: *I am Theron Mobius. I am myself. My mind is my center...*

"Get it out of me! Please!"

JarNay pulled away from me. "Stand back!"

"Won't you help me?"

"Help? How?"

"You have devices that can send people across the universe with a thought. You've built ships the size of planets. You have twenty-one million years of technology and you can't help me? I'm just one man with something in his head."

"Those are usually the most dangerous of men. You're now the enemy." JarNay started to call out.

I grabbed her, pressing my hand tightly on her mouth. She struggled, but I contained her. "I'm sorry. I won't hurt you." I dragged her to a back room, where I found an empty stasis chamber. I pushed her inside and shut the door. My fingers hit random buttons, apparently a successful combination since JarNay became still. "Forgive me."

As I considered how to deal with the others, Orsteen entered the room with Morion limp in his arms. Orsteen set him on the table.

"We discovered him a ways down the boulevard, collapsed from exhaustion. He's not hurt."

Morion came to his senses. "I defeated the beast, Theron."

"You've done well," I said.

Morion drew a long breath and stood. "Despite my triumph, we shouldn't remain here. The clamor of our battle no doubt echoed throughout the corridors of the Guardian Sphere. It was such a battle that if I mentioned the details, you might think I was prone to embellishments and self-glorifications."

"A true hero is always humble," I said impatiently. "As for our departure, everything's ready. We should leave immediately."

Orsteen retrieved three bags from the hallway and handed them out. "I found weapons for our trip."

"Well done," I said.

Stimple walked into the room and looked around curiously. "Where's JarNay?"

I didn't know what to say. "Uh... she said something about disabling the dimensional archways in the Antechamber, so to stop the migration of the Fume's beasts to the other Guardian Spheres. She was confident in her plan and, citing time as an issue, left through a back passageway. Before she left, she wished us luck on our journey. So, let's go."

I stood beside the transportation carapace and was joined by all but Stimple, who spoke: "A person of my unique characteristics doesn't do well in remote lands. I'll stay here, where the surroundings are to my advantage, in that I know all the best hiding places."

"Take care, little man," I said, glancing nervously toward the back room.

"Do me a favor," said Stimple. "Get revenge for Fandoral's murder."

"We'll do our best," I replied sincerely. In a gesture of farewell, I extended a finger.

Stimple placed his tiny hand upon it. "Goodbye, Theron Mobius."

CELESTIAL PHENOMENON

We found ourselves on the world Fallgate, in the middle of a junkyard. The wrecks of old spaceships were scattered around us like the giant skeletons of old sea monsters.

"Amazing," I said. "I'll never get tired of dimensional travel. I still don't know why I can perceive the journey and the two of you can't."

"For me, it was again instantaneous," said Orsteen. "Across the universe in the blink of an eye."

I looked skyward and saw a monolithic construct floating in low orbit—a space station of breathtaking proportions.

"Beautiful," I said.

Orsteen glanced to the surrounding hulks. "Probably built to escape a devastated planet."

I removed a scanner from the supply pack Orsteen retrieved from the armory. I couldn't get it to work until I realized it was voice activated.

"Are the surroundings safe?" I asked.

The scanner responded: "Ambient radiation levels are safe. The atmosphere is breathable for common double-helix species."

"I'm becoming tired of these double-helix stereotypes," said Morion. "Even the computers are racist."

The scanner continued: "There is an unidentifiable energy signature a half-kilometer ahead."

We moved forward and discovered a pipeline of flowing liquid hovering twenty feet off the ground. The fluid was contained by a tubular energy-field being emitted from rings spaced every hundred feet. I asked the scanner to identify the liquid.

"The fluid in question is ninety-nine percent deuterium," replied the scanner.

"Where's the port city Neubius?"

"My database does not include topographical information for this planet."

Orsteen threw a piece of metal debris at the pipeline. It vaporized on contact with the energy field. "Spaceships need deuterium. Let's follow the flow of the pipeline."

"Agreed," I said. "First, help me hide the transportation carapace under that pile of garbage."

We moved forward with determination, only occasionally slowing our pace to allow Morion to catch his breath. Darkness soon fell and stars blossomed in the sky. We came upon a small shack built from the hull panels of old spaceships.

"It appears to be abandoned," said Morion. "Let's rest for the night. I can't go any farther."

"Not so fast," I said, noticing a wisp of smoke coming from a metal chimney. I inhaled deeply. "Someone's cooking their evening meal inside."

Orsteen put a hand on his belly. "A bite of food would be nice."

"You can't be serious?" I said.

Orsteen shrugged his shoulders. "What's the harm in asking?"

As we contemplated the thought, the front door creaked open to expose the silhouette of an oddly-shaped man. Between bowed legs drooped two plump buttocks, giving the man an unwieldy, underslung appearance.

"Who are you?" called out the man. "Why do you loiter at my doorstep?"

"I apologize," I said. "We're travelers in need of shelter and food."

"Come closer, so I may be certain you're not rogues." We did so and the man carefully examined us. "You're off-worlders?"

"We are," I responded.

"Excellent! I'm always willing to accommodate off-worlders. Your timing is perfect. I've just prepared a sumptuous meal. It'll now be in your honor. Come, join me."

Morion moved forward excitedly. "I didn't expect such hospitality, considering the rumors of lawlessness on this world."

I grabbed Morion, bringing him to a halt.

"What are you thinking?" exclaimed Morion. "Release me!"

"There's a blade concealed behind his forearm," I whispered. "It glistens under the starlight." I turned to the man who eagerly awaited us. "On second thought, we should continue to our destination. Can you direct us to the port city Neubius?"

"It's bad judgment to travel tonight. There's no moon to protect you from lurking cockatrices and rotmouth chimeras. Moreover, a strange celestial phenomenon hangs in the sky like a phantom." The man pointed to the sky, where a glowing haze was barely noticeable.

I tilted my head up. "It looks like a nearby nebula, nothing more."

"So it wants you to believe. Come, you'd be safer inside. As will those overstuffed bags that hang on your backs."

"We'll take our chances," I said.

The man responded with a snarl and disappeared within the shack, slamming the door shut.

Disappointed, we continued following the pipeline. An hour had passed when Orsteen pointed up at the stars with excitement.

"Do you see them!"

I looked into the sky and noticed what seemed to be an occasional star descending. "Ships! Your instincts to follow the flow of deuterium were right, Orsteen. Judging the distance, it should take us a half-day to get there."

During our travels, I found Morion at a standstill, looking off into an oasis of trees, appraising something in silence.

Orsteen and I joined him.

"What are you looking at?" I asked.

Morion pointed among the trees and I spotted a young girl tied to a tree trunk. At first, she appeared dead, but soon enlivened, struggling against her bonds and screaming for help.

Orsteen moved to assist the girl, but Morion held a hand in front of his chest. Orsteen angrily pressed the hand away.

"Why do you hesitate, Morion?"

"Who are we to judge her situation?" said Morion. "For all we know, she's a murderer serving her sentence. As far as I'm concerned, we have no business interfering. We're foreigners, ignorant of the ways of this world."

"I agree with Orsteen," I said. "She needs our help."

As we approached, the girl looked at us timidly. "Your generosity is a credit to all strangers."

"It's truly nothing," said Orsteen. "Have you been hurt in any way?"

"Not at all, I'm fine. In fact, I've never been better."

As we untied the girl, three large metallic-mesh sacks suddenly fell from above, trapping us. I struggled to free myself from the sack. I heard cheers of triumph from all around. Moments later, a crushing blow took my consciousness.

I woke up, no longer inside the metallic-mesh sack. A hood made of similar material was now pulled over my head. It had three holes in it—two for my eyes and one for my mouth. I tried to pull it off, but it was secured at my neck by a metal ring, clamped and padlocked.

I peered through the holes and found myself imprisoned in a cage hanging from the ceiling of an exquisitely decorated dining room. Its walls were lined with a cherry-brown wainscoting, and the ceiling was opened to the stars by means of a large skylight. Beside my cage hung two others, containing Orsteen and

Morion, who both wore matching hoods and seemed unconscious.

Orsteen stirred. "I've been faking sleep so to assess our situation and our captors. The Masters of the house, as they're called, are three fellows in ridiculously tall top hats. They're currently refreshing themselves before the evening meal, which is being prepared by a lumbering oaf called Palook. Unfortunately, this is all I've learned. Why they've taken us captive, I don't know."

In the corner of the room, I noticed four lifelike statues sitting in chairs holding stringed instruments at the ready. "They seem prepared to pluck the first notes of a great masterwork."

Orsteen nodded. "Bizarre, aren't they? I'm still not sure if they're real or wax."

"They're a creepy quartet," I said. "If they are real, they command a remarkable muscle control to maintain such a pose."

"They look sad and tortured," said Orsteen.

"Agreed." I focused on their faces. "They have no eyes, only hollow spaces. And there are electronic implants at their temples."

The door leading to the kitchen swung open and the oaf Palook came lurching through. He set the dining table with fine porcelain plates, crystal goblets, clean linens, and an array of silverware.

"We're on an important mission," I announced, watching Palook light a pair of candles. "Do you understand me?"

Palook looked at me dumbly, blinked, and then, with clumsy footwork, went back to the kitchen. He promptly returned carrying three metal bowls, which he fit through feeding slots in the bars of our cages.

"Butterbeans. Eat!" Palook grabbed a sharp piece of silverware from the dining table and poked Morion awake. "Eat!"

Morion pulled frantically at his hood. "I'm being smothered!" He at last aligned the holes for his eyes and mouth. Once calm, he ate the bowl of butterbeans, stuffing handfuls of the gummy porridge through the hole of his hood and into his mouth.

I pushed my bowl away defiantly. "I won't eat your slop. I want answers!"

The oaf Palook didn't respond verbally, instead, he went to the far wall of the room, where a panel of switches was located. He pointed to each as if counting them, and then flipped one on.

My cage conducted a powerful current of electricity, sending shocks through my body. "I'll eat! No more! I'll eat!"

An hour passed and the Masters arrived for the evening meal dressed in fancy suits and tall top hats. They walked with a hobbling gait apparently typical for their race, given their bowed legs and underslung asses. They took their seats and the quartet of musicians came to life, plucking and strumming a serene melody.

Morion clanged his empty metal bowl against his cage. "Is this how you greet strangers to your land? Let us go, you bastards!"

"I apologize," I said. "What my friend intended to say was that there must be a way to negotiate our freedom. You look like a civil group of gentleman, who—"

"Silence!" exclaimed one of the men, holding up a hand. "You've broken etiquette by interrupting our evening meal."

I tried to further reason with the men, but the most offended of the three signaled Palook, who, standing by the panel of switches, administered punishment.

Fearing further shocks, we remained quiet as Palook began serving the three Masters course after course of culinary delights.

Five small courses were consumed before Palook rolled out a long cart carrying the final course, which was covered by a white cloth.

"Main course is served," said Palook. He pulled away the cloth with a sweeping flourish, making the presentation ever more dramatic.

Upon an oversized platter lay the body of a man cooked to a golden-brown crisp. His chest cavity had been split open and filled with aromatic vegetables, roots, and spices.

From the sight of the main course, I now knew why we were captured. "You plan to eat us? You're animals!"

One of the Masters pulled a crisp of skin from the carcass and ate it. "A misguided classification. We're not animals, but simply people who enjoy the flavor and succulence of other people."

"I do admit," declared Morion, "these bones of mine probably bear many delicious and tasty cutlets."

All in attendance waited, expecting Morion to beg for his life or give some such appeal, but Morion had come to the end of his announcement.

Orsteen looked to Morion as if he'd lost his mind. "Morion's not only delusional, he's an idiot. We're from a polluted land of many toxins. Our bodies have become tainted, and are probably poisonous. I doubt we'll be appetizing."

The Master with the tallest of top hats disregarded Orsteen's statement. "I commend your companion's enthusiasm. It's not often our food appreciates its situation. I promise that when the time comes, you'll be prepared by Palook with the utmost care and expertise. Then, unlike your friend believes..." He gestured to me. "...you won't be devoured in snaps and gulps as if we were animals. Rather, you'll be relished and savored. Be proud of what you'll become."

I scoffed. "If we're privileged to be your meal, then why do you conceal our faces with these hoods?" I pointed to the main course. "Even after your victims are prepared and cooked, they still wear hoods over their heads. Are you afraid you'll relate to them on some personal level, or do you not wish the faces of your food to haunt your dreams?"

Just then, a girl in a fashionable gown strolled into the room.

One of the Masters tipped his hat in greeting. "You're late, Felia. The main course grows cold. We were just being entertained by the food, which has been sharing its insights in regard to our psyches."

Taking her seat, she loaded her plate with a large scoop of the stuffing that bloated the main course's chest cavity. She then cut a generous portion of thigh meat.

She was the same girl who had lured us into this dreadful situation. Despite her charming appearance, she was no less a monster than the Masters of the house.

I looked at them scornfully. "Am I wrong to assume that this angel-eyed devil was once on your menu? Why wasn't *she* allowed the privileged fate you now give us? Was she so innocent in appearance that, out of guilt, you allowed her to live? In my opinion, she's suffered a fate far worse than digestion."

One of the Masters signaled Palook, who electrified my cage.

The meal continued, with the four cannibals eating slowly upon the victim who'd lost his life for the epicurean psychosis of three madmen and a child.

Over their meal, the Masters spoke of past hunts and plotted future hunts using new and innovative luring and trapping techniques. At one point, they paused and gathered around us, examining and prodding, discussing the best ways to prepare and garnish us.

At the end of the meal, the four diners sat in silence, apparently intoxicated by their eating binge. A yellow tinge of oil stained the perimeters of their mouths and their bellies protruded so much that they appeared pregnant.

Palook took the leftovers of the main course to the kitchen. I could see him through the open door as he removed the metallic-mesh hood and indulged on the head meat. It made me sick.

As the days passed, we grew tired and depressed as our bodies grew fatter from the rich butterbean porridge. To diminish our spirits further, we were forced to shit and piss into buckets attached to the bottoms of our cages. It was a level of humiliation I'd never felt before.

When the Masters of the house were not out hunting, they busied themselves by competing at a game called Demons of the Majestic Onslaught. I found it similar to chess. Its board was a large hexagon composed of many smaller hexagons. The two opponents each commanded a set of twenty figurines, all of unique character and power.

With nothing else to do, I observed the game matches, eventually learning the rules and strategies. It proved to be my only source of entertainment.

At night, when the household was at rest, we made our best efforts to escape. We tried to pick the locks of our cages, but were unsuccessful.

I pled for help from the quartet of musicians who slept in their chairs: "I know you can't see, but you can hear me. If you help us, we'll lead you away from this awful place." They didn't respond. "Don't my offers interest you? There's more to this life than music and butterbeans!"

"They're zombies," said Morion. "Those implants at their temples must be control devices."

"I think I'm getting through." I continued coaxing the musicians. "There's a fork on the floor. Bring it to me and I'll pick our locks. In no time, you'll be playing venues throughout this world and the next. Your music is too profound to be wasted on the ears of murderous monsters."

Eventually, I gave up for the night. I leaned back and gazed up through the skylight. I noticed the celestial phenomenon we'd been warned about during our travels along the deuterium pipeline.

"Did you see that, Orsteen?"

"See what? I've been busy unraveling the fabric of my shirt, which I plan to use as a grapple to capture the fork on the floor."

"The celestial phenomenon," I said. "The one we were warned about. I believe it came alive for a moment."

"You've become stir crazy," said Orsteen. "The fellow who warned us about it was only making excuses to lure us within his shack."

I rubbed my eyes. "I swear it pulsed, becoming twice as bright. Then, like an amoeba, it consumed a cluster of stars. Doesn't it look bigger? Morion, what of you? Did you see it?"

Morion responded with snores as he slept soundly.

I shook my head in wonder. "Maybe I'm having a reaction to the butterbeans. I do feel strange. Goodnight, Orsteen."

The next day, the Masters of the house trotted into the dining room. "We bring the three of you excellent news. You'll soon be free."

"You've at last realized your evil ways?" said Orsteen.

"You embrace my statement too liberally. You'll be free from your cages, not from our bellies. We were successful in our morning hunt, giving us a surplus of food. Thus, the three of you will be prepared tomorrow morning."

Morion grabbed the bars of his cage and pulled back and forth, swinging the cage haphazardly about. "I curse you wretched souls with all the power of my spirit! There's a shit-load of karma to be dealt upon you in the next life!"

One of the Masters lifted a decorative walking cane and poked Morion's stomach through the bars. "You're a spicy one, aren't you? I'll have Palook prepare you accordingly."

Morion shrank back to avoid the poking and made no reply.

The Masters left the room.

Morion looked to me. "Why do you stare forth, as if entranced? You're supposedly the smart one. It's about time you devise our escape. Theron! Do you hear me?"

"I... am..." I heard Morion's statement but couldn't reply. My head felt heavy and my brain burned.

"What's the matter?" asked Orsteen.

"He's broken under these conditions," said Morion.

"Don't fret, Theron." Orsteen pointed downward. "Palook hasn't discovered the fork on the floor, and I've nearly completed my grapple of fabric."

My hearing diminished and Orsteen's words became muted. I struggled to overcome the strange paralysis. *It's the evil incubating inside me. It's the Fume taking control?*

The walls around me seemed to heave with each breath I took. The bars of my cage wiggled and bowed. Out of nowhere, another cage appeared next to mine. Allienora was in it, screaming and flailing. I wanted to save her, but I couldn't move.

It isn't real, I thought. *She isn't there. I'm losing my mind.*

It was midday when two of the Masters came to the dining room for a game of Demons of the Majestic Onslaught. I still couldn't move or speak. One of the Masters placed a key on the dining table. It was the key to our cages. It was our freedom. I focused on it.

I can feel it in my mind. The cold metal. Its meager weight.

Incredibly, the key moved in my direction. It slid slowly across the table and fell to the floor.

The Master of the house quickly responded by snatching it up. He looked suspiciously around, attempting to locate the ghostly culprit who had knocked it to the floor.

I emerged from my stupor, gaining full control of my faculties. *Was I dreaming? Did I really force the key from the table with some tendril of thought?*

I grunted softly to gain Orsteen's attention, making certain the Masters didn't hear.

"You've at last snapped out of it," whispered Orsteen. "I thought we lost you."

"It's begun."

"What's begun?"

Before responding, I thought about my condition. I moved my hand in front of my face. *It moves by my will alone. This power is merely a side effect of the Fume's energy in my mind. My thoughts are still my own. I shouldn't tell them about my new ability.*

"Never mind," I said.

When no one was looking, I gave my full attention to the fork on the floor and attempted to summon the power to lift it off the ground and into my hands. The fork responded to my beckoning by moving only ten centimeters across the floor. I was filled with disappointment as I realized the weakness of my new telekinetic ability. Then it came to me.

"I have a plan to escape, Orsteen. You must do as I say, when I say."

"Without question," said Orsteen.

I indicated a stray butterbean at the base of Orsteen's cage. "When I signal you, throw that butterbean toward the lead musician in the quartet. Aim for his head." I turned to Morion. "You do the same."

Morion searched his cage frantically. "I have no butterbeans! I've eaten them all!"

Orsteen rolled his eyes and then handed Morion a butterbean through the bars of his cage. "Theron, we wait for your signal."

I watched as the Masters studied their game. I then signaled Orsteen and Morion. The butterbeans went flying. The lead musician, who was absorbed in the heavy notes of a complicated melody, became startled by the assault of butterbeans, causing his fingers to trip over the strings of his instrument, making a mess of the music.

The Masters turned to the musicians in outrage. "What's this dissonance that rattles our ears? If this is a prelude to your enfeeblement, you'll all be playing your music to the flames of the oven."

While the Masters' attention was drawn away from the game, I summoned the power to move a single figurine on the game-board, and then waited.

Once the musicians continued with their music, the Masters returned to their game, at which time one of them released a hideous cry.

"Cheater! We've played this game for decades. How many times have you beaten me by the sleight of your hand?"

"I'm speechless," said the other Master, whose figurine had been moved to his advantage. "I can't explain it."

"Come now, your stupefied reaction won't pardon you! It only enhances your guilt!"

The accused Master sat puzzled, wringing his hands. "Uh... well... we'll start again and disregard this astonishing and unintentional event. It's possible an earthquake shifted the piece—or maybe it was the collision of an insect."

"I've detected neither earthquake nor insect!" The deceived Master swept his forearm across the many figurines, scattering them across the table. "I'm done here!" he shouted, and then stormed from the room.

I turned to the remaining Master, who stared at the toppled figurines.

"Your thoughts spin in disarray for no reason," I said. "You've fallen victim to a clever trick. May I continue?"

The Master's eyes widened. "Speak on. I'm listening."

"First, you were—and I'm sure you'll agree—at an advantage before the piece was moved."

"Correct. I was at the top of my game."

"And then, when the musicians fumbled, your own figurine was moved. But why would you cheat? You had the advantage."

"You've hit the nail on the head. I certainly wouldn't have. Please, continue."

"Isn't it obvious?" I said. "Your companion himself moved the figurine. He was so confident of his own defeat that he framed and accused you of cheating before the game's conclusion. Thus, the game was voided and he was able to escape defeat."

"A diabolical scheme! I may have never known!"

I lowered my voice to intensify the weight of my words. "I've overheard their conversations when you're not around. They talk as if you're gullible and stupid."

"I'm greatly disturbed and infuriated!"

"But you're still a superior player. Otherwise they wouldn't need to cheat."

"At least I'm reassured on this point." The Master looked at the game-board with dreary eyes. "Who will I play now? I trust no one. Shall I sit here and twiddle my thumbs for amusement?"

"May I suggest myself as your opponent? Since I'm unable to reach the game-board, you may be assured of my inability to cheat. However, you'll have to move my figurines for me."

The Master laughed. "You know nothing of this game. Your skills and intelligence are insufficient to rival my own."

"I admit as much, and for this reason, I propose a modification to the game. Each time you capture one of my figurines, you'll be required to consume three stout chugs of that fine yellow wine. As you, the more skilled player, capture more and more of my figurines, you'll in turn become more and more drunk. Naturally, your abilities will decline and an equilibrium of skill will be reached between us."

"An interesting, if unusual, challenge. I accept!"

As I expected, the game progressed at an accelerated pace. The Master of the house captured my figurines skillfully, while I only captured a few of his. By the time the Master had captured half of my figurines, he had consumed an entire flagon of wine and was totally drunk.

On schedule, Palook entered the dining room with three bowls of butterbean porridge.

"Halt," I cried, stopping Palook in his tracks before he could dispense the porridge. "Your Master is furious. Can't you see his goblet's empty?"

"This is exactly so," slurred the Master. "Another flagon is required on this instant."

Before Palook moved to the cages, I again spoke: "It would be inappropriate to serve the lowly captives their gruel before you serve your Master his wine. I recommend you place those bowls on the table."

"Damn right!" said the Master with drunken anger. "I am, as my title indicates, the *Master* of the house, and should be treated as such!"

Palook's eyes blazed in my direction. He then did as I suggested and placed the three bowls on the table before heading to the kitchen.

I was confident of my plan, since the bowls of porridge sat on the table directly beside the key to our cages. While the Master was busy assessing the game-board through his swollen eyelids, I focused all my mental energy on the key. It moved by my will, slowly but surely, up the side of a bowl, over the rim, and into the thick porridge. The Master, in his current state, was none the wiser.

Palook returned with a fresh flagon of wine and then dispensed the bowls of porridge. When no one was looking, I rooted my finger through the porridge and retrieved the key.

The game concluded with the Master being not only the victor, but too drunk to realize the key was missing. He propped himself up from his chair and presented me with a horse-toothed grin.

"When you put forth this challenge, I neglected to divulge that I hold my wine exceptionally well. Your loss was inevitable." The Master paused as a belch escaped his lips. "My victory will make each bite of you, at tomorrow's feast, even more enjoyable. Pleasant dreams."

When all in the household were fast asleep, I made use of the key, opening our cages and releasing the metal rings that secured the hoods over our heads. Orsteen removed his hood and I noticed his strange gaze.

"What's wrong, Orsteen?"

"The way you acquired that key wasn't in accordance with the natural laws of the universe. I find myself reminded of the promise I made to intervene if I found the Fume's influence overcoming you."

"You're overreacting. I'm in control, Orsteen. We'll discuss the matter later. Come, let's leave before the Masters wake up."

"I agree," said Morion, moving with fast footsteps to the front door.

Orsteen and I followed behind. As Morion prepared to open the front door, I stopped him and looked to a nearby staircase. "Wait a minute, Morion. We're not done here."

"What are you talking about?" asked Morion.

"We can't allow these cannibals to continue."

"You're right," said Orsteen. "I believe the karma Morion had warned them about has found its way to them—through us."

"You've taken my words too seriously," said Morion. "I was only venting my anger at the time. It would be stupid to risk further endangerment. The door is here; we need but step to the other side and we're free and clear from this nightmare."

"Let's first find our bags," said Orsteen. "We'll need our weapons."

On an impulse, I reached into my pocket. I was missing more than my bag. "Cassandra's necklace! How could I forget? We can't go anywhere without my necklace."

"Calm down," said Orsteen. "We'll find it."

We at last located our bags in the cellar among a collection of clothes, weapons, wallets, and other valuables acquired by the Masters over the years.

Where is it? I panicked. *Where's my necklace? I can't lose it. It's all I have.*

"Here," called Orsteen, holding open the lid of a metal chest.

I sighed in relief when I saw the cobalt-blue gleam of the infinity spiral pendant on top a pile of old coins and jewelry.

"Thank you, Orsteen. I've lost too much already." I tucked the necklace into my pocket.

Morion retrieved a purse of coins from the chest. "Excellent, we'll need some native money for food and lodging when we reach the port city Neubius. Can we leave now, or do you still want to force the hand of karma on the Masters?"

"Orsteen and I won't be long," I said. "Take this key and release the other captives. I assume they're being held in the shed at the back of the house." I paused. "One more thing, Morion. Give me your clothes."

Palook awoke in the predawn hours to see to the preparation of the evening feast. He fired the ovens and made a basting agent of pungent oils and choice spices. After all was in order, he went to the dining room to fetch the three main courses. In his attempts to remove the captives from their cages, he found them uncooperative and belligerent, flailing their arms while producing ugly, unintelligible sounds.

"Cooperate!" said Palook, as he electrified the cages in warning.

Still they struggled, grabbing at the bars and pulling on their hoods. Retrieving a club of considerable girth, Palook bashed each captive repeatedly on the head to tame their resistance.

Palook transferred the unconscious captives to oversized platters and relieved them of their innards, replacing them with a stuffing of sweet fruits and nuts. Half the day passed as the three captives cooked, during which time Palook basted them rigorously.

When dinnertime came, Palook pounded four times on a bell that sounded throughout the household.

Felia was first to arrive in the dining hall. "It smells remarkable, Palook."

"Where are Masters?" asked Palook, rolling out the first course of the anticipated three-course meal.

"How should I know?" replied Felia. "I've been frolicking along the pipeline most of the day, seducing travelers that walked by." Her gaze fell upon the first course as Palook removed the white cloth that concealed it. "Palook, this specimen you've prepared seems familiar. It even wears a ring similar to—" Felia stammered. "You senseless brute, what have you done? You've cooked the Master!"

Seeking his own verification, Palook removed the hoods that concealed the faces of all three courses. "No mistake. I cook Masters. How I know? They wore clothes of captives." With a knife, Palook wedged open a Master's mouth and looked within. "And tongue cut out." After a few silent moments, Palook presented Felia with a bottle of wine. "Red wine circa '29 from special reserves?"

"I have no doubt the Masters themselves would've selected such a luxurious wine to complement their own robust flavors." Felia proceeded to sample a spoonful of fruit and nut stuffing that filled the chest cavity. It had been thoroughly steamed and basted in the blood, fluids, and juices of her Master. She spoke with her mouth full: "Succulence."

13

SPACEPORT

After a long night's journey along the deuterium pipeline, we arrived at the outskirts of the port city Neubius. I moved forward with a slow gait. My bag hung heavy on my back. I felt fat and tired from the weeklong fattening regimen of butterbeans.

The sun rose and a gentle morning light warmed us. We came upon a cluster of shacks that seemed on the verge of toppling to the ground. From the sky a silver air-car appeared. Its pristine condition was at odds with the surrounding slums.

The vehicle swerved in our direction. As it approached, I noticed a colorful emblem painted on its side—a spaceship overlapping a blue and green planet.

The vehicle stopped beside us and a large head popped out a window. "You lost? With those fine clothes, someone might think you're from the Overworld." He pointed his thumb up to the sky at the massive space station. "There are many criminals in these parts. They might take you for ransom, or at least steal your shoes and harvest your organs."

I pulled my Intersplit gun from my belt. "We're already aware of the dangers. What's your interest in us? Speak fast!"

"I'm a courtesy taxi provided by the spaceport for off-worlders. Since I've just finished a fare and my taxi's vacant, I'd be willing to take you away from this unpleasant area—for a small fee, of course."

That won't be a problem," said Morion, removing a small collection of silver coins from his new coin purse. "Will this be sufficient?"

The taxi driver seemed to restrain a grin that pushed up at the corners of his mouth. "By coincidence, you've removed the exact price of the fare. Hop in."

We entered the taxi.

"Where are you headed?"

"We're in search of a man named Fanbert Manderwall," I said.

"Unfortunately, the name isn't familiar."

"How does one go about finding a stranger in these parts?"

The driver tapped two fingers on his chin. "The only modern infrastructure in the city is the spaceport. They keep records of all who pass in and out of its gates, though it's unlikely you'll be given access to such information."

"We'll get the information one way or another," said Orsteen.

"I wouldn't trespass," said the driver. "The spaceport is guarded by many armed men eager for target practice."

"Take us to a hotel near the spaceport," I said.

"I assume one of high quality," said the driver.

"You assume correctly," replied Morion promptly. "We want a hotel with the softest beds and finest food."

As the taxi neared the spaceport, the condition of the city improved with the appearance of many street-side bistros, pubs, hotels, and storefronts.

"Do you get many tourists?" I asked.

"Very few tourists," said the driver. "Most of the ships arriving from off-world are delivering and receiving cargo. The businesses around the spaceport cater mainly to the spacemen who wish to find a break from the long boredom of space travel." The taxi driver motioned to a strip of kiosks at the side of the road. "It would be wise to ignore the solicitations of street peddlers. Their goods are both costly and cheaply made. They'll rob you blind if you let them. I recommend you apply the same philosophy to prostitutes, who'll squeeze your genitals only to keep you distracted as they reach for your purse."

"Your advice is appreciated," said Orsteen. "However, we're not here for trinkets or pleasure."

"As you say." The driver brought the taxi to a halt. "We've arrived at your destination."

As I opened the door, I noticed a badge clipped to the driver's shirt. "Are documents required to book transport off-world?"

"Only a certified planetary identification card."

"How does one obtain such identification?"

"You must apply at the registrar's office, where you must show various personal information, including birthplace, current residence, age, and business. You must then wait until a spaceport agent can verify your information."

"And if one doesn't wish to wait for such verification?"

The driver pursed his lips. "Counterfeiting identification cards is a deed tangled in risk. The spaceport authorities punish severely for such acts."

"You're right," I said. "Forgive me. I spoke merely on a whim. Good day."

The driver extended a greasy finger. "You give up too quickly. I was only attempting to express that such a service isn't cheap. It'll cost your friend half his purse for three identification cards."

"Only *one* is needed, for which we're willing to pay a quarter of his purse."

"A done deal," said the driver, extending his hand for payment.

I pushed the hand away in a thrust. "Fortunately, I've adapted your earlier advice concerning street peddlers and prostitutes to also include greedy taxi drivers. You'll be paid in full upon delivery. Additionally, I require the identification card to be issued in the name of Fanbert Manderwall."

"You strike a hard but reasonable bargain. I'll return in five hours to this exact spot."

The taxi pulled away and Morion threw up his hands. "How do you expect us to afford comfortable beds and flavorful foods when you give our money away?"

"You're right," I said, snatching the coin purse from Morion. "We can't afford such luxuries. I'll arrange the most economical room and board."

Our room was a shit-hole. Its complex stench was a layering of foul smells that told of the room's history of drunken spacemen and cheap whores. A single bed with stained sheets and clumpy pillows was apparently meant to accommodate the three of us. We took turns to rest and bathe.

Five hours had passed when I left Orsteen and Morion in the room. I stood on the street-side waiting for the taxi driver. At last he arrived and I got in the taxi.

"Were you successful?" I asked.

"Yes." The driver handed me the identification card.

I inspected it carefully, acting as though I had experience with such documents and could interpret the alien writing. "I'd like to see your own identification card for comparison."

The driver sighed. "There. Are you satisfied?"

"It looks good." I gave him the agreed-upon sum. "Here are a few more coins. Take me to the spaceport."

"As you wish."

"One more thing," I said. "What's the closest inhabited planet to Fallgate?"

"That would be the world Illpheria."

We arrived at the spaceport and the driver let me off at the front gate. Over a hundred spaceships sat within the fenced perimeter. I watched as ships were loaded with cargo. The shipments going off-world appeared to be raw materials such as lumber and precious ores. To a lesser extent were exotic animals, edible vegetation, and a variety of simple goods probably made cheaply on Fallgate. The main resource was obviously the deuterium being piped in. Large tanker ships were being filled directly from the pipeline.

I approached the gates, where two guards held weapons at the ready. "I'm here to book passage off-world."

"Prepare to be searched!"

I remained calm as one of the guards confiscated the Intersplit gun at my belt. "We'll return your weapon when you leave."

"Thank you." I nodded and made my way to a facility at the side of the shipyard. There I was put to a second search.

"What's your business?" asked the guard.

"To book passage off-world."

"Up the stairs, ten doors to the right."

There, I found a bald man with a great hunchback sitting behind a desk. Holo-projectors displayed an overhead map of planetary systems. The man was apparently plotting cargo routes between the inhabited worlds of the Crux Galaxy.

"Pardon me," I said.

The man looked at me through the hologram with a pinched-faced expression, as though he sucked on a bitter pill.

"I'm clerk Bodel. How may I help you?"

"I wish to book passage to the world Illpheria."

"One moment, please." Clerk Bodel studied a view-screen embedded in the surface of his desk. "You're in luck. The cargo ship *Arobourou* departs tomorrow morning. The *Arobourou* has set their cost for passage at eleven coins, and the spaceports fee for booking convenience is an additional eleven coins. This brings your total to twenty-two coins. May I see your certified identification card?"

I handed it over. "I've recently changed residence. Your files may not be accurate. What residence of mine do you have on record?"

Clerk Bodel examined the identification card and brought up a file onto the view-screen. "Let's have a look, Mr. Fanbert Manderwall." He reviewed the information before him. "Humph..." Clerk Bodel paused momentarily and then slid his hand under his desk.

A great metal claw swooped down from the ceiling and caught me in its grips.

"What the fuck!" I screamed, struggling against the cold metal fingers.

Clerk Bodel pointed to his view-screen. "Apparently, you're a walking and talking corpse."

"I assure you I'm alive and well."

"Not so! According to your spaceport file, you've been dead for over a century. Cause of death—old age."

I knew that as a Guardian, Fanbert Manderwall couldn't have died of old age. "Your records are obviously wrong."

Clerk Bodel's eyes nearly disappeared under his brow as his face pinched tighter. "Here at the spaceport, we're thorough down to every jot and tittle. To suggest otherwise is a crime in itself. I believe the truth of the matter to be such—you're a space pirate using a dead man's identification card to gain passage aboard your next conquest."

"You've missed the mark completely. I'm merely in search of the man named on that identification card."

"Congratulations. You've not only discovered his whereabouts, but you'll soon be joining him." Clerk Bodel reached for a communication box.

"Please! Maybe we can resolve this another way. My coin purse contains a large sum of money, which you may find useful."

Clerk Bodel hesitated, pulling his hand away from the communication box. "Are you suggesting I'm open to bribery? Such insults won't help your case. Your coin purse will be added to the spaceport treasury."

"And who commands the spaceport treasury? Who controls the flow of deuterium? Where does all this profit go?"

Clerk Bodel showed an expression of curiosity, as though he'd never thought to entertain such an obvious question. "To be honest, even after being cooped up in this office for half my life, I'm uncertain."

"Allow me to enlighten you," I said. "The money, goods, and resources are sucked from this planet you call home, by some greedy off-worlder who dwells deep in a mansion, getting fat from the hard work of you, your family, your friends, and your neighbors. He pampers himself with sweet meats, bitter cheeses, and robust liqueurs, while you eat stale bread and drink brown water."

"You've painted a picture of many unpleasant colors."

I shook my head. "It's unfair that your hard work makes someone else a rich man. Don't think of my money as a bribe, but as due payment for your dedication to the spaceport. Tonight *you* can be washing down mouthfuls of sweet meats and bitter cheeses with a robust liqueur."

"You make a compelling point." Clerk Bodel paced back and forth for a moment. "Since you're not a space pirate, I see no danger in letting you go quietly. However, I don't want to see you at the spaceport again. Understood?"

"Absolutely!"

Clerk Bodel disengaged the great metal hand, which retracted back to the ceiling to again look like a chandelier. "I'll now graciously accept your coin purse."

"As promised." I tossed it in his direction.

Clerk Bodel's pinched-face momentarily relaxed into a smile.

I started to leave but stopped short. "Would it be inappropriate to ask about the children of Fanbert Manderwall?"

Clerk Bodel, more cooperative with the coin purse weighing down his belt, went to his view-screen. "He's survived by a grandson named Adel Manderwall, who resides in a loft above the Drunk Bird Saloon."

With the sun on its downward journey and a cool breeze in the air, I decided to walk back to the hotel. On the way, my thoughts echoed with questions.

What am I becoming? Am I even the same person?

Fear and uncertainty played upon my mind. The weak telekinetic power I had developed indicated the Fume's energies were stirring within me. The one thing that seemed clear was that Nara-Narayana, if as wise and powerful as told, might be the only person able to help me.

I stopped short on the road and was compelled to look to the sky. I was confronted by that strange celestial phenomenon I'd observed earlier. Even with the light of the sun veiling the heavens, it still managed to be seen as a faint haze.

I can feel it, I thought. *A deep drumming within me... but so far away. Why does it beckon me?*

I felt like a wild beast with the urge to howl at the moon. I tried to look away, but was unable. I slipped into a powerful trance and stood frozen.

When I finally snapped out of it, I found myself alone in the dark. The sun had set and the celestial phenomenon loomed above me. It was larger than I remembered from previous nights.

Aggravated by the loss of time, I moved quickly back to the hotel.

I found Orsteen and Morion asleep. "Wake up! It's time to leave."

Morion's eyes opened. "You've interrupted the flow of a pleasant dream. Now I'll never discover its end."

"We were worried," said Orsteen. "You've been gone a long time."

"I think I've found Fanbert Manderwall."

Morion splashed his face with sink water. "Can't we rest longer?"

"Do what you want," I said. "I leave now with the possibility of never returning. Orsteen, are you coming?"

"What's wrong with you, Theron?" said Orsteen.

"Nothing," I said defensively. "What do you mean?"

"There's a strange air about you."

He knows, I thought. *He can sense the change within me. I should tell him. He's my friend.*

"Well?" asked Orsteen.

"I'm tired, weak, and worried about Allienora."

"You know what I'm talking about," said Orsteen. "The Fume."

"I'm still in command of my faculties. I promise, my friend. Shall we go?"

Orsteen stood silent for a moment and then nodded. "Lead the way and I'll follow."

I glanced to Morion. "Are you coming?"

Morion groaned. "I'm right behind you."

From the hotel's front desk, we got directions to the Drunk Bird Saloon, which took us three blocks down the main strip.

"This is the place," I said. "The grandson of Fanbert Manderwall is said to live in the loft above."

Orsteen poked his head into a dim alleyway at the side of the establishment. "There's a staircase which may very well lead us to our man."

We climbed the staircase and knocked on the door. After no answer, Orsteen thrust his shoulder at the door and the bolt broke free.

We entered cautiously, finding only a small cot, a chair, a toilet, and a hotplate.

"The place is extremely clean," said Orsteen, "but the air is stale, as if no one's lived here for some time."

I threw up my hands in frustration. "This seems to be the way our luck's running."

"All isn't lost," said Morion. "We're only steps from the Drunk Bird Saloon. We could use a drink and a bite."

"You're right," I said. "We can also ask about the loft."

The Drunk Bird Saloon was filled with a colorful lot of spacemen from many different planets in the Crux Galaxy. They flushed their organs with the local rotgut, and entertained each other with the tales of their travels, grandly exaggerated.

I led the way to a magnificent wooden bar, where we awaited the notice of a serving girl, who tolerated the drunken ramblings of a petite man.

"I used to be an important man," the drunk informed the serving girl, who returned an empty gaze. "However, the times change and the progress of the universe can't be stopped. Now, I sit here obsolete and unemployed. Some may soon be calling me a relic or even a timeworm, and maybe they're right, maybe I've become nothing more than a cinder of the past. It's unfortunate my memories can only be appreciated by myself."

The serving girl at last saw us and moved away from the petite man, who continued talking to himself.

"What's your pleasure?" she said.

I looked to the mugs of the surrounding patrons. "We'll have three of your house drinks, and a word with the owner."

"I can help you with the drinks, but as for the owner of the Drunk Bird, he's away on an errand."

"Then maybe *you* can help us. We're seeking the tenant who lives upstairs."

"Sorry, but I've only worked here a few days. The previous serving girl may have been a greater help. They say she vanished one late night on her way home. A common occurrence when young girls work around so many drunk and lusty-eyed spacemen. I, however, have devised a method for dealing with such perverts." She pulled a blade from her pocket. "This fillet knife will quickly relieve any man of such urges."

My jaw dropped. "We'll take our drinks now."

The petite man turned to me and scooted a stool closer. He spoke loudly, as if to ensure he was the center of attention. "You and your friends are mismatched with the rest of these space bumpkins!" His comment caught the attention of a group of spacemen whose eyes flared in his direction. "In fact, I've never seen your kind before, and I've traveled far and wide, to each and every inhabited planet in the Crux Galaxy!"

Before I could respond, one of the nearby spacemen approached. At his sides hung two enormous arms like restrained dogs.

"I've never heard such large words from such a pathetic wisp!" announced the spaceman. "Your claims of travel are absurd. You insult the real adventurers who surround you! It would take a lifetime to visit every world in the Crux Galaxy. You're a gas bladder venting a vile bilge!"

The petite man tilted his mug to a vertical position, and then slammed it to the bar. He inspected the monstrous spaceman with apparent difficulty, as his vision must have been blurred from intoxication. "Let me reassure you, big fellow." He nudged a finger into the spaceman's chest. "I've even been to your planet, and can confirm that the females of your race are the most ugly in all the Crux Galaxy. Their stench, if I were to guess, is from the practice of bathing in fish guts."

The spaceman's face flushed and his hands trembled. He swung his fists at the petite man, but with each swing, the petite man successfully, but clumsily, moved aside at the last moment.

"Is this your best?" taunted the petite man, who just then was struck by an unexpected punch to the back of his head by one of the spaceman's companions. He hunched forward with hands on knees, stunned by the impact.

The spaceman stood above him preparing to deliver one final blow to the back of his head. "Your words have killed you, small fellow." He dropped his fist with full force.

A wail of pain was released, not from the petite man, but from the spaceman, whose fist shattered upon the petite man's head.

Everyone in the Drunk Bird Saloon was witness to the petite man and the armor that had blinked into existence around him. The petite man stood upright and presented the spaceman with the single fiery eye of a Guardian.

The spaceman and his companions fled the saloon.

I turned to Orsteen and Morion. "I think we've found Fanbert Manderwall."

Fanbert disengaged his armor, sending it back to its unseen realm, and then, as if nothing had happened, returned to his position at the bar. He signaled the serving girl. "I'll have another drink, darling."

She bowed nervously and fetched his flavor.

I joined him. "Fanbert Manderwall?"

Fanbert raised a crooked eyebrow of puzzlement. "You speak of a past life. I now go by the name Adel Manderwall. Although, I suppose that name, too, describes a past life. You see, I now dance to a new music. One that's carefree, unrestrained, and possibly reckless."

"I didn't expect you to be so... coarse."

"And who are you to pass judgment on me?"

"You're a Guardian, aren't you?" I said.

Fanbert's eyes became sober as he looked suspiciously at us. "You yourselves aren't Guardians." He touched a finger to his temple. "I would detect the distortion of space around you if you commanded a dimensional transporter carapace and the Guardian armor. Who are you and why are you looking for me?"

Orsteen looked harshly to Fanbert. "I'm disturbed that you, a Guardian, sit drunk in a bar and neglect your duties as a protector of the Brahman Sprawl. Don't you know what's happening beyond these walls?"

"Apparently you know something I don't. As far as I know, the threat of paradox has passed and the Brahman Sprawl no longer requires my services."

I ordered a second drink. "I assume you're aware of the Fume, and his presence in the Seven Galaxies."

"I haven't drunk myself stupid yet."

"Then let me be the first to inform you that the Obelisks have failed to push the Fume out of our universe. Furthermore, the Fume has sent an army of beasts onto the Guardian Spheres. The Guardian Army is in ruin."

"Impossible!" cried Fanbert. "I would've been called into action if such were the case." Again, Fanbert tapped at his head. "I'm directly linked to the trans-dimensional Guardian network."

"The Fume's beasts have disabled many systems on the Guardian Spheres, including communications."

Fanbert stood, his poise altered as if infused with renewed purpose. "If you're telling the truth, I must leave at once to battle these beastly forces."

"They're too dangerous," said Orsteen. "You wouldn't survive long."

Fanbert became oddly silent, staring into space.

"Are you all right?" I asked.

"I'm attempting communication with the Guardian network." A pause. "Something's wrong. I can't make contact with anyone. Even if the Guardian Spheres in the seven galaxies were overtaken, I should still be able to contact other Guardians. There are communication nodes scattered throughout the Brahman Sprawl. The three of you will wait here while I find answers."

"No!" I said emphatically. "We can't risk you jaunting off to another galaxy and never returning. We're depending on you to lead us to Nara-Narayana."

"Nara-Narayana?" Fanbert looked to me skeptically, as if my statement was insane. "You ask the impossible. Nara-Narayana is a demigod, beyond the reach of mere mortals. No one knows her location. This is the reason she can't be corrupted or compromised, and this is why she's able to bring order and control to the Brahman Sprawl."

Morion tapped an inquisitive finger on the bar. "And how can she rule so effectively while being so detached?"

"It's in her power to see all that's happening in the Brahman Sprawl. And if she's compelled to give orders to a single Guardian, she'll whisper in their ear like a ghost. Her wisdom is profound, and with it, she's guided us for over twenty-one million years without paradox."

"And it's this wisdom we require," I said. "I've been told to tell you that we seek the forgotten world where the Prophets sleep, and that their awakening is overdue. Does this mean anything to you?"

"It means you've been in contact with one of only two people still alive who know of the Prophets." Fanbert leaned forward eagerly. "JarNay survived the attack?"

I hesitated. "She'll be fine."

"Although JarNay's a truehearted woman, I can't allow her judgment to rule my actions. To help you locate Nara-Narayana would be against one of the most important laws of the Guardian Army."

"Things have changed," I said. "The Fume's manipulations in the seven galaxies—and, more specifically, on Earth—were only the beginning of a plot so grand in scope that it's almost beyond comprehension."

"You have my attention," said Fanbert. "Continue."

"The temporal displacement of the Brahman Station wasn't an accident, but a part of the Fume's plans. Somehow he has anticipated the development and evolution of the Brahman Sprawl and all the people within it. The Fume told me the Brahman Sprawl and all its inhabitants are a critical part of his plan."

Fanbert was at the edge of his seat. "Which is?"

"He claims his manipulations will cause our universe to evolve into something like himself, and his own universe, at which point he'll be able to absorb the energies of our universe, so to become a more powerful entity."

"Evolve into something like him? What do you mean?"

"He claims our universe is evolving into a god."

"A god?" said Fanbert.

I nodded. "An entity whose constitution will be formed from all the matter and energy of the universe."

"By what process?" asked Fanbert with disbelief.

"I, too, asked this question, but was left to wonder. However, when he spoke of this evolution, it was as if he spoke of a metaphysical process by which the souls of the people in the Brahman Sprawl would be assimilated and utilized to some extent. He said the soul is the precursor to godliness."

Fanbert's eyes sparkled with wonder. "A precursor to godliness? Astonishing."

"The whole process seems quite complex," I said, taking a chug from my mug. "Such a concept of god being born from humankind turns all religions on their heads. The assumption has always been that man was born of god."

"What of the Fume?" said Fanbert. "Technically, couldn't he be considered our god?"

"A god maybe... *our* god, no. The Fume didn't create the energy of this universe, or even the first life on Earth. He arrived after the fact, and manipulated what was already there."

"So, if gods are born from universes, then what created the universe to begin with?"

I looked ponderously at the contents of my mug and then polished it off. "The basic energy of the universe has always existed. Isn't it more logical to believe this, rather than to believe an all-knowing god has always existed? Where did he gain his knowledge? How could such knowledge have always existed? It's a paradox. Gods, too, must have beginnings."

"It's an inspiring concept that humankind is the beginning of a god."

"It is," I said. "But that doesn't mean the birth of this god should be allowed to occur. How will the universe be better? I'm comfortable with the universe and the state of humankind, as it is. If each of us has a soul, then each of us is divine. There's no need for a god."

"I tend to agree," said Fanbert. "Change is unnecessary. The human condition is a magnificent thing that need not be lost. What's more, if the creation of this god does occur, it's apparently the plan of the Fume to destroy it and then absorb its energies... in effect our energies."

"And this is why we must find Nara-Narayana."

"We need not actually find Nara-Narayana to give her this message. I'll relay the message to her by certain channels of communication."

"No!" I blurted.

Fanbert's eyes widened. "What?"

"You said you were unable to make contact with anyone."

"This is true, but I'll find a way."

I rose to my feet. "May I speak with you in private, Fanbert?"

"Be quick."

Orsteen and Morion looked at me suspiciously. I ignored their expressions and led Fanbert to a table hidden in a corner at the other end of the bar.

I must be careful with my words, I thought. *How can I explain this? He can't lose trust in me.*

I eased into my seat. "There are other revelations that only I can deliver to Nara-Narayana."

"Which are?"

I scratched at the table nervously. "I can't tell you."

"You'd better tell me something, stranger, or I'm off."

With truth I'll find trust, I thought.

"I believe I hold the key to the Fume's plans." I drilled my index finger into the side of my head. "Long ago, he instilled in me a part of his essence, or exotic energy, or whatever his constitution, and now it grows in my brain like a cancer. If I deliver myself to Nara-Narayana, she may have the power to extract this spark of evil from my brain. Maybe it'll help her learn the mechanics behind the Fume's plot, so to stop him."

Fanbert drew back in his seat as if I had become the villain. "This is troubling, Mr. Mobius. You admit that you've been corrupted by the Fume, and are possibly an instrument in his plans to absorb the energies of our universe." Fanbert's eyes widened. "No, no, no—I can't allow this. I won't help you. I won't lead you to Nara-Narayana. In fact, I'm compelled to kill you on the instant."

"Wait!" I called. A pressure ran through my head as I strained to find a solution to this fragile moment.

"Speak fast!"

"Your eye," I said.

"What?"

"There's something in your eye. A strange glimmer."

Fanbert ran a finger along his bottom eyelid. "There's nothing in my eye, you lunatic."

"It grows," I said, looking at the shimmering fracture that lengthened across Fanbert's eye. It opened wider, like a second eyelid. Light spilled outward. I looked inward and marveled.

A fissure into his mind.

Fanbert's teeth chattered. "I can't move. What's happening?"

"I don't know," I said. I felt the path before me. I focused harder on Fanbert's glowing eye. My perceptions slipped inward, like rainwater into the gaps. Fanbert's mind was before me. Thoughts and emotions swirled around me like objects. "I see you, Fanbert. All of you at once."

"What are you saying?" uttered Fanbert. "What are you doing?"

"What is consciousness?" I said in excitement. "What is thought? What defines you, Fanbert? What defines me? The totality of a man sits between the gaps of his skull."

"You're speaking crazy," cried Fanbert.

I grabbed Fanbert's hand and felt an energy travel between us. I felt his every atom. "Be still now, Fanbert."

"I don't understand."

"Don't worry," I whispered. "I'll make you understand."

Fanbert and I rejoined Orsteen and Morion at the bar.

Orsteen looked at us suspiciously. "Have the two of you agreed on our next course of action?"

"We have," said Fanbert. "We leave to find Nara-Narayana."

Orsteen raised his thick brow high. "What of the Guardian laws, which ban you from such action?"

"Theron has made clear the errors of my earlier thinking. In dire times a man must reevaluate laws and break them if necessary."

I felt guilty. Fanbert wasn't deserving of such deception.

I've done the unforgivable. I thought back on the sanitarium and how the Fume had violated me. *Am I becoming the monster I hate?* My heart fluttered, my chest hurt.

"Let's go!" I said.

Morion squirmed in his seat. "Before we go, I have to shit. This beer is rank." He signaled the serving girl. "Where's your bathroom?"

"The alley's as good a place as any."

"You wouldn't be pleased if a breeze found its way through the front door. Now, I demand the use of proper facilities!"

The serving girl hesitantly pointed to a door next to the kitchen.

"We'll be waiting outside," I said. "Be fast with your duties."

Morion frowned and then disappeared to the back of the bar.

Upon exiting the Drunk Bird Saloon, Fanbert looked up to the stars and sampled a generous gulp of air, as if trying to taste the beauty of the heavens. It wasn't long before his expression shifted to surprise.

"I'm not one to become easily startled, but I find myself worried by this glowing haze lighting the night sky." Fanbert pointed to the celestial cloud that couldn't go unnoticed. It now covered an area equivalent to a large moon. "What is this celestial phenomenon?"

"We don't know." I didn't look at it, for fear of another episode. "Over the past week, it's expanded four-fold, enveloping all the stars in its path."

"You underestimate the scale of this formation," said Fanbert. "Those aren't stars being enveloped."

I was perplexed by his statement. "Then what are they?"

"They're galaxies in the Brahman Sprawl."

"Impossible," I said, slack-jawed.

"I'm not mistaken!" said Fanbert. "As a Guardian, I command a quantum control plexus. I have an advanced perception of the universe, which allows me to navigate galaxies. I know the sky like I know myself." He indicated a dense band of stars. "That's the main disc of the Crux Galaxy, which we're in. And over there, where the celestial phenomenon hangs, is a gap in the stars affording us a view of the many galaxies in the Brahman Sprawl."

"If this is true, then I fear we're too late." I looked out into the universe. "This may be the beginning when all becomes one."

As we stood on the street, marveling at the sky, more than a thousand people materialized by some mode of dimensional transportation. I inspected the crowd of people that filled the street. They were in a state of frenzy, like a herd of panicked livestock.

"Like you," said Fanbert, "these people aren't from the Crux Galaxy. Their anatomy is strange to me."

From the crowd emerged four Guardians. They moved toward Fanbert and disengaged their armor.

"I'm Rygel," said the tallest of the four. "This is Tambo, Crenum, and Deakin."

"I'm Fanbert. Why have you come here and who are these people?"

Rygel gestured to the sky. "If you haven't noticed, a doomful swell of mystery consumes the Brahman Sprawl. We're fleeing its wake of destruction. I was the closest to the phenomenon when it first appeared. I tried to contact my superiors, but found the Guardian network down. It became obvious this wasn't a force to be reckoned with. After gathering as many people for rescue as possible, I fled to a galaxy farther from the phenomenon. There, I was able to locate another Guardian by the telltale of his dimensional transporter."

"And consequently he found me," said another Guardian. "The planet I was stationed on had highly advanced astronomical telescopes, which we utilized in an attempt to identify the phenomenon."

"And what did you learn?" I asked.

"We learned that it's unlike anything in the universe. It displays characteristics that defy logic. The word supernatural comes to mind. When it decides to consume a nearby galaxy, it grows outward at an impossible rate, as if the laws of the universe don't apply. If I tried to define its constitution, I'd say it's composed of an indefinable energy organized into a highly complex pattern. Even the dimensional fabric of space itself is being restructured."

I looked fearfully at the glowing celestial phenomenon. "I've heard a similar description regarding the Fume's constitution."

"The similarity is frightening," said the Guardian Rygel. "But the Fume has only ever manifested himself in the seven Galaxies, which are far from the borders of the Brahman Sprawl. It may have a likeness to the Fume's exotic energies, but this isn't one of his outpocketings into our universe. This is something different, something occurring independently within our own universe. The very fabric of our universe and all its dimensions and energies are restructuring into something fundamentally different."

Orsteen leaned close to Theron. "The universe is evolving, just as the Fume said it would."

"And without my influence," I replied, somewhat relieved.

The Guardian Crenum stepped forward. "The most inconceivable aspect of the phenomenon is that we're capable of seeing it at all. It should take millions of years for its light to reach us, given its distance. Somehow we're able to see the phenomenon growing in real time. When does light travel faster than light?"

"When the universe is unraveling," I said.

Crenum looked up at the celestial phenomenon with something like admiration. "Whatever it is, it's extraordinary."

The Guardian Rygel looked skyward as well. "Since the phenomenon continues to expand, we've had no choice but to move farther and farther away, skipping from galaxy to galaxy, locating fellow Guardians and rescuing as many people as our dimensional transporters will accommodate. Will you join us, Fanbert?"

Before Fanbert replied, I read his thoughts. He was on the verge of revealing the details of the Fume's plan and our current quest to find Nara-Narayana.

More Guardians with this knowledge will only cause further conflict with my plans.

I seized upon Fanbert's mind, so to fashion an adequate response for Fanbert to convey.

"I cannot," said Fanbert decidedly. "My companions and I head closer to the phenomenon. We're on a quest to find an ancient people, who command great insights into the universe. They may have a better understanding of the celestial phenomenon."

"You risk death moving closer to the phenomenon, for what seems a mission of little promise." Rygel looked at Fanbert doubtfully. "Who are these ancient people you speak of? I know nothing about them."

"Their existence was hidden long ago on the orders of Nara-Narayana. I apologize, but I can't tell you any more details. I suggest you continue moving farther from the celestial phenomenon, rescuing as many people as possible."

For a moment, the four Guardians stared with distrust at us until at last the Guardian Rygel spoke. "As you wish. Good luck with your quest."

With that said, the Guardians returned to the crowd. A minute later they were gone, and the streets were once again empty.

"I'm confused, Fanbert," said Orsteen. "Shouldn't we have enlisted their help and told them about the Fume's plans to evolve the universe?"

Fanbert pulled at his ear. "It's strange. I had every intention of doing just that, but was compelled by some deep impulse to do otherwise. Now that I contemplate my decision, I regret it."

What am I becoming? I thought. *A liar? A monster? Forgive me.*

I patted Fanbert on the shoulder. "We'll be fine without them. Let's continue on our quest and find the lost world where the Prophets sleep."

Fanbert nodded in agreement. "Before we leave this planet, we must stop at my bunker. We'll require a special device to awake the Prophets when we find them. Also, the three of you should change into more suitable clothing. Yours are far too fancy for where we're going."

"Here's Morion," I said.

"Very good," said Fanbert. "Gather around me and prepare to transport."

We arrived in an enormous room. Despite its size, it provided little space to move around freely, since the floor was cluttered with heaps and mounds of random effects.

"We're a hundred feet underground," said Fanbert. "I excavated this place long ago to ensure my identity would remain safe. I possess many devices beyond the understanding of the natives of this world. If found, there would be many questions concerning my origins and intentions."

Morion glanced around the room. "It looks like a dump. Why do you keep these stacks of newspapers? They appear useless, outdated, and a fire hazard."

"Those are important historical documents. When the threat of paradox lingered, it was my duty to carefully monitor and archive them." Fanbert looked harshly at Morion. "My job wasn't an easy one. I alone was responsible for all the planets in the Crux Galaxy."

Orsteen picked up a magazine with a scantily clad alien woman on the cover. "Was there ever really a possibility that anyone from this galaxy could've found Earth and caused a paradox?"

"I'm trained to underestimate no one. To do otherwise would be reckless." Fanbert gestured to me. "At any time, the next Theron Mobius could've been born into this world with a mind for dimensional mechanics."

Morion opened a glass case filled with crystal spheres. He picked one up and peered at its center, where a sparkling light was contained. "And what of these? What universe-toppling significance do they hold?"

"Be careful with that!" said Fanbert. "Those are my prisoners. Each crystal sphere holds a criminal serving their sentence in a dimensional realm—a self-contained prison. If you break them, they'd be released."

Morion tapped on the sphere. "Are you saying there are people living in these crystal spheres?"

"Very bad people," replied Fanbert, grabbing the crystal sphere and carefully returning it to the glass case.

He then led us to a table, where lay various devices of apparent complexity. Fanbert selected a device ten centimeters long, with the shape of two slender rods, fused and convoluted. "This is the device required to wake up the Prophets."

I looked at the thing. "Tell us about these Prophets. Why are they sleeping and how do they know Nara-Narayana's location?"

"About two hundred thousand years ago, the Guardian Army came across a rebel group that had discovered Nara-Narayana's location. They were determined to undermine Nara-Narayana's rule over the Brahman Sprawl by assassinating her. Since they didn't have the convenience of dimensional transportation, they built massive ships capable of traversing the long distances across the Brahman Sprawl. Before they launched their ships, myself and a hundred other Guardians arrived at their planet. We tried to establish peaceful talks so to understand their motives, but they said they wouldn't speak to the servants of the beast."

Fanbert paused in a moment of recollection. "They then tried to overtake us. Consequently, many of them were killed. Once we took hold of the situation, there was only a handful left. We decided to put them into temporal stasis until the threat of paradox had passed. Since the planet was so remote, we left them there in stasis, along with their ships."

"Why do you call them the Prophets?" asked Orsteen.

"Some of the Guardians gave them this nickname as a joke, since when we asked them why they wanted to kill Nara-Narayana, they responded: 'We've seen the future.' We assumed they were talking about Earth."

"So you never understood their motives?" I asked.

"Once we put them into stasis, we searched their ships and their encampment, but found few clues to reveal the reason they were against Nara-Narayana. However, after examining the remaining dead, we discovered they had performed strange mutilations upon their brains. We believed this might have contributed to their delusions."

"Yet, if they were delusional," I said, "how did they know Nara-Narayana's location? Are you certain they even knew?"

"Nara-Narayana seemed positive they knew, and demanded swift action. We never figured out how they knew. And after two hundred thousand years, we still don't."

Morion whistled. "Are you saying you're over two hundred thousand years old?"

"It's hard for even me to comprehend my age. Now wait! You've made me think of another item we may need." Fanbert retrieved something like a hand-cannon. "Two hundred thousand years is a long time to be in any one place, even when in temporal stasis. The Prophets have, in all likelihood, been buried by the sediments of time. This entropy gun will help us excavate them if necessary." Fanbert handed it to Orsteen and then disappeared into a maze of alcoves formed by his massive collections. He at last reappeared with a stack of clothes. "These should fit you. Their lack in style is made up by their durability and comfort."

"Did you say we're headed closer to the celestial phenomenon?" asked Morion.

"We are," said Fanbert. "To a galaxy at the near edge of the celestial phenomenon."

I grabbed a set of clothes from Fanbert. "The phenomenon has been expanding at more frequent intervals."

"It'll be dangerous. Everything could go bad in a second." Fanbert's mouth gaped wide from a yawn. "We should get some sleep. The world we're headed for has been left untended by man for many millennia. We may need our strength."

I didn't feel like sleeping. I lay motionless, contemplating my mental state and the powers I was gaining.

What is the energy of the Fume doing to me? Right now it festers inside me.

I shuddered—I thought to feel it squirm, like a parasite tunneling through my brain. I bit my lip till I tasted blood.

What of the celestial phenomenon? Why does it pull on my mind with such force? Am I connected to it? How? Why?

There were too many questions. My thoughts turned to Allienora—her round blue eyes, her soft skin, her vanilla smell.

I miss you, my darling.

At last, I slept.

FEEDBACK

We arrived on the planet where the Prophets slept and were captivated by the celestial phenomenon, which saturated nearly half the sky. It cast a brilliant glow on the landscape before us, and only from the absence of a sun did we determine it was night.

"It's both breathtaking and terrifying," said Orsteen. "Our eyes gape wide at the end of the universe. We're too small to stop this. We are but men trying to move mountains."

I experienced the scene more viscerally—I felt the power of the phenomenon pulsing in and out of my being like the ebb and flow of an ocean tide. After a while, the sensation faded to become no more than a second heartbeat. "We must do what we can, no matter how impossible it may seem, Orsteen. Even an insect can cause an avalanche."

"Speaking of mountains," said Fanbert, looking off into the distance at a snow-capped peak. "I don't remember this peak. The landscape has transformed substantially more than anticipated." Fanbert retrieved an ocular device. He held it to his eye and looked to the ground. "If I remember correctly, the Prophets should be three meters below us. Yet, I don't detect them."

I surveyed the jagged and mountainous landscape. To the right meandered a canyon cut deep by a small river. To the left and at a more immediate distance was a wall of sheer cliffs supporting a forest of peach-leaved trees.

"Could they have moved with the shifting landscape?" I suggested.

"Unlikely," said Fanbert, shaking his head with conviction. "The temporal stasis device attached to each Prophet will maintain their exact location with relation to the center of the planet. In effect, nothing can move them. They're fixed in space as well as time." He again pointed the ocular device in the direction of the supposed resting place of the Prophets. "Then again, anything's possible."

Orsteen repositioned the large entropy gun over his shoulder. "Is there another way to locate them?"

"No," said Fanbert. "I had expected to locate them by their planetary coordinates."

"We should move to higher ground," I said. "Maybe we can get a better view of our surroundings."

Everyone agreed and we moved with determined strides in the direction of the snow-capped peak. The sun started rising, warming our backs.

Morion pointed into the distance. "Just above that cliff, I saw an unnatural glimmer, like the dance of light reflecting off metal. There it is again!"

"I also see it," said Orsteen.

After a brief assessment of the terrain, we plotted the best route to avoid the steeper and more dangerous parts of the cliff. A short but exhausting hike brought us to the top of the cliff and into the presence of three behemoth spaceships, each partially buried, protruding up from the ground at haphazard angles.

"What craftsmanship!" said Orsteen. "Such creations aren't meant to be trapped in the dense atmosphere of a planet, but free to float in the ether of outer space."

I pushed my head forward. "For being abandoned for two hundred thousand years, they appear unblemished by the elements. In fact, they're polished to a mirror's surface."

Fanbert looked up from his ocular device. "I'm in agreement. Their preservation over the eons is surprising."

Morion squinted. "What are those things clinging to the surfaces of the ships?"

Fanbert trained his ocular device on them. "People! With lank limbs, plump bodies, and suction cups attached to their knees and elbows. I think they're cleaning the hulls."

"I thought no one was left on this planet," I said.

Fanbert shook his head in wonder. "There shouldn't have been. It's possible they're an alien evolution."

I stepped forward. "Let's get a better look."

We moved closer to the ships, but were soon confronted by the same kind of alien as those attached to the ships by suction cups. He looked male. His skin had a light blue tinge. His large eyes had great big pupils rimmed with green. He seemed primitive, wearing simple white garments and holding a long, rusty blade in his hand.

"Halt, strange creatures! You trespass on sanctified land!"

Fanbert implemented his dimensional transporter and appeared directly behind the alien. With little effort, Fanbert snatched away his clumsy blade.

The alien extended his lank arms in a defensive posture. "Back! Stay back!"

"Interesting," I said. "If I'm not mistaken, our ability to understand him indicates he has a biolinguistic lobe, and is thus a Brahman descendent."

"You're correct." Fanbert waved the man's blade in front of him. "What are you doing here? How have you come to this planet?"

"Your questions suggest my people's claim to this land is in dispute. Our history here extends back through the ages."

"And when did this history begin?" asked Fanbert.

"The details of the past are blurred like a drunk man's vision. My people find it unhealthy to fixate on the past, and instead concentrate on the future, where we're all headed."

Fanbert stabbed the man's rusty blade into the ground. "These people aren't the Prophets' descendents. It's possible they're from the only other inhabited solar system in this galaxy. Since its distance is so great, we didn't think they'd find this planet. I guess we were wrong."

"In any event, they're here now," I said, turning to the local inhabitant. "Why do you polish these ships so diligently?"

"Only those who remain loyal until the return of the Elevated Ones are allowed passage to the Celestial Homeworld."

"The Celestial Homeworld?" said Morion.

"A paradise where all your desires are granted and all hardships alleviated."

"So you're a religious people?" asked Orsteen.

"We prefer the term Devotees. Come, I'll show you our practices—unless you're going to kill me. In which case, I'd prefer to be knocked on the head so my body is unscathed for the Rite of Preservation."

I returned the man's rusty blade. "We're not going to harm you or your people. Please, lead the way and we'll follow."

"Very well. My name's Marden. I'm head of territorial security and maintenance. Since you're here peacefully, I'm obligated to invite you to join us in the service of the Elevated Ones. We don't discriminate or turn away those willing to be devout in our ways. Though, I must admit, you'd be the first not born into them."

"Thank you," I said. "We'll consider your offer."

Marden led us to the closest ship. It was farther than we expected—its size was so great that its distance was misleading. We moved through a small farm, past a cluster of primitive dome-roofed dwellings, and at last came to the base of the ship.

Marden touched the ship thoughtfully. "If you place your hand on the surface, you'll notice it's warm to the touch. This is the divine heat, which doesn't dwindle on even the coldest days. As you can see, there are many Devotees presently giving their daily service to satisfy the Elevated Ones." Marden looked up to a dizzying height at the many figures attached precariously to the ship's hull. "With a passionate, counterclockwise motion, they polish the hull with a sacred cloth weaved by our women from the delicate underbelly hairs of a burrowing animal called a droobsy mouse."

As Marden continued to detail the exact weaving pattern of the cloth, Fanbert continued to peer through his ocular device, searching in all directions. Marden noticed his distracted behavior and, with a brisk hand clapping, called for his attention.

Marden indicated a Devotee descending from the ship's hull. "When a Devotee finishes his daily service, as brother Darden has, the cloth, which has become positively charged with the divine heat of the hull, must be taken to the fire beacon. Come, we'll follow Darden."

We followed the man along a dirt path that curved through a tree-covered hillock, across a cold rocky stream and finally ended at a grass carpeted clearing. There, we found a large fire pit surrounded by over a hundred enormous telescopes, all pointing over the snow-capped peak.

Marden continued: "Darden now throws the positively charged cloth into the fire beacon, which remains lit at all times. The rich gray smoke produced from the burning cloth is a signal to the Elevated Ones that his daily service is done. He's now free to look to the heavens through a great eye and pray for the Elevated Ones to return, so they may pilot their chariots back to the Celestial Homeworld with him aboard."

I noticed an elderly Devotee limping to the fire beacon. "And your ancestors also performed this ritual?"

"They did, with as much pride and zeal as we do today."

"Isn't it discouraging to know your ancestors worked their entire lives in the service of these Elevated Ones, only to die without being delivered to the Celestial Homeworld?"

Marden laughed. "This is an understandable concern that's easily resolved. Those who have died before the return of the Elevated Ones are allowed the Rite of Preservation, in which their bodies are submerged in a potent brine derived from a local plant extract. After thirty days of submersion, their bodies remain preserved until the return of the Elevated Ones, who have the power to resurrect these loyal Devotees." Marden made a sympathetic look. "If the four of you are to gain favor from the Elevated Ones, you'll need to start offering your services immediately. We believe the appearance of this awesome light in the sky is a sign of their return."

"We'll keep this in mind," I said, nodding with fake concern. "However, before we join you in worship, we'd like a better look at these fine lands composing your community. We wish to know the full quality of your lifestyle."

Marden raised his brow curiously. "I see no reason to hesitate in your devotion. Who in their right mind would refuse the promise of paradise? When a thirsty man is presented with a glass of water and a mug of ale, doesn't he leave the water for the dogs?"

Orsteen puffed his chest out. "This may be a truth to live by, but only if you know the ale is a quality brew."

Marden contemplated for a moment. "Very well. You're welcome to look around, but first we should announce your peaceful intentions to my people. Otherwise, they may sneak up behind you and cut off your heads with a pair of farming shears." Marden led us onward. "Since the appearance of the great light, we've been holding a continual feast at the Pantheon Gardens, where all but those performing their daily services are celebrating. I'll take you there now."

We arrived at a beautiful stone-paved patio open to the sky and surrounded by gardens of bell-shaped flowers wafting a honey-sweet aroma. The blue-skinned residents were caught up in a joyful celebration. A group of children blew vigorously into large, twisted gourds, creating an uplifting music that resonated throughout the patio. Everyone in attendance was invigorated by the glow of the phenomenon and let loose their inhibitions, moving rhythmically to the music.

Marden led us to the stage and stopped the children's music with an authoritative gesture. All who danced became still and gazed with big pupils to the stage. Marden introduced us, and we were met with little interest. Marden again gestured to the children, who resumed huffing and puffing into their gourds.

"Your presence is acknowledged," said Marden. "You may roam our lands as you please. Help yourself to the beverages and cuisine laid out for the celebration. You'll discover the droobsy mouse to be a versatile creature."

Marden departed and we found our way to the perimeter of the patio, where long serving tables were piled high with many foreign dishes. Morion was quick to find a large cask full of small animal bladders filled with a golden ale.

I noticed Fanbert continuing to utilize his ocular device. "Have you discovered any sign of the Prophets? Ten minutes ago, I noticed the phenomenon pulse and shimmer, as if it could barely maintain its current size."

"It may take more time than we have. This ocular device is inefficient for searching large areas."

Orsteen devoured a cheese-filled droobsy mouse. "Why don't we just ask Marden if his people have seen these Prophets?"

"Why not, indeed?" I said, now searching the crowd for Marden.

"No need!" proclaimed Fanbert. "Our search has ended."

Fanbert looked down the length of the flower garden, where stood a row of statues, chiseled from a lustrous jade stone. They were unlike the race celebrating on the patio. They wore a modest garb indicative of a lifestyle unconcerned with fashion. Yet, on their heads they wore skullcaps decorated with a unique arrangement of feathers, suggesting rank or status.

"They're just statues," I said.

"Statues of the Prophets!" replied Fanbert, who rewarded himself with an ale-bladder. "Don't you see? These are the Elevated Ones. I'll show you. Gather around me."

Fanbert transported us back to the grass-carpeted clearing, where the many telescopes pointed to the sky. He guided us to the closest telescope and peered through the peephole. He raised his head and smiled triumphantly. He signaled me to take a turn at the peephole. "Behold, a Prophet!"

The telescope was fixed on a single figure floating, motionless, high above the snow-capped peak and left to exist in a frozen moment. I manipulated a knob near the peephole, so the telescope zoomed out. All the Prophets came into view. They hung close together, forming a disc of bodies, to the effect that the mountaintop wore a halo of men.

I withdrew from the peephole. "And I thought Marden and his fellow Devotees were wild-eyed lunatics, awaiting gods born from the imagination of their ancestors."

Orsteen took his turn at the peephole. "How do we get them down? We don't have a ship or anti-gravity belts."

"We only need one of them," said Fanbert. "I can grab him from the sky with the help of my dimensional transporter."

"Can you do it now?" I asked, feeling the tug of the phenomenon on my mind.

"Absolutely." Fanbert opened his bag and retrieved the device required to wake the Prophet from temporal stasis. He sharpened his attention above the mountain and vanished.

Through the peephole, I saw Fanbert materialize above the Prophet he'd selected. During the subsequent three-meter fall, Fanbert activated the device, causing the Prophet to come out of stasis and fall alongside him. Fanbert grabbed on to him and engaged his dimensional transporter.

I pulled away from the peephole. Fanbert and the Prophet appeared beside me.

The Prophet stomped his foot on the ground, apparently to guarantee he was no longer falling. With eyes conveying great intelligence, he inspected us. Before he could speak, he was thrown to his knees by an invisible force. He clutched his skull with two large hands, disheveling the arrangement of feathers on his skullcap. He then applied to his skull what seemed the full force of his grip, as if trying to break an unbreakable egg. His face twisted in pain.

"The feedback's too powerful!" cried the Prophet. "It's too much! My mind can't handle it!"

"What's he talking about?" I asked.

"I haven't the slightest idea," responded Fanbert.

The Prophet struggled to control his seizure. I tried to help him from the ground, but he pushed me away. He examined me with odd intensity and then focused on the sky, where the celestial phenomenon shimmered and pulsed.

"It's begun!" said the Prophet, looking to Fanbert with familiarity. "We could've prevented this, but you stopped us!"

Why does he care about the celestial phenomenon? I thought. *Weren't they trying to assassinate Nara-Narayana?*

"You're confused," I said. "The celestial phenomenon is the work of the Fume. He's trying to birth a god from the souls of all humankind. We must find Nara-Narayana. She's our only hope to stop this apocalypse."

The Prophet made a mocking laugh that progressed into a cough of pain. "You fools! Do you think I'm ignorant? Of course this is the work of the Fume! You don't know what the celestial phenomenon is, do you?"

I grabbed him by the shoulders. "We only want to find Nara-Narayana."

The Prophet laughed insanely. He pushed his hand toward the sky and pointed to the celestial phenomenon. "Are you blind? She's right in front of you, oozing out upon the universe. The celestial phenomenon *is* Nara-Narayana."

"My God," I uttered. "If the phenomenon is Nara-Narayana, then we're fucked."

Fanbert's nostrils flared. "You're just as crazy as the day we put you into stasis, two hundred thousand years ago. If you knew this was coming, why didn't you tell us?"

"No more questions! I can't tolerate the feedback!" The Prophet's eyes bulged, as if a pressure from inside his skull grew to uncontainable levels. "Take me to my ship. I must stop this pain."

Fanbert transported us to one of the ships. The Devotees clinging to the hull caught sight of the Prophet and apparently recognized him as an Elevated One.

Hysterical cries rained down: "An Elevated One has returned! He has come to take us to the Celestial Homeworld!"

And, from even higher above: "We've served you with all the diligence and zeal possible! We praise your return! Take us to the Celestial Homeworld. Please!"

A hundred Devotees frantically descended. The squish-squelch of their suction cups produced a bizarre chorus.

"Where's the entrance?" I cried. "Fanbert! Transport us inside the ship!"

"I can't," responded Fanbert. "The Prophets built it so Guardians couldn't transport inside. From what I remember, the main portal is at the base of the ship. It's now buried."

I shook the Prophet who kneeled on the ground in pain. "Are there any other portals?"

The Prophet lifted his head. "No."

"I have a solution," said Orsteen, presenting the entropy gun. He raised it to the hull and let loose a stream of energy that vaporized the metal. "The door's open," he said, nodding with satisfaction.

I turned to Orsteen and Morion. "Keep the Devotees at bay. We don't have time to deal with their fairy tales."

"You got it," said Orsteen.

I lifted the Prophet over my shoulder and entered the ship.

The Prophet pointed a finger, guiding us. "Take the lift up twelve decks, veer left, and then proceed to the end of the corridor."

There we came to a small chamber. Within rested a single metal chair. I placed the Prophet into the chair and three metal posts rose from the floor and surrounded him. I heard an electrical buzz as the silver posts glowed.

With great care, the Prophet began removing the skullcap from his bulbous head. When finally he pried it free, Fanbert and I noticed a substantial part of the Prophet's brain protruding from a hole in his skull.

"Why have you mutilated yourself?" I asked, approaching the Prophet.

"Keep your distance!" said the Prophet. "I must undergo a special treatment to undo the modifications made to my biolinguistic lobe." He spoke a command word and the three silver posts projected energized beams toward his head. They carried through the air like ripples of heat rising off hot sand. The Prophet closed his eyes and accepted the strange energy.

"Will this take long?" I asked. "Time is a noose around our necks, constricting tighter with every passing second."

The Prophet opened his eyes. "It might take a while."

"Can you speak during the process?"

"I can, but at any moment my biolinguistic lobe may fail, in which case, you won't be able to understand me. If this occurs, I'll probably die."

"Then immediately tell us about Nara-Narayana and the Fume's plans to birth a god from the souls of humankind." I looked at the Prophet's protruding brain matter and saw it undulate. "And what exactly have you done to your biolinguistic lobe that needs undoing?"

"I'll start at the beginning, twenty-one million years ago, when the first world, Brahman, was colonized by the survivors of the Brahman Station." The Prophet paused, as if coping with a surge of pain. "After two millennia, Brahman became a thriving world of high spirits and great minds. And, like their ancestors of the Terran star, the adventurer within their human souls awakened. They yearned to travel the stars and discover new worlds.

"The threat of paradox, however, hung rich on the minds of scientists, philosophers, and laymen alike. And for this reason they established the Guardian Army. But they soon realized that even the greatest army wouldn't be sufficient to monitor over twenty-one million years of human expansion into the universe. There would be too many worlds, too many people, and too many possibilities. Paradox could be caused by even the slightest contact with the Terran solar system or any of the seven galaxies inhabited by the Fume.

"To appease these concerns, a great thinker named Sensimion created Nara-Narayana—an incorruptible entity who would serve as the leader of the Guardian Army. She was engineered with a genome beyond any deca-helix species that has ever existed. But the true nature of Nara-Narayana, the true depth of her power and awareness over the Brahman Sprawl, is undeniably the greatest secret in the human universe." The Prophet was again struck to silence.

"Are you all right?" I asked.

"I'll be fine." The Prophet continued his story: "The secret that's been kept from all who've lived in the Brahman Sprawl has to do with the architecture that allows Nara-Narayana to monitor them." The Prophet again paused.

"What architecture?" said Fanbert. "What do you mean?"

"Before anyone from Brahman was allowed to use the dimensional gateway technology to travel beyond that first planet, Sensimion released a virus into the population. Once it entered a host, it induced a genetic alteration, causing the next generation to be born with biolinguistic lobes. No one but Sensimion was aware of this genetic alteration. It was eventually believed that the biolinguistic lobe was a miracle of evolution, allowing human races to understand each other on a psychic level, thus eliminating any language barriers. But this was only a side effect. The true purpose of the biolinguistic lobe was to connect the thoughts of every human in the Brahman Sprawl to Nara-Narayana. In effect, she was created to be a nexus of thought for all humankind. We're all connected to her. She's the ultimate Guardian, able to hear the thoughts of the one quadrillion people inhabiting the Brahman Sprawl. She's a demigod to humankind."

"My god!" said Fanbert. "Such a feat of biological technology would be a challenge now—even more so twenty-one million years ago."

I touched the back of my head. "Can she hear my thoughts now?"

"She can hear the thoughts of everyone," said the Prophet.

Fanbert made a distant look. "This is how she ruled over the Guardian Army. This is how she prevented a paradox."

The Prophet looked at us ominously. "The creation of Nara-Narayana *did* prevent paradox, but at the cost of falling victim to the Fume's ultimate plan. Fanbert, you're correct in your impression of the level of biological technology required to create Nara-Narayana and the biolinguistic lobes. For it was, in fact, the Fume who planted the design of Nara-Narayana's architecture into the mind of that great scientist, Sensimion, who ultimately created her."

I couldn't believe it. Sensimion had also been manipulated by the Fume in the sanitarium.

The Fume has planned everything.

Fanbert was visibly agitated. He had served proudly under Nara-Narayana's command for hundreds of millennia. "How does Nara-Narayana's ability to read the thoughts of all humankind equate to the Fume's plan to evolve the universe?"

"Isn't it obvious?" said the Prophet. "She's the center of all humankind—she's the bond that ties us all together. The biolinguistic lobe is attached to a very specific point in our brains, within the Corpus Callosum. The Corpus Callosum not only connects the hemispheres of the brain, but it's also the path to the soul."

I marveled at the Prophet's exposed biolinguistic lobe. "Then Nara-Narayana is literally connected to each of our souls?"

"Indeed," said the Prophet. "And Nara-Narayana is the center of the next human evolution, which is occurring now. It's ironic, Nara-Narayana was the cornerstone of the Guardian Army—the ultimate intelligence to protect the Brahman Sprawl from paradox and the Fume's manipulations—and all along she was the Fume's greatest accomplishment."

"You're lying!" yelled Fanbert, eyes aflame.

"Calm down, Fanbert." I faced the Prophet. "How is it that, after twenty-one million years, only your people became aware of this frightful revelation?"

"Long ago, my people, by an accident of medical research, modified the biolinguistic lobe of a single man. Soon after, he claimed he was in touch with God. He became overwhelmed with an amazing wisdom. Many more underwent the modification and eventually it became understood what was occurring. The biolinguistic lobe is a transmitter of thoughts. Normally, this transmission goes in one direction—from the person with the biolinguistic lobe to Nara-Narayana. Our modification, however, distorted that signal and created a feedback, in which a person's biolinguistic lobe would receive an assortment of thoughts and memories from Nara-Narayana. The modification enlightened us with her wisdom. We gained certain insights on the most fundamental properties of the universe." The Prophet went silent, apparently finding awe in his own thoughts. "Everything and everyone in this universe is connected.

"This universe and our existence are ruled by wondrous complexities that the human mind can't fully fathom. Beyond the perceivable universe, there are other realms, other levels of consciousness, other plains of existence, and invisible forces that bind us together. But even with all its complexities, the universe is still ruled by chaos." The Prophet's eyes glowed with profound intensity. "It's the human soul that's the first step in bringing true order to the chaos of the universe."

I again touched the back of my head, wondering if Nara-Narayana now read my thoughts. "And Nara-Narayana, by unifying all humankind, becomes a sort of collective consciousness?"

"Precisely," said the Prophet. "And the celestial phenomenon we witness in the sky is the final step, when the collective consciousness becomes one consciousness. Nara-Narayana will assimilate all matter, all energy, and the soul of every person with a biolinguistic lobe, to eventually evolve into a being like the Fume. The Fume's plans will come to fruition once this wake of evolution reaches the seven galaxies where his outpocketings are located. He'll then be able to move freely into our universe and absorb all the divine energies composing Nara-Narayana's new transcendental form."

I shook my head. "If Nara-Narayana is becoming an entity on the same order as the Fume, couldn't she resist him once her evolved state reaches the seven galaxies?"

"It's possible," said the Prophet. "She may be hoping for such an outcome in her favor. Either way, we'll have lost our lives. Our souls will be dissolved into a greater consciousness. Whether Nara-Narayana's or the Fume's, it won't matter."

Fanbert seemed more accepting of the revelation. "Why only now has Nara-Narayana begun this final transformation?"

The Prophet pondered a moment. "Maybe she required a certain number of people, a certain number of souls, to be contained within her collective consciousness before she could begin the transformation."

Holy shit! I thought. *It all makes sense now.*

I turned to Fanbert. "I require private counsel with—"

"My name is Torell," said the Prophet.

"I'm Theron, and this is Fanbert." I again turned to Fanbert. "I must speak with Torell alone."

Fanbert studied me for a moment. "As you wish. I'll check on Orsteen and Morion." He then walked from the room, stopping once to glance back in suspicion.

I waited till Fanbert was gone, and even then spoke to Prophet Torell in a secretive tone. "I think I'm the cause of Nara-Narayana's final transformation."

"What? How?"

"Not only am I a creation of the Fume, but I was seeded with his energy... or essence. I think that when I was finally implanted with a biolinguistic lobe and connected to Nara-Narayana, the energy of the Fume hidden in my brain acted as a catalyst for Nara-Narayana's evolution."

"This would explain my initial impression of you, when I still commanded the full insights of Nara-Narayana."

"What do you mean?" I asked.

"I could sense a strange force spilling from the crevices of your soul."

"An interesting turn of words. This modification of the biolinguistic lobe truly gives you access to the full scope of Nara-Narayana's mind?"

"The feedback allows only a glimpse of her great intelligence."

"I wish to undergo the process."

"It would be pointless," said Prophet Torell. "Her consciousness has become a tempest of thought, too intense for any physical being to process. Why do you think I'm disconnecting myself from her? If I were to have tried to cope with her consciousness any longer, my mind would've ruptured. Besides, there's nothing left to do. We can't reverse her evolution. We sit on borrowed time."

"Please," I said calmly. "I'd rather not force you."

Prophet Torell shrugged. "Your threats are hollow, since we'll all soon be surrendering to our mutual and ultimate nemesis—death."

"There's more to my condition than I've revealed. As the celestial phenomenon, or Nara-Narayana as you've indicated, has been expanding, I've been undergoing extraordinary changes. At first, it was merely an odd sensation, as if the celestial phenomenon beckoned me in some way. Then I was changed. I was left with a heightened awareness of my surroundings, able to move objects with my mind. Days passed and the celestial phenomenon grew larger and I was again altered. I found myself not only able to read people's minds, but I could also manipulate them. I could change their thoughts and memories at will."

"Interesting," said Prophet Torell. "It seems you're connected to Nara-Narayana on a more fundamental level than merely sharing her wisdom, as my people have. You're evolving, although to a lesser degree, parallel with her."

"Whatever the case, it's a powerful connection." I tilted my head upward. "Even now, I can feel her invigorating my soul. It's a euphoric—though terrifying—sensation."

"And you believe your current connection with Nara-Narayana will allow you to cope with the intensity of the feedback?"

"I do... and it must. I need answers to explain what I'm experiencing. I believe I'm becoming something greater than the Fume had planned." I stepped closer to Prophet Torell. "Are you paying attention?"

Prophet Torell's eyes had become droopy, and his neck collapsed from the weight of his head. The three silver posts disengaged. They were either finished with the process or found it pointless continuing on a dead man.

I jolted him about. "Are you alive?"

"There's a node," said Prophet Torell, his words barely audible. "It protrudes from my biolinguistic lobe."

"I see it." I located what appeared to be a small pearl resting on his exposed brain tissue.

"Take hold of it and pull delicately."

I did as instructed, and as I pulled on the small pearly node, a matrix of nearly invisible filaments drew out of Torell's biolinguistic lobe. "It's done."

Prophet Torell put the skullcap back on his head, concealing his exposed brain tissue. He looked around as if his surroundings had changed. "It's odd. Now that I'm not linked with Nara-Narayana, I'm overcome by a sense of... insignificance. What were we discussing?"

"My need to experience the feedback."

"Even if you find answers, Theron, they won't solve our biggest problem—impending doom."

"Will you help me or not?"

"I see no reason not to. If you were indeed a catalyst to initiate the final evolution of Nara-Narayana, you've done all the damage you could possibly do."

Prophet Torell guided me to another room, where he prepared for the procedure.

I watched as he removed a collection of surgical tools. "I'm curious, Torell. Is it absolutely necessary that my brain is exposed to daylight? There could be a number of complications from putting my brain in such a vulnerable state—not the least of which is infection, necrosis, and the unavoidable release of vital fluids."

"Don't worry. The process, after centuries of implementation, is tried and true. Now, lie on the table and remain still. I must measure the dimensions of your head so I can make your skullcap."

"Are you saying that after the process, my brain will remain exposed, as yours is?"

"Yes. The process will cause your biolinguistic lobe to swell in size. Your skull won't be able to accommodate your brain tissues, thus the need for a properly fitted skullcap."

I heaved a dreadful sigh. "I should be use to such procedures by now."

Prophet Torell first applied a chemical to my dark hair, which melted away and left me bald. He then injected me with a pain killer, and began removing skin and skull, eventually leaving a ten-centimeter hole at the back of my head. Finally, he placed a pearly node to the surface of my exposed biolinguistic lobe.

Once the node extended its matrix of filaments, Prophet Torell smeared an oily substance over all exposed brain tissue. "These nanites will prevent infection and cauterize the perimeter of incised flesh." He led me back to the room with the three silver posts and sat me in the chair. "I must strap you in. You might convulse violently during the process."

"I understand."

Prophet Torell spoke a command word, and the silver posts released their energies toward me. My biolinguistic lobe began to change. I sat in anticipation, waiting for some kind of mind-altering epiphany. Instead, I found an overwhelming terror. It was as if every neuron in my brain was firing at once. My muscles tensed and my jaw clenched. Pain, memories, and emotions cluttered my mind until at last I blacked out.

FORGING REALITY

I woke up in a standing position, as if sleepwalking had taken me to a place of mystery. I was surrounded by a forest of crystalline trees shimmering with a range of rich colors, from aquamarine to the deepest magenta.

Such beauty, I thought. *It must be a dream.*

I approached one of the crystalline trees and came to the conclusion that the slightest disturbance would cause the structure to crumble into a pile of shards.

The sky was bright with a million points of white light.

Are they stars?

I ambitiously reached up to grab one. In my hand, I discovered a glowing, winged insect sitting calmly on my palm and looking back as if wondering why it had been disturbed. After a moment, it returned to flight and took its place overhead.

I walked on. Eventually, I came to a small pond of placid water, reflecting the sky of glowing insects with perfect clarity. It was a calming sight until I noticed two large eyes staring up from just below the water's surface. I sprung back as I imagined the eyes were attached to a beast stalking the water's edge for a meal. But, as I reeled, the two eyes slowly descended out of sight and into the water's depths.

The surreal landscape elicited an uneasy sensation within me.

Someone's watching me. I can feel it. My every movement's being scrutinized. I turned in a dizzying circle. *Or is it the forest itself that watches me?*

I moved forward nervously. The crystalline trees swayed in my direction as I walked on in search of the unknown.

From the shadows of the forest, I saw another pair of eyes. But as I moved to discover who spied on me, I found only empty shadows. On another occasion, I swore I saw an AI-droid with a human head, sipping from Orsteen's flask of Neuro-Rapture. But it too, when approached, dissolved into the crystalline forest.

At last, my wandering ended when I arrived at some nightmarish replica of the Brahman Station. It wasn't constructed of diamond-fiber composite, it was built of bricks formed from human body parts, mingled and compressed. My stomach shivered.

What the hell is this place? It's horrible. Disgusting.

I placed my hand on a brick composed of an arm, a collapsed torso, and other unidentifiable folds of flesh. I felt warmth as the grotesque masonry pulsed with life.

From a nearby brick, an eye emerged from a wrinkle of flesh. It took an interest in me, but when I neared, it retreated back into a fold, possibly fearing the poke of a curious finger.

I moved along the perimeter of the horrible replica, searching for a docking bay to enter. I suddenly saw a figure darting around a corner.

Impossible!

I recognized the figure—that lovely girl I'd adored so long ago in the sanitarium. But how? She had been murdered by the Fume.

Is it her? Could it truly be Mage?

I again caught sight of her. She stood in front of an open docking bay. I cried out to her, but she vanished into the station on pattering feet.

I entered the repulsive structure and found the girl boarding a lift. Again I called for her, but the door slid closed and she was taken up a level. Every time I caught up with her, I'd lose her around a corner or she'd board another lift to move upward.

I followed her up one final level and arrived in the glass-domed arboretum of the nightmarish station. It afforded a beautiful though haunting panorama of the crystalline forest. There, I found a woman dressed in a long gown of white silk. She stood with back turned to me, apparently enjoying the view. Strangely, Mage was nowhere to be found.

"Who are you?" I asked. The woman turned in a whirl of flowing fabric. I stood frozen with joy and relief. "Allienora! You're alive!" I moved to embrace her, but stopped short. "Something's wrong. I remember now. I was with Prophet Torell. He was modifying my biolinguistic lobe so I could find answers from Nara-Narayana. Am I dreaming?"

"No, you're not dreaming," spoke Allienora. "Your search for me has ended. I am Nara-Narayana."

"Why do you look like Allienora?"

"I know you gain pleasure from this form. And since I'm everything in this place, I thought you'd be more comfortable if I took her appearance."

"This place..." I said, looking around. "...what is it?"

"This is the new universe, where I am God."

I gestured to the floor, composed of more bricks made of living flesh. "You've become unbalanced over the eons, even deranged. This place is the work of insanity."

She disregarded the brickwork with a wave of her hand. "A work of whimsy, which I see is only appreciated by myself."

"I beg you, Nara-Narayana. Stop this evolution that consumes humankind."

"This is a strange request, coming from you who delivered me the key to this evolution." Nara-Narayana took a deep breath, as if relishing her current state of existence. "Divinity isn't something one refuses. It's what humankind has always aspired for."

"You're becoming exactly what the Fume wants you to become. Once your energies reach the seven galaxies of the Fume, you'll be overtaken by him."

"The Fume has underestimated my mastery over this universe. It's he who should fear me. He's powerless against me in my universe."

"*Your* universe!" I scoffed in defiance. "What of humankind? By proceeding with your evolution, you disregard the lives of so many. Are they really so insignificant to you?"

"To the contrary, they're as much a part of this evolution as I. Isn't it wondrous, Theron? Out of many... one. Their souls will bring this universe to a state of perfect consciousness, where anything's possible." Nara-

Narayana gestured to her surroundings. "Where my mind's eye forges reality."

"Your mind's eye! Your consciousness! The individual human may be inferior to your newfound greatness, but they have a right to their unique consciousness in this universe. Yet you give no credence to this, and without their consent, you devour them to satisfy your need for ultimate power. You're no better than the Fume and may even be kindred spirits."

"The Fume and I are of the same nature, yes. Kindred spirits, we're not." Nara-Narayana struck an elegant pose. "This body conjures deep-felt emotions within you. I won't object if you wish to comfort it. Come closer, Theron Mobius. Comfort me."

I was about to tell her off, but something shifted within me. I became aware of something passing just within the limits of my perceptions.

"Illumination... I can see... far away."

"What are you saying?" asked Nara-Narayana, apparently sensing discord. "What are you doing?"

"You know where Allienora is, Nara-Narayana. Yes... there she is... on one of the worlds in the seven galaxies of the Fume, an outpocketing of his consciousness. It's not Earth, though."

"You shouldn't be able to share in these thoughts! I forbid you!"

I remained focused on Allienora, disregarding Nara-Narayana's cries of authority. "Of course! You're connected to her by her biolinguistic lobe. You have the power to see as Allienora sees, and now I, too, have this power."

"You're a leech on my thoughts. Be gone!"

Images and sensations flashed in my mind. "At this moment Allienora looks at the Fume. She's afraid. He wants her to be. His current manifestation is an alien form, unlike any I've seen him use before. He's tall, muscular, and has olive skin that gleams like silicon. His eyes are blood-red spheres deep-set into a chiseled face. There's no nose, only two pinholes that flare and contract as he speaks to her."

Where is your dear Theron now, my sweet? He has abandoned you without a second thought. Don't worry. You may devote yourself to me. I'll be your one true love. The Fume laughed.

Allienora struggled against him as he stripped her down and led her to a stone elevation, like an offering table. Above her a mirror reflected her nude figure. She was trembling.

What are you going to do to me?

The Fume leaned in close, his blood-red eyes widened. *I'm going to teach you the meaning of unthinkable agony.*

Horror filled my mind and I lost sight—I no longer saw as Allienora saw. Once again, I looked upon her imposter, Nara-Narayana. "Why does he torment her? She's done nothing to deserve such treatment."

"The Fume's motivations are beyond my understanding. Nevertheless, I can comfort you in the fact that he won't have long with her, since I'm expanding ever faster into the universe."

My chest felt tight and my head hurt. "Neither you nor the Fume will succeed. I promise you."

"You're a single raindrop attempting to quench an unquenchable flame."

My thoughts intensified. My emotions made me stronger. My presence in Nara-Narayana's realm enlarged. She showed signs of unease. I felt power.

I smiled. "I sense something within you, Nara-Narayana. You have a secret of great consequence to your existence. It would reveal your single vulnerability. Tell me your secret!"

With all my being, I pushed my perceptions into the depths of Nara-Narayana's continuum of thought.

"Out!" roared Nara-Narayana. "Get out!"

"You didn't anticipate my mental energies. Do you feel the burden of me upon your mind? Tell me your secret, goddamnit!"

Nara-Narayana released a thunderous scream that broke the glass of the surrounding dome. Shards rained down.

My body—which, in this place, was but a representation of my real self—shimmered and glowed, until a pulse of thought rippled out from my being and into the landscape of Nara-Narayana's mind's eye. In its wake, the crystalline forest shattered to pieces, and the insects giving light to the forest smoldered and fell dead from the sky.

Darkness consumed all. We were left without form, to exist in a gloom of thought.

My presence emerged from the darkness in the form of a whisper: "I'm now aware of your single vulnerability. Stop your transformation or pay the consequence."

Nara-Narayana released a fury so profound that she finally summoned the power to expel me from her conscious realm.

THE CATALYST
OF
EVOLUTION

My eyes opened to the real world. I felt a chill on my head as Prophet Torell placed a metal skullcap on me.

"Excellent. You're awake." Prophet Torell held up some kind of medical sensor. "Are you under any mental distress, Theron?"

My body trembled. "No."

"Are you able to tolerate the feedback?"

"I think so."

"I'll take you to a meditation chamber. It may take time to decipher the feedback."

"That's not necessary, Torell." I stood up between the three silver posts. "I found my answers."

"Impossible! It'll take days to separate the feedback of Nara-Narayana's thoughts from your own."

"I've experienced something beyond the mere feedback you're familiar with. While unconscious, my mind was drawn away from my body and delivered to Nara-Narayana's realm of consciousness. There, I walked through the landscape of her mind, a surreal and twisted reality. I even spoke with her face to face—or so it seemed."

Torell's eyes showed a gleam of envy. "What did you learn during this encounter?"

"I learned that Nara-Narayana isn't the unstoppable force we thought. We can, and will, stop her. And, in doing so, we'll also stop the Fume."

"How?"

"First, where's the Guardian Fanbert? I must speak with him on other matters."

"He's helping Orsteen and Morion, keeping the natives from entering the ship."

I found my companions oddly cheerful. They stood within the entrance that Orsteen had made in the ship and looked outside. They had used the entropy gun to make a five-meter pit below the entrance, forcing the Devotees to make their way to the entrance by suction cup, one by one.

I watched as Orsteen gently thrust an incoming Devotee into the pit below.

Orsteen's eyes lit up. "Theron! Thank God you're alive! It was crazy to undergo this procedure Torell described. I'm happy to see you're not cross-eyed and drooling."

I looked out from the entrance and into the sky. It was completely overcast with the glow of Nara-Narayana's divinity. I thought of my biolinguistic lobe.

I hope she can hear my thoughts. I formed them loud and clear: *I will stop you, Nara!*

"Is there any hope?" asked Fanbert. "Or is it time to take the final measurement of our lives?"

"There's always hope," I said. "We may still be able to reestablish the balance of the universe. Come." I waved them into the ship.

"Wait!" called Morion. "You forget the Devotees. They're persistent beyond reason and will prove a nuisance when they overrun the ship, screaming for their Celestial Homeworld. They just finished building a catapult at the other end of the pit and are loading it with the bravest Devotee."

At that moment, a Devotee soared through the air, apparently prepared to smash through the strangers blocking his passage to paradise. To his misfortune, he had too much arc in his trajectory. Instead of smashing through us, he fell short and grabbed the base of the entrance with hooked fingers.

"Hijackers!" he shouted, still hanging on. "You're not worthy to enter the chariot of the Elevated Ones. Why do you withhold an Elevated One from us? Release him, so we may be rewarded for our worship."

I approached the edge of the entrance and, with an outstretched arm, lifted the Devotee from his peril. "Don't worry, my friend. You'll be rewarded."

The horde of Devotees at the other side of the pit let loose a roar of triumph.

The Devotee trembled. "Then the Elevated One will take us to paradise?"

"There's no need to travel. I'll make you realize paradise." I sent out a wave of thought.

The Devotee's religious passion faded. At first, he appeared sad, but soon showed something like awareness. He waved to his people. "We've been in paradise all along! Paradise is now!"

The rest of the Devotees showed a similar enthusiasm and marched away from the ship with purpose.

I smiled. I had done something right with my new power. It felt good. "They'll bother us no more."

"How have you done this?" asked Orsteen. "You've altered their minds."

"I've enlightened them with the truth of these ships and their so-called Elevated Ones. I've made them realize that paradise is a state of mind."

"Are you saying you've moved these people to happiness by glancing at them?"

"More or less," I said. "Is this a bad thing?"

"You've been changing," said Orsteen, "ever since Nara-Narayana has been growing in the sky. And since I know you're a part of the Fume's plans, my fears are not without merit. You haven't been truthful about your condition. Tell us now, or I'll be forced to take action against you, my friend."

"I have nothing to hide from you anymore, Orsteen. My part in the Fume's plan has already been executed. I think these powers are just a side effect. Come. I'll explain."

We sat in the ship's congregation room and I revealed my secret.

The Guardian Fanbert glared at me. "Even now part of the Fume whirls in your head. How can we trust you?"

"I'm ashamed of what I am, but I didn't deliberately cause the final transformation of Nara-Narayana. I never consciously acted on the Fume's behalf. I'm not one of his minions and have no allegiance to him. I was merely an ignorant carrier who transmitted the disease that catalyzed the evolution of the universe." I looked to Orsteen and Morion. "The two of you believe me, don't you?"

"I believe you," said Orsteen. "Through all of this, we've learned one enormous truth. The soul within each of us is a powerful and complicated force. I believe each of us is a divine entity, capable of our own choices. I know in my heart you're not one of the Fume's soulless minions."

Morion leaned forward in his seat. "How can you be certain the Fume's minions are soulless?"

"They don't have free will," said Fanbert. "If they did, they'd see their loyalty to the Fume is without reason. They'd see the Fume uses them like pawns."

"Theron, you said earlier you could stop Nara-Narayana's evolution," said Prophet Torell. "What did you learn while connected to her?"

I can't tell them, I thought. *Not now. Not until I save her.*

"Well?" said Prophet Torell.

"I'll tell you as soon as Fanbert transports me to where Allienora is being held."

"Who?" asked Fanbert. "Is she significant in the plan to stop Nara-Narayana's expansion?"

"No," I said. "But she's significant to me."

"Am I hearing you right?" said Fanbert. "Humankind is about to be obliterated. She's just one person. Tell us how to stop Nara-Narayana!"

"You've heard my terms. I must get her back."

Fanbert paced back and forth, eyes darting in thought. "Where is she?"

I turned to Prophet Torell. "I assume this ship has advanced stellar cartography?"

"It does. Follow me." Prophet Torell led us to a room designated for stellar cartography. He showed me how to use the controls of a star projector. "We're in this galaxy, here. You may pan and zoom using the control pad at the base of the unit."

"Thank you, Torell." I guided the projector through the virtual universe. I didn't know how, but the stars and galaxies seemed familiar to me. I zoomed in upon a particular galaxy, and then upon a star orbited by a blue-green planet.

The mere sight of the planet brought Fanbert to an uproar. "Are you insane? That's one of the Fume's outpocketings. Not only do you wish to waste precious time in the name of love, but now you wish to serve us up like delicacies directly into the mouth of the monster."

I can bend you to my will. I clenched my teeth. *I must stop these thoughts. I'm not this person. I'm not a monster like the Fume.*

"I swear, Fanbert," I said. "We won't be in his outpocketing for long. Once we rescue Allienora, I'll tell you how to stop Nara-Narayana from spreading farther into the universe."

"Why not simply stop Nara-Narayana first?" asked Fanbert visibly frustrated.

"There's no telling what the Fume will do once his plans have fallen into ruin. For all I know, he'll kill everyone within his outpocketings just to spite us. I won't risk Allienora's life."

Bickering continued and I couldn't be persuaded.

Fanbert's shoulders slumped in resignation. "The entire universe is at your mercy, Theron."

"You concede to my terms?" I said.

Fanbert looked to Orsteen. "Tell Theron your opinion of his terms."

I turned to hear Orsteen's opinion, but instead received the full weight of his fist between my eyes.

Orsteen looked down at Theron's unconscious body with guilt. "I'm sorry, brother, but it was you who wanted me to judge your mental disposition. I didn't think love would be the cause of your corruption."

"Good work, Orsteen," said Fanbert.

Orsteen knelt down to check Theron's condition.

Fanbert turned to Prophet Torell. "Your people, Torell, seem to be masters of all that's cerebral. Do you have the power to extract from Theron's mind the information on how to stop Nara-Narayana's evolution?"

"Yes. It shouldn't be a problem." Prophet Torell rubbed his metal skullcap. "I also look forward to a closer examination, so I can see what he's made of."

"Be gentle," said Orsteen, uncomfortable with Torell's enthusiasm.

Fanbert grabbed Prophet Torell's arm. "And remember, he must remain sedated. We can't have him playing tricks on our minds, like he did to the Devotees."

Prophet Torell nodded. "Bring him back to my laboratory."

Orsteen caringly lifted Theron into his arms and followed Prophet Torell.

A day passed as Prophet Torell worked tirelessly on Theron. Orsteen, after a short nap, walked into Torell's laboratory. Theron floated erect in a fluid-filled cylinder with a tube down his throat.

"How's he doing?" asked Orsteen.

Prophet Torell's eyes were wide with wonder. "Exotic energies fill his head. A spark of divinity, indeed. Whatever he's becoming, it's more than any mortal man has ever known."

"What of the information we seek?"

"I'm having difficulty. Not only is there interference from the foreign energies, but his neural activity is at extraordinary levels. I'm cooling his body in an attempt to suppress the fire within him."

Orsteen set a gentle hand on the glass cylinder in which Theron floated. "She would understand the sacrifice that needs to be made, my friend. Why couldn't you just let her go?"

Theron couldn't reply.

SOULESTIAL
REALM

I wasn't awake but I was aware, trapped in a chasm of consciousness, looking through the inner eye of my mind. Like a sightseer on a tour of my own life, I roamed a convoluted landscape of memories, emotions, and dreams. It was a place that found balance in extremes—love and hate, triumph and tragedy, life and death. I felt confident that, in the entire universe, the mind of man was the most unique of places.

I abandoned my introspection and scolded myself: *Wake up, you fool! Beyond the confines of your skull, the end of the universe unfolds... Why won't you wake up?*

No amount of will or want proved sufficient to transport me back to the waking world. With little hope of escaping from my mental prison, I was again caught up in a moment of introspection. With the sum of my life splayed out before me, all at once and in such perfect clarity, I felt I had a chance to gain some further understanding of not only myself but the human condition.

As I explored my inner self, I perceived something greater than myself back-dropping my mental confines. There was something more, something beyond my inner self, as if my mind was a medium into another realm.

Is this one of the realms which Prophet Torell had spoken of? A realm only to be perceived with the inner eye. A place within one's self that goes beyond one's self.

My perceptions focused, and I realized my bubble of consciousness was not the only one. I was surrounded by a countless number of other bubbles of consciousness. They seemed to be the minds, or maybe the souls, of all humankind. Each connected to the next by some fundamental bond.

Even in this metaphysical universe, Nara-Narayana couldn't go unnoticed. She spread like wildfire, absorbing the souls of the Brahman Sprawl.

I became aware of an awful pain coming from somewhere in the eternal distance. It fell on my mind with weight. I traced its source to another bubble of consciousness and then heard her voice sing in agony.

"Help me, Theron. Where are you? Why have you abandoned me?"

"Allienora! I hear you, my love!" I pushed my consciousness out beyond the perimeters of my mind, into the myriad of souls surrounding me. I traveled in and out of the spiritual spheres of others, whose lives flashed before my eyes. I felt as though I journeyed down the length of a string of pearls, moving by some uncontrollable pull toward Allienora's own bubble of consciousness.

I came into Allienora's inner self and became intoxicated by my surroundings. All my previous perceptions of her were verified. I could now see her virtue and inner beauty. It was obvious why I felt so strongly for her—the soothing radiance of her soul negated all the pain burdened upon me during my life. She was a balance, a cure, a way to happiness.

"I'm with you, Allienora! Do you hear me?"

She didn't respond.

I pressed deeper into her soulestial realm. She was all around me, but nowhere to be found—everywhere her past and nowhere her present. I witnessed vignettes of her life, from her inauguration as prime minister, to her graduation from the University of New Paris, to the breakup with her first love, to her mother's funeral, to her first kiss, and to her childhood. Oh, what a wonderful childhood it was. Something I wished I could've had myself.

I continued my journey, drifting through the layers of her life and, at last, came to her beginning. It was sometime in her mother's womb that the spark of her existence came to be. I marveled at the event. And as I gazed into the light of her first moment, I glimpsed something more, something before her inception, a hidden layer.

I couldn't believe what I perceived—I saw my wedding day through the eyes of my dead wife, Cassandra. I saw my life with Cassandra, and Cassandra's life before we had met. I felt joy and confusion.

Does this mean what I think it means? Allienora was thirty-five years old, and Cassandra died thirty-five years ago.

As I admired the overlapping lives, I discovered yet a third layer, a life hidden beneath Cassandra's life. It was a short life, but another life nonetheless. I found the memories of a girl whose life was taken too soon. Her entire existence defined by her heart, which she gave to a boy. A boy named Theron.

A strange ecstasy flushed through my mind as I relished in the revelation. I had loved three women in my entire life—Mage, Cassandra, and Allienora. All incarnations of the same soul.

It was always one girl—one love—one soul. It was always you.

Just as I found true peace in Allienora's soulestial realm, I detected a disturbing distortion. Like the clabbering of cream, her soul began to turn.

What's wrong, my love?

It was the Fume. I knew it. He was responsible for this foul change. With all my mental strength, I maneuvered my perspective so I saw the outer universe as Allienora saw.

She looked at the Fume, who loomed over her reclined body. His face was that of a madman, with oversized eyes gleaming with satisfaction and a mouth that split his face like a gloom-filled gulch into hell.

Horror! Pain! Despair!

I felt her emotions. The scent of blood filled the air. And as Allienora peered down the length of her body, I discovered the source of the bloody smell—the Fume was in the middle of dissecting her torso. He had folded back her ribcage, exposing her organs to the air. The Fume's hand crawled upon her innards as if to make inventory, starting at the intestines and moving upward, from liver to stomach to lungs and finally to rest upon her beating heart.

The Fume clutched down on the vital organ, causing Allienora to gasp in pain. He smiled, apparently relishing in her misery. "Can you see the precipice of death? It's the greatest burden upon the mortal mind."

The Fume relaxed his grip, giving her heart a moment of reprieve and then again pushed his sharp digits into her center organ.

Allienora's pain became my pain.

Why does the Fume torture her? I must stop him! Maybe I can take control of Allienora's body?

I tried to move her lips to speak against the Fume and his senseless acts of torture—I failed. I tried to move her arms to push away the unwelcome fingers impinging on her heart—it was hopeless.

I sent out my sharpest thoughts to the Fume, hoping to do harm.

As I worked my ineffective mental assault, the Fume halted his gruesome work, as if he knew my consciousness was eavesdropping on the other side of Allienora's eyes.

The Fume cradled Allienora's heart in his hand. "Is this what your dear love, Theron, wants? Does he wish to feel the heat of this romanticized organ against his chest?" The Fume glowed with satisfaction. "He'll never again feel its vibration, unless he can perform miracles."

Allienora pushed thin words through the pain: "What does it matter to you... a god... a monster... whatever you are?"

The Fume's only response was a smile.

Allienora's mental anguish sat like an anvil atop her head. Her anguish became my anguish. Her mind fractured. I felt the effects of a miniature apocalypse within her. It became my miniature apocalypse.

In that moment, I found the power to turn all that negative energy into strength, giving me the means to wake myself.

I returned to the waking world with such force that a burst of mental energy escaped my mind, shattering the fluid-filled cylinder containing me. I stood wet and naked, steam rolling off my body into the cold air around me.

Orsteen, Morion, Fanbert, and Prophet Torell were all present. They were speechless, shocked by the spectacle of my awakening.

I felt powerful. "You'll do as I ask."

They nodded their heads and the Guardian Fanbert spoke timidly: "Where on this planet do you wish to be taken?"

I led them back to the stellar cartography lab and indicated the planetary coordinates. "We must leave immediately. Nara-Narayana is going to try to accelerate her absorption of this galaxy. She wishes to take my soul, so I won't have the opportunity to stop her."

Fanbert gave me a final pleading look. "I shouldn't help you. I hope you know what you're doing. If we delay, we might not stop Nara-Narayana in time."

"I'm aware of the risk," I said. "Take me to Allienora!"

"If I must," said Fanbert in a grumble.

"If you don't need me," said Prophet Torell, "I'd like to stay here and prepare for the end."

"As you like," I said. "I couldn't have found Allienora without you. Thank you for this."

Orsteen, Morion, and I surrounded Fanbert. In an instant, we vanished.

WITHOUT VESSEL
OR
DEVICE

We arrived on the planet of the Fume's outpocketing. Before us sat the ruins of an ancient city. Its buildings were blighted by the synergy of time and the elements, leaving them crumbled and worn. In the distance, an Obelisk towered. It was a reminder of the Guardian Army's failed attempt to stop the Fume.

I staggered forward and fell to a knee. My breath was sucked from my lungs. I gasped for air. I tilted my head up and looked above the dead city. The sky was a swirling vault of the Fume's exotic energy. I no longer needed the eyes of the Scions of Sensimion. I no longer needed technology. I saw it through a lens of new awareness.

"This is insanity!" said Fanbert. "The Fume overwhelms you, even now. Tell us how to stop this! How do we stop Nara-Narayana's evolution?"

I gazed into Fanbert's eyes. He was an honest man, a good man. "You're right, Fanbert. You're the only one who commands a dimensional transporter." I looked beyond the Fume's exotic energy to Nara-Narayana's evolution which, in this far place beyond the Brahman Sprawl, was less prominent in the sky. "At the center of Nara-Narayana's divinity, she still maintains her corporeal form. Not until she assimilates the entire Brahman Sprawl will she completely transcend her mortal being."

"And you believe if we kill her mortal body, it'll stop her evolution?"

"I do. Will you be able to transport there, Fanbert?"

"It's an unusual destination," said Fanbert. "I'll need to focus long and hard before I can confidently transport to the center of her growing divinity."

"Do it now!" I yelled. "Leave me here! Before I do something to you... take control of you. I've done it before. I can't be trusted." I fell forward, palms flat on the ground. I wept.

Why have I led these fine people here, jeopardized their lives? I've become selfish, my soul wretched. I am the monster I hate.

I felt large hands lift me up. I looked into Orsteen's eyes. They were the most compassionate eyes I'd ever seen.

"You're a good man, Theron Mobius," said Orsteen. "You do this for love, for her. I'll stay with you. I'll help you find her."

"You must leave me, all of you," I said. "Fanbert, take Orsteen and Morion with you."

Fanbert looked at me for a moment. "You look so familiar... I used to have such passion. I used to know love—a long time ago. I wasn't always a Guardian." He closed his eyes and smiled, as if relishing some old memory. "We all have our moments to shine." Fanbert placed a hand on my shoulder. "It would be a wasted trip if we didn't at least try to save her."

I felt my heart beat faster. I was reminded of something Mage had told me in the sanitarium, ninety years ago. *With friendship, hope is forged.* These people cared about me. These people were my friends.

Morion wrung his hands impatiently. "All is settled, then. Let's hurry up and save her. Where is she being held?"

I studied our surroundings, slowly sweeping my gaze across the city. My eyes fixed to a direction. I could sense her, as if I smelled a faint, familiar smell. "She's this way."

"How can you be sure, Theron?" asked Morion.

"I just am. Trust me." I moved forward with the determination of a monomaniac.

We traveled onward, guided by my unnatural pull toward Allienora. Night quickly came and, with a swollen moon overhead and a fog coalescing, the dead city was drenched in an eerie murk.

The surrounding haze served to create two great halos around both the moon and the glow of Nara-Narayana's divinity.

Orsteen looked up in wonder. "They're like two heavenly eyes, staring down at us, mocking our significance in the universe."

I put a reassuring hand on Orsteen's shoulder. A moment later, Nara-Narayana's divinity brightened and my pace quickened.

After twenty minutes, I stopped the company in front of a massive domed structure. Its condition was no better than the rest of the crumbling city. It had a disturbing ambiance, leaving me to wonder if it housed the ghosts of the city's long-forgotten inhabitants.

"This is the place," I said. "We can't be seen or heard. If the Fume's inside, and we're found, we'll be forced to flee and Allienora will be lost."

We entered the domed structure through a partially toppled wall, rather than the main entrance, and arrived in a dark corridor, which circled the perimeter of the structure. We soon came to a portal providing a view of the structure's center, which accounted for the majority of the structure's volume. We looked out on a vacant field surrounded by many levels of stone seating. Above was a transparent dome, which had become half shattered over the eons. It now allowed Nara-Narayana's divinity to shine down in its fullest splendor.

"It's a coliseum," whispered Orsteen. "Possibly used at one time for musical concerts or sporting events, if such were the pastimes of the city's inhabitants."

"This is the place," I said. "This is the place that surrounded me when I saw as Allienora saw."

"Where is she?" asked Orsteen.

"There." I pointed to the center of the field. "She's still lying on the stone altar." I kept my eyes on her. "The Fume isn't manifested in any form around her. I see no one but her. This may be easier than I had expected. Fanbert, transport us next to her, and then transport us all to the center of Nara-Narayana's divinity. Are you ready?"

Fanbert replied with a weird gurgling sound. I turned and found Fanbert's throat gushing with blood.

"What the fuck!" I screamed, discovering a bloody blade in Morion's hand. He had slit Fanbert's throat.

A final glottal sound pushed up from Fanbert's throat and he fell dead to the ground. His armor and dimensional transporter shifted out of their unseen dimension.

Orsteen seized Morion and restrained him. "What have you done!"

"I've done what's necessary," said Morion hysterically.

A rage burned through my body. I could barely suppress the urge to kill Morion on the instant. "You fuck! You just ensured the destruction of humankind. Why?"

"I couldn't allow you to leave here and destroy Nara-Narayana," said Morion.

I held up a white-knuckled fist. "What are you talking about?"

At that moment, from the shadows, six of the Fume's black beasts appeared. They were followed by a tall, muscular man with olive skin that shined like silicon—the very same form the Fume took when torturing Allienora. His blood-red eyes widened as he caught sight of me.

I was frozen, unable to speak. The Fume's close proximity caused a strange sensation within me. I felt as though my heart was being torn from my chest. I remembered my mantra.

I am Theron Mobius. I am myself. My mind is my center. I glanced at Orsteen and sent out my thoughts. *Save yourself, my friend. Run!*

"I have nowhere to run," responded Orsteen, throwing Morion to the ground and then discharging his Intersplit gun at the Fume's manifestation. The energy blast merely dissipated on impact.

The Fume's mouth curled from a smile. "Come now, Mr. Orsteen. I didn't think you were stupid. You can't kill me. You can't even harm me. This form isn't made of the foul flesh that encases your soul. It's an illusion of flesh that allows me to interact with you mere mortals."

Morion picked himself off the ground and stumbled to the Fume. "I've done well, Master. Haven't I? They never suspected my allegiance was to you. I blended among them with little effort from the beginning."

"You did fine work," said the Fume, patting Morion on the head like an obedient pet. "Your timing with the Guardian's death was superb."

I couldn't believe Morion's admission. I wanted to rip him apart, but was still overwhelmed by the Fume's proximity.

Orsteen apparently sensed my thoughts and spoke: "Morion, your betrayal is deserving of punishment beyond my competence. Regardless, I'll resolve the matter." Orsteen turned his Intersplit gun toward Morion.

"Wait!" called Morion. "You'll be no better than me."

"Wrong!" declared Orsteen. "You have no soul." He fired and Morion instantly fell dead. Orsteen turned to the Fume. "It appears your minions, unlike you, *are* composed of the foul flesh of men."

The Fume ignored Morion's death and engaged his black beasts. "Disarm them and bring them down into the light of the universe's evolution."

The black beasts led us to the field below. I felt a pain, a pull, a fracture at the very center of my soul. I felt myself being torn between the Fume and Nara-Narayana, both of whom I was connected to on a level beyond my comprehension.

The Fume brought us to the side of the field opposite Allienora. I couldn't see if she was all right.

The Fume held up his hands in a grand gesture. "This planet was once home to a species I created long before humankind. My current manifestation represents them. Not the prettiest creatures, but they were peaceful, as well as brilliant architects. Notice how their structures still stand after eons of decay. Unfortunately, their souls were much too thin for the purpose of evolving your universe." The Fume placed his hand under my chin, admiring my features with lustful eyes. "Humankind was my first success after many failed species. Creating conscious matter with a soul deep enough to evolve a universe is a complex and daunting task. But, as you can see, I've succeeded." The Fume looked up with a prideful grin to the glow of the universe's evolution. "Isn't it spectacular? The birth of a god!"

This is the end, I thought. *I must look at her face and hear her sweet voice one last time.*

I started to run for Allienora, but the Fume's black beasts grabbed me. I thrashed and screamed.

I spit at the Fume. "You've won! This universe is yours! Just tell me why you needed Allienora!"

"With pleasure," said the Fume. "I needed her to lure you here."

"Why!" I screamed. "My part in your grand design is over. Wasn't I the catalyst for Nara-Narayana's evolution? Didn't I fulfill your needs when I was implanted with a biolinguistic lobe?"

"You're more important to my plan than you think."

"You still need me?" I said. "For what?"

"When we spoke on the Guardian Sphere, it was essential you accomplished two things to ensure the progress of my plans. First, I needed you to get closer to Nara-Narayana, since the potency of my essence within you would only catalyze her evolution if you were within the Brahman Sprawl. After this was accomplished, I needed you to return to one of my outpocketings. You see, Theron, you're a vital element in my plan to absorb this universe's energies once they're evolved. You're the hybridization of my energies and Nara-Narayana's energies. I needed you here, because you're the conduit by which I'll be able to freely move into this universe and absorb Nara-Narayana's transcendental energies."

"How did you anticipate our travels so precisely? If we hadn't found the Prophets, I would've never been linked to Nara-Narayana, thus I would've never found Allienora."

"The human mind is predictable and easily influenced. From the beginning, I left you a trail of breadcrumbs, and you gobbled them up like a greedy mouse. If you recall, in Fandoral's quarters on the Guardian Sphere, I had my soldiers leave that homunculus Stimple alive, for I knew he'd lead you to the training facility of the Guardian Army, where you encountered JarNay, who was also left alive by my soldiers."

"And then there was Morion," I said. "I had wondered how he defeated the goliath beast guarding JarNay."

"Yes, Morion was at your side the whole time, acting the part and reporting back to me on the progress of your journey."

"And you knew that JarNay could lead us to the Guardian Fanbert, who in turn could lead us to the Prophets."

"Precisely," said the Fume, inclining his nose to a boastful angle. "And the Prophets gave you the means to communicate directly with Nara-Narayana. At that point, I was counting on love, that human condition that weakens the mind so the body will bend in irrational directions. Once you linked with Nara-Narayana, who is connected to every soul in the Brahman Sprawl, I knew your love for Allienora would take you to her."

"And what now?" asked Orsteen.

"We wait for the wake of Nara-Narayana's evolution. Once it reaches my outpocketings, all will be done. This universe will be mine for the taking."

I looked to the sky. "Nara-Narayana believes you'll be powerless to overtake her. She thinks you underestimate her mastery of this universe."

"She's just a child, drunk with a power she doesn't know how to wield."

"You've orchestrated your plans flawlessly," I said, gazing to Allienora in the distance. "Will you grant me one last request before the end?"

"I'll consider it. Speak on."

"Let me say goodbye to Allienora, before we're all sucked into your continuum of thought."

"A harmless request. I'll allow it." The Fume caused Allienora and the stone altar to glide through the air until she came to be in front of me.

I held my breath in horror. *My sweet. My love.*

Below me lay the ruins of a once beautiful and delicate woman. Insects swarmed like an aura around her. I swatted them away desperately. Her face, although untouched, was left in a contorted expression of pain. I wept.

"Why?"

"It was necessary that her thoughts travel with intensity into her biolinguistic lobe, so your connection to her wouldn't diminish. I had to be certain you could locate her." The Fume ran his fingers through Allienora's soft golden hair. "I hate to flaunt my own accomplishments, but I've brought 'agony' to a whole new height of meaning."

Above Allienora's head, I discovered a repugnant and inhuman organ. It pulsed and quivered with an unsettling rhythm. It was connected to her head by a network of nano-fibers. What was its purpose? At that moment, as I looked into Allienora's dead eyes, she blinked.

"She lives!" I exclaimed. "What is this? How is this possible?"

"Of course she lives. This is the genius of my work." The Fume gently caressed the organ above her head. "I created this organ to keep her brain and nervous system alive, so I could torture her beyond her body's breaking point. Have no fear—her mind will soon join her body in death. You look unwell, Theron. Don't let hate spoil your experience of these momentous events."

My shock turned to absolute sadness. *I've lost her again.* I reached into my pocket and removed the infinity spiral pendant. I placed it at her neck.

"This is yours, my dear... it's always been yours... from the very beginning."

I looked up from my one true love and into the Fume's eyes. Within me, a dark emotion was born—it was fast to poison all others. But with the darkness came control, power, and determination.

"You've taken that which is most dear to me, and from my loss, I've come to accept the fate that everyone in this universe will be assimilated into a greater conscious realm. However, it won't be your conscious realm that rules this universe. It'll be Nara-Narayana's."

My head throbbed with the mental powers I had been mastering during my recent journey. I focused my thoughts on the two beasts standing beside me and they crumbled to dust. I took control of a third black beast and it returned my Intersplit gun.

"Your mental feats are unimpressive," said the Fume. "Your small powers can't help you. As for your weapon, it's useless against me, as you already know."

I looked to Orsteen. "Forgive me, my friend. There's no hope left to save humankind." I turned a hateful gaze to the Fume. "Consider your conduit into this universe closed."

I pressed the Intersplit gun to my own head and fired.

In that moment of suicide, as my head was completely obliterated from the point-blank impact of an energy blast, I found that my thoughts and existence persisted beyond the flesh. Something miraculous ensued. I gained a different perspective of the universe and realized my part within it.

The Fume had once told me how the universe was composed of intangibles that pulsed and seethed through its ethos. Maybe it was the rapture of my body, but I suddenly understood those intangibles. It was as if a veil had been lifted from my eyes, and the universe was no longer that complex monster I had once thought it to be. I felt as though countless threads of thought radiated from my unique node of consciousness, connecting me to everything in the universe.

Suddenly, I found myself returned to my body. I was back in the coliseum, facing the Fume.

The Fume laughed with such abundance that his current manifestation could barely maintain definite form. "Your attempt was unsuccessful, Theron. As a result of your new function, acting as my conduit into this universe, your vital forces have matured beyond the normal limitations of the body. You've reached a condition in which you cannot die."

Orsteen stepped toward me and touched my face. "The whole of your head regenerated in a strange and miraculous way."

I laughed, stifling the Fume's laughter.

"What do you find amusing?" asked the Fume.

"You underestimate what I've become, and what I'm capable of doing. Just within that small moment of disembodiment, I tasted the secrets of the universe. Whatever you've put inside me, it's caused me to evolve beyond your expectations."

I tilted my head up to the light of Nara-Narayana's divinity, spread my arms wide as if to embrace the infinities above me, and proclaimed: "With awakened eyes, I can fathom all the depths of the universe! I can travel through it without vessel or device, but by thought alone!"

My body underwent a fantastic dissolution, after which I existed as a shimmering wisp of energy, thought, and soul. In an instant, my new constitution sped out into the universe, leaving the Fume snatching with desperate hands at the empty air left in my wake.

TRANSCENDENCE

L ike a ghostly comet, I traveled across the universe at impossible speeds. In short time, I arrived at the center of Nara-Narayana's growing divinity, at the heart of the Brahman Sprawl.

As if by second nature, I reconstituted my body and was again my former self of flesh and blood. The transformation left me disoriented and trembling. *What is this place? Where is she? Is this the center of her divine consciousness?*

I looked up and found myself standing within a spherical structure, at least a kilometer in diameter. Ancient machines surrounded me. The sphere's inner walls were lined with thousands of mechanical nodes. They shot forth rivers of shimmering blue energy.

It's beautiful, breathtaking.

I followed the flow of the energy streams. They cascaded toward the center of the sphere and converged on a floating mass that I couldn't identify. What was it? I examined it with wonder. It was alive. It was monstrous. A heap of brain matter, pale and glistening. It absorbed the rivers of energy into its cerebral tissues, as if feeding on them.

My God, this 'thing' is Nara-Narayana.

She had once been that awkward young girl in Sensimion's care, but was now an enormous creature of brain matter. I noticed something dangling from her surface. I strained my vision and found it to be a withered body, attached to the cerebral mass by a long, drawn neck, all tendon and sinew. After twenty-one million years, Nara-Narayana's vestigial body remained attached to her great sensorium like an obstinate fruit refusing to fall from its branch, shriveled and old.

As I marveled at Nara-Narayana's magnificent form, two great eyes protruded from the cerebral mass. My head echoed with Nara-Narayana's thoughts: "You're too late to stop me, Theron Mobius. I've spread far into the Brahman Sprawl, successfully evolving the universe into a realm of my pure consciousness. I know why you've come here. Even if you kill my corporeal form, I'll survive, since my thoughts stretch beyond this archaic structure, which has imprisoned me for an eternity. My transcendental energies are all around us. Just beyond the walls of this sphere, I'm a god."

"If such is the case, then why does this place still exist? I believe your assertions are premature. I believe that until you assimilate all the souls and matter within the Brahman Sprawl, this corporeal form remains necessary for you to maintain the cohesion of your evolved self. This hideous form is still the nexus of your thought."

At that moment, the entire spherical complex underwent a volatile episode, during which the matter of Nara-Narayana's sensorium went into a state of flux.

"You see," said Nara-Narayana, "even now I'm absorbing galaxies in the Brahman Sprawl. And as my divine consciousness expands, this form becomes more and more obsolete. As you just witnessed, I'm barely able to maintain this corporeal state."

"What are these rivers of energy you absorb?"

"Each river is a linkage to the thoughts and souls of an entire galaxy of human beings within the Brahman Sprawl. Their thoughts flow directly into me."

"This is how you're connected to everyone?"

"Indeed."

I noticed a dozen of them extinguish. "Why do they dissipate?"

"When I transform the energies of a galaxy, I'm also transforming the souls of all the people within it, utilizing them to form my matrix of consciousness. Thus they become a part of me, and since they're no longer with body, my connection to their biolinguistic lobes cease."

I waved my hand in a careless gesture. "Since you're so confident I can't stop you, there'll be no harm if I destroy your corporeal body."

Nara-Narayana paused. "And how will you accomplish this feat?"

"I myself have become a demigod of sorts." I felt a rush of power as I gave my full focus to Nara-Narayana's great sensorium, striving to do her harm.

"I'm a thousand-fold your superior," proclaimed Nara-Narayana. "You're a speck on my thoughts. Be gone from me, maggot!"

"I'm not the maggot!" I howled. "I'm the maggot's disease that'll bring you death."

As I pushed forth my mental energies, I felt Nara-Narayana pushing back, not a thousand-fold but a trillion-fold. She was indeed my superior. Death was upon me. Despite being the hybridization of the Fume and Nara-Narayana, I still wasn't a god. Nara-Narayana had a power over me that I couldn't match. And as my soul was on the verge of collapse, I experienced a strange moment, as if time slowed or my perceptions accelerated. I noticed a thread of energy hovering above me. It emanated from my head and meandered through the air toward Nara-Narayana's sensorium. I batted my hand at it, trying to interrupt its flow. It stretched and curled, unfazed by the assault.

This is her power over me. This is her strength. My biolinguistic lobe connects me to her.

"I'm no longer just human. I'm not one of the many. I'm more. I am Theron Mobius." I focused on my own body and mind, and went into a state of flux. I reached for the back of my head and pushed my fingers inward. I gripped onto a piece of my brain and tore it out. In my hand, I presented Nara-Narayana with my severed biolinguistic lobe. The thread of energy emanated from it for one last moment and then dissipated.

"My soul is free of you!" I dropped the brain organ to the ground and smashed it under a vengeful foot.

A new fire blazed in my heart. A deep droning resonated from my center. It grew louder and louder. With all my spirit, I unleashed my power on her. I felt the very substance of her sensorium. Her brain matter undulated and writhed. Her vital fluids boiled.

"Stop this!" she wailed. "You can't destroy me without consequence? You were correct when you said my corporeal form is maintaining the cohesion of my divine self beyond this complex. If you kill me now, all the energy composing my divine self will be released in a wave of destruction that will sterilize the universe of all life. No one will gain if you destroy me—not myself, not the Fume, and certainly not humankind."

I withdrew my attack. "Lies! You're stalling since you're so close to completely assimilating the Brahman Sprawl and reaching your full potential."

"I assure you, what I've said is true."

My mind reeled with panic and dread. *She's not lying. I can sense it. What do I do? How do I stop her? How do I save them? She's close to transcending her corporeal form. Do something! Do it now!*

My thoughts came to a moment of epiphany. "I've been changing, you know. At first, I thought these powers were just a side effect of my connection to you and the Fume. But I now realize they're not merely abstract powers I command, but the universe itself. I believe I share the same understanding and dominion over the universe as you do. I believe I have the power to stand here at the center of the universe's evolution, and replace your consciousness with my own."

Nara-Narayana's cerebral form trembled as if from laughter. "I've lived a life of extraordinary duration, during which I've been connected to many souls in the Brahman Sprawl. I've grown into an entity of unparalleled power and influence over this universe. You're delusional, Theron Mobius, to think you could stand in my place and control the forces swelling just beyond these walls."

The remaining rivers of thought extinguished.

It's now or never, I thought. *She's completely assimilated all the souls in the Brahman Sprawl.*

"I've nothing to lose," I said, as I released the full force of my powers to destroy her sensorium. It was more difficult, since her substance underwent a volatile flux as she strived to transcend her corporeal form. I feared my powers weren't enough. I thought of Allienora lying dead on that altar.

I've already failed my one true love. I won't fail again. This is for Allienora. This is for humankind.

From the depths of my soul I summoned all my energies.

Nara-Narayana released a miserable wail that shook the fabric of her universe. Her great sensorium ruptured, and a discharge of vital fluids sputtered and spilled, raining down upon me. The long, thin neck of her vestigial body at last snapped, and the withered remains of her former humanity fell only meters from where I stood.

The size of Nara-Narayana's sensorium quickly diminished, as lobes of brain matter sloughed away, piece by piece.

The final remaining core of Nara-Narayana's sensorium fell away, and I sent myself adrift. I floated up to the center of the sphere and took Nara-Narayana's place.

"I am Theron Mobius! I am myself! My mind is the center!" A devastating wave of energy closed in upon me from every direction. I felt pain and ecstasy. The walls of the sphere dissolved and my corporeal body transcended.

Stillness... clarity... I felt as though the entire universe rested on a single point of thought. I had become a god.

LULLABIES
TO
OBLIVION

Orsteen watched as the shimmering silver-white matrix of consciousness slowly filled the breadth of the sky. He prayed Theron could stop Nara-Narayana before she completely transcended. If not, the end of humankind neared. Orsteen looked at the Fume's manifestation, which stood less than five meters away. It stared at the growing divinity so intensely that Orsteen imagined its gaze might split the very fabric of the universe asunder.

As Orsteen understood it, even if Nara-Narayana's divine energies made it to the Fume's outpocketing, the Fume still couldn't carry on with his plan. Theron was supposed to act as the conduit for the Fume to move freely into the universe and absorb the divine energies. But Theron was gone.

Orsteen stepped to Allienora's remains and paid his respects. She was a beautiful woman, undeserving of such cruelty. He tore off a piece of his shirt and placed it over her face.

"It'll be over soon, dear girl."

Orsteen pondered his own mortality. And though he stood at the end of his existence, he felt at peace. He had lived a full life, a great life. He had known love, seen beauty, and felt joy. Regrets... there were none. He looked skyward and smiled, realizing the magnificence before him. His last sight would be the birth of a god.

"It will be an epic death."

Orsteen felt it was time to get comfortable. He eased himself to the ground, arms and legs sprawled, belly to the heavens. He breathed slow, deep breaths and cleared his thoughts.

"True serenity is to welcome death."

An hour passed... then two... then three. And Orsteen realized serenity was boring in long doses. He addressed the Fume's manifestation. "Where's my death, Mr. Fume, my permanent peace?"

The Fume gave no reply and remained frozen, looking to the sky. Orsteen shrugged and began singing lullabies his wife had sung to their children. These would be his last memories—reminiscing on those sweet moments of love and innocence.

As he sang his second song, he thought to hear voices singing along—voices from somewhere above. He became silent and lifted himself to his feet.

"Something has changed, Mr. Fume. Why are we still here? It hasn't grown or intensified in hours." Orsteen smiled widely. "Don't you see, Mr. Fume? The evolution of the universe has stopped."

At that moment, the divine energies above showed a perceivable lessening. An impossible reversal ensued, as the radiant cloud receded at a slow but steady pace. By some miracle of reincarnation, the galaxies of the Brahman Sprawl began to reconstitute. The divine energies of this newborn god began reverting back into planets and stars.

Orsteen swung a triumphant fist upward. He looked at the Fume fearlessly. "The human spirit is stronger than you. You stand here defeated, your grandiose plan in ruin."

"I don't take lightly to the hiss and spit of insects." The Fume roared and the sky became overcast with a black haze that accentuated his dark emotion. His manifestation grew to an impossible stature, greater than any exaggerated beast of fable that Orsteen had been told of during his youth—its eyes were two swirling fireballs; its mouth an abyss into nothingness.

The Fume lurched in Orsteen's direction, but when his great fingers swooped down on Orsteen, his grip was empty. Orsteen had vanished.

I took human form. I stood next to the stone altar where Allienora had been tortured. I had transported her far from the Fume.

I've done it. I've saved her. This is all that matters.

I smiled coolly at the Fume. "Despite all your power, you're incompetent at producing an appearance pleasing to the eye. Even now your ugliness excels into new frontiers."

The Fume showed an expression of renewed confidence. "Your return was a blunder you'll regret." The Fume moved to overtake me, but I produced an energy field around me.

"You're powerless against me, as I not only killed Nara-Narayana, but I took her place at the center of her transcendence." I gestured to the divine energies filling the heavens. "It's now my own consciousness that controls the evolution of this universe. You can no longer manipulate my thoughts and actions. I am my own entity, with powers as great as yours. You overlooked a simple truth when you helped bring the human soul into existence—a soul deep enough to evolve the universe is a soul deep enough to rule the universe. And with this rule, I deny myself the power to be a god. Soon the entire Brahman Sprawl will be reconstituted."

The Fume's manifestation, in all its hideous glory, began growing larger and larger until a moment of transformation caused its substance to separate into a trillion particles of exotic energy. The sky became filled with an ocean of light as the Fume's outpocketing became energized with his divine consciousness. It swirled and shimmered, becoming more intense as the Fume summoned forth a wave of consciousness from his universe.

I was surrounded by the Fume's divinity. It constricted my movement with a hundred wisps of consciousness. I felt as though I were back in the sanitarium, once again experiencing the inner realm of the sphincter beast.

I was lifted from the ground and floated in a vortex of consciousness. I felt the Fume attempting to access my inner being. "This is no longer my body! It's no different from one of your manifestations! I'm no longer your conduit! You cannot travel beyond this outpocketing! You must accept your defeat!"

"Never!" replied the Fume with a disembodied roar.

"You forget," I said. "You were a part of me, and I was a part of you. I knew your thoughts, and I know of your blight. I now remember your words as you manipulated my soul into existence: 'A thread of thought, I forge in flesh, I cast it out into the light and await its return to cure the blight.' Your consciousness is withering—your universe is dying. This is why you're so desperate to absorb the energies of this universe. You wish to replenish your own."

The ground shook and winds blew. The world contained within the Fume's consciousness went into upheaval. The coliseum collapsed around me. I could feel the volatility within the Fume's outpocketing, as the Fume frantically moved a tremendous amount of his conscious energies within it. As it reached critical saturation, a plume of the Fume's consciousness exploded out into the universe, successfully escaping the confines of the outpocketing. It stretched with desperate purpose toward the evolution that *was* me, that *was* the collective souls of the human race, that *was* the universe itself. The Fume's divine consciousness reached the boundaries of my divinity. And just as the Fume thought victory was at hand, and prepared to assimilate the energies before him, I proclaimed: "Face your fear! Not even gods are forever!"

With that said, I implemented all the power of the universe against the Fume, whose plume of consciousness was sent reeling back into the confinement of his outpocketing. In one final heave, I expelled the Fume and his outpocketing from the universe.

21

ENLIGHTENMENT

Allienora woke up to convulsions—not of death but of life. Her mind worked to find a mutual stasis with her new and pristine body. The spasms at last subsided, and although her thoughts were barely coherent, she became overwhelmed by a rich sensation of déjà vu.

She hung naked upon a great machine, secured by a cold metal restraint across her chest. Her view was of a windowless wall that swirled with yellow electric-light. As her jumbled thoughts at last became clear, she became aware of a group of familiar beings. They stood before her upon legs with backward-bending knees, exchanging whispers.

One of the beings approached on odd strides. "Do you know where you are?"

"I think I've been here before," replied Allienora. "Although these memories may be of a past life."

"You're in the floating city of Azimoir. You were recently here in need of medical attention due to a case of impalement. At the time, I also implanted you and your companions with biolinguistic lobes."

"And how have I come to be here again?"

"Of that I'm uncertain," he said as he released the restraint across her chest, sending her to the floor clumsily. "When you arrived, your condition was beyond wretched. Your brain, however, was intact, and we were able to give you a new body."

Allienora lifted herself off the floor. "My friends... do you know where they are?"

One of the individuals manipulated a control podium and the walls of the room drained of their color and vanished, revealing Orsteen on the other side. He rushed to her and gave her a caring hug. "They've returned you from death! How do you feel?"

Allienora felt the weight of many unbearable memories. "I've dreamed of hell, and I fear that dream has changed me."

Orsteen hugged her again. "Even the most terrible memories become dulled with time. Forget the horrors you suffered. You'll heal."

Orsteen led Allienora to a terrace overlooking an ocean painted in the rich colors of twilight. In the distance, a jagged shoreline crept past as the floating city migrated south to warmer weather.

Allienora looked skyward. "The evolution of the universe still swells! How much time's left?"

"Don't worry, Allienora. It's no longer a threat. In fact, even now it dwindles in size."

Allienora reflected on her abduction. "The Fume told me of his unbelievable plans, and said many awful things about Theron. Was he telling the truth, Orsteen?"

"In the end, the Fume's own creation turned against him. Theron saved us all. I don't know how, but Theron's the reason the evolution now reverses. And not only is the process reversing, but the planets and people once absorbed by the divine evolution are being reconstituted. The Brahman Sprawl is being given a second chance. Even *this* planet had been absorbed, but by some miracle it has returned."

"And what of Theron?"

"I don't know. I believe he's become something incredible, something more. I saw it. The things he could do. Death couldn't contain him."

"How did I get free?"

"Theron freed you. Somehow, he transported us here. He knew these people could save you, Allienora." Orsteen looked at her sincerely. "It was his love for you that drove him to do everything he did."

Orsteen told Allienora what had transpired after her separation from the company on the Guardian Sphere. She listened passionately until the end, at which point they were approached by an Azimoir native.

"Excuse me," he said, "but we've received a communication from someone calling himself 'Impresario Stimple.' He claimed to be one of a few survivors on the Guardian Sphere near Earth and simply stated: 'The Fume's outpocketings around Earth and elsewhere in the seven galaxies have collapsed out of our universe. And all his beastly minions have vanished from existence.'"

Orsteen nodded with satisfaction. "It appears it's safe to go home."

Allienora thought of returning home. She opened and closed her hands in an uncomfortable manner, as if her new body wasn't properly worn in. "I don't think I can bring myself to return just yet. I fear the scent of the Fume still lingers in the air of Earth."

The native bowed his head. "You may remain in Azimoir as long as you like. I'll arrange for your accommodations."

Orsteen held her hand. "We have all the time in the universe. We'll return home when you're comfortable."

Allienora kissed his cheek. "Thank you, my friend."

Many weeks passed. Allienora stood in the night, on the white beaches of a tropical island, where the city of Azimoir had settled. She looked out on the starlight-drenched ocean and then up to the heavens.

The universe's divine evolution had diminished to a single glimmering node, and at that moment it extinguished, leaving Allienora only a small sense of relief. She still found her thoughts infected with overwhelming anguish—the Fume had broken her. A tear rolled down her face, as she realized something significant was missing inside her. She scanned the heavens.

"What's become of you, my dear Theron?" She waited, but there was no reply.

With a caring finger, she touched the infinity spiral pendant that hung from her neck and wondered where it had come from. She didn't know, yet it was the one thing left in her world that brought her a small amount of comfort.

Allienora remained on the beach all through the night. She watched as a predawn light seeped up from the horizon and stained the atmosphere in a mingling of crimson and lavender. As she stood there, mourning the loss of her past happiness, something changed within her. A smile spread across her face and her blood warmed. She felt a presence nearby and was compelled to turn around.

"Theron!" she said with great joy.

I stood before her. My physical appearance, although normal, emitted a soft radiance—my skin had taken on a phosphorescent quality. She ran toward me, and I caught her. I held her in a long embrace.

We kissed. An amazing energy ran through us—connecting us.

She stepped back and drew a deep breath. "What was that?"

"Just a little help," I said.

Her eyes gleamed. "I remember."

"Everything?"

"I remember the sanitarium. We were there together. I adored you with all my heart, Theron. We were so young."

I placed my hand on her cheek. "What else?"

She laughed. "We're married." She touched the infinity spiral pendant at her neck. "I remember our wedding day." She kicked the sand at our feet. "It was a beach, much like this one. The birds were singing, the waves crashing. We stood at the water's edge as we said our vows."

"Not even death could part us, my wife."

401

Her eyes filled with sorrow. "I was pregnant."

I nodded.

She placed her hands on her stomach. "We died?"

"I lost you both that day."

Her lips trembled. "I remember. It was a girl. I had just found out. I never got to tell you."

I looked up to the stars. "You'll meet her someday, my dear. She's out there right now, living another life."

Allienora smiled and began to cry.

I held her close. "I love you so much."

"And I love you, Theron." She caressed my skin in wonder of its radiant nature. "What's happened to you?"

I looked out on the rising sun. "Enlightenment."

"And with this enlightenment you were able to save the universe from evolving into a single conscious entity?"

"I was able to save the universe, because it was I who came to command that amazing continuum of thought."

"And you chose to refuse this transcendence?"

"My time as a god was short. However, I'll remain more than just human."

Allienora shook her head. "I know the evolution of humankind and the universe was the orchestration of the Fume. But, I wonder, will this evolution someday occur naturally? Was that the ultimate condition that humankind is destined for?"

"No. Humankind can be so much better. Within each human is the means to attain enlightenment. It's merely fear and ignorance that stops the soul from reaching its potential."

"And what of this potential?"

I moved my arm with a sweeping flourish toward the ocean and focused. In a marvelous display, an enormous island of rock rose up from the ocean depths, and from its surface raised mountains. The barren landscape soon sprouted trees, which grew at impossible speed.

Allienora looked with wide eyes at the island's birth. "How have you done this?"

"We're all a part of this universe. It's our body, and we're its consciousness. We can all be gods in our own right. You need only to look within yourself and open your mind." I leaned close to Allienora, kissed her with passion, and then whispered in her ear: "Wake up, my darling. It's time to wake up."

FROM THE AUTHOR

I hope you enjoyed MOBIUS. If you've taken the time to read the entire novel, I hope you'll take a minute to review it on Amazon or Goodreads. As an independent author, your reviews are so very important to me. They'll let others know about this novel, and help me to become a better writer. I can't wait to hear what you thought!

Thanks so much,

Vincent Vale

Goodreads: www.goodreads.com/VincentVale

Email: vincentvale@vincentvale.com

Twitter: @VincentValeNews

~SOULESTIAL~

~PRESS~